IT COMES FROM THE RIVER

IT COMES FROM THE RIVER

THE RIVER

Rachel Bower

BLOOMSBURY CIRCUS
LONDON · OXFORD · NEW YORK · NEW DELHI · SYDNEY

BLOOMSBURY CIRCUS
Bloomsbury Publishing Plc
50 Bedford Square, London, WC1B 3DP, UK
29 Earlsfort Terrace, Dublin 2, Ireland

BLOOMSBURY, BLOOMSBURY CIRCUS and the Circus logo
are trademarks of Bloomsbury Publishing Plc

First published in Great Britain 2025

A catalogue record for this book is available from the British Library

ISBN: HB: 978-1-5266-7266-7; TPB: 978-1-5266-7265-0;
EBOOK: 978-1-5266-7262-9; EPDF: 978-1-5266-7261-2

2 4 6 8 10 9 7 5 3 1

Typeset by Integra Software Services Pvt. Ltd.
Printed and bound in Great Britain by CPI Group (UK) Ltd, Croydon CR0 4YY

To find out more about our authors and books visit www.bloomsbury.com
and sign up for our newsletters

as I watched for it to appear through the dusk, I remembered certain of Bessie's tales wherein figured a North-of-England spirit, called a 'Gytrash'; which, in the form of horse, mule, or large dog, haunted solitary ways, and sometimes came upon belated travelers

– Charlotte Brontë, *Jane Eyre*

you crack the live branch –
the branch is white,
the green crushed,
each leaf is rent like split wood

– H. D. 'Storm'

Prologue

NEW YEAR'S EVE

I can't do it, a woman in a baggy hospital dress is screaming. Nails scarlet gloss; violet-ash hair poker-straight. *Make it stop!* Her mouth is open, black egg.

The midwife's nails are red too. You're doing really well, just breathe.

You breathe! Head thrust dramatically back into a pile of starched pillows, knees bent, legs apart, crotch tented to the knees by a crisp sheet. *It's hurting! Get off me!* The strip lights make obscene eyelash shadows on her cheeks.

The midwife is saying I know you can do it, nearly time to give a really big push – I'm sorry, darling, it's too late for an epidural, you've missed the window, you're too dilated. Wry smile. Have a bit more gas and air.

It's not working! I want proper drugs. The woman is sobbing now. *I'm scared.* Boyfriend squeezing her hand. *I've done bad things. I'm really scared.*

Three lonely women watch this birthing in bright windows of electric light.

Lauren, on the sofa, in a frayed dressing gown, drinking cheap yellow sunshine. She turns down the volume, doesn't want to wake her boys.

Alex, ghost-faced, on a faux leather chair, maternity joggers sagging, blare of TV wild in her hair. Her body postnatal, in shock.

Nancy, rooted in a high-backed green velvet chair with wooden arms. Cardigan wrapped tight under crossed arms. Telly blazing in the corner, no warm dog chin on her slippers.

The three women feel no truth in this labour: it is pure surface and dazzle. It is a brawl in the pub, a blow job in the garage, a slanging match over dinner, an affair with your sister's husband. There is nothing of slick chasm, three fingers open: a dreadful oily boat rising on a wave. There is no soft thud of dislocated knee, no lighthouse cracking raw yolk on rocks. No fire in the coccyx, the anus, the cunt. No reek of lavender vomit, purple-induced panic. No house is a shit-tip, unfit mother, talking about me as if I am cattle.

The three women flinch: feel something pass outside. A reek of singed fur, scorching damp. Flaming eyes. A creature. It knows these women. They feel its wanting. A noise unlike the voice of any known animal. It leaves no footprints. From the river it comes; to the river it always returns.

Lauren will be alone tomorrow. Everything will be shut and she's skint anyway. She will take the boys to the park again.

Alex can't see tomorrow, startled by her pale hands, sick. Belly, hollow and slack, baby-blue boy asleep in a sterile bassinet. Her daughter at home, without her.

For Nancy, tomorrow will be the same. Festive sherry sits on a glass-topped table next to her, untouched. Thin brownish blood to the brim.

They all watch the boyfriend saying it's the gas and air talking; the pain. *No. Something awful is going to happen. Make it stop. It's because I'm bad.* Hyperventilating. The midwife can see the head below the styrofoam dome of stomach. You're doing really well, pant now. Keep going. Pant. Like this. Mouth open like a puppy. You can do it. There is a long, shattering shriek from the woman. Her forehead glassy. She suddenly turns to the camera, one hand gripping the bed frame, the other clamping a white Entonox pipe to her jaws.

Lauren hits mute, sick of the screeching. Alex sits motionless, trapped. Nancy stares at the screen, frozen.

The fake midwife has a glove on each of the woman's raised knees. *No! Get off me. I'm bad.* Come on now, you're lovely. On the next contraction you need to give me a really big push. *I'm really scared. I'm rotting inside. It was me.* Push now, come on, big push. I need you to give me one big last push.

The women feel sick: charred shadow wrapping their faces, yeasty and rank, blood-black fur, soaking paws. Upon them all.

That first cry, clean into the bright set, everyone falling on each other, sobbing and laughing, a neat package in the woman's arms, the boyfriend leaning over to hug them both, but that final shot – a look on the woman's face over his shoulder – he does not see what Lauren and Nancy and Alex see. The actress has made a mistake: leaked something of herself into her eyes.

And then the creature has gone, shadow spilt to earth, soaking into bedrock, and the women are left only with colours: scarlet nails, violet hair, yellow wine, green velvet, baby blue, brown sherry. It is not, yet, their time.

PART ONE

Nine Months Earlier

April

Alex

Alex can taste Paul's spit, even with her tongue burning mouthwash. She is in bed, curled into herself like a shell. Pearl slime inside. The room is pulpy black, deepest ocean floor, TV thumping up through the carpet. Glint of gold earrings on the bedside table, pebble pendant hot on her chest. She can hear Paul laughing downstairs. The crash of river, always surging through the open window.

He wasn't happy with the pudding: the custard was lumpy, she knew he hated it like that. And he'd made such an effort with the necklace, bespoke for his geology-loving wife. *Close your eyes, darling, lift your hair at the back.* The tickle of small stone as he fastened the clasp at her nape. He had the mirror ready. *Look. I had it drilled specially. It's slate from our river.*

But the custard had lumps. He'd smashed the glass bowl at the wall, crumble and all, spatters of silly yellow in her hair. A clownish splat on the paper, before he shoved her into the lounge, forwards onto the sofa, to make up for it. River pebble reeling. No protection. She'd told him before it was too soon – Isabella still a baby, only fifteen months, sleeping upstairs. He whispered she wanted it, it would do her good. Alex was silent. She didn't want to wake Izzy.

Afterwards, she'd swept cold globs and glass into the dustpan, the brush caked solid with weeks of toddler food. He'd stayed

9

in the lounge, TV up loud. She fretted about missing a shard: Izzy's fat little feet in the morning. She smeared the rug, making it worse; kept rinsing the brush under the tap.

Upstairs, under the duvet with her eyes closed, Alex tries to block the images. Flashes of her daughter drowning, cholera rising, an arrested mother, an illegal oil well in flames. She is going mad. The river grit in her teeth, the overcrowded vision. River pebble burning. It is not like the seeing-stones of her childhood, worn by the sea into holes over centuries: circular windows into the future. Old folk in the seaside town said you should spit on these witch stones, toss them over your left shoulder for luck.

But this stone is different: drilled, distorted. The futures it holds have been rent. When Alex closes her eyes, it all floods in: river broiling, heart of a saint returned, daughter wailing. She was supposed to be meeting her friend Reema in town tomorrow, for a treat. Maybe she'll say something about how things have been. But Reema will only think she's losing it. Alex flings the necklace under the bed but it is no use: she lies awake for hours, images flashing like a crazy film. A giant black dog on the river; eyes like saucers, burning coals.

Lauren

Oliver clings to my leg outside the Co-op while I try and get hold of Mum. She always takes forever to answer. What the bloody hell is she doing. Daniel's in the buggy, bawling, snot running in his mouth. The coppers are nicer than that security guy, on his power trip – failed footballer, failed life. I shouldn't have lost it, but what else was I supposed to do – shaming me like that in front of all them people, grinning – *I've had my eye on you for weeks, you thieving little madam, you've had this coming.*

They might have let me off if it weren't for him – it's not like I robbed a bank. Powdered milk, tinned peaches. Fun-size Milky Ways for my boys. *Come on – let's have it – empty your pockets.* I'll never show my face there again. And *Mmm, what's this, in with* the bairn – tweezers – let's see – lip balm, deodorant. Smirking. *What kind of person gets their kid involved in crime before they can even walk? You'll go down for this – think on that.* Who the fuck does he think he is. My stomach blathering acid. He's coming out the shop now, talking to the coppers – *To be honest, officers, I was scared of what she might do.* My arse he was scared. He's had it in for me since the day I didn't take his number.

I beg with the woman – look, please – but she sees shit clothes and single mum and stashing stolen goods in a raggy pushchair – with a child! – and says you do not have to say anything but it may harm your defence if you do not mention when questioned something which you later rely on in court. My mum finally answers her mobile. *What is it now, Lauren?*

I tell her. *What the hell? Lauren!* I know, Mum, I know. I needed the money – it was only a couple of things – Tania said she'd pay me for them, and the food was only for the boys. Mum, oh God, I don't know what to do, I couldn't let them go hungry. I'm not in debt or nothing – you always said. *Stop talking, Lauren, stop it. Just don't say anything. I'll be there in five minutes.* She's only round the corner. Just let her get dressed. I pull Danny out the buggy, hold both boys too hard. I tell them look, you're okay, we're fine, aren't we? – you'll have a good time with Nana, Mummy will be back really soon. It's like an adventure! Anything you do say may be given in evidence. I don't want them to hear this. To remember me like this. Both boys go quiet, faces in my jacket.

People stare as I wait for the disappointed shape of Mum – the humiliation in her walk, the spark of steel in her eyes. Oliver says *but, Mummy, it's boring at Nana's, I want to stay with you.* I tell him I love you – shaking, a mess – kiss him goodnight, just in case, and Danny too, I'll be back really soon love. Be good boys for Nanna. Come on, Oli, you need to look after your little brother now. That's it. I'm so sorry, baby. Mummy was just trying her best. Oliver's face making strange, silent shapes.

Mum appears from the snicket behind the Co-op, from the river, marching past all the old shoes and knickers hiding in the bushes. I can't meet her eyes. She rubs my arm – a surprise – then picks Danny up and grips tight to Oli's hand. As I walk away, she yells after me – *don't say another word, Lauren – just make sure you talk to someone legal at the station* – and I'm leaving in underwater motion – my boys, my life – ducking into the car like a criminal.

Nancy

Pip drives me there with my handbag in my lap. Everything else is boxed up: he did the packing. That wife of his probably did nothing, as per usual. Pip will go back for the rest of my things, and my little spaniel Ruby. He thinks that's easier on me. He'll look after her until I get back on my feet.

Pip puts the radio on to cover the silence. I stare out of the window until we turn into the car park. Only a five-minute drive, but a different part of the river. It churns here, rough. Not like the glossy curve of water by my apartment. My home.

There's a gigantic sign: River Garden Residential Care Home. The car park smells of washing powder and stewing steak. Standing on gravel facing the red building, I see the silhouette of a fat caged bird in the window. It looks like a pigeon. Who would … *Come on, Mum.*

The air is thick with the sound of unruly women. Rushing like wings in my ears: humming, singing, laughing. Not white-permed women, but sleek-bobbed flappers, strung with pearls; pin-curled women, bouffant waves and silky bloused women. Girls. I can't make out any words. Pip takes my arm and walks me forward; presses the buzzer. An automatic glass door judders open to let us in.

Come on in, the woman says, *welcome to River Garden.* I look at my shoes. *I'm Bev, the manager here. You'll get to know everyone soon enough.* Pip is saying something ridiculous about me losing my words a bit since the accident. *We want you to make yourself right at home, love.* I don't look up. Pip told me it's a good place: clean and modern. We were lucky they had space at such short notice. None of that cabbage smell. He showed me the website, *look at that nice decor, Mum — cocoa, cappuccino and cream.* But there's no old people in those decor pictures.

The gushing Bev marches us round: corridor, lounge, dining room. My swollen feet follow. I can't hear the women singing now we're in. Everyone wearing shoes instead of slippers. Practical brownish carpets. Safety plugs. Skirting scuffed from trolley wheels.

Your son says you've a sweet tooth, Nancy? Bev's flat loafers are matt at the toe, where she's rubbed black polish into the scuff. I keep my eyes on them. *Well, we've pudding every day here, so you'll never go short.* They laugh together, into the tension. In the lounge, I want to look up at the caged pigeon, but don't want them to see me looking. My auntie always kept birds: knew everything there was to know. She sometimes let us feed them through the bars when we went round with unsold loaves from the shop.

It's nice, isn't it, Mum? I look at Pip's new squash shoes, laces double-knotted. Adjust the chain on my mother's locket, her words always with me. Pip never could tie his laces properly. *Come on now, Nancy, let's get you settled, you must be shattered.* He whispers, *Mum, can't you just say something? It's a bit embarrassing — it's not her fault.* I look at him: my boy. His whispers more urgent now. *Mum, you have to promise me you'll tell them if you need anything — they won't be able to look after you right otherwise.*

My Ruby will never take to living with him and that woman: she'll think I'm gone for good. Everyone knows little dogs like her can die of broken hearts. The bedroom is fogged with the scent of lilies. Ugly grab rails everywhere. A woman's voice from the open window. *Ain't she sweet.* Safe to look up: Bev's mouth moving but no sound cutting through the clotted air. I grip my handbag to my chest. The river sounds wrong. White static. I go over to the window to check. A flit of shadow in the bushes.

It's a nice view of the water, isn't it, Mum, just like your old place? I shudder. Pip thinks I'm chilly: comes over to shut the window. The sound is dampened, but still there, hissing beneath the fog. Plastic fuchsias on the bedside drawers. *What more could you want?* It's his wife's fault. He'd have let me stay with them while they cleaned up the smoke damage in my kitchen if it wasn't for her. She's never liked me.

They leave me to it. *I'll come back tomorrow to check how you're doing, Mum.* Pip drove here last night to unpack some of my things, but nothing is where it should be, everything's wrong. He said my valuables are in the safe in my wardrobe: my documents, brooches, his dad's gold pocket watch. But other things are missing: where are the tickets and coins from my underwear drawer? Betty's funeral memorial card? They've got it into their heads that I'm staying, that I'm confused. They've even put my special spoon rack on the wall, rows of tiny silver spoons. I use the travel hairbrush from my handbag before bed, so I don't have to ask where my usual one is. A quiet knock at the door: one of the girls checking on me, like a child.

I'll never sleep in here. The ceiling is cold: green ghost of emergency lighting; sprinkler system; ugly metal hooks and hoist pulleys. Smoke detectors, like at my flat. No soft wisp of Ruby's breath, only the river rattle, inescapable, even with double glazing.

In the morning, I use the small sink in my room. The only mercy: I don't have to wash in everyone else's muck. The toilet's shared, though. I just hope I don't meet anyone in the corridor. My stomach a ball of hard wax. I've always been an early riser: it suits Ruby. She'll be hungry now, always whines to be fed by six. I find a skirt and blouse in my wardrobe and venture out, averting my eyes from a tall woman with flat breasts in a long nightie. She stares shamelessly at me. I shut the bathroom door on her. I am not like these people.

I'm terrified I'll end up in the wrong room. I need to mark my door, so I don't get muddled. Back in my room, I sit on the single chair, big thighs spilling over the edges. It's unreal: I can't be here, with no breakfast to make. Defunct. The sky thick white over the river.

I try the TV but there's no signal so I put my wireless on. At least I've that. A woman eventually knocks to see if I need anything. *Morning, pet, how're we getting on? I'm Kerry – second in command – you can always go down early and help yourself to breakfast*

14

if you're up. She walks me down to the dining room, chatting on. *It's a bit of a maze, but you'll get used to it, don't you worry. Just in here, pet.*

I'm too polite to say that I'm not planning to be here long enough to get used to anything. The dining room is talc and morning breath and sour yellow daffodils. I will never be able to eat in here.

Kerry sits me down opposite a woman with a neat white perm and bright green eyes. *Nancy, meet Gladys.* Gladys smiles good morning politely and offers me the rack of toast: stiff triangles of sliced white. She says *it's lovely out* and I try to smile my mouth. I've never got on with women. The one from upstairs with the nightie has a brown dress on now, screeching loudly across the room.

Where have you moved from? I try not to look at the cackling woman and Gladys doesn't seem offended when I don't answer. She keeps taking neat bites of toast and sips of tea, gazing into the distance. The woman across the room stands up, shouting now. *You! What are you doing here?! Get out! You're a whore!* My stomach lurches: she's pointing at me. Screaming. *Intruder – security! Help! Police!*

Kerry hurries back in, *now now, Patricia, settle yourself down, let's get you back in your chair. This is just Nancy, poor hen. Let's try to be nice – it's her first morning. The last thing she needs is you bawling at the top of your voice.* Smiling over at me, *don't mind her, Nancy – she doesn't mean anything by it.* Gladys offers tea from the pot, and I nod, grateful for something else to look at.

May

Alex

Alex takes the plastic stick down to the river in her pocket. Her brain feels swollen, too big for her skull. She hasn't looked yet, but knows it will be two pink lines: she's been bolt awake in the night, feeling sick all the time. Her period was due a week ago. She sits on the gravelly bank, just past the otter holt. Compensation for new houses on wild river land. This is flood plain: the ground should be soft damp under Alex after all the rain, but the construction people carved a huge ditch at the edge of the site. Unrivalled flood defences for peace of mind.

Alex pulls off her boots and socks and lowers her feet in the water, silky green. It is deep, murky. She would have swum here, when she was younger. She was never out of the water: training in the lido, the sea, the pool. Her dad always said she was born with gills.

Paul doesn't know about the test. He can't see her from the house but knows where she is. She told him she needed some air before he went to work; left him finishing breakfast. Izzy in front of CBeebies. There is a movement in the trees on the opposite bank, but it is nothing. The cold pierces her feet, painful deep in the bones. The early sun shines amber green through the leaves, dappling her hair. She raises her face to it, doesn't know if she can get through this again. It all started last time when she was pregnant, full of bloom. Something about the pregnancy unsettled Paul. It had all been so perfect until then. She startles as a frond of slimy weed catches her ankle, shakes her foot violently to get rid of it. She feels the river call, the promise of oblivion.

There is a crackle on the towpath and Alex pulls her knees to her chest, but it is only a man in a suit cycling past, commuting to town. She drags her socks over damp feet. She should be back by now. A cloud blows in, the air suddenly chill; another flicker of movement on the opposite bank. Nothing. She hauls herself up, wrenches the stick from her pocket and looks at the tiny display. Two definite pink lines. Positive.

Lauren

The Union Jack's flying. Mum's shoes are killing my feet. The solicitor told me dress sensible – we're doing the caring, decent mother – no bare skin, nothing low-cut or short. Nothing flash neither. My cousin Hannah has driven up – thank God I'm not by myself. My teeth are chattering. Hannah always looks gorgeous – nails and hair to die for. She's salt of the earth though, not up herself. We've been in this tiny corridor room for hours. I just want it over now, just need to know.

On the way in, I saw a massive black dog by itself in the distance. People shouldn't have dogs like that if they can't look after them. The council need to get on it before a child gets bit. The metal detectors screamed at me on the way in. It's like an airport – a sick joke. The woman in the cloak ticked my name loudly off her clipboard. So relaxed, sweeping round, laughing with the others. I'm with the laughless ones – tense on metal chairs, screwed into the ground.

I run to the loo again, chest tight. There's a nappy bin and a pull-down baby changer. Yellow and grey. Sickly. I rush back, my number blaring on the tannoy: 364 to Court Two and they're all going in, bright lights, everyone moving. Lauren Turner. Hannah kisses my burning cheek, *good luck, darling, I'll be there the whole time*, then she's gone – whisked to a row of chairs, miles across the room, where the public people sit. I shake my head, try to uncloud my eyes. The cloaked woman crowds me, pointing me in – people everywhere. Market day. My jacket too tight across my back.

Sit down, all rise, people at the front in suits, the middle one, a prehistoric man, in red. I thought there'd be wigs. I look round for Hannah. I've lost her. I scratch my head but put my hands down when my solicitor looks. She's nice – posh but doesn't talk down. To be fair, she's tried really hard to help me understand everything. All these people watching me in the hush. We sit, the ones at the front whispering loudly like they've forgotten we're here.

Then he looks right at me, that old man in the red, suddenly massive – *can the defendant please stand* – and I am weighted to my chair, can't move, rooted and he's a giant staring down and I'm doing my best and there's Hannah again – yes beautiful Hannah who's driven all this way – and my boys without me at my mum's – and I shudder to my feet and yes I am Lauren Turner and yes I live on Lowfield Road and yes that's me, standing there in my body. A voice booming from the sky.

Lauren Turner, you are charged with low-value shoplifting. And I stand and I stand. The carpet slipping blue to grey to blue. Sucking me down. Water. I try to think of grass, solid and sweet, fields and fields of green.

A man near the front gets up, his voice swimming slow, addressing the giant who will eat us all – the accused – at the bottom of the beanstalk – clear evidence – left without paying for eight items – wash her away – bed without supper – and I wish for an axe, for gold, for a singing harp – three food items and five toiletry items – nettles that sting – lip balm, tweezers, fun-size chocolate bars, honeyed peaches – and they all lived – not for her personal use – and they all lived – climb now, climb through the burn, Lauren, hold on – evidence that she was planning to sell these items – and my boys – brave Jack, he forgave his mum and climbed – she admitted she was planning to sell these items on – escape the wrath – premeditation – felled that beanstalk – this theft was planned, Your Worship – the swift silver blade – CCTV footage – plummeting – secreting items in a pushchair which also contained her young child – brains dashed out – her own baby, Your Worship – and they all lived – we have witness statements – the mum looking up – left the shop, clearly not intending to pay – and they all lived – paying only for a single tin of beans – magic beans – it was not the first time – and they all lived – offensive language – and they all lived – she has confessed – happily ever after.

The judge tells my solicitor I can sit down if I'm not fit to stand. I try to breathe more quietly. My solicitor has been saying I'll never be sent down for this but how does she know – I just can't go to prison – my boys need me. My legs judder and they're all so stuck up, these people talking on – no idea about real life and now my solicitor is standing up – Your Worship, my client fully accepts this offence of theft: she was hungry, her benefits had been sanctioned; the food was for her children. My client has a clear history and a good character, Your Worship. This is her first offence. She is a devoted mother and these are difficult times for her, as they are for many people. Sir, my client found herself in a desperate situation. She had no money; her children depend on her; she felt that she had no other choice. She fully understands and accepts the harm she has caused.

Hannah is smiling over at me, nodding her freshly high-lighted hair. Hope. And then the man in the middle is staring down at me again, giant unslayed. Lauren Turner. Turner. Turner. We do not readily accept that you went into the shop to steal just for being hungry. You had other options: support from your family or a food bank. He has no idea. I know I shouldn't of, but I was so hungry. This is a serious offence: many people erroneously believe that shoplifting is a victimless crime, but people have been harmed by your actions – not only the business owners, but the staff and every single customer who has to pay more to cover the items that people like you have stolen. It is unacceptable: your behaviour; your foul language; your abuse of a security officer – a man who was purely there to do his job.

And there it is, guilty or not guilty, I am Guilty – guilty of swinging that axe, of taking more than I deserve, of being poor, of loving without competence, of not being a good enough mother. And then we're out, and it's done, quick as a cut. Back on dry land. My solicitor guides me across the corridor to a room; hands me water and tissues, says take a few deep breaths. But I need to make sure I can stay with my kids, that it's definitely not prison – I need to get home to them now, but no, I need to stay until everything is done properly. The solicitor says the magistrate wanted to make sure I understood the harm I had caused – there was evidence of premeditation and intention to sell what I stole – but my clear record and good character means that they gave me the lowest community sentence – eighty hours of unpaid work. And as long as I stick to the plan that will be it, as long as I don't do it again. The court probation officer will explain it to me now – book me an appointment and then I can go back home to my kids, and we'll bring down the duvet and watch films together on the sofa and I'll hold them tight until bed.

Nancy

Time here is ruled by meals and the fat bird in the cage. A bird like that should be flying free, like the sparrows on the feeders at my flat. It has a grey body like a pigeon but when it turns round you see its face, made up like a clown: yellow paint, red circle cheeks, grey spike of hair. Sad. It sleeps through breakfast, coffee, dinner, tiny padlock on its cage, but starts up the squawking after pudding, fiery eyes and sparking beak, until someone loses patience and throws the blanket over the cage.

The staff smother us too – a constant flow of squash and biscuits and crafts – hoping we won't make a fuss. Activity Room, Timetable of Fun: crafts, baking, bingo. There's no oven so lord knows how they do the baking. If only I could get back to my kitchen, I'd rustle up some proper scones and biscuits to cheer everyone up. I sneak a look in the Activity Room at 3 p.m., just to see. It is all set up: boxes of cornflakes, bun cases, small pile of example crispy buns dripping with microwaved chocolate. No scalding; no risk. I think of the toasty rooms above my parents' baker's shop, where I grew up with my brothers, always scorching from the ovens, floorboards silky with flour. My father would turn in his grave. I head to the garden in disgust.

The damp of the bench soaks through my nylon trousers. The ornamental arms match the lamp post, shining into my room all night. I have to close the window on the women and their lonesome songs, and the awful crash of the river. I never cry, but today I can't help it.

Dogs feel it. Ruby always knew when to push close to my leg. I used to take her to the park and we'd sit on a bench and share two eclairs by the river. Such an art to get the choux light. Then she'd race ahead, past the playground, along the path to the old bridge, glossy fur rippled by ribs. Our usual loop and back along the towpath home.

A carer appears – *just checking you're alright, Nancy* – but I look away. There's no privacy in here. She goes back in to make a note. Nancy still appears upset and isolated – does not want to talk. Build opportunities for connection and expression into her care.

My ragged nails dig into my palms: I need a plan. I've been letting everything go by in a haze. They keep us here in a fog of meals and chatter, hoping we won't notice the singing women – the women that seep from the river to murmur you are trapped, if only you will listen. I am listening now. Watching. I get my notebook out of my bag: get the record started.

Alex

Alex has her booking visit with the midwife at 10.20 a.m. She eats white cheese before they set off, tart and creamy, to help the nausea. Paul insists on coming, even though it's routine – long forms, Bounty pack, protein test – exactly like with Izzy. But he wants to support her every step of the way: he will drive her there with their daughter, then drop them back home before work. It's all sorted, flexitime, no hassle.

She can't feel the baby yet, but sees it when she closes her eyes: a floating creature, in a swirl of ink. Tea-bag infusion, drops of blood in hot water, darkly spreading cloud. Everyone will see it at the scan in a few weeks, brighter then, feathery bones, more coherent, a pulsing white seed at its heart. The midwife welcomes them all in, cheery, tells them to take a seat. She has a twitch in her left eyelid.

Alex is flustered and hot, arms full of jumpers and raincoats. Izzy clambers onto her lap in yellow wellies, suddenly shy. The forms take ages, and the girl starts putting her hands down Alex's top, pulling at her hair, complaining. Bored. The midwife says Paul can take her outside to splash in the puddles if he likes – there's not much today apart from the forms. But he doesn't want to miss a thing.

Alex does the urine sample in the disabled toilet. The midwife's pregnancy wheel said eight weeks, five days; further on than he thought. Why didn't she tell him sooner? There is a big poster on the door with a sepia photo of a crying woman's face and a helpline. Alex looks away. It's so awkward with the cardboard pot. She tips the yellow liquid into a tube, wipes it dry, and takes it back to the midwife, who dips two sticks in and casually tosses them into the bin. Fine.

Paul drops her back home after the appointment; tells her to rest while Isabella has her nap, to take care of herself and their baby. Alex is wrung out like a permanent hangover, but spends the rest of the afternoon by the river: lets Izzy nap in the push-chair. They float sticks in the river, so lucky to live in such a beautiful part of town.

Later, he says she needs to drink more water: she is dehy-drated, *it's not good for the baby*. Alex is exhausted, the visions jolting her awake in the night. She has put the necklace out on the landing windowsill, with her rock collection. But there is still the drilling, vibrations, the violence done to the stone: future split, contorted, strange shadow of dog flashing, drowning women, daughter tripping into the road, tower in flames. Alex is not superstitious, knows that logically the visions cannot be connected to the stone. It is the pregnancy waking her, making her confused. But still she lies motionless in the night, sweating, itching, terrified that she will somehow make the stone's visions come true.

Lauren

I've always hated charity shops – the smell of scummy perfume under steam, the heat, all those interfering old women. I used to take the boys into Pet Protection and let them pick three cars for 50p, until the stupid old cow on the till started bossing us around, thinking she was so much better than us. I never, in a million years, thought I'd end up working in there.

My probation officer said she'd been round the houses to get me in – that I could do better than painting railings. I'm supposed to be making up for what I've done – understanding the harm I've caused – getting skills for the future. She's always saying it's not only about punishment. It feels like it, but she's not so bad. I said I'd give it a go, since she seemed so chuffed with it – not that I've got much choice. At least I don't have to wear one of those stinking orange vests. Mum said her cousin's friend's son got a shitload of abuse wearing one – he had to paint the same park toilet three times on the trot.

She said casual clothes would be fine for the charity shop. I don't want to turn up in jeans though so I squeeze into some Primark trousers – from before I had Oli, pinching the loose skin at my waist. The post comes while I'm getting ready – some circular from the TV licence people. I rip up the envelope without opening it, shove it in the recycling. I can't keep still – just want it over and done with. I don't want the kids at my mum's – they can tell she doesn't like having them. I told Oli that Nana will let him watch TV and she'll give him fizzy pop and biscuits.

Some grannies would kill to spend more time with their grandkids. My mum's done her time though – finished with nappies and all that. It's her turn now, for herself and her blue eyeliner and clicking plastic jewellery. *Alright, I'll have them once a* week but I don't know how I'll explain it to Marge next door, Lauren – I'll die if it gets around. What if she sees you in the shop? You'll have to say you've always loved animals – it's a foot in the door – you want to get back to work after the kiddies. Like Margery doesn't know anyway. But Mum's always on at me – I never brought you up like this, Lauren. I walk away from her house, coated in a thick slick of guilt.

The pissing rain soaks my jacket and frizzes my hair. I arrive at 9.30 – the shop's already open. The old guy at the till thinks I'm a customer. I try to say that I've come on the scheme, to work, cheeks burning, but he can't hear me – just looks confused and shouts for Dee from the back. Dee appears from behind a purple curtain, rosy-cheeked and glowing, high ponytail swishing, not a lot older than me. She shakes my hand, beaming, *hiya, oh it's so lovely to meet you, Lauren – let me give you the tour! Leonard – it would be super-duper if you could hold the fort for ten minutes – thank you, darling.*

Leonard is about a hundred. Ready to pop his clogs. The room out back is piled high with bags – *you'll start here, Lauren, sorting and steaming, and when you get used to it we'll have a little think about the shop floor.*

Floppy clothes seep out of bags all around me. I think I'm going to vom. At least no one can see me back here.

One of our volunteers – lovely Clare – you'll meet her soon – well, she was supposed to be in at 10 a.m., but she's just phoned in sick, poor thing, so you'll be by yourself this afternoon, Lauren, sorting bags, once I've shown you the ropes – I hope that's okay?! I put my best smile on and stand up straight.

You can go on your dinner at twelve – you get an hour – and then we close up at five. Dee doesn't even stop for breath, words pouring from her mouth. She flicks the kettle on and says she'll walk me through everything. *Don't worry about anything. We're just so behind on sorting – you'll be a fantastic help.*

She cuts open the top of a black bag and beams – *it's a good bag!*

It doesn't look good to me. She's so weird. *And this is my very favourite bit – opening the bags – it's always such a surprise – a bit like a tombola!* The clothes and shoes are squirming in the bin liner. I step back, shocked – there is a woman in the bag.

Dee pulls out a baby-blue jumper. She holds it up, turning it from side to side in the light, then pushes a hanger up through the neck and hooks it on the rail. The woman looks like she's trapped in the soft wool – staring out at us, caught, motionless. *Lovely! It only needs a quick steam that one – I'll show you in a minute, don't worry about it for now.*

Dee doesn't seem to notice – just goes back to the bag. The thin plastic splits down the seam as Dee rummages around – sandals, scarves and skirts spilling out – creeping, floating, filling the room with their lives, women suddenly wrapping my face, suffocating. My lungs squeeze – what's happening to me.

I look at the rack – a fat woman bursting out of a pencil skirt – a bony girl with dark eyes in a tiny sequinned dress – a pregnant one in maternity jeans smiling sadly, topless and cow-heavy, naval sticking out madly.

I run for it, tripping through the curtain onto the shop floor, where Leonard's serving a customer. I realise there are women everywhere, that I hadn't noticed before – hanging on every rail. Silent, flickering, almost invisible but definitely there. My breathing's too fast again. The lights are on because it's stormy out – the brightness hurts my forehead. I have to go back – I've brought this on myself – whatever's going on, I have to go through with this, for the kids. I can't mess up. For my probation officer. My cousin. My mum. It's insane though – what the fuck *is* this place. Old Leonard's bagging up a customer's books. Dee comes out from the curtain behind me, her mouth smiling too sweetly. I'm so sorry, I tell her, I just came over a bit dizzy or something – I'm fine now – it would be great if you could show me the steaming.

Nancy

All my clothes have to be labelled. I haven't sewed name tags since Pip started school. My big tears plopping onto bright new shirts and cardigans. He was so sensitive after his dad died, seemed too little for school. Here, someone comes into my room to take dirty washing when I'm not looking. Freshly pressed slacks magically appear in the wardrobe. I'll try harder to catch them at it.

This morning I opened my drawer and found a pair of peachy-coloured knickers: not mine. I slammed the drawer shut, heart racing, sat back on the bed. And where is my underwear. And who is laughing at my huge pants and the big saggy cups of my bra. I decide to write it in my book. But still don't know what to do with the knickers.

I can lock my door so people don't wander off with my belongings, but the handle is always rattling up and down when I'm listening to the wireless: people forget which is their room. Bev gave me a lanyard to keep my key around my neck but it's an illusion: the staff have a main key that works all the doors.

I've come up to get ready for the private dining. Bev keeps dropping hints about visitors joining residents for meals. I know Pip will hate it: brought up on my home cooking. Although it's probably still better than what he gets at home. Everything she makes comes from a jar or packet.

I hold the knickers, finger and thumb, at arm's length. If I put them in my washing basket they might come back, but if I leave them outside my door the staff will think I'm losing it. In my notes. Leaving underwear strewn around, inhibitions going.

I can't exactly walk the corridors with a pair of someone else's knickers: it would be humiliating for everyone. And what if they think I'm the wanderer – that I took them from somebody's room. There's a tap on my door. My stomach clenches and I fling them in my washing basket, praying they'll go away. It's Krystyna, one of the staff. *We are ready for you, Nancy, if you want to come down.*

Private Dining comes off the main room. I walk through, past the usual women: neat Gladys, mad Patricia, scrawny Joyce who likes the same programme as me. It's all high-back chairs with sashes and tablecloths: embarrassing sitting by myself in the quiet. I fiddle with my locket, the clatter of soup coming from the trolley next door. It was my mother's, left to me when she died with its tiny piece of paper: *To my only girl, I will always be with you, no matter what.*

The staff said they'll keep my dinner hot until he gets here. At least you can't hear the river or the singing women from here. The car park is shadowy through nets: lumps of cars and walls. I straighten my cutlery, worrying there's been a crash. Write timings in my book; start a list of suspects about the knickers. Krystyna startles me when she pops her head round. *Just check-ing you are okay, Nancy? I'll bring your food so you can make a start.* I keep hearing tyres on gravel, but when I look, it's only rain against the window.

I've started my soup by the time Bev bustles Pip in, hair plastered to his head, blustering about traffic and weather. Bev saying, *he's made it, poor love, what a day!* Krystyna hurries in with another soup, slopped up the sides. It tastes green. Lukewarm. I smile at Pip as he sits down and dips his spoon. *It's not very hot, is it, Mum? Shall I get them to warm it up?* I carry on drinking mine, not sure what he expected.

I saw you on the website, Mum, for the VE Day thing. It looked nice.

It was swaying and clapping and staring at knees. An ex-care worker with red lips singing off a crib sheet, everyone flap-ping Union Jacks. We'll meet again. My flag flat as a pancake on my lap.

That nice girl was on there too – the one who brought the soup. I nod, put my spoon in the bowl. It's not his fault. And Krystyna is nice. On cue, she appears with two plates before he's even finished: meat, potato, soft veg. He nods towards my notebook. *Do you need anything?* I shake my head, slide it in my bag.

I ask about Ruby. He mumbles that she's settling in. *Start on your main, Mum, don't wait for me.* Something he's not telling me. It'll be that wife of his. She's never liked dogs. I ask him, what is it, love?

He doesn't reply. When it finally comes, the apple pie is soggy and too sweet: brown liquid. The only crunch from tiny rectangles of sugar on top. Custard from a tin. My husband would never have stood for that. I'd arrived with him, newly-wed, at that mossy cottage by the river, full of hope. My family had been the bakers in our little pit village; his the barbers, red-and-white-striped pole outside their shop. George had ambitions for his own shop in town. All I'd known was scorching ovens and the battle to keep coal dust out of the vanilla custards, but everyone said town would be an adventure: George would smoke, twirl me in the new dance halls, sharpen up in a suit.

But I'd never bake the damp out of that house. He slapped my face, grabbed my throat. Clammy pale fingers like fish, leaving big red welts on my skin. On at me about wasting fuel from the off.

I push my pudding away. *Mum, careful.* Tablecloth sprayed finely with custard. I screw my napkin in a ball. Pip doesn't like the pie either. He's only eating it because he feels bad, he's always been that way.

I had a look at the timetable, Mum. I nod, pushing out my chair. *The hairdresser's in tomorrow.* He's trying so hard. I'm used to my mobile hairdresser coming over once a month to tidy up my ends. In here, it's all set perms and pampering: they're always badgering me. *A bit of me-time would do you the world of good.* If anyone thinks they're touching my hair they've got another think coming.

We have a quick walk around the garden, peonies bursting, and then Pip's gone, a few minutes before my programme. I give the bird in the cage some bits of sweetcorn from earlier: she hops across to take them from my fingers. Nothing like a dog, but she's okay. I go to my chair and the telly.

The girl's alcoholic father is lurching around as usual: on the bridge tonight. The volume's up too high, so the deafer ones can hear. *You can't even look after yourself, never mind a baby.* Bev comes round with barley squash and a plate of Nice biscuits. Obsessed about dehydration.

The father lunges at the girl, fist raised, but she's too quick. On his knees, spitting blood. The staff are always interrupting, especially Bev: she puts on a good show of looking after every-one. *Did you enjoy your special dinner, Nancy?* I smile, try to peer

28

round her. The girl is screaming above the river. *What would Mam say if she saw you now?*

The bird is squawking so Bev throws a blanket over the cage. Joyce is next to me, skin and bones, crumbs down her blouse; in the pleats of her skirt. She flinches when the father clouts the girl. Then tuts. *That's it,* the girl's screaming back at him, *I'm done. You're not coming anywhere near me or this baby.*

I hand Joyce my two biscuits, eyes still on the TV. She needs them more than me. *Come back, you're all I've got. I'll prove it!*

Joyce stops munching: the father on the railings now, legs dangling over the water. What's he up to? *Dad, get the hell down.* We all hold our breath. He laughs. *You'll never be free of me.* We lean forward in our ugly chairs, willing the girl on. She storms at him. A close-up of his face – surprise, sudden jerk – and he's plummeting from the bridge. Joyce cackles loudly, spitting biscuit, pointing at the TV. A lingering scream and he's gone: white-clawed river flowing fast.

Alex

Alex has a hole in her stomach and ninety minutes to fill while Izzy does her first settling-in session at the nature nursery. They had agreed to wait until she was two, but Alex needs a break: Paul says she's not coping. At least it's the forest school, the one Reema recommended, not the baby factory place Paul wanted.

The key worker said *it's okay – you just try leaving for a bit, she'll be right as rain.* But Alex insisted on staying too long. Neurotic mother as usual. She'd sneaked out while Izzy was in the garden, distracted by a worm: a betrayal of her daughter. Alex is marching now, bereft. She can't go far. Izzy's too young to understand: what if she thinks Mummy's not coming back? She should have said goodbye. She's only ever been left with her parents for a few hours when they've come up from Brighton, and that's a rare thing. A text comes in: *Isabella is fine, we'll call you if we need you :)*

The graffiti starts before she reaches the river: chalky scrawl on T Motor Mechanics, purple tags on trees, blue cocks and tits on lamp posts. Ivy catches at her arm as she walks down the high-walled snicket: urine and moss, soft wind, narrow strip of blue sky. She once read an urban nature book about ground-sunshine, pale gold primroses, but everything here is soiled with dirty wipes and crushed Volvic; the warm day sneering: why aren't you paddling splashing ice cream. Bad mother.

Ten weeks: *The ears are starting to develop on the sides of your baby's head, and the ear canals are forming inside the head.* It is his baby, not hers. The river is shallow grey, objects rupturing the surface: wooden crate, tyre, upturned trolley. Murky. She's bigger this time, bloated. She shouldn't even be showing yet. Her blue vest is missing. Paul gave her two floral maternity dresses last night: bought them on his lunch break. Says she's blooming. Too soon. She'll put one on later, before he gets home.

There's a sudden burning smell: tyres, rust, meat. It's the pregnancy; a nightmare. An abrupt movement downstream, through the stone bridge. Jerky in the undergrowth. The river's usually like a painting through the arch: a fairy world of babbling green, but Alex freezes – there's a blot in her vision, somehow bleeding into the foliage, spilling itself. Migraine lights flashing in her eyes.

The paving is sticky and cold: Alex can't get up. Drenched in sweat. She vomits water, tries to move out of the way, coughing so hard piss leaks into her jeans. She's a mess – Paul's right – she's totally losing it. Why isn't she in a cafe making the most of this time, treating herself like the key worker said. What if somebody sees.

Alex hauls herself up by the railings, shaking. Wipes her mouth with a baby wipe, tidies up. Checks her face on her phone camera. There is nothing in the bushes. She'll head to the old cemetery – there are benches there – then she can head back early to collect her daughter. White garlic flowers everywhere. *If you could look at your baby's face, you'd be able to see an upper lip and two tiny nostrils in the nose.* She gets to the bench, birds scrabbling like rats in the bushes: scrolls the news on her phone. There's a Family Tracker app which she hasn't seen before. She decides not to pick Izzy up early, after all.

Lauren

Morning, morning, says Dee in the shop, shining in her cherry-red jumper. I nearly puke on the spot – a shadow vanishes into the knit. *Am I glad to see you, Lauren – we've got such a massive backlog!* Last week she sent me home at dinner time – *it's your first day – you really shouldn't be here if you're not feeling well – it's a lot to take in.*

But today I'm on my own, unpacking out back all day. *Leonard's here for a couple of hours and then you'll meet Pam – she comes in once the carers have been round for her William. I'll be out and about at meetings, but don't worry – Pam'll sort you out. She's a superstar!*

Pam turns out to be the old cow who's precious about the kids' cars. She looks like the judge. She's *oh good morning* when she comes in, sickly sweet, head popping through the purple curtain, *it's really nice to meet you.* I can see right through her peachy lips. She's got brassy hair, set tight, and a pearly blouse – wafting Estée Lauder and cats. Mum said there'd be crazy cat women.

There's a mountain of bags in the back, pulsating. It's disgusting. Most them are packed tight, lumpy shapes pushing the plastic from inside, lives trying to get out. It's like the boys in my belly, knuckle lumps hard against the skin, deforming my belly. I can hardly breathe with it.

I drag a white bin bag with a yellow tie down from the pile and slice into it with scissors, shitting myself. Careful not to damage anything. But it's only a bag of uniform – faded red cardies and pleated skirts; greyish polos, well-worn – a pair of pumps, pegged together. Nothing else. No women. I breathe out heavily – maybe I'll go back to normal now, stop seeing things.

I gently cut the name tags out of each bit of uniform as I hang them up – no kid wants everyone knowing they're in second-hand gear. There are boys' trousers and V-necks at the bottom of the bag. I smooth them all out – family life swaying happily on my rail, neatly divided into reds, whites and greens. It's not so bad.

There's a Sainsbury's bag next, stuffed with more uniform – from the same family. They must be chucking everything out and buying all new, unless they've changed school or something. I want my boys at a good school – to wear nice stuff. I keep hanging the clothes and I've nearly emptied the bag when I see her, flattened at the bottom on orange plastic. Cheek against the floor. Pam pokes her head through the curtain to check if I'm alright – she heard a scream. I stutter about unpacking this bag but I think there's something in it. Her face is blank except for the mouth, curling upwards. Oh my God, she knows. *Oh we get all sorts,* she says slickly, *you won't believe what some people send in – there was a dirty nappy in one of my bags last week. Here, let me look.* Pam pulls out the tunic dress with the woman in it, then turns the bag inside out and gives it a sharp shake. A stray bit of Lego, a hair bobble: nothing else. She grips the dress by the shoulders and holds it high: *White Stuff, size 12, good condition. This'll be nice in the window with some beads – let's have a think about it later this aft.*

Pam pushes the dress at me and goes back through to the front. I throw it down – kick it away from my feet. It crumples next to the wheels of the yellow dump bin. I can't see the woman, but I can feel her, exhausted and sad, almost invisible on the floor. There's no way I can pick her up.

There's a box of books, so I go through them next, checking for scribbles and missing pages like Dee said, trying not to think about the woman. The box is noisy, full of bickering and interruptions but nothing to see. There are so many bags, I'll never get through them. I pick one that isn't sealed – a big blue Ikea bag overflowing with jigsaws and baby toys. Stained breastfeeding cushion. The puzzles need to be checked for their pieces. Pam said she's happy to do them at the till. I push back through the curtain with a stack of boxes – the shop is empty and she's chatting to Leonard. *I'm making a cuppa – do you want one?* Pretending to be nice. I say yes please, milk no sugar, hoping it'll get me out of unpacking for a bit.

The sad woman's still on the floor. I can't leave her there – what if Pam tells Dee. I pick up the tunic, hold her at arm's length. She stares back, scorn in her hollow eyes. I brush off the dust, shove the hanger in and get her on the rail. I work faster after that, trying not to see anything. Last week, Dee said *you need to give all the pockets a quick check before you steam them, Lauren*, merrily plunging her hand into a coat and pulling out scraggy tissues and sticky wrappers. I can't bring myself to do that, not yet, so instead I just try and shake them out. Anything with holes, rips or stains gets chucked in the dumper. I'm surprised when Pam asks me to join them by the till for my tea. She's probably poisoned it. She gestures to the sanitiser, then offers the pack of digestives. I take one and eat it upside down, slowly, chocolate melting warm on my tongue. Leonard dunks his; doesn't notice Pam's disapproval. She gives me a look, shaking her head at him. I hope she'll offer me another, stomach rumbling, but know it'd be politer to refuse.

Gytrash

The security guard takes the shortcut along the river, sky already streaked raspberry pink: past the new-builds, out of town towards the hospital. She is on a day shift, a good job for security work, but she will still miss the heatwave everyone's raving about.

She whistles while she walks. Nothing you'd recognise. Swings her arms, all the world hers. New green everywhere. There is a sudden crack in the bushes up ahead. She freezes. She often disturbs squirrels and birds at this hour, but can't see anything. The towpath is deserted, as usual.

She takes two slow steps forward, watching. Again, the snap of branches. And a stink – like the abattoir – boiling the bones. She can't turn back now: she'll be late signing in.

She squares up: can take anyone on. But it is not anyone, blocking the path, fierce pain in her arm and heart, huge shaggy head, fiery eyes, big as a horse

and it all floods in: built like a brick shithouse, gobby shite, you're a lesbo, cornered in the yard, batting harder than any lad, what the fuck you wearing? In the wrong job, look at the tits on this, women on crutches, with babies, in wheelchairs, women who see straight through her.

Glue in the bins, blinding head, spots around her mouth and she clutches her heart, but then it's gone, pink-jam-ripple sky washed into dawn, birds singing, gentle breeze, and she has to get on, get up off the ground: she'll be late for work. She will take a different path next time.

June

Lauren

Dee says we have to get the shop looking *tip-top, sparkly hop* before the area manager gets here. She's so fucking weird. I'm sorting again today, but old Pam's out back too, as Dee's taking care of the front. I've put my tatty jeans on – I'm not ruining my best clothes going through other people's shit any more. Pam's still doing my head in, but I'm hoping I won't start seeing things if she's around.

Pam's wiping shelves and manically hoovering round the heap of donations – doesn't want it looking a disgrace. She tuts – *I can't believe some people* – *leaving all that rubbish outside the shop again last night* – *it's basically fly-tipping, Lauren.* I nod along – the pile of bags getting bigger instead of smaller. Dripping with sweat, hardly room to breathe. *Just what are we supposed to do with all these dirty duvets and broken toasters and soggy bags of rubbish? You know* – *I said to Dee she should phone the police.*

Pam stops abruptly, neck flushing red. *Sorry, Lauren. I didn't mean anything about you, I mean the police might put people off doing it.* I nod in agreement, it's bad yeah, trying to paper over her embarrassment. People probably mean well though, Pam. I don't know why everyone thinks I'll go to pieces if they so much as mention the cops. Pam puts her vac back on, but keeps gawping at me. My throat blocks with dread – I won't get away with leaving the pockets while Pam's watching my every move. I turn away – drag a black bin liner out from the front. Pick up my scissors. Take a massive breath – pray that it's a normal one. I'm going mad in here.

Two women rush straight out through the slit as soon as I cut the plastic. I want to push them back, stuff polythene and cushions in their faces, run out of here for good. They circle my head, mouths gaping, laughing silently to the sound of Pam's Hoover. They've flaky red lips, stained with wine. It's not a good bag. Mucky cushion covers, odd socks, used knickers. Pam glances over when she's done but doesn't flinch.

I flap at my head when she's not looking. The only thing worth saving's a leopard fake-fur coat, but its pockets are so far into the fur that I'm tempted to trash it. Pam's already seen though – I have to do the job properly – think of my boys. I try to push the pockets up from inside the coat, but they're in the lining. It's impossible. I roll up my sleeves and get ready.

I put my hand gently into the first pocket. Something warm and soft. I recoil, pulling out quickly, almost dropping the coat. I could just leave it. But she's watching. I go in again: pull out a black leather glove. The women shriek with laughter. Bitches. I grope around for more, trying to scoop all the bits out in one so I don't have to put my hand in again. There's a scrunched ticket and a foil-wrapped bit of chewing gum, crumby. Scraps of life. Grit and bits from the seams have got under my nails and I shake my hand hard, trying to get rid them, the women batting my face. I race on to the other pocket – I need those women fixed on the rail. More crumbs and 20p – no mate for the glove. It's a battle now. Pam watches me put the coin in the special box on the shelf.

I rush to the toilet to wash my hands and face. It's cramped, everything in one tiny whitewashed cubbyhole, and I sit on the toilet lid, forehead on the little chipped sink, sobbing. I don't know what to believe – I just want to do this right so I can get back to my kids. I need a proper job. Always having to do everything myself – why can't I get a man like Jody's or

Chelsea's? I always end up with the bad ones. We need a garden, not even a big one – and a trampoline, to get the kids off the telly, get some energy out – I need someone to help me, just a bit. Fuck's sake.

My mascara's a state in the rusting mirror, but I do my best to clean up, and eventually head back. Pam pats my arm a bit as I go past but I don't show I notice – I don't want to end up like her.

I'm out in the yard by the fire door having a smoke when I hear men's voices in the back. I listen to the river, sucking sweet cherry mist to help with the stench of the bags. When I go back in, there's two men stood next to the dump bin with Pam. Her face shining pleased. The fit one puts out his hand, how very lovely to meet you. Zegna shirt, sunglasses on his head, kind face. Relaxed. Italian-looking arms. His polo shirt is fresh in the suffocating room of limp clothes. I pull my T-shirt down, suck my belly in, shoulders up, back down. Meet his handshake, steady and cool, well, nice to meet you too, and I shake the other man's hand as well – they're both from head office – and then they're off again, back through the curtain. I hear them laughing out front with Dee as I slice into the next bag.

Alex

Alex arrives at Kaffeine ten minutes early, excited to see Reema. She texts: *I'm early, what can I get you? On me :)* A reply. *Just parking, won't be a min. Coffee pls xx.* Alex orders two cappuccinos, a salted brownie and a wedge of lemon drizzle. She has cash left over from her birthday: they will share the cakes, like they used to, on maternity leave. She sinks into an air-cooled chair: a relief to be out of the heat. Thirteen weeks, five days. The sickness dissipating. A celebration.

Gap maternity jeans, left over from Izzy. Stripy vest, pebble necklace on show. Second trimester: You'll notice a small bump developing as your womb grows and moves upwards. Paul says she's spilling like a whale. Already. But she feels oddly lighter than at six weeks. Guilty, for being so excited about chatting to a grown-up while Izzy's at nursery, but lighter. She hasn't seen Reema for months. Air-conditioned chill blows her cheeks. A man and woman at the back of the cafe, shy: looks like a first date. She checks her phone, feeling good: a big breath into her lungs until her ribs can't expand any more. Then she does it. Deletes the tracker app; the app she never installed in the first place.

She has an hour before she picks Izzy up. Reema's driving straight over from Sunnyside. She keeps telling Alex that she loves being back at work, *nothing's changed though, Al – except they'll never find a geography teacher as good as you!* Her energetic laugh. *At least I get my coffee while it's hot. I super miss Rudi though.* She wants him to grow up with a strong female role model.

Reema bursts into the cafe with a big hug: *Oh my goodness, come here, you – I can't believe it's been this long! Am I late?!* She's not really. *Tell me everything, Alex!* Alex says yeah, it's all good, Izzy's just started nursery – it seems to be going well. *Will you be coming back to work then?* Alex stands up to wave at the lost-looking waiter. He brings their tray over.

Alex – you're so naughty! I'm on a new regime. Alex smiles conspiratorially. *Oh, blow it, who'll know?!* Reema laughs, and Alex joins in, relieved: she's just the same. Alex demands the latest Sunnyside gossip, cafe jazz silking through their hair, Reema rattling rumours about Pete and Liz, bouncing in her seat, blinking her perfect curve of eyeliner. She's always rocked tracksuit and trainers like a skin: ever the PE teacher. But suddenly. *Are you okay, Alex?* Alex panics: she must have been staring. She'd thought she was on good form today; presenting well. She's a total fucking disaster in social situations these days; she's forgotten everything.

She feels tears coming. *Oh, Alex, what is it?* Reema leans forward; squeezes her hand. Alex says she's pregnant – not planned. But nice, just a bit emotionally all over the place, you know. *Oh – that's amazing, congratulations! Wow! Look at me rabbiting on when you've got this massive news! Why didn't you stop me?!*

Big hug. *Absolutely everything used to set me off when I was pregnant with Rudi – don't you worry about it.* Another big hug. *Oh, Paul must be over the moon.* Gush gush second child. *It's so exciting that you've taken the plunge. We've been thinking we'll wait a bit longer, you know – so I can get back into the swing of work, and so Rudi's just that bit older.* Alex tries a smile while Reema babbles on. *You've got me all broody now though!*

Alex blows her nose; presses tissue under her eyes. I'm so sorry, what am I like? Reema rubs Alex's knee, just like when Alex started at Sunnyside: newly qualified and petrified. PE and geography: a good pair. Both had restless bodies; both found it easier to talk on the move. Reema helped her navigate staffroom politics, and Alex did the logistics for their weekend camping trips.

Have you the photo from the scan? Reema asks. Alex shakes her head and smiles. Not on me, but everything's fine. There's lots of movement apparently. It's too soon to feel anything yet, of course. About the size of a lemon. Reema shrieks. *Oh my goodness, I remember that – all those different fruits they bang on about! My Rudi was a watermelon from the off!*

Paul used to say that Reema was one of those attractive pregnant women: neat bump, tidy up front, not a flabby tyre round the middle. She looks better pregnant – less like a boy – not so flat-chested. He didn't like them seeing each other though. *You're too smart for her, Alex.* You have an extra organ in your body that wasn't there fourteen weeks ago. The placenta. Fine hair is growing on your baby's head and body. Alex focuses hard on the buttercup drizzle of the cake, determined not to let anything spoil it. She slices through cracked white sugar into the sticky yellow heart, splitting the cake with a smiling mouth.

They chat about Friday's match against Belgium; why the World Cup never gets called the 'men's' football; their book group, which Alex keeps missing because of Paul's work meetings. He does his best though: last month he double-booked with squash, but cancelled the second he realised. Even came home from work early so Alex had time to get ready. He knows she wants to meet more people: that her only friends here are still through work.

Alex tries to ignore the images that come crowding in: the heatwave, throwing hot coffee at the waiter, Germany's knockout, blaze on the moor, soldiers fighting fire. She blinks hard. Focus on the nutty smell of coffee. She's been using a birth hypnosis CD to calm her mind but it flares up whenever she stresses out. She takes off the pebble necklace and slides it in her bag.

Alex heads off for Izzy at 4.30 and arrives home with her, hand in hand, at the normal time. She feels better for the tears: her heart rinsed a little. She's promised her daughter pink milk and curly pasta. A cosy tea. But when they come up the drive, Paul's already opening the door. Home earlier than he said. Sticking his hand out, palm to Alex. *Phone, Alex.* She hesitates, mobile in her back pocket. Paul! Come on, let's go in, Izzy's tired. *Do you think I'm stupid, Alex? And her name's Isabella.* What is it, Paul, what are you talking about? They go inside, shut the door. Alex kneels to take Izzy's shoes off.

Why did you delete it?

Alex keeps working on Izzy's shoes, head down. *You know full well what I'm talking about, Alex. I obviously don't matter to you any more.* Alex finishes the shoes and stands up. Paul – come on – why would you say that? – you know I love you. We both do. Izzy holds on to her leg. You look like you've had a really hard day – Isabella's been talking about you on the way back – she wants to play – that'll make us all feel better.

Isabella can watch TV – we need to sort this. Go on, darling, into the living room.

Paul, she needs her tea – she needs her daddy – come on. Let's all have tea together. We could get pizza? A hesitation. A hope. But. *In here, Isabella, I'll put* Teletubbies *on while Mummy and Daddy have a little chat – that's what you want, isn't it? – Mummy doesn't even know what you like does she, silly Mummy.*

Please, Paul. Alex begging now. Please. *Alex, you always have to be different. All the other dads look out for their wives – I've never heard anyone else complaining. It's my job to keep you safe.* I know, Paul, you know how much I appreciate it. Alex feels faint with the heat. The baby has started to crackle inside her. *You're not right in the head, Alex. What if something happens to you – or Isabella – or our baby?* He's right. Izzy drowning. Ballistic missile. Fever.

Alex stands, not moving, just staring at his blurry mouth. *You've got me down for a fool – I know you're hiding something from me.* Alex shakes her head, no, Paul, no. *Well, why else would you delete it? What's that woman been putting in your head?* Paul – I didn't really know what it was – I was just having a quick tidy-up on my phone – I can get it back if it's important, no problem – look, I'll do it now. I'm always getting these things wrong.

It's too late, Alex – damage done. Paul, don't say that. Please. You know – you and Isabella – you're all that matter to me – come on, let's ring for pizza. You know I love you.

You think you can talk your way out of everything, Alex. You're such a manipulative bitch. Paul, please. Isabella – go back in the living room, my love. *Scheming to see other men behind my back.* Paul – she can hear – she's upset. Paul closes the door and blocks it with his body.

You're suddenly so bothered about your daughter? Don't give me that – the only person you care about is yourself. You and your fancy coffee – out spending my money and then drivelling on about pizza. Goddamn pizza? Why haven't you made dinner like a normal person?! Paul's face stretching like a shiny red balloon. Alex knows there is nothing she can say now. *Down on all fours like the animal that you are. Now.* Alex shakes her head. Izzy is shouting for her. No. Not in front of her.

Mummy, Mummy. Crying. Alex smiles at her: it's okay, Isabella – go back in the living room, Mummy's fine. As long as he stays away from Izzy. Please – go on, love. But. *No, darling, come here. Mummy's just playing doggies, aren't you, love – come on, Isabella – we'll all play together.*

Nancy

My stomach lurches when I open the drawer. It's been nearly a fortnight since I put the knickers in the basket, but someone obviously thinks they're mine. I've no idea what to do. Throw them away. Hide them. I wonder about trying the washing basket one last time: it might work in my favour, to distract from the butterfly of blood, folded in on itself, probably nothing, hidden among yesterday's skirts. It's been happening since I got here: I'm far too old for it.

I switch off the fan for a bit of peace. They're everywhere, whirring like water. I can't sleep for the heat, so I've been going down to sit with the bird at night. Luna, she's called. The best company I'm likely to get in here.

A troop of Brownies are coming to sing to us today: an afternoon concert with tea and cake. A good turn. Bev said I should get a nice shampoo and blow-dry at the weekly salon, to get ready for it. Lord help us.

Gladys knocks for me, so I close the drawer and walk with her to the lift. We're early. It's embarrassing, sitting like lemons waiting for the girls. Legs sticky in crimplene trousers, fans whirring hot air. I go over to the birdcage: post a little treat from my handbag through the bars. The bird hisses back. She's female. Gentler than the males. One of the staff ushers me to my seat so they can parade the Brownies in. It's in their faces: all they see and smell is old people. I clap politely next to Gladys: in her element now, twinkling for the girls.

One of them, at the front, has nice curly hair. She meets my eyes while Brown Owl does her speech. She sees white plait, snaking over my shoulder, thick glasses. Tries to smile. Fat old woman. Past it. I don't smile back and her face goes like a beetroot. I have a pain, deep below my belly.

We never knew if the baby before Pip was a girl, but I always thought of her like that. You didn't talk about things like that then. George was good to me, for once, arm around me, cramping on the floor. Making excuses for me after, when I couldn't face anyone. He'd wanted it badly too. It's not your fault, love. The toilet outside the kitchen, always freezing. Urine and offal stinging bright red in the bowl, whitewash from the walls in my hair. I've never told Pip, not even to this day.

Pip was our miracle – we'd thought it was too late for us by then. George wet the baby's head in the pub, glad it was a boy, but I would have loved a sister for him. And then, all those years after, Pip's daughter came along. My second chance. We'd go to the swings, play Poohsticks on the old bridge. Bake sponges the old way: egg whites whisked into glorious peaks; the perfect wobble of yolks, so easily split. But his wife always got between us: rushing the little girl off here, there and everywhere when they could have been round at mine. Always twisting my words. In the end, they only came round at weekends, when Pip wasn't working, and it was obvious she didn't want to be there, even then. She's never been right for him.

I look up. The Brownies are singing now: out of tune, but slightly better than expected, although I refuse to sway my skirts or tap along. The curly-haired girl sings to her toes. I will never understand girls.

July

Alex

Alex pegs a muslin over the pushchair to shade Izzy from the sun. Curls plastered to her head, cheeks flushed, sticky, cherry lips. She looks so little when she's asleep. Alex thought there would be a breeze at the river, but this bit of towpath is blazing midday heat. She leans into the walk, muscles lethargic, her brain toddler-slow: snails, stones in shoes, stopping every five steps. Nap-time the only rest. Sweat trickles into Alex's mouth, her cleavage; shoulders burning, inner thighs rubbing. Salty. Worrying about a lost gold hoop earring. A special birthday present from Paul when she was pregnant with Izzy. Down the river will be shadier. Alex prays her daughter will stay asleep; book-club novel ready in her bag. She needs to read it this time: wants to be able to join in the conversation.

The river sparkles cold in the sunlight. Alex's stomach itches; her feet are swollen hot. If it was the sea, she would plunge in, rinse herself cool. Paul used to love this about her: would stand on the beach when they visited her parents, watch her swim, towel over his shoulder, laughing.

They should go down to see them again: get away, get sea air, start again. The crackle of waves pulling pebbles in and out; the excitement of sand at spring tide. Her parents have always loved Paul, the perfect guest: armed with wine and flowers, a super

44

help in the kitchen. Maybe it would help her get back to her usual self. She will ask if he can get a few days off.

Alex strides along, thinks I will be better this afternoon, more patient with Izzy. She's only a baby. We'll paddle in the shade; cut through the park for ice cream. There is a sudden splash in the river up ahead: a splintering shriek. Alex rushes forward, shielding her eyes. There is a woman in the water, laughing. Space-black cap covering her ears, like a rugby player. No obvious danger. Alex puts the brake on the pushchair and peers down the steep bank. The woman beams up at Alex, then hauls herself onto a boulder and waves. She is a pale lizard now, crêpe skin on bone: her swimming costume loose and green. Strands of white hair leaking out from under the cap. She beckons enthusiastically. *Come on in!* Star-blue eyes bright at Alex.

Alex waves back, hello. Her forehead hurts: it is too bright. She says it looks lovely – but – shaking her head, talking too much, gesturing to the pushchair – another time. The woman unglues her lips, speaking slowly – *come back a different time without it* – stressing every consonant. *The water is very exquisite. I swim here every day, all the year round!* Alex has never seen this woman before. There is something peculiar about her voice. Then she is gone, white under green, undulating. At home. Alex closes her eyes. Should have brought her sunglasses. Racing at the city pool, lungs burning for the squad. In the water, she used to be part of something bigger, before she moved north for uni. Wrinkled fingers, chlorine tang for days. She used to tell everyone she'd swim the Channel: stripped to the skin by salt.

But the river is not the sea. The woman's sleek green. Moss and frogs. Alex opens her eyes: this river pool must be deep – muddy at the bottom, sucking. She calls a polite goodbye and turns away – the woman gone from her – then rummages for the sports bottle under the pushchair, throat burning, legs tight and stiff. Her back aches. Her phone on silent in her back pocket: three missed calls. Tears prickle her eyes. Lips sore. She needs to reach the shade, to rest, to read her book in time for the group.

She gently lifts the brake, trying not to jar the girl, but it is too late. *Mama. Mama?* Alex peeps under the muslin. It's alright, darling, I'm here. Mummy's always here.

Lauren

I lent some rubber gloves off Mum this morning to help with the unpacking. They'll stop stuff getting under my nails at least. I'm elbow-deep in a bag of tweed suits when the area manager appears at the curtain. I look up, caught in my Marigolds – nobody mentioned he was coming. *I just wanted to pop back in to see how you're getting on.* Thick dark hair. Eyes clear like water on a sunny day. Me and the boys sometimes go down to the old bridge and look for fish. My face is hot. I stand myself up tall and peel off the gloves – tuck my hair behind my ears. *Don't mind me,* he says, *I just wanted to say hello properly. Why don't you finish off and I'll put the kettle on?* I say that'd be nice. Worrying about the stink of rubber on my hands. He opens the fridge. *Dee always has some proper coffee in here – it'll be our secret. I'll do us a cafetière!*

I'd been right in the middle of a set of sad bags, getting in a rhythm with them, sorting through the old man's life – gardening tools, ship in a bottle, smart shirts and jackets. It looked like his family wanted rid of everything. There were no women – these were gentle bags. Breather bags. Old Spice and tobacco bags. Dee would've said they were good bags – not much for the dump – but it's not as straightforward as that. While the manager's getting the mugs out, I push everything together, tidy, and disappear into the toilet – scrub my hands and nip my cheeks for blush. I put my head upside down and rake my fingers through my hair. When I come out, he's moved two wooden stools across to the fridge. I hope he isn't going to report me. Accuse me of something. I've been doing exactly what they said – right down to the pockets.

Dee tells me you're working really hard, he says. I smile, non-committal, perching on a stool. *It sounds like you've got your hands full at home.* I do a giggle. You can say that again!

Boys or girls? I tell him two boys – not at school yet. They're with my mum today. He has dark eyelashes: tree-brown eyes. I look away: he's so intense, staring into my face like that. He pours the coffee and offers a mug, turning the handle my way, burning his fingers a bit. Awkward. We laugh. *Milk? Sugar?* I tell him white, please, no sugar. I cross my legs, lean in, maybe he's not so bad. He asks, *are you from round here?* I tell him I grew up down the road – went to Hall Cross – just downriver. What about you? He sounds a bit southern. *We moved here from London when I was a teenager, so I can't really claim it as home.* He laughs again. *My accent's a bit of a mash-up isn't it?!* Maybe he really does just want to chat. Dee suddenly appears through the curtain.

Ah, Dee! Why good morning! Well, you've truly caught us red-handed! He stands up and smiles for her. *I'll get you a brand-new bag of coffee for next week – your favourite. Promise.* Dee tinkles laughter and shrugs, no bother, but her face is like thunder. Wants a quick word with him. He heads through the purple curtain with her – *so nice to have you here, Lauren – part of the family.* A wink. *See you another time.* I'm suddenly desperate for a smoke but should wait til he's gone. He didn't mention my probation, but no one ever does. I stand up, take a gulp of the coffee, bitter-sweet burning my throat, and then go back to the trowels and tweed jackets.

Nancy

I can't sleep again. The birds are loud outside, the light whining through the curtains. Breakfast isn't til eight. You're allowed it earlier, but I don't like to stand out. I overheard Joyce asking for a sandwich in her room last night, but bedrooms are no place for eating. I should be walking Ruby at the river by now.

I would be if it wasn't for that wife of his. Pip always said he'd be there for me, even after she moved in with him, but she made it perfectly clear she wouldn't have me to stay after the fire in my kitchen. And now she's got her way: I'm stuck here and she's got him all to herself.

47

I should have seen it coming. She needs to watch her back though. People don't realise how I've had to fend for myself, what with my brothers and husband. That time I woke George with his own barber's blade glinting at his throat: swore I'd kill him if he ever touched my little boy. He was worse with me after that, but never went near Pip. Just wait until I'm out.

The front door has a code. Some residents go out, but there's regulations: signing out, expected return, all in the book by the front door. They're looking for a volunteer to walk out with me: until my nerves are more steady after the accident. I get up and put the kettle on, stomach swirling acid.

I open the drawer while I wait. More knickers. I need to put a stop to this. No name tag again. I get my notebook. Possible owners. Gladys and mad Patricia at the top. Try to think logically. I turn to the log in the back of my book: shift patterns, movements in the building. First-floor corridor mostly unguarded in the day.

A carer sits on my corridor some nights, to stop Patricia wandering. She's up all the time, moth at a light bulb, traipsed back to bed, inky purple ridges under her eyes in the morning. The staff caked them with concealer yesterday, at the weekly salon, crystal-pink lipstick on her mouth. She looked appalling: she's not the make-up type. Gladys looked away, tactfully, but I couldn't help staring. Abysmal fairy lips, black cave of mouth, thread of spittle. The tears filled up in my eyes, big great lump rising in my throat and chin, blocking.

I decide to try Gladys's room first: she's the most predictable. The cleaners do the bedrooms during mealtimes, leave the doors unlocked when they're done, working from her room, past mine, up the corridor to the second floor. I tuck both pairs of pants in my bag, under my purse. An hour until breakfast. I get dressed, thinking it all through.

Downstairs, Gladys is tapping delicately at her eggs, pearls perfect around her neck. I sit with scrawny Joyce for a change: don't want my face to slip anything. Krystyna is on the breakfast shift, as my notebook predicted. *Morning, Nancy,* she smiles at me, *did you sleep well?* Not so bad, thanks. I take a slice of stiff toast from the rack and start buttering. Keep it normal.

Halfway through I push my plate away. Triangle toast unfinished. *That's not like you, Nancy!* Krystyna doesn't miss a trick. Actually, I'm feeling a bit off – could I have a sandwich in my room later on? Polite but casual. *Of course – I will let the kitchen know. You get some rest.* Old Joyce frowns at me, suspicious. She's as sharp as Gladys, in her own way. Krystyna murmurs on. *You can change your mind later if you feel a bit better, it is not a problem, Nancy.*

I'll have to spend the rest of the morning in my room; hope that Gladys doesn't do anything unusual. The deputy knocks to check my temperature. *You need to keep yourself hydrated, Nancy pet.* High alert. She puts a pile of magazines and a glass of squash on my bedside table. *This should keep you going. I'll bring your paper up when it comes.*

My stomach clenches when I hear the gong for dinner. I can't go anywhere until they bring my sandwich. I stay in bed with my paper. Five minutes later Kerry arrives with a thermometer and ham salad on triangle white, with a little pile of crisps. A kiddies' party plate. *I told the kitchen to do it extra special for you, pet.*

The moment she's gone, I polish off half the sandwich, listening for the cleaners: they're at the last room on my floor. The lift doors signal action. I give them a minute to launch off with their mops and trolleys and slowly open my door, wincing at the click. I quick-shuffle up the carpet to Gladys's room, blood rushing in my ears.

A tiny knock, just in case. Nothing. I try the handle. Another click, then the door opens to lavender light. Last glance, corridor clear, and I slip in and shut myself in. The room is tidy and fresh like Gladys's hair, not a strand out of place. With the door shut, I've no idea what I'm doing in here. If anyone sees, they'll report me as a wanderer, and then I'll never get out. They'll think I'm a thief. Or I have a weird fixation about knickers.

I swallow, trying to calm my blood. It's too late now. Gladys has glossy white drawers and a spotless matching dresser – she must have brought them from home. I hear something in the corridor and stop dead. A trolley going past. At the wrong time. Mad, criminal, deviant. I wait, rooted to the spot, until I hear the lift. Gone again.

I pull the knickers from the bottom of my bag, shake off the crumbs. If I can only get them back to their owner, everything will be sorted. I get lucky. The first drawer is rows of underwear, neatly rolled. But there's something wrong. Pearly satin, a bit of lace, not a peachy pair in sight. I think about stuffing them in anyway, but that would give the whole game away. I push the drawer shut, shove the knickers back in my bag, bang a few more drawers, reckless now, praying for something else.

I'm scurrying for the door when I notice a pale yellow sticky note under the mirror. Four digits in black marker. 2104. There is a rumbling: the lift on the move. I scrabble for my notebook, but the lift stops. No time to write it. I'll have to rely on my head. I burst into the corridor, back to detergent and steak pie, down the carpet to my room. A glimpse of the manager coming out of the lift. She'll just think I came from the bathroom.

Alex

Nineteen weeks: Alex is exhausted already. She remembers those hazy night mornings when Isabella was new, feeding into blur. Padded thick between the thighs, slack, bruised. How will she do it again. Propped up with pillows, constant giving, desperate to sleep. Paul has just signed her up to Audible: said she should enjoy this time, like the other mums. Wishes he could chill out all day with books, instead of working. He slept in the spare room when Izzy was born: needed his rest for work. Bringing in hot tea at first light; sending photos to the NCT group. Mums texting: lucky you!

Alex's head was stuffed with clouds after Izzy, confused. The health visitor gave her a questionnaire and Paul watched her fill it in. Her score was not depressed. He booked parental leave for all the appointments. Her parents came and went in a flurry: stayed in a nearby B&B to give the new family space. His mum was the opposite: Alex realised she had been expecting to move in. Alex had put her foot down: we can't have her living here, Paul, it's too much. We need some space to get used to everything. Not that that stopped his mother criticising. Alex couldn't do anything right.

Izzy was down on her birth weight at first – normal for breastfed babies – but she regained it quickly. All those yellow nappies to change, milk going straight through, drudgery. We'll keep an eye on her, nothing to worry about. Paul and his mum were obsessed with the growth chart. Alex failing to feed his child properly.

The health visiting team are always available to chat at the weigh-in clinics. Paul said they should be formula feeding: that way they'd know how much the baby took. Alex's milk might be deficient. He joked. He booked a long lunch every Wednesday so they could go to the weigh-in clinic together: her and the baby should be ready outside at 2 p.m. so that he wouldn't be late back. The weekly test. He charmed all the nurses at the clinic: such a keen first-time dad.

One Thursday, the doorbell went when Alex wasn't expecting it. She ignored it at first, feeding upstairs with the curtains shut. But it wouldn't go away. The health visitor stood there, bright as a daisy. *Hiya, love – only me. I was just round the corner seeing another mum and I thought I'd pop by on the off chance, to check how you're both getting on.* Alex's heart racing. A checking up. A bad mother. Erm, it might be better to come back when Paul's in – he's at work right now. *Oh, we don't need him, poppet, he'd only get in the way. Why don't you put the kettle on and I'll get my scales out? Milk no sugar please.* Alex dithered around, then left Izzy on the play gym in the living room, squawking. The health visitor on the sofa with the baby's red book. It was weird in the kitchen – quiet and shivery.

Alex carried two mugs back to the living room, trying not to slop. She was always so clumsy. *Ooo, love, it says you've been weighing her every week, you don't need to be bothering yourself with that.* Looking up enquiringly. Alex nodded – we just like to make sure she's putting her weight on. *Well, we won't disturb her today then – her chart's looking excellent. You're doing super!* She put her mug carefully on the coaster that Alex put in front of her. *I've brought you some vitamins, love – for you and baby – I forgot to drop them off last time I came. You can tell Dad I just popped round with those.*

Alex sat down, relieved, gazing at Izzy on the play mat. The health visitor leaned forwards and smiled. *So, how've you been keeping?* Alex replied fine – but tired – more than I expected. She doesn't mention that she keeps getting confused. Some of the babies in our group are sleeping through the night, but Isabella wakes up at least every two hours. We don't know what to do. *Oh, it's normal normal – their stomachs are teeny tiny at this age, like little marbles – they need to wake up so they don't starve! It's nature's way.* The baby's arms and legs were waving a bit too wildly on the mat. Alex stood to pick her up. *But what about you, love?* Yes fine. Fine I think. Scooping up the baby, rooting for milk.

You get yourself settled, I'll bring you some water. The health visitor passed her a cushion. Alex nodded, unclipping her bra. Thanks. The tumblers are in the cupboard above the sink. The health visitor went out and came back with water: *I always got parched the second I sat down to nurse – and then you're stuck!* Alex nodded again, eyes on Izzy. Paul always left the remote out of reach so that she could concentrate properly on the baby. She tried to think of something normal to say. Listening for wheels on the drive. The health visitor picked up her mug and held it in two hands.

Have you got any family close by, love? Alex adjusted the baby's head. Not really – my parents are down south so it's a bit of a drive really. We're okay though.

The health visitor nodded. *Well, I'm glad I've caught you by yourself for a bit.* Alex looked at her, startled. *Oh, don't look like that – it's nothing to worry about – it just gives you a chance to ask about things that feel a bit more private, you know, all these things that men don't understand about having a baby!* Alex did a small laugh.

How's it been – with you and your husband I mean? It's a big change for everyone, having a baby.

Fine, Alex smiled, yeah fine. Tried not to nod. She's always nodding. He's really good, looking after us both. She glanced at the photo on the windowsill: honeymoon couple laughing, faces close, after their seven-hour trek up Mount Baker, cold blue skies stretching out behind. Alex is sun-freckled and flushed from the climb. In her element. She'd done the planning and itinerary: she always used to be better at that sort of thing. It was an incredible trip.

Alex turned back to the woman. He's always been amazing. He can't take his eyes off the baby. *And how's that, love?* Izzy came unlatched, crying. Alex focused on getting her back on.

The woman's voice going again. *I did notice how attentive he is – never wants to miss anything when I call.* Alex didn't reply, face crimson. *Alex?* The health visitor looking directly at her now, speaking more slowly. *If there's anything ever that doesn't feel right, I'm always here.* Alex kept staring down at the baby. *Or I can put you in touch with people who can help. It's all confidential – we don't go round telling the world and it definitely won't be written in your notes for anyone to see.*

Alex's cheeks burning. Hot and cold. Little laugh. Izzy's sucks were always too noisy: clicks and clacks. The health visitor speaking quietly – *abuse comes in lots of forms, Alex. We do see a big rise when ladies have babies – so it's something we always have to ask about. If there's anything your husband does that makes you feel uncomfortable, you can always talk to us.* Alex shook her head. Grinned brightly, teeth bared. No, nothing like that. Thank goodness! *Okay, love, well, I've got a little booklet here with some information and a helpline – I'll just put it here while I nip to the loo if you don't mind. I'll need to take it away with me as I only have the one.*

Alex sat, frozen, the pamphlet searing a hole in the coffee table. Silence on the drive. Pastel dandelion clocks on the front. She reached forward and flicked through. Does your partner belittle you blame you isolate you Pressure you hurt you make unwanted demands Keep cash prevent you Take your money? She heard movement upstairs: put the leaf-let back exactly where it was. Well practised. The woman came back in, cheery. Knew she had peeked. *I'll be straight with you, Alex, before I head off. It's hard to talk about these things. But there are people who can help – who'll believe you. Like me. Places you can go.* Silence.

Alex stroked Isabella's soft scalp, the baby asleep at the breast, lips ticking in sleep. Angry with this woman, judging her. Silence. And then she was off again. *Okay, I best be getting on or they'll think I've got lost! I'm down to see you in a couple of weeks anyway, but don't forget I'm only at the end of the phone – my clinic number's on the vitamins – you can leave a message any time.* She swept everything into her bag – notes, folder, pamphlet – and with a last look at Alex, she stood and turned to leave.

Lauren

The plastic model in the leopard-print coat in the window isn't happy with all the chintz. It cheers me up when I arrive – that offended look. Anything's better than fucking desperation. And then I'm off again, seeing faces – woman caught between a swirly orange blouse and a string of beads. Long denim skirt, peeling gold belt. That'll be Dee's doing. Propped up in a load of clutter – tasselled lamps, plastic flowers, lace doilies, spiral candlesticks – it's a wonder they sell any of that crap. A gull-ible porcelain milkmaid lifting her skirts. Dee keeps saying we're doing vintage. There's a new sign on the door: *Check us out online! Give us a follow on Depop! Whatever your style.* It's got Dee all over it. The woman in the coat gives me a knowing look – rolls her eyes. Bloodshot. We're in this together.

The shop blasts my face with the usual foisty perfume when I walk in. Pam looks up and says hi, not too over the top. She's calmed down a bit, now I've been here a few weeks. Doesn't have to constantly pretend she's not scared of me. *Morning, love. The kettle's just boiled if you want to help yourself to a cuppa.* I'm actually starting to think all the dodgy goings-on are down to

Dee. I say thanks and head into the back. Someone's dumped another lorryload of bags.

The boys are at Mum's again. She's been obsessing about food – keeps sending me home with budget tins of beans. She'll give them a good tea before I pick them up. Like I can't look after my own kids. Although it's not exactly like it's a secret now – dirty washing strung up for the world. What a fuck-up. I have to make it right. Only a few more weeks. I make my tea milky so it's less acid on my stomach – I didn't manage to get breakfast this morning. Pam's droning on – *Leonard's in later. Dee's out on training all day at head office, so it's just me and you for now.* She's weirdly perky, busting to tell me something. But waiting to be asked. We take our teas through the curtain and I ask her how things are. *Ooo, Lauren, you wouldn't believe it. I'm going to be a granny!* I smile at her. Congratulations, Pam, that's lovely. *But it's not public yet, not until after the scan, so keep it to yourself for now, love.* Who would give a shit if I told them anyway. But that's nice for Pam. Even though she never sees her son. She starts sorting the baby rail and I head back through to the bags.

I've been sorting for an hour, hands scratched bloody from a vicious bag – tangerine tan with sharp acrylic nails and thick fake eyelashes, clawing at me, jealous – when I come across the leather purse. Fat with cash.

Fuck only knows how you could lose something with that much money in. I take it straight through to Pam in the front. She looks pleased – looks at the ID, logs it, gives it a ticket, and says she'll give the owner a ring straight away.

I've only just gone back to the bags when I hear Pam gushing up to top speed. *Oh, what a nice surprise! We weren't expecting you back again so soon.* A man – *the pleasure's mine, Pam. Always a joy to see you. I was just passing and thought I'd pop in to see my favourite team.* I shove everything down into the bag, tie a knot and throw it away from me, back to the pile. I zhuzh up my hair, pinch my cheeks and reach for a safer-looking bag of baby toys. Pam's still going on. *You've missed Dee, I'm afraid – she's out all day – it's just me and Lauren holding the fort. She's out back.*

The curtain opens in a rush of spearmint and the area manager is there again, looking me directly in the face, like he's over the moon with me. *Lauren! I was hoping to catch you! How's tricks?* I stand up, weight into right hip, left knee forward, stomach in, head tilt, and tell him fine, thanks. The kettle's still hot. He perches on a stool and watches me. I'm not sure whether to carry on with the baby toys. I ask him how he is, polite. He suddenly looks at me sad and I think I've said the wrong thing. *To be honest, I'm struggling a bit at the minute, Lauren — juggling a lot — family troubles, you know.* I nod, holding a teddy with a shiny green bow. Kind of.

Sometimes you just don't know what to do for the best, you know what I mean? I try a sympathetic smile. Tricky. Hmm. *Anyway, look at me, already nattering on — you're so easy to talk to, Lauren.* I put the teddy on the good pile, pick a few bits of fluff off my jeans, sprinkling them like seeds on the carpet. *You know what — why don't we get out of here for half an hour, get a proper coffee? Pam can hold the fort — I always like to get to know new recruits.* A whisper. *It'll give you a break from her too.*

I hesitate — I've got all this to get through. Sweep my arm towards the bags. I can't let anything go wrong. *They'll still be here when you get back — come on, get your coat — it's on the company account.* I grab my denim jacket and handbag like a teenager, excited. We head out, giggling, Pam staring after us. I've never been out with anyone like him. I bet he looks after his wife properly — opening doors, nice house, smart. Proper gent.

I look at his left hand, trying not to be too obvious. But it's just a business meeting. And my probation's the top priority. At least I'm not in a neon vest. He walks slightly ahead, *we'll go to the place on the high street — it's only a few minutes.* There are women in floaty floral dresses buying ice creams at the Thorntons' hatch, sticky kids, summer shopping. I take my jacket off and drape it over my arm, sunshine warm on my skin. I feel him watching. I'm not likely to know anyone up here — I can do what I want. The floral women might think we're actually together.

I'm dying for the vanilla frostino but say black coffee. He tells me to find a table – he'll bring it over. I choose one at the back, in the darker bit. Goose-pimpled arms from the air con. Makes them look even bonier. I cross my legs, sit up straight. Then put my jacket on the table and head to the toilet to check my face. When I come back he's got his tea, legs wide, looking towards the window, relaxed. My jacket draped neatly around a chair. He looks up like he's missed me, asks how I really am. *It's impossible to talk in that stuffy shop, with Pam listening in.* I say fine, know not to give much away. But he keeps his eyes on my eyes all the time – he really wants to know. *I admire you, you know, everything you're holding together – having to be Mum and Dad all rolled into one – and with everything you've had to get through – I don't know how you do it. You're one strong woman!*

Half an hour dissolves like sugar. I let my guard down, probably too much. Who knows what he really thinks of me. *We'd better get back, Lauren, but I'm glad we've finally had a chance to talk.* I'm standing up, tucking in my chair. *I tell you what, why don't I give you a missed call so you have my number, and then if we ever need to talk shop again we can? It's so nice to have someone intelligent to chat to.* I laugh. *And beautiful.* Then he looks panicked. *Sorry, Lauren. I shouldn't have said that – not very professional, is it?!* Hand on his face, slight alarm. *I hope I haven't offended you.* I tell him it's fine, no drama.

Pam's serving a customer when we walk back in. He calls over – *I need to get off now, Pam, but a joy to see you – as always. And no need to go bothering Dee with this, okay?* Pam looks up at him, frowning. *Okay,* she says, *fine.* She understands. *See you later then, Pam.* She comes through to see me when the customer's gone, hands on hips as if she's my mother. I grin and carry on sorting. Have you heard anything else about the baby, Pam? You must be so excited for the scan. *What's going on, Lauren?* I don't know what you mean, Pam. I think there's another customer. Pam says *just be careful – okay?* then disappears through the curtain, while I get back to the bags for the afternoon.

Gytrash

The woman is walking home from yoga, rolled mat under her arm, bright silk scarf in her piled hair. She takes the river path in summer, likes the small birds: water birds, wood birds, wild as leaves.

But tonight the air is thick and quiet: without birdsong. The light greener than usual. The woman hums her own tune to fill the silence.

There is a sudden dank smell. She looks at the water: strange today, the surface yeasty like an old beer bottle. Midges pestering brown glass.

She picks up her pace: to be home for her little son before bedtime. She tries not to run, spine needling. Keeps humming into the hush.

The sun sinks crimson and thick behind the trees. As she approaches the old wooden bridge, a twig cracks loudly on the opposite bank. The woman shrieks.

There is something huge there, at the edge of the woods, bundle of oiled rags, big as a cow.

The creature fixes the woman with giant red eyes. She doubles over, guilt dragging her forwards, burning belly, head, lungs

for the girls at school, wrapping her face, hiding in the toilets, on the bus, spitting on estate girls out of the window, suffocating diesel: girls with the wrong shoes, bags, hair, all the girls she might have been in a different house, street, country

girls trampled, bullied, left behind to rot. The woman flings her yoga mat and sprints past the bridge, fire in her lungs, not looking back

pausing only when she reaches the park, old bridge far behind: no sign of the creature but the stench of burnt hair still filling her lungs.

Nancy

Four numbers. 2104. The Queen's birthday. Not very original, but possible. Would Gladys really leave the code displayed like that though? The number sears into my brain for the entire day. Twooneohfour. Branded like cattle flank. I have no choice: I have to try it. Not to escape, just to know what's possible. I look at my notebook and decide on breakfast time: it's a muddle then, natural to want to stretch your legs.

Bev's office is right by the front door. She calls it Reception to be grand. There are a couple of desks, one piled high with folders: our records. The door is only shut when nobody's in. There are visitor coat hooks and a small table with a fan of leaflets in the corridor. No reason for us to go there.

I'll say I'm looking for Bev: they won't be able to prove I'm lying. That is, unless they actually catch me in the porch. The inside door opens automatically with the big button: the code must be for the second, outside door. It always swings open for eight seconds, before it shudders shut.

Deliveries are Tuesdays and Thursdays at 8.15 a.m. Always a commotion, trolleys stacked high with milk cartons and plastic bread. I miss the clink of glass bottles at home: you could set your clock by my milkman. At Christmas, he brought me salted yellow butter and orange juice in tall glass bottles.

I'll try the code while they're putting away the delivery as well as juggling breakfast. Maybe I'll say I thought they dropped a loaf. I'm down at eight o'clock prompt: plump myself down opposite Gladys and her boiled eggs. She smiles at me, as always, *did you sleep well?* I can't be too nice: they'll know something's up. I reply, as usual, fine thanks, and you? Eat my cornflakes, not really listening to the news.

Did you hear that? Gladys asks. *It's terrible, isn't it?* I look at her, questioningly. I can see she's disappointed in me: all she wants is someone to talk sense to. Her son brings her *The Times* every week – they chat away, but no one here is much interested. I try to tune in: they're talking about a building collapsing in India but I'm thinking about 2104. And the news moves on to the Queen, which must be a sign. I look at Gladys suspiciously to see how she reacts. She doesn't meet my eyes: dabbing at her lips with the napkin; tapping her second egg.

I dash off my cereal and tea, and head to the lounge at 8.13 a.m., where there's a good view of the car park. So hot with all these extra layers. Just in case. The lorry not here yet. I look back at my notebook: delivery timings can vary. I pretend to read the *Morning Post*, my stomach lurching at heavy tyres on gravel. It is here.

My fat Luna bird looks asleep, but I know she's also biding her time. The keys to her padlock are by the front door, in the little table. Banter echoes down the corridor, the delivery guys having a laugh with the girls. No one's flirted with me like that since the early days at the barber shop. I've always been good with customers: my mother said I was babbling in the baker's before she could get my plump legs in lacy knickers.

George knocked all that out of me though. By the time Pip was born I was bloated and lethargic with the moisture of the cottage. Big flabby arms and sweet breath. All that remained in me from childhood was jam tarts and stone baking, crisp pastry, maypole ribbons and thrift. My mother's locket. And an ember of defiance, still smouldering to this day, deep in my belly.

I sit in the living room, alone, everyone else at breakfast. The girls trundle past with the trolley, laughing – the blokes shouting from the entrance, *see you Thursday, ducks!*

I stand quietly and peep into the corridor: coast clear. Clanging from the kitchen, everyone jolly. Stomach cramping, I head up the corridor towards the front door. Darker than usual: the office door shut. My answers suddenly make no sense: I am looking for Bev; I thought you dropped a loaf. What have I been thinking. But I'm already where I shouldn't be.

I press the big silver button. The inside door judders open into the porch, with its thin panes of glass. Chilly. And then I'm there, on the Welcome mat behind the front door, and I can hear the river gassing past, women singing loudly. I tap in the code. Two-one-oh-four. Nothing happens. Again. I jab it again. A rush of water and song in my head, twooneohfour toow-unohfor. Nothing. Stabbing at the keypad. Come on. But there is nothing.

Krystyna sees me coming back down the corridor, tears streaming down my face. *Nancy, are you okay? Come, what are you doing up here?* She thinks I am lost, *Nancy, it is okay, you are safe in your home.* In my notes. Nancy is confused and disorientated this morning: arranged urine test with nurse. Useless. I go back to my room, exhausted, passing mad Patricia on the way. My face like a big purpling ham in the mirror. I turn away in shame, and throw my notebook at the wall.

Alex

Alex wipes porridge from Isabella's round cheeks with a flannel, then dives in with a dry cloth before the little girl can shriek. Tiniest sparkle, low in the belly. Suds popping. Nineteen weeks. Your baby is putting on a bit of weight, but still does not have much fat. The sun is out and Paul is at work: she will take Izzy on a road trip. He made them a lovely breakfast before he set off, like he used to.

Girls only, out to the hills: away from the river, from the house. Alex stacks the picnic in her walking rucksack: cheese sandwiches, crisps, chocolate, apples. Slides in an ice pack to keep it all fresh. Ignores the pregnancy massage book that has magically appeared on the worktop.

Nappies, spare clothes, cash, phone. Come on, Izzy, shoes on now. The keys are not in the kitchen where she left them. She thought she left them. She finds them easily though – in the bedroom, near the mirror – and it is strangely easy to get her daughter in the car. A good day. No my socks are scrumpled, I'm hungry, arched back, don't want to. But perhaps she is too quiet. Alex puts a cool palm to Izzy's forehead. No fever.

If you could see your baby now, they would look a bit wrinkled. Like the apples, but overwintered. The scan is next week. Alex starts the car. She sends the windows down; turns Radio 1 up loud. Giddy. I'll be riding shotgun, underneath the hot sun! Ready for an adventure, lovely?! Izzy giggles in the back, bobbing her head with the beat. Alex steers the saccharine curves of the estate, big identical houses shining sandstone in the light. They stare accusingly at her scuffed Fiesta.

Her heart lifts as they drive away, breeze on her face, in her hair. Going who knows where. She puts the windows up a bit: doesn't want to blast Izzy. There is a bird of prey circling above: the red kite again, rusty brown. It keeps stealing little birds, but she loves the white splashes on its dark wings, the deep fork of tail. Keep your eyes on the road. They leave the town behind, surrounded by fields already, the sky bigger, opening Alex's lungs. Last night's rain has rinsed the world clean: salad-green fields and cornflower sky. Her mind is clear. The earth still soft from scented raindrops, fresh with honeysuckle and rose. She glances at her beautiful girl in the mirror, kicking her legs, as they belt out their songs together.

At the roundabout she exits at the brown sign: National Trust house. Of course. Fountains and mazes in the gardens; cafe with ice cream and scones. Izzy will love it. They should be spontaneous more often. She will tell Paul all about it later, knowing he already knows. Tracker app. But it doesn't matter. Alex drives slowly past the sheep, down the long sweeping drive. Paul loves the National Trust – maybe they can come together at the weekend.

Lauren

There's obviously something up with Dee. When I walked in, she just kept pricing up with one of them old-fashioned sticker-guns, not even looking over. I thought I saw a frozen woman with a black O mouth staring out of the back of her Adidas hoodie, but when I looked again it was gone. I'm losing it. Pam gushed good morning, red-faced. I headed into the back, worried sick. I was on time, wasn't I. I've been trying to get everything right.

The area manager texted again last night, asking if I'd like to meet up. A work meeting. I've sorted it with my mum – she's having the kids Friday morning, just for a couple of hours. I've said I'm going to the dentist's so she doesn't give me the third degree. He said we could meet at that little Italian cafe on the other side of town. No one will know me over there. I was buzzing last night but now I'm thinking I've got it all wrong.

As I snap my Marigolds on and slice into a white bag, Dee sashays in with a silk scarf in her hands. *Can I have a quick word, sweetie?* I straighten up and look at her, ridiculous in the yellow gloves. Maybe she doesn't want me wearing them. It's a desperation bag – melting all over my pumps, wavy-mouth woman, seeping edges. I look down. Elasticated waists, Asda jeans, cable knit. Snivelling at my feet. I am breathing too fast – don't want her to sack me. Not that this is even a proper job to get sacked from. I look back at Dee, trying to breathe like normal people – quiet and calm.

But she's out of breath too. Maybe the air's too thin in here. I'll open the fire escape. *Lauren – you just need to check in with me if you're planning any more outings.* Dee folds the scarf while she chats on. Refusing to look near my feet. *It's nothing to worry about – just health and safety. We don't want you getting in any bother now, do we?* A shrill giggle. I smile my mouth and yes, of course, yeah. I didn't realise.

Good! Easy-peasy, isn't it! Our area manager is such a sweetheart but he can get a bit carried away! The cheeky bitch. She passes me the folded square of silk, and lifts the curtain to go back to the shop. *I've been asked to take care of you, Lauren – and you know I like to do things properly!* Another high-pitched laugh. *I'm looking forward to talking to your probation officer on Friday and telling her how hard you've been working!*

Dee vanishes through the curtain and I kick the sad jeans and jumpers away from my feet. I hear her sing-song goodbye to Pam, the door swishing shut behind her, and I'm suddenly sorry for the kicking. I bend down to gather the clothes – the heat of six shameful weeks in this place burning my face, broiling up from my belly, hands shaking. I crumple and sob – drop the clothes then rip the rubber gloves off and fling them on the pile, hands velvety with the stink of teats and johnnies and flaccid hot-water bottles. I've had enough.

Lungs burning, I thrash through the curtain to face Pam. It was you! What do you think I am? – I went for a coffee – coff-ee – not even my fucking idea! Pam holds a hand-knit baby cardigan up high in front of her like a shield. Just who do you think you are, you old cow? – grassing me up like I'm some kind of whore, ready to open my legs at the drop of a hat – it was a work meeting!

Pam keeps backing away, face flame-red. Mumbling. Do you know, Pam – my boys – actually, my fucking everything – is riding on this going right – and I'm spending hours on end going through bags of people's shit without a single complaint and I go for one coffee for less than one hour with one manager – who asked me, as part of my job – and you go telling tales to Dee! It's on your head if I end up inside and my boys are left with no mum! I'm too close to her, tears streaming, jabbing my finger. Water trickling from her pale eyes.

Lauren – I'm sorry – I didn't mean anything by it – Dee asked me – she was worried, and I couldn't exactly lie, could I? I step back. Fold my arms and keep staring at her face. *She just likes to look after everyone, Lauren, and I, I. I don't know. I didn't think.* Yeah, well, I tell her, spinning away. You might want to think next time, Pam. Think. I march back to the bags, shaking, and don't speak for the rest of the day. Send a text to him on my break: *Sorry, can't make Friday now. Will have to do it another time. Lauren.* No kiss.

By the time I get home I've got three missed calls, a voicemail and a text. *Please call me ASAP – about work.* It seems a bit much, but I put the boys in front of the TV and ring him back. Once I talk to him, I understand the rush – there's a paid job coming up in the shop, perfect for me, and he's talking to probation about it on Friday to tell them how brilliantly I'm doing. If I keep working hard, he's sure the job'll be mine. He said they got a thank-you card at head office from a woman who'd been reunited with her purse and its contents. She'd made a big donation and he'd heard it was down to me. Excellent work. He wants to talk it all through in person, before Friday, so he can get everything in order for probation. He'll bring the paperwork.

August

Nancy

I've been here four months already. I know from my diary, not like some of them in here. I told Pip: look at them, they've no idea even what day it is. I can see he feels terrible, know I should hug him; tell him it's not so bad after all. He's got enough on his plate at home with her.

He told me last week that they've managed to find nice tenants for the flat. I thought I was getting mixed up: what flat? *You know, Mum, we've talked about this – we're having to rent your flat out to pay for your care.*

But they were only supposed to be cleaning it up, getting rid of the smoke damage, ready for me to go back? He looked shocked. *Mum, you know about all this. We agreed.*

But what about Ruby?

He stuttered. *Ruby's fine. Like I said before. And the tenants aren't forever. It's not like you're selling up.*

He went soon after, but I didn't let go when he bent over to give me a kiss: just clung round his neck and dug my talons in. Don't leave me. Please. His skin marked red when he finally wriggled free.

Bev cornered me in the garden about it yesterday, by the rose bed. The yellow ones with the scent of sherbet. *You're not being fair, Nancy.* I kept my face near the petals, not turning round. She didn't take the hint. *I know it's hard, but you need to accept your life*

65

here. Believe you me, I've seen enough play hard done by — you've got it better than you think. I grabbed one of the wide-open sunny hearts and pulled hard until it plucked.

Nancy — no! Lungeing at me. *What do you think you're doing?!* I turned away, crushing the big juicy flower in my fist: graze of small thorns, strange crack of petals. *You're hurting yourself more than anyone, Nancy.* I marched inside, rose clenched fat in my fist. Bev shouted after me, *those nails need sorting. I've booked you in for tomorrow.*

Jessie, one of my favourites, took me to the lounge this morning for my nails. Anyone else and I'd have refused, but I like her. She wouldn't force me into the salon. The nails girl was waiting in her spa tunic, hip jutting out, bored. Plumped-up lips and big eyelashes. Jessie explained. *This is Nancy — she just needs a little tidy-up. Nothing too extravagant please.* The girl followed me to my chair, took one look at my hands, and rummaged for alcohol wipes in her case. I winced as she sterilised the scratches and mud.

I stared at daytime TV as she trimmed, filed, painted the moons of my nails sugar pink. Bev put her head in and smiled to see me: stuck in my chair with *Cash in the Attic*, under control. I escaped to the garden as soon as she'd done: set to picking off the candyfloss polish. My hands didn't look like my own.

They've met their match though. I told the girl straight when she said *I can squeeze you in this aft if you fancy a little wash and blow-dry.* No thank you very much I said. No one's going near my hair. I always had it short, for a girl, until I married a barber and he left it long. The barber pole, red and white, the butcher, the blood, the cloth. Pip stroking and combing as he grew up. Mama, your hair smells like green apples.

I'm back in the living room now, waiting for his visit, next to Gladys, with her hair freshly set, like a new lamb. I scrape at the last of the nail polish.

He's due before tea. I post a snack through the bird's cage, heavy plait swinging down my back, then walk to my chair. Gladys keeps asking me crossword questions, even though I never know the answers. Mad Patricia suddenly screams across the room, *cut my toenails!* I ignore her, sweeping sugary flecks off my trousers. She's mad as a hatter, always pointing at me with her knuckly fingers. The nails girl did her feet this morning. *I'm in agony here – you – sort them out!* Gladys smiles sideways at me, conspiratorially, but I can't smile back. Patricia makes my skin crawl.

There's a car on the gravel but it's only one of the girls for the teatime shift. Lisa. I write it in my book. Jessie's on activities today: she bounces in and puts on some eighties pop, all ready for chair aerobics. The lounge starts filling up: everyone loves her. I move to the edge to wait, some of the women agadoo-ing in their seats already. Jessie never pressures me to join in.

Pip's due any second. Gladys and the rest start obediently pushing up their arms to the ceiling, and then Norman saunters in muttering. He sits in his chair by the door, no intention of joining in. He's a rude sod. Glint like drink in his eyes. Bloodshot. He starts talking to me, voice too loud. *Look at her.* Arm stretched, pointing at Jessie. *The likes of her shouldn't even be in here.* My stomach twists. I hope she can't hear over the music. Jessie's got her primrose leg warmers on, and headband to match: the works. She puts her heart and soul into everything. *Allus taking our jobs. She should go home – back where she came from.* I hit out at his legs with my magazine. Stop that. But he's purple-faced, spittle on his lips. Shouting now. *All of them – we should send them all back.*

I jump up, tell him shut your mouth. Standing over him. Shouting. You're bloody pig-ignorant, you are. Gladys is staring at me, arms frozen in the air, shocked, but Jessie shakes her head and calls over, *it's alright, Nancy, you sit down. He doesn't know what he's saying.* Jessie carries on pumping her arms and beaming at the women. *Come on, girls – hands up, baby, hands up.* Like it's nothing.

I march out into the corridor to get someone. Pip should have been here twenty minutes ago. I almost bump into Bev, and then I'm screaming, it's downright appalling – I'm not staying here with that man. You don't give a fig about anything – your staff, any of us – it's only money to you, isn't it? Bev watches me calmly, sweet smile on her face. When I stop, slow words glug from her mouth, exaggerated lips.

Calm the toddler with a lollipop. *Come, Nancy, now, let's get you back to your room for some breathing space. Your son called to say he can't make today after all, something has come up at work, so we can go upstairs.* I stare at her candy lipstick. Look away too late. *It's teatime soon – we've got mushroom soup today, and a proper pudding. I know how you love that.*

My feet follow her to the lift. She escorts me upstairs and into my room, then seizes my key from the bedside drawers when I put it down. *It's best you don't lock your door while you're feeling so distressed. We need to be able to get to you in an emergency.*

When she's gone, I pace the lockless room, window-to-bed-repeat. Check the safe, everything still there: pocket watch, documents, jewellery. But how will I sleep now? Anyone could walk in. I should have seen it before – that woman is clamping, stamping down on me, on all of us: snatching every last scrap of freedom we've got. It's all down to me now.

Lauren

The front door is unlocked like always. It's only me, Mum! The boys come running at me. *Mummy!* My mum appears, following them into the hall, click-clacking with her plastic jewellery and snapping her gum. The dog yapping in the back. *Hi, Lauren love! I've got an egg flan in, and some coleslaw, if you want to stay?* I see Neal hovering behind her in the kitchen doorway. So that's what the quiche is about.

How was the dentist's then? Yeah, all fine, I tell her, just routine like I said. Mum's done her lips with dark brown liner and shimmer-pink, nineties style. Zebra-print plunge top. *Well, I hope you didn't let him charge you an arm and a leg – they're awful down there for that – isn't that right, Neal?* Neal slinks forward, mumbling agreement. I haven't seen him since the row at the Bull, the drunk bastard.

68

Even Neal's not getting me down after this morning though. Treated right for the first time in my life. The area manager took my coat, pulled out my chair, and treated me to posh coffee with little pastries. He was so understanding about why I'd texted to cancel – *that's what I like about you, Lauren – you're so sensitive and honest.*

Okay, thanks, Mum, I say, taking my shoes off. She looks surprised that I'm stopping. Gives me the once-over – best jeans and all made up. Happy eyes. *What's up, Lauren?* I wink and huddle the boys into the front room and pull them up on the sofa, both of them talking at the same time, regurgitating some shit Neal's told them about chickens and rabbits. Come here, you two. I give them both a big squeeze. Whisper – we'll just have some quick dinner with Nan and then we'll go to the swings if you want? Oli's straight up, jumping on my head, chanting *park park swings, park park swings!* He's crackers.

Mum brings me a sugary Nescafé in a chipped Minions mug. She's being nice – hoping I'll spill the beans. Oliver's jumping on the sofa. I pull him onto my lap. Calm down now, Oli, come on, sit with me. Everything looks cheap after the glam of Cafe Florian with its gold letters and lush ferns and mirrors. Antique tiles and chandeliers. I tried to make out like I was used to places like that. He gave me a kiss on each cheek when we left, like the Italians do.

Mum goes back to the kitchen and I sip my Nescafé, careful of Oli. The glaze of cartoons in the corner. I told him I'm not sure I can keep working in that shop but he said if I stay on as a volunteer after my probation there'll be a sure-fire paid job at the end of it. Showed me all the paperwork. I can get those free hours at the nursery now Dan's two, and it'll keep the social off my back as well. They're always on at me about job prep – last week the woman said I'll get sanctioned again if I don't get on it, especially once Dan's three. They're having a laugh expecting anyone to spend sixteen hours a week looking for work. But I can't let them stop my money again.

He said the shop's just a start – I could go far – work my way up. Mum would be well chuffed if I got a proper job. And he'd give me a reference, he said – a good one, no need to mention the past. The bags in the shop are so manky though. And Dee's such a bitch. But he said she'd have to train me up proper – show me the tills and everything – I wouldn't just be her skivvy any more.

Mum shouts from the kitchen like a foghorn – *it's ready!* Me and the boys scramble in and Mum plonks triangles of yellow flan and handfuls of crisps on all the plates, talking too loud like always. *Coleslaw?* I shake my head – can't manage much after all the sweet cakes at the cafe. Nerves sparking off in my chest.

Mum's ogles my plate, barely touched. *Now I know something's up, Lauren!* Neal just sits there, waited on hand and foot as usual. Swilling his Friday beer. Not even afternoon yet. I'm dying to tell her about my posh morning and the job – but my throat suddenly mangles with a bad feeling. Next week, back in the shop. Dee. Pam. Seeing things. All them bags. Too much stupid hope. I put my knife and fork together and push my plate away. It'll wait.

Alex

Alex looks in the mirror at a bloated toad. It is overcast and muggy: filling her skull. Paul has set her up with Ruth, his squash buddy's wife. Doesn't want her getting lonely. She is due at the church playgroup on the high street at 10 a.m. Alex is too hot and exhausted to walk, but can't find her car keys. She remembers putting them in the key-tidy, but they are not there, or by the front door. She searches the house, top to bottom, Isabella shouting *Mummy, Mummy* from the living room every ten seconds. She texts Paul, already off to work. He calls her straight back, laughing, *I'm not sure what's getting into you, darling – you'd lose your head if it wasn't screwed on.*

She looks at her arms while he talks, still shiny from the pregnancy massage last night. She'd wanted to sleep but he'd researched the benefits: soothes tension; relieves puffiness in the legs. He'd bought safe oils: sweet almond and tangerine, making such a big effort. Brought her camomile tea afterwards, and left her with low lights and calming music while he went to watch TV.

Alex had lain under the duvet, oily and ashamed for suspecting an ulterior motive. *She always has to think the worst of people. He's trying his best. Lack of sleep is common in pregnancy. When you are trying to sleep, your baby may be wide awake and moving about.* Pirate attack, daughter burning up, a van ploughing into a crowd. Paul put the TV on low, not to disturb her. Only the sound of the river. Her pillow soaked with tears. *Why couldn't she be fairer on him. She has to make more effort.*

He has always adored her, trusted her with his secrets. His father chasing him up the stairs, his mother's body absorbing the bruises. Watching every time, instead of protecting her: the guilt, tears, shame. Alex makes him feel safe. *If only she could sort her confusion, he wouldn't get so frustrated. They both know how good they can be together. All couples have bad patches. They can get through this.*

On the phone now, Paul is saying *your keys are in the bathroom – where you left them. Are you feeling dizzy, darling?* Alex says no, sorry for interrupting you, I'm still waking up.

Look, I've got to work – you'll be late for Ruth if you're not quick. Check in with me at lunch, won't you, so I know you're okay? Alex trudges up to get the keys from the bathroom windowsill: no memory of putting them there. *She's going doolally.* Legs lifting boulders. She is late: Izzy not even dressed. Upstairs, downstairs, nappy change, sandals. The car seat is in the hall: Paul must have been cleaning the car. She finally gets everything in her cramped Fiesta and straps Izzy in. As they drive off, Alex remembers snacks, but it is too late to go back.

The church is only five minutes away, but Izzy screams the whole way, juddering Alex's heart. She can hardly drive with it. The wife of the friend is waiting in the car park with her toddler, looking serene. Hair piled and wrapped with a silky green scarf. Scarlet lips and nails. Perfect yoga posture. Alex gets out, shaking, Izzy streaming with tears. The woman comes over smiling. *Hiya – I'm Ruth – you must be Alex.* She peers through the window as Alex ducks into the car to get her daughter. They both see it at the same time. As she is lifting Izzy out of the seat. It is unmistakable. A wobble. Alex pushes the seat forward in disbelief. It can't be. It is completely loose. Not strapped into the car. She has driven her daughter in a death trap.

Alex straightens up and looks at Ruth, aghast. How can it, I'm sure I, oh my God, what have I done? Little Izzy in her arms, gripping her neck. Ruth is brisk, *come on, it's okay, look – she's alright. No harm done.* Alex squeezes the girl, face into her hair. Both sobbing now. What on earth is this Ruth going to think? No wonder Paul needs people to keep an eye on her: she is a liability. He is going to kill her for this. Alex tries to open the boot with one hand, but Ruth steps in. *Let me help.* The buggy is in pieces, but Ruth whips them out; snaps them together in seconds. She pats the pushchair seat, *come and sit here, Isabella – I've got a nice gingerbread person each for you and Edward.* Whispers to Alex. *Don't worry, they're sugar-free, all natural.*

Izzy takes the biscuit and quietens, streaky-faced: lets Alex fasten her in. As Alex bends into the car to sort the seat, Ruth gently touches her arm. *I tell you what – why don't we give the group a miss and walk to the river for a bit? It's too nice to waste the day indoors, and you can sort the car when we get back?* Alex looks at the sky and forces a laugh – yes it does look like a nice day. The sky a shroud of humid grey. She has sunblock and nappies in the bag. Yes. Okay. Whatever this woman plans to report, Alex wants to go with her, away from that echoey hall of perfect mothers; away from rhyme-time and wooden trains; away from dry aching eyes.

They push the buggies to a stony little beach by the river in the park. Ruth flaps out a picnic rug, and they unstrap the kids. The sun comes out, drying the air. Alex takes a big lungful, expanding her ribs, Izzy squirming to be free. Ruth has aqua shoes for her little Edward. Alex leaves Izzy's sandals on, in case there is glass. They will dry. At the edge of the water Alex stoops and takes both of Izzy's hands, guiding her into the shallows, big steps, high knees, splashing and shrieks, juicy legs shining in the sun. Both children end up sitting in the water together like teddy bears, cherry-legged with cold, spattering diamond water and plopping pebbles.

Alex and Ruth sit on the rug. Alex picks up stones out of habit, sorting them into little piles: sandstone, granite, shale, always an eye on Izzy. She will take one for her collection, even though she has too many already. Ruth asks how the pregnancy is going. *My husband says it's a boy?* Alex smiles, looking at Ruth's son.

Yes. It will be strange not to have a girl baby. Ruth isn't as bad as she expected, but Alex is still mortified about the car seat. She nods again, yes a boy, then asks Ruth a stream of quiet questions, hands busy with the pebbles, trying not to let anything slip in return. Ruth doesn't seem to mind, happy to chat about her husband and holistic education and the worrying confines of the school institution.

The children inevitably end up cold and crying, but Ruth is ready with dry flannels and a flask of warm milk. She is a wonder. Alex a fountain of excuses: I didn't realise we were coming, I would have, I usually, but Ruth glosses over it all – *let's do this again – before the autumn sets in. Thanks for coming off-piste with me!* A whispered confession. *To be honest, I find those groups so tedious.*

Izzy falls asleep in the pushchair on the way back to the car. The baby is moving but there are bricks inside Alex too, weighing her down with dread. Ruth is bound to say something bad to her husband. Alex secures and triple-checks the seat. She waves goodbye to Ruth, who is walking so that her Edward can have a good nap.

At home, Alex frets all afternoon: can't settle to picture books or jigsaws. Her inner thighs rubbed sore with heat rash. Stretch marks may become noticeable when you are twenty-two to twenty-four weeks pregnant. They may appear on your stomach, breasts, thighs. At first red, then fading to a silvery grey. When Paul finally gets back it is almost a relief. Get it over with. She has tea ready: home-made spaghetti bolognese with secret veg. Simple but wholesome. His mother would approve for once. Paul gets changed and joins them at the table. *I spoke to Chris on my way home, Alex.* Alex nods and pours water into his glass. Chris is the squash buddy. The husband. Heart hammering. How's he doing? *What did you get up to with Ruth?* Alex doesn't miss a beat: answers ready. Oh, it was lovely – she took us to the river – it was such nice weather. He picks up his fork, smiling. And the children got on super well – it was sweet. Her voice catching a little. She coughs to cover it up. Excuse me. We brought Daddy a special stone, didn't we, Isabella? Izzy laughs, mouth stuffed with tomato pasta.

Well, that does sound nice! I told you you'd get on. You'll have to meet up with them again! And that is it. Nothing else. She asks about his day: he is pleased with the new performance figures. A boost for the team. She tells him their news. Isabella counted to five. The baby has been kicking. He reaches over to feel, delighted. *How's my boy?!* She smiles, knowing how quickly he can turn, any second, back to Ruth, everything collapsing under them, sucking down chairs, table, spaghetti; red mince staining her face, matting her hair. Lost keys, loose car seat, wet sandals, forgotten snacks. Losing, incompetent, you fucking, you'd forget your head.

But there is nothing. Only his hand and the thick hot air. And a swollen blue fly, dying in the window. Paul stands up and finishes it off with the newspaper, then takes Isabella into the living room for tickles. Alex clears up and fetches strawberries and cream. Like a normal mum – a normal family – nothing like she almost killed her daughter.

Nancy

I write the new discovery in my book. Spare key to birdcage. The girls dangle the normal key from a ribbon twice a day like clockwork: opening Luna's door to give her fresh seeds and water, then back to the drawer in the table by the front door.

I always say hello before breakfast. They've even moved my chair so I can talk through the cage more easily. She expects me, when I pop my head under her grey blanket like a photographer, ready for her treat. Red cheeks, yellow spike, grey head: trussed up as they want her. I overheard one of the girls asking for the spare key last week and caught Kerry getting it out of the same little drawer.

I go to see Luna before the afternoon activities: slop my whole cup of tea on old Norman's chair as I go past. It's easy, with it being by the door. That'll teach him to pick on young girls. You can't see it with the pattern, and it'll be nicely cold by the time he sits down. The staff keep thinking he's wet himself, taking him off to change his pads. They're clearing the dining room now; we're supposed to be snoozing or sitting in the garden. Joyce is in her chair, singing about nothing, and Gladys is across the room with her crossword, trying to scribble her biro back to life. She tuts, rolls it between her palms to warm the ink. I try not to think about knickers. Need to concentrate.

I give it five minutes by the mantelpiece clock, then get up smoothly, not wanting a ruckus. Joyce glances up, then goes back to her sing-staring. My slippers are soundless in the corridor, but I spot the problem immediately. Sunlight on the table by the front door: the office is open when it should be shut. I hum a little tune, to show I'm relaxed. Plan B: the fan of leaflets on the table. I reach the front door and pick a leaflet. Bev calls out across the corridor in her cloying voice, *are you alright, Nancy duck?*

I turn and smile. Yes thank you, I just noticed these lovely leaflets. Actually I was looking for a pen for Gladys's crossword – hers keeps running dry. Bev's machine face smiles on me. *Hang on a sec.* She loves a practical problem. *I'm sure I've some new ones in here.* While she's banging about in her desk I slide open the drawer. The little key's fiddly for my fingers, but I manage to slide it up into my palm. I turn back, fistful of leaflets in my other hand. Bev's holds up a crinkly plastic pack with three new biros, triumphant. I've messed up her display.

I take the pens, thank you. Realise she'll prove it's me if no one else has been here. She comes over to tidy the table and sends me on my way. Back in the lounge, I hand Gladys the new pens. You'd think Christmas had come early. I ask if she'll come and see Bev about magazine subscriptions. You're better at talking than me, Gladys. She looks surprised, but keen, and scrawny Joyce springs out of her chair: she wants to come too. I tell her there are some beautiful glossy leaflets to look at – let's go and see if we're in any photographs! We all troop back to the office. Bev stands up, frowning. *Can I help, ladies? It's like Piccadilly Circus up here this afternoon!*

I start the speaking. We wondered if we could get any other magazines? Or papers? Gladys chimes in. *My son brings me his every week, but it's out of date so quick – and we all like the cross-words.* We nod, except Joyce, at the back, not listening, scattering leaflets on the floor. Then mad Patricia appears too, trundling down the corridor towards us, cackling her head off: she wants in on the action. *Okay, ladies,* Bev says, *let's get back to the main house – I'll look at the sums and we'll see what we can do.* She comes across and starts picking leaflets off the floor; gives me a suspicious look.

She shoos us like chickens. *Come on, you all need a cuppa before cooking club.* We troop back to the lounge, except Patricia, who wanders off fretting, as usual. I sit next to Luna's cage and hum her a little tune. Nobody takes a blind bit of notice. The tea trolley is due in five. The bird gazes at me with her dark pink eyes. I smile at her and murmur. Tonight's the night, Luna, tonight's the night.

Lauren

I haven't even managed to get my jacket off when Pam comes through the curtain with an open pack of digestives. *Look, Lauren, I'm sorry about last week. I honestly didn't mean to get you in trouble.* I look at the biscuits but don't take one. I'm surprised she's bothering after the grief I gave her. She should wash her hands of me. *It's been lovely having you here, you're such a hard worker. I can see you're trying to make a real go of it. Go on, love, have one.* I turn away and hang my jacket up. *And just think of all the*

76

donations we've had in these last few weeks — I don't know what's got into people. We'd never have managed without you. I turn back and take a biscuit. Ta.

I take a deep breath. It's me that should be saying sorry, Pam. I get the bottle of apricot nail polish out of my pocket, and hand it to her. Here — I got it given but it's not my colour. It's not been opened. I thought it'd suit you. Pam thanks me and looks like she's going to start crying again. I shouldn't have taken it out on you, Pam. It's not your fault.

But. I take a deep breath. Pam — I think there's something weird going on here. Pam looks like she's going to say something but stops. She holds up the bottle to the light and reads. *Rimmel. Scratch Resistant. This is lovely!* I keep looking at her. *It's a busy time of year, love — people are definitely odd, the stuff they bring in, but I guess that's just the business.*

She must be too scared to say anything else. It's still early — no customers yet — so we perch on stools in the back and drink our tea. I eat four biscuits. Fuck it. Pam takes our cups over to the sink and asks me to help out with the shop window. *Let's trim it up, shall we, love, for back to school? You've got a better eye for these things than me.* I go through and help her button little uniforms onto mannequins, grateful for the light and air up front. Dee prances in just as I'm straddling a mannequin, wrestling with a cardigan. *Morning, ladies! Wow — that window is looking super-duper — look at you two go! My Dream Team!*

She heads into the back to do her admin in her broom cupboard. I get back to sorting bags. Mainly objects. A relief. Dee tip-taps at the keyboard with her new acrylics, door open. Watching my every move. I take a boxed silver fountain pen through to the special glass case at the front and Pam gives me an encouraging smile. Then on to a bag of thimbles and scratched postcards.

Are you doing anything nice this weekend? Dee interrupts my flow. I shake my head, just the usual with the kids, you know — we'll probably go down the park and see my mum for a bit. I don't tell her I've shaved my legs for the first time in months.

Plucked my eyebrows. He texted again this morning. He'd like to get to know me better. Cafe Florian again soon?

I carry on pulling objects from bags like a magician, wondering why Dee was so bothered about that coffee. Maybe she's got a thing for him. My chest tightens – maybe they had something going on before. The nice bags at the front came in yesterday. Books: *Grow Your Own Veg, The Magic of Thinking Big.* Glass lampshade, greenish pearl and lead. I've let my guard down, thinking it's all normal, when there's a sudden flash in one of the glass hexagons. Fractured face. Ghostly. Open mouth, soundless scream.

I flinch but hold on. I know if I look away it'll vanish. I keep my focus soft on the face – stroke the tiny cheek, gloss on fingertip. Shudder. The woman closes her mouth. Gold hoops tremble in her ears, pleading somehow. My breath is fast and shallow – I can't put the lampshade down. A jingle on the radio jolts me out of it. Then someone spouting crap about the legalisation of drugs. I nearly drop the lamp – I'm going bat-shit crazy. Last week was a phone-in about lead poisoning. Nearly impossible to spot, even when the blood is totally toxic. I turn away, petrified. I'm going mental. Headed for the loony bin.

Dee's still typing, oblivious. I look back at the shining lampshade. Nothing. I shake the bag, to check it's empty and a gold hoop falls out. I pick it up, inspect it closely. There's a hallmark – the real deal. Heavy in my hand. I put it on the shelf while I carry on sorting.

Alex

Izzy is asleep when they pull up to the little stone cottage in the Peak District. Paul opens the passenger door for Alex, helps her out. She has pelvic pain already: not even third trimester. The sky is streaked pink and gold, the valley below in hill shadow. The landscape calms her: she chose a uni up north for the promise of these hills.

The unearthly call of a tawny owl. Paul takes her hand. *It's stunning – you've done us proud again, darling.* She squeezes back: it looks good. The journey was easy and they have three nights together in this beautiful place: a place she researched and booked, like old times. It feels good to be back in charge of something.

All she wants is for them to be happy. A proper long weekend. She drank three litres of water this morning, before the midwife, to make sure her urine was clearer this time. She is desperate to pee again now. Paul took a couple of hours off at lunch and took them to Pizza Express after the appointment to celebrate the heartbeat. Hooves stamping racing wind. He is pleased with her: hard work paying off.

Paul gets the key from the lock-box by the front door, while Alex stands at the car with their daughter sleeping in the back. Inhales deeply: the cooling air of hills. Izzy wakes when Paul returns to carry her inside, cries out, but Alex wraps a blanket over her and she snuggles in. Alex says she'll be inside in a minute, hunting for Izzy's soft rabbit in the front. She remembers squishing it into the glovebox to be safe. Bashing it shut. It would hardly close: she definitely put it there. Izzy's cry suddenly cuts the twilight from inside. Alex rushes to the boot, grabs the bedrail and heads upstairs. Paul has put her in the twin room upstairs, on top of a duvet. *She needs her bunny, Alex,* he says, sounding agitated.

Alex whispers she can't find it, not wanting the girl to hear – I'll go back and look – but Izzy is weeping *Mummy, Mummy* so Paul says *I'll go then – always second best.* Alex tucks her under the covers and puts her face close, smoothing her hair, murmuring Mummy's here now. Just a second, lovely, let me make your bed nice and cosy. Alex wrestles the heavy set of bedside drawers away from the wall, towards the door, then uses her weight to push Izzy's bed against the wall. She slides the bed guard under the mattress on the other side and slots it up. There, she tells her, just like at home: you can't fall out now.

Paul bursts back in – *I can't find that damn bunny anywhere,* which sets Izzy off again. *Bunny! Mummy, I want Bunny!* Alex says, Paul, I'm sorry, I'm sure it was in the front. It must have gone under the seat or something.

Everything was supposed to be perfect.

Paul sulks – *nothing's ever simple with you. Look, I need to fetch everything in before it gets dark.* Alex strokes Izzy's hair. You do that, Paul, we'll be okay here. *It's not easy with that roof box though, Alex – we need a bigger car, you know.* She nods at him, shushing Isabella, yes, fine, I know, yes we do. Come on, lovely, goodnight now.

Paul goes out and leaves them in the dark. Alex sits on the floor by the bed, twisting her wedding ring. Her fingers are already swollen with the pregnancy: she will put it in the drawer with Paul's for safe keeping when they get home. He never wears his: always says rings don't look right on men. She takes Izzy's small hand and holds it until her breathing calms and her fingers unfurl. Alex's right foot is a wooden block when she finally stands. She hobbles out of the room, suitcases and bags piled on the landing. Paul is sulking on the sofa with the paper. *I boiled the kettle for you hours ago.* She tells him thank you, electric pins and needles inside her foot like a plasma globe: too painful to move. *Go on then*, he tells her.

Alex winces across to the kitchenette. The ground floor is one big room. I need to get Bunny from the car, Paul. He replies gently. *Get a drink first, you'll exhaust yourself.* Hope. This holiday will work out after all. She asks if he wants anything. *I'm alright thanks, I've got a beer.* He has left a mug on the side for her with a herbal tea bag inside. The mug has photos of their honeymoon: he has brought it from home. She feels sick, tells him what a lovely surprise, so thoughtful, pouring hot water, steam rising into her face. She joins him on the sofa, hoping for the best. *I thought you'd like it.* He smiles at her, opening a packet of Jaffa Cakes. His phone lights up with a message from an unnamed number: he puts it face down on the arm.

You know, Alex, you always have to be so strong. He offers her the open pack. *Why can't you let me help? Let me in.* Alex takes a biscuit and puts it on her knee, then swirls the tea bag around with a spoon. Hot spoon. *I could have moved those drawers. Made sure the toy rabbit was packed.* Alex squeezes the tea bag and puts it on the saucer he's left on the table for her. He eats Jaffa Cakes whole. Mouth wide like a snake. *You need help. I don't want you hurting yourself.*

Alex used to nibble the edges and save the circle of orange jelly for last, but he hates that, so she takes a normal bite. Orangechocolatesponge. Maybe it was a different day she'd smashed the glovebox on Bunny. Or a dream. Everything so slippery in her brain. She gets up to close the curtains. I'd better get Bunny. She'll be so upset. Paul says, *it's too dark now. Sit down. It'll wait til morning.* The windowsill is deep behind the curtains, kohl-black sky, flashing pins of gold. Alex wants to race out, pluck the razor-sharp stars, shriek and stamp. School shootings, virus outbreak, giant icebergs calving. Your baby gets all their oxygen from you via the placenta. They will do so until they're born. She trudges back to the sofa, remoulding her face to pleasant, a mug of tears behind her eyes.

Lauren

I take the river path to the cafe again. I thought it would be out of the sun, but the glare gets past the trees onto the water and kills my eyes. I need sunglasses, then I could push my hair back when I get there, sophisticated, like other girls. If I had one of those loans Tania keeps banging on about, I could look half decent for a change. She's always saying, *how do you think everyone else round here manages, Lauren?* But Mum'd murder me. She looks down on me for even having a debit card – you'd think it was the work of the devil. She's got her post office account for her benefits then it's cash only for everything else.

It's boiling. I'll be soaked in sweat at this rate. Hopefully I'll get there first so I can sort myself in the toilet. I'd love that Strawberry Iced Tea. I get my phone out – Mum told me to text her to let her know how it went with probation. I told her I was going into the office, but my probation officer said a phone call was enough. I'd talked to her sitting on the bench outside

Greggs, stomach rumbling, sausage roll wafting round my face. A man chucking bits to the pigeons. Some people are made of money.

She asked how it was going and I launched in, saying I've honestly been trying my best – there's just a couple of people who are a bit tricky to work with, but she interrupted me. *Well, you wouldn't know it, Lauren – I've had glowing reports, including from a senior manager who rang me specially – he said you've been going the extra mile, putting your heart and soul into everything!* I was surprised, but told her I've done everything they said. She told me *keep on it, Lauren, good work – only four weeks left now – keep your head down and behave, don't let anyone wind you up, yeah? We don't want you breached when you've got this far.*

It was good of him, speaking up for me. Risking his own reputation. I keep marching down the deserted towpath – everyone inside in the cool – lick my lips, taste salt. I owe him big time. I go under troll bridge, crumbling and damp. A shiver, into blind dark, then back out into white light. The boys love that bridge. Who's that trip-trapping.

The scuffle behind me nearly makes me jump out of my skin. I turn round but can't see anything. I'm worried it's that big fucking dog again, following me. It could have rabies or anything. I leg it – racing forwards – totally stupid, nothing even there. And then I'm choking with all the women who've ever hated me – my teacher, Gran, the police – red-blasted cheeks, saggy, skinny, so clumsy, useless, and the panic takes over – like when I was at school. I sprint along the narrow path, lungs burning, and even though there's only my feet pounding gravel, I force myself on, legs shaking, til that little gap onto Bridle Close. And then I'm through, spilling on the pavement in front of all those bungalows, braying for breath like a donkey, a total fucking mess.

The houses stare down at me with their wide grins, fat cheeks and posh paving. My nose dripping blood. I try to calm my breathing like the school nurse used to say. In and out. I should sack it all off and go home. In and out. I look up but there's no one around. I rifle through my bag for a tissue but there's only bus tickets and receipts. What a state.

I stumble up the cul-de-sac, feeling watched. I can't go back to the river. What the hell's wrong with me – seeing things, hearing things. It's not like I'm even scared of dogs. He's reading his book at an outside table – jumps up when he sees me. *Lauren, what's the matter? Come here. What's happened? Are you hurt?* I let him lead me inside, arm round my shoulders, say I'm fine, honestly, I've always had nosebleeds – ever since I was a kid. I can't shut up. I just had a bit of a shock – I don't know what got into me! He takes me to the back of the cafe and sits me down with a stack of napkins, then goes off to order me hot chocolate and a sticky bun.

Nancy

I wait in my room with the lights off until I hear Patricia screeching upstairs, then sneak out in my dressing gown, blinking at the light, sweet sesame bird treat in my pocket. The key to the cage hidden in my bra.

I creep down the stairs, into the lounge, feel my way to Luna's cage. She hops over to watch me fumbling for the key: pink sadness reflecting in her dark eyes. I know she understood me earlier. Tonight's the night. She can't go on like this forever, the living dead, but she wills me to understand as I look into her eyes. *I can't do it.* I take no notice. We have come too far: she has no choice.

There's a noise in the corridor, so I quickly pull out the treat and plop into my chair. Krystyna's on nights: she pops her head in and flicks the light on. *Why are you sitting here in the dark, Nancy?!* She's not worried: it's only dotty Nancy with her bird. It's good that she takes comfort from it. *Don't stay down too long, you will catch cold.* She drapes a blanket around my shoulders.

I wait until I hear her off down the corridor, then nip round the room, opening windows. I'll say I was too hot. There are safety catches, but Luna can squeeze through the narrow gaps. I stand on tiptoes and open two of the top windows for good measure. Perfect for birds. I go back to the cage and finally extract the key, embedded in my droopy flesh, manage to push the fiddly thing into the padlock. It turns easily. I swing open the door, tears blocking my throat, and reach in.

Luna hops straight onto my fingers, tickle of claw on my skin. She knows me. I bring her close and cradle her to my chest. Feathers soft as water. Head tickling my lips. I murmur. You can do this, girl – it's your time, do you hear? Go free now. Go safe. I fling her in the air then, a sputter of feathers and dust. She hasn't flown since she got here. She spirals unsteadily then lands shakily on the curtain rail. I hook the padlock back on the open door, push the key back in my bra. It will look like a simple mistake: someone forgot to click the padlock; the door swung open when the bird pushed it with her head. I leave Luna perched on the curtains above the open window and switch off the light. No one will be in until morning. Goodnight, Luna. God bless.

Lauren

I spit on a raggy tissue and scrub Oliver's chin at the big iron gates to the park. I've told both boys – very best behaviour or we'll be straight home. It's the charity's staff picnic – they do it every year apparently – families welcome! Old Pam told me to bring the kids – she'd love to meet them. Oli twists free and races off the path onto the field. He's been up since 6 a.m., hyper. I spoke to Mum before I set off and she said *it's nice they invited you, isn't it, love?*

I scan the field and spot a group in the distance, under a tree by the river. I bounce the buggy down over the grass towards them and Oli loops back to me, panting. I remind him, don't forget to say your pleases and thank yous – but he's off again, like a puppy. My breath snags when I see they've all got special picnic blankets – I nearly keep on walking, but Pam spots me and starts hollering, patting her blanket, *Lauren! Over here, love!* so I push the buggy over to her mat and tell Dan say hello. He waves at Pam and beams his lovely face. Pam gushes – *what a sweetheart!* – then Oli races over to say hi too. I take a deep breath and smile. It's okay to be out here in the sunshine – to have the boys with me – to see Pam. I should never have been so vile to her.

I lift Dan out and stand him on the rug. Old Leonard from the shop's at the edge on a fold-out chair, glass in hand, but I can't see any others I know. Pam gets us sat down with her, then starts introducing us to the other mats, sweeping her arm – *this is Lauren – she's been volunteering at our shop a couple of months now.* My chest goes tight. I'm sure everyone knows why I'm at the shop. I sit myself down, cross-legged, not making eye contact, and settle Dan on my knee. Oli crouches down and presses close to my arm, suddenly shy. Pam smiles at him. She gave me a massive cuddle in the shop last week when I told her I'll be staying on as a volunteer after my probation.

She's keeps gushing on, as if we're her very own – *and these are her kiddies – Oliver and Daniel – aren't they beauties?!* Everyone's nodding and smiling in the sparkling river light and the woman next to me passes three paper plates and a bowl of cheesy Wotsits. It's going to be fine. I notice Pam's done her nails with the polish I gave her and I tell her it looks lovely on. I'm dishing out orange puffs when I catch sight of the area manager, sauntering across the field on his own, spotless in his sports gear. I turn back to Pam, my face hot, pretending I haven't seen him and say yes please to lemonade. Pam doesn't skip a beat – calls out to the woman with the giant bottle of pop. She appears above us with plastic cups, and glugs it in, just like we're meant to be here, laughing as a bit fizzes over on the grass.

The bubbles tickle Oli's nose and make him giggle, and then we're all laughing and I sit up straighter, warm breeze on my face, glancing over at the manager, on the far side of the group now, greeting everyone with brilliant smiles. Even from here, I can see how he breathes life into people – standing up, moving closer. Shaking hands, clapping backs, kissing women's cheeks, hand lightly on their waists.

We've been meeting every Friday – talking, holding hands, kissing. It's all happened so fast. He said he couldn't make it this

85

week, but then texted me Thursday, saying he needed to talk. He picked me up from the main road, same as every Friday since my pathetic panic on the river. He had stubble and purple-brown under his eyes – not his usual self. He drove us out of town to a pub, and caught my hand in the car park. We walked in like that – a proper couple. It was an old man's pub with those black-and-white beams and little windows with dusty light.

He started talking as soon as he sat down – words pouring out. *I have to tell you about my ex-wife, Lauren.* I looked at the cutlery and thick tablecloth, stomach plunging. *It's complicated, and you deserve the whole story.* I picked up a heavy, shining fork. I didn't know he'd been married. I mean, we hadn't talked about our exes, so why would I know? He carried on. *I've been thinking maybe we should stop seeing each other. I like you too much, and I don't want you getting hurt.*

I put the fork down and looked in his face. It's not like I come without baggage, but it was all a bit out of the fucking blue. And then he started telling me all about how lonely he's been – his wife not well – mentally – for years now – and the pregnancy's made it worse than ever. He started welling up, so sad about how it's all turned out. *I didn't want to mess things up between us, Lauren – I've told her so many times it's over – but she can't let go.* He reached his hand across the table, but I didn't take it.

I told him, honestly, I'm not sure what you want me to say. Is she your wife or your ex? Did you say pregnant? He left his hand, palm up, in the middle of the table and looked into my eyes. *It's complicated, Lauren. I know how it sounds. But it's over between us. I told her I'll stay in the house until the baby's born and that's it.* I sit back and let out a big breath. So, the baby's yours then?

He glanced down, his hand still upturned on the table, waiting for me. *Who knows with her? She's all over the place. We can't know for sure until the baby's here and we do the tests. But what I do know is that I can't just abandon her – not in her state – she's the mother of my daughter. Once the baby's arrives we'll do the tests and I'll move out. With my daughter, and the baby if it's mine.* I clasped my hands in my lap and said but what if it *is* yours? It's a big thing. How will you cope with two kids on your own?

Water shining in his eyes. *I don't know, Lauren – sometimes I look at you and think – you're doing it. But you're so strong. I don't know.*

It was a lot to take in. A waitress came over with our coffees and some food menus, so he moved his hand. I looked down blankly at my menu, and he kept gazing at me. Almost whispering. *It's a waiting game, Lauren – I've spoken to a solicitor about getting custody. It's not safe to leave her right now – no one will help or listen – or do anything. Not unless she gets so bad apparently. Well, you know.* Tears fell into his coffee. *It's hell, Lauren.*

I've never seen a man cry like that, in public and all. Grief in his eyes, wrecked. You wouldn't know it now, at the picnic, out here on the grass, in the sunlight, clean-shaven and minty fresh, always so charming and open. Popular. But I can still see the little boy in him – desperate to please, so easily hurt. He glances over and catches me looking – gives me a huge wave and grin. Silently mouths *Lauren! Pam! I'll be right over!*

I couldn't sleep last night, for it all going round in my head. I really like him – I've been buzzing these last few weeks. For someone like him to be interested in me – it's like I'm alive – a woman with a proper body, not just a skivvy for a change. It's so complicated though, I have to step back – I'd tell anyone else to steer well clear, especially with a baby involved. I asked about his wife, and he said she didn't love him – she was manipulative, had only ever wanted control. *I know it's all a bit intense, Lauren – especially when we haven't been seeing each other long – but I didn't want it to fester, you deserve the truth from the outset. I want you to have the chance to walk away now.*

I wanted to take his hand but instead I asked in a hard voice how the baby came about. He said his wife had always wanted another – she'd gone on and on – said that'd make everything okay between them, but he'd already made up his mind to leave – had always said no. *I thought she was on the pill, Lauren.* He rolled up his sleeve and showed me a pale crescent moon on his bicep, silver on tan, where she'd bit him. She's been saying he must hate her, otherwise he'd be happy about the baby.

I know too well how babies don't make things right – you only have to think of me and Jamie – but I can't make it my business – I've got enough on my plate with my boys. Another woman, baby involved. But he was saying all he's been thinking about is a future for us together, like he knows it's too soon for all that, but he's let himself get carried away, and I can't get him out of my head.

I look at Pam – flying a toy helicopter around little Dan – he's smitten with her. Shrieking with delight. Brrm! Oli gets up and starts pulling at my hand – he's finished his Wotsits, wants to play. Pam says I should go, she'll watch Dan, so we go over to the kids by the bubble machine. There's balls and Frisbees as well – they've thought of everything.

Suddenly he's there, next to us. *Hey, Lauren. You look lovely.* Even though I don't – in my only jeans without holes. He crouches down. *And you must be Oliver?* He holds his big hand out. Oli looks up to check with me. I nod so Oli takes the hand and they shake. *Well, it's very nice to meet you!* He picks up a ball and takes a step back. *Do you like football?* Rolls it to Oli. And that's it, they're playing, Oli in hysterics. It's more than Jamie ever did. Pam comes over with Dan tottering, holding his hands in the air, and he pauses, *hello, little guy, you must be Daniel?* then we're all laughing and jumping for bubbles and balls and when it's time to leave he says *we'll have to do this again some time, eh, boys?* and I can see on their faces just how very much they'd like that.

September

Alex

Paul is ready for work, bag in hand, when he delivers the blow. Alex is off guard: dressing gown, cotton-wool head, watching Izzy eating her porridge at the table. Mesmerised by the way she spoons food so methodically when she is hungry. A small animal. *I'm off,* Paul shouts from the doorway. Alex looks up, have a nice day. *Oh – and by the way, love – good news!* Alex waits. *I've found a buyer for your car.* She can't stop her face contorting. What is he talking about. What?

Wake up, darling! Remember, we talked about it – at the cottage – a new car before the baby gets here. Pause. *You don't remember, do you?* Alex opens her mouth. I do remember but. He talks over her. *It's not exactly practical, cramming everything in your three-door hatchback. Is it?*

She stands up too quickly, silver sprinkles in her vision. But, Paul. We didn't agree we'd sell it.

Well, money doesn't grow on trees, love – how did you think we were going to finance a big new one? I took it in for a valuation last week. We'll both sell – that way we can club together for one proper family car.

But, Paul.

Look, I have to go – I'll be late.

Paul – we both need our cars – you know how hard it is to get places from here. Paul laughs. *Love – I'm sure you'll cope – lots of people do! We'll share, won't we? And you know I'll always give you a lift anywhere.* Another laugh, hand on the door. *The extra walking will help you shed the baby weight anyway!* Alex puts her palms flat on the table to steady herself. But.

Look, I really have to go. Warning. *I'll ring you after my meeting if you're going to insist on a protracted discussion.*

As Paul pulls out of the drive, Alex clears the table, crashing dishes onto the worktop. She slams one of the cupboard doors shut: cracksplinter of china. Leave it. She can't deal with that now. She buttons a thick cardigan over Isabella's pyjamas, and straps her in the pushchair. We're going out. The girl is bewildered but goes along with it. An expedition. Alex marches down the lane, buggy thrust in front, arms outstretched. She needs that car, needs to get out of town: will not give it up without a fight.

Sunlight pours on the dark fields for miles around: tea-coloured scalps with spiky stubble. Too hot for September: sapphire sky; tiny birds singing their hearts out in the hedgerows. Rosehips glowing. They do not fool Alex: the ferment of autumn cider is in the air. Blackberries starting to shrivel; wasps pestering yellow leaves in the ditches. The dark days approaching, tiny birds or not.

A car races past, making Alex jump. What is she doing – she shouldn't be on the road. She turns at the footpath sign: lifts Izzy out and plonks her through the gap in the stone wall into the field, then heaves the pushchair above her head, twinge in her belly. Let him see where she is on his app: the danger he has put them in. Izzy leaps around in the tractor grooves, while Alex paces back and forth on the packed earth and tries to think. Breathe.

The static of the river, even here, stuffing her head up. She wants to rip that thick dirty noise from the air: needs to think clearly; needs a bit of peace. Pain in her skull. She damn well needs that car. A different pain, stabbing low in her belly. Alex sinks to her knees on the soil, crusty on her palms, her forehead.

Come on, Mummy! The girl brings her back, leaping from rut to rut. Always bringing her back. Alex gets up, mud dust on her forehead. She lifts her feet, one by one, over to the girl. Puppet woman. We will get through this. Let's go home. When they get inside, she leaves him a voicemail. We need to talk about the car.

He doesn't call back until the afternoon. She is in the garden, Izzy asleep inside, insects buzzing a headache of fuchsia, pink and purple, so ultra it aches her eyes. Unnatural at this time of year. *It's all done, Alex, piece of cake! We should have done it years ago – all signed and sealed over lunch.* Alex takes the phone from her ear: puts him on speakerphone on the floor. Let the neighbours hear. His voice from the grass. *Don't you want to know what we got?! It was a good price, especially considering the miles you've racked up.*

Alex stands up and shouts: coming, Isabella! Her daughter asleep after their morning in the fields. His voice still echoing up from the grass. *Now we won't have to faff around with silly little cars. And I've phoned the showroom – we can do a few test drives at the weekend!* Puffed chest like a rooster. *Hello? Are you there?*

Alex crumples. Tries to hold her voice. I'm really sorry – I've got to go, Paul – Isabella's shouting for me. Too late for logical argument. The deal is done. He does not let on that he has noticed. *See you later then, darling. We'll drop your car off at the weekend.*

Gytrash

The teacher took up hiking when she retired. She welcomes autumn now: without planning, marking, dread. To face the season without bloodshot eyes and nerves; to open one's heart to twirling yellow, blush of stars. Air on skin.

Today would be back to school and she is walking the towpath by the river. She smiles to herself; still has so much to give. She is mentoring a young PE teacher later, on the Women as Future Leaders scheme. She dawdles, bending to pick up the brightest leaves, gleaming conkers, acorns complete with caps. She has done well for herself. There is no rush, no one to please. No swearing, short skirts, battles.

At noon, the teacher spreads her carrier bag on a bench and sits down on it, satisfied: unpacks cheese sandwich, crisps, apple. The crisp sour of a Granny Smith.

The sun seems too low, making silhouettes of the trees. Bright but balmy: the cold has not yet snapped. The teacher shivers, despite the warmth: something is not quite right. She bites into the sandwich but struggles to swallow. The crisps too loud. She rewraps the bread in foil; folds the crisp packet down. It's too early: she will enjoy it more at the bench by the playground. It is only a mile or so.

She stands, brushing crumbs from her trousers, sticking behind the knees, then sets off again, more quickly now. The towpath is empty. Even the dog walkers missing. Only her boots and the sound of the river. She wants to be out of the woods: away from the wasps and sour tang of leaves. There is no rush, but she wants out: there's no shame in that. She keeps marching, sweating now: not even pausing to remove her Karrimor jacket.

There is a black smudge ahead in the distance, but she loses it every time the river curves. Each time it reappears, it is bigger. She realises she is getting closer, catching it up from behind: the shape of a dog. Like a pony. An old one, lopsided and slow, heading away from her, back legs dragging, out of rhythm. She looks for the owner, but there is not a soul in sight.

An old dog would not worry this teacher, but something is bothering her: suddenly alert to every rustle and shadow. That dog does not look lost. Its owner could be anywhere. Hiding, ready to pounce. The teacher shakes herself: she has been watching too many police dramas.

The teacher closes in on the dog. She slows her pace, but can't fall back more without stopping. She tries not to glance around. Head high, looking forward. I am not your woman to attack.

When she is close enough to hear the ugly drag of back paws, the dog halts and turns its eyes on her. Flaming orange. Big as plates. She stumbles back – back to school, the slap of guilt, the girls she shrieked at, crowding in, the ones she dropped, too busy, the girls she judged, should have carried like her own, smothering her face, sucking at her mouth, the shamed, the overlooked and the teacher claws at her face – at the sluts, the wasted, the smokers – get away getawayfromme – but the cloud is too thick, she has been fleeing too long, so she says it, I'm sorry – she screams at the hot choking air – I'm sorry, I'm sorry – it wasn't your fault, I tried my best but we should have done better by you all.

Nancy

I hardly slept, wondering if Luna managed to fly out. Downstairs there's a commotion: the lounge cordoned off for cleaning, Bev on the phone blethering about a health hazard. I go into the dining room, innocent as a buttercup. I ask Kerry, second in command, for two soft boiled eggs with soldiers, same as Gladys please, small yolk of hope in my heart.

Kerry's in her element, dashing about with coffee and tea, telling everyone, *who'd have thought one bird could make that much mess?* Laughing her wicked laugh. She plonks a metal jug of milk on my table. *There you go, Nance!* I look up at her, thanks. White splash on the tablecloth. I cross my fingers under the table.

At least you'll be happy this morning, Nancy?! I smile up at Kerry, absently. *Haven't you heard?* I shake my head. She's almost beside herself with glee. *You'll never guess – that precious bird of yours very nearly escaped last night!* I try to keep smiling at her, glass falling, thickening between us now, harder to see.

I squint, try to focus on her mouth. Pane of glass so thick. *Honestly, Nance, I know you're fond of it but the stupid bloody thing – the mess it's made!* I shake my head like I've water in my ears, can't hear properly. She looks at me oddly, but carries on. *Just sat there in its cage this morning, bold as brass, and with an egg as well!* I look down at my pale brown tea, spoon clenched in my hand, tears on my cheeks. Kerry reaches through the glass, oblivious, and pats me on the shoulder, *we shouldn't laugh – Bev's having to get the professionals in!* then skips off, chuckling, to see to Gladys.

Lauren

My first day as a normal volunteer. Freedom. Butterflies battering my bowels. I've had my official letter – HMPPS – completed community sentence, discharged. I thought it'd be more different, being off probation, but when I walk in there's still old Leonard muttering by the till and Pam's still out back getting the kettle on. I go through the curtain, morning, Pam! She turns, arms wide for a hug – *come here, you – you did it* – when I see Dee's broom-cupboard-office door opening. And there she is in a sing-song of Impulse and hairspray – *good morning, Lauren sweetie – well, this is a big day for you, isn't it?!*

I've no idea how she breathes in there when the door's shut. Office my arse. She thinks she's God's gift. I give Pam a quick squeeze, then stand back to look at Dee. Ponytail swishing as usual, gold eyeshadow glittering – she's got the hold on us all. My chest tightens, but I try not to flinch – I'm here on my own merit now. A proper volunteer. I do my smile. Morning. Take my jacket off. I can leave any time I want.

But if I left I'd have no chance for the job. A proper paid job and all. For the boys, for my mum, for myself. I can suck it up – whatever she throws at me – I've got to make a go of this. Pam goes back to the kettle, asks Dee if she wants one. *Not for me, sweetie – I'm on a detox.* She looks back at me. *Lauren – I hope today's not going to be too much of a let-down – it'll just be more of the same – we're drowning in donations!* I tell her that's fine, thanks. Coffee for me please, Pam.

I'll get straight to it then. Dee seems a bit disappointed – maybe she was hoping for some backchat – and goes back to tapping the computer in her cupboard. *I'm popping out in five, but I'll see you ladies later this afternoon!* Fine. I open a bag of creased books, and start sorting them into piles. Women fluttering on the rail at the edges of my vision, but not bothering me so much today. Pam leaves my coffee on a shelf and goes out to see to a customer. It's quiet, so she comes back once Dee's gone. *Let's have a little break, shall we, love?*

We perch on stools and she asks after the boys. I tell her they're still buzzing about the picnic – they proper loved it! *Oh, they were smashing,* Pam says. Then more quietly. *And they seemed to take a shine to our area manager?* Everyone's got a soft spot for him. I try to be casual. Yeah, he was good with all the kids. He has his own, doesn't he? Pam loves a gossip. *Ooo, he does, Lauren – he's got a little kiddie he dotes on, but we don't see them together at the dos.* I swallow the dregs of my lukewarm coffee and look at her, eyebrows raised. Pam whispers. *Between you and me, Lauren, it's not plain sailing with his wife. A lot of us have never even met her – I think they're one of those couples who tend to do their own thing – you know?* I wipe a drip from the side of my mug with my finger and nod, non-committal, while she carries on. *I can't pretend to understand it. Take me and William – we did everything together before he got – you know – before he stopped going out. But I suppose it's all more complicated these days.*

It sure is, Pam, it sure is. We get back to work – my head spinning, I can't think straight. He texted after the picnic – said the boys were a real credit to me. *You're an inspiration.* I sat at the table and read it a few times then opened my post. Another red letter from the TV licence. *Despite having written to you a number of times. To stop this investigation you need to act now.* I put it on the side while I made my tea, then another text came in. *Can we meet Friday? We could do something special. Just as friends if you like.* I folded the letter back into the envelope and ripped the whole thing up, then made myself wait twenty minutes before replying. Ok – sounds good x. He messaged straight back. *Excellent! Let's celebrate you officially joining the team!*

Alex

The mushrooms have popped up, overnight. Soft white heads, pushing through, arriving as a clump. Gaggle. Cracking tarmac: upsetting the Residents' Association. Last year, a man kicked at them, angry, boot into grey flesh, feathered sponge across blue-black tar.

He didn't realise that fungi scatter invisible spores: trod them all over his landscaped garden. Next year they will sprout across his lawn. Laughing white heads circling the foot of his ornamental cherry. Revenge.

Alex moves away from the window on the landing, back to bed. Lurch in the belly, doesn't know how long she's been standing there. She was only going to pee. Always has to pee. She draws the curtains on the river light; gets back in bed.

Photo on the wall looming down: a wedding present from a girl on her teacher training course. Friend of a friend. Alex and Paul, tipsy, close and grinning, out for a group meal, a few weeks after they met. You can see how happy they are.

Nothing else good here. Paul has taken Izzy to nursery. Alex will not eat or wash before they get back. She knows he will shout but she can't get up. Legs so heavy. Body too thick. River static. Flashing water. Blank. Third trimester pummelling. Numb. Stupid baby.

Nancy

Pip popped in this morning. I was in the garden, by the lavender, not expecting him. Empty bird feeders swinging. I was staring at the snapped stems, where Joyce has twisted bits off for the little scent bags she's always making. A late bee pestering at the purple. *What are you doing out here, Mum?* Pip asked. Forehead crumpling like a little boy. *Everyone's inside having cake.*

I told him it's too stuffy in there. We sat on the bench and he showed me photos on his phone. Little girl laughing: ice cream, balloon, tower of bricks. She probably wouldn't even know me by now. Her own grandmother. *I'll bring her to see you next week-end, Mum, how about that? We could all come?* I shook my head. Not if *she's* coming. Not after everything. I wouldn't even be here if it wasn't for that wife of his.

From the moment she moved in, barely out of college, she's been out for what she can get: manoeuvring into a ready-made house and job, cosy set-up from the off. She's never had to make her own way, not like me. Even after the baby was born, always moaning on, don't feed her too much sugar, always carting her off to fancy places when they could have come over to mine. Breastfeeding a grown child, turning her against me. It's too late for reconciliations: she's made her feelings quite clear. She wants nothing to do with me.

I know it's difficult, Mum, but maybe we should try to move on? I kicked at the crispy leaves crowding my feet. They're really starting to fall now. The rowan berries beading bright blood. I shrugged. I'm sorry, Pip – I'm not really up to talking about this right now. He sighed and looked so disappointed I agreed to go in for cake. Come on then.

We sat in the conservatory under Patricia's sparkly birthday banner and he said *good news, they've got a volunteer to go walking with you!* Krystyna appeared with two pieces of synthetic sponge. *You missed the candles, Nancy, but there's plenty to go round.* I said thank you then told him quietly I don't need to be paraded around the streets: I'm fine as I am.

Well, why don't we go out for a walk somewhere nice instead? I stopped and looked at him, paper plate awkward on his knee, uninvited boy at the party. I'd love that, a smile that hurts my cheeks – I really would. With Ruby.

She always loved it on the river, sniffing at everything. Down at the old bridge, fetching sticks. You could bring Rubes, I said, that would be smashing, love. He's always said it would be too upsetting before. I sat forward on my chair, excited, but his face went a strange shape and his words started distorting like a robot running out of battery, *I'm so sorry, Mum – I don't know how to tell you.*

A horrible pause. *We've been looking everywhere for her, honestly.* I stopped chewing and stared. What are you saying?

I've put pictures all over social media. She just spooked, I don't know why – we were down by the river and she just ran for it. I've not known how to tell you. His face like a sad little boy.

Pip, she can't have just vanished into thin air – I need to get out there and look. He stopped me. *Mum, sit down, you know you're not well enough. I knew this would set you back. I've rung round the vets, everyone's searching. I'll tell you the second we have news.*

I sat down. We've such a strong a bond: I'd know if anything had happened. He nodded, leaned forward and took my hand. *That's it, you're right, she'll be fine. We'll find her.*

I'm sure that woman is behind this: she's never liked dogs. She always sat in Ruby's chair on purpose. He'd never say: loyal to the last. But I've done without her so long. I stood up, said I had a headache, then went off to my room, knowing the hurt on his face.

Upstairs I set to cleaning: swiping everything off my dresser and drawers; scrubbing every surface with a wet flannel. I flung the teaspoons off the rack into my wardrobe, metal clash; pulled clothes out of the drawers, kicked them under the bed. I didn't come out until teatime, everything still racing, specks of silver, little bits in space, but even then, what happened after, it wasn't like me.

I went down to the dining room and sat by the door without speaking, but when they brought me that tepid green soup it was the last straw: I jumped up, overturned the bowl, dark slime on the carpet, then I saw Norman coming in, so stuck my foot out and tripped him. He half tipped a table, but caught himself. Even so, the staff were straight on me, escorting me out, time-out in my room to calm down and reflect.

I'm in my room now, tray of stone-cold food on my dresser. This is very serious, Nancy – Norman could have landed up in hospital. We know you're finding things hard but this kind of behaviour isn't tolerated here. We'll meet in the morning to talk it through, and I realise they're right – it's the only way out of here. Hospital. Slips and trips. And now they've left me sobbing even though I never cry, and they'll be watching my every move, sitting me where they can see me, away from the door, press your buzzer if you want to go down at night, we only want to keep you safe, Nancy.

Lauren

He's picking me up from the bus stop on the main road at 10 a.m. Just friends, keeping it simple. I'm usually at the shop Wednesdays but I haven't missed one since I started and Pam says I deserve a break. I can do what I want, now my probation's done. There's graffiti tits and cocks all over the shelter and rubbish on the floor, but the weak sun shines down through the mucky glass.

I stand into one hip – grimy spray fizzing up from cars and lorries. Wet tyres shining in the sunlight. The clouds still brooding but backlit by heaven – what a weird day – it can't make up its mind for two minutes. I hope it clears up. I smooth my hair, then check my lipstick and eyes in my mirror.

We've gone out a few times since the picnic – but nothing's happened again between us. I don't know how I can help someone like him, but he says I'm a good listener. He's the one who listens though – it's like I'm the only person in the world when I'm speaking. I've told him too much. About Mum. About Jamie. Not how we made Oli by accident behind the bandstand, wet grass on the back of my head, skirt round my middle, mud and blood thighs in the morning; everyone necking White Lightning by the tennis courts. But a bit about how Mum went mental, how Jamie did right by me for a bit, walking proud with my bump in the streets, linked arms – little kids, full of jelly beans.

A rainbow appears across the road – I could do with some gold. I close my eyes and make a wish – for it to stay. So I can show him. For good luck. So this works out somehow. I rang Mum after I got his text on Wednesday and told her, for a change – who I was meeting, that it's a work thing. Which it is. She ruined everything like always, saying she doesn't want me taking advantage, minding the boys so much. I went straight on the loan website after, filled in my details, and got the money straight away. Fuck it. It's only two hundred quid and I can't turn up looking a state. And now I can get the boys shoes and all. Mum'll never know. I caught her looking at my skinny jeans and ankle boots when I dropped the boys off, but she didn't say anything. She'll think I lent them off Hannah. If I get that job I'll pay it all straight back.

Be careful, Lauren. She'd nudged me with her elbow into the wallpaper. *Don't do anything I wouldn't.* I told her that didn't leave much then, did it? But she said I looked nice – *go on – have a good time then.*

The rainbow's gone by the time he pulls up. He leans over with his two-kiss greeting when I climb in. Crisp shirt. Spicy ginger and mandarin, like autumn whisky. He always smells gorgeous. Even the car is wood polish and leather. There's no sign of kids, or another woman. It's his car only. Everything sophisticated, gleaming. It must be over between them. He surely wouldn't risk this otherwise.

I wondered if you fancied somewhere different today, Lauren, with it being your day off? I tell him I'm up for anything – the kids are at Mum's so we have the whole day to play with. Flicking my hair. World's our oyster! *You said it. Right, let's go then.* We set off and he says *you're looking beautiful today.* I just laugh.

At the train station he turns into the multi-storey. I ask where we're going but he says it's a surprise. *I promise I'll have you back at your mum's before you turn into a pumpkin.* He pulls a wad of cash from his wallet for the tickets. Birmingham New Street, day returns. It's not even noon, but he gets mini bottles of Prosecco from the trolley on the train – *what the hell!* Packs of nuts and crisps to share. We giggle over the plastic glasses like kids, fields flashing past, salt-licking fingers – the old couple across the way looking down their noses at us.

It's hectic at the station – everything crowding and blaring, tannoys, suitcases, engines, and we're buried underground with all that heat and roaring. I come over a bit giddy and he guides me up the escalator and out. I'm flustered, tide of blood rushing in my ears – sorry – it's the wine, what a fucking lightweight! *Let's get you some lunch,* he laughs, and glides us past glossy shops and a starlit tunnel into Selfridges, straight to the fancy restaurant for food and champagne. I know everyone's staring at me, even in my new clothes, but he takes my hand and walks me past the glittering glass and cutlery as if he's proud of me, *come on, you, I'm starving!*

We head outside after, daytime tipsy, and he leads me to a swanky hotel bar for cocktails, velvet drapes, red bricks and candles on low tables in the middle of the day. He orders two Bad Boy Good Girls – spritz of blue vodka, rhubarb, strawberry, champagne. *It's all on me* – he insists – *my treat – it's the least I can do. I wouldn't have got through the last few weeks without you* – and we sit together on a red leather sofa, friends, chatting and laughing like it's a night out, legs touching, holding hands after the third drink, tangling up.

I sip at the thin black straw when he goes to the loo. Fuck it – why can't I just lighten up and enjoy myself – especially after he's been so straight with me – life's complicated and Mum's always saying I'm too independent for my own good. He orders more drinks on his way back. We should slow down – I can't go home wasted.

I'm shocked it's still light when I next go to the loo – we've still got two hours – and I redo my lipstick and pout at the mirror, why shouldn't he like me? – and when I stride back, stomach sucked in, head up, willowy in the candlelight, he's looking for me – not at his phone – just waiting, smiling, wanting me back. He looks at me – funny, beautiful, sexy – and his mouth tastes of sugar and lime and I trace the silver scar on his arm with my fingertips and I'll be there for him. We'll work it out. Two hours later we get speciality coffees that'll never sober us up, and then stumble outside, sparking off each other, his hand on my bum all the way back to the station.

October

Alex

Paul turns the engine off and Alex clambers out, bigger than ever. Hippopotamus. *I'll be back after the group to pick you up and drop you home.* Alex tells him no need, honestly, we'll walk, the air will do us good, but he insists. *I'm on my break at half eleven anyway, so it's no drama.* Alex unclips Izzy from the car seat in the back: easy with a five-door. Her heart lurches as she catches sight of Ruth, breezing into the car park in a crimson coat, hair piled up as usual, orange silk scarf today. Wife. Squash buddy. Car seat. What if she says something. Alex lifts Izzy and slams the door too hard to distract Paul, but he's already seen her: stepping out of the car. *Ruth! Hey there! How are you and the A-team?!* Ruth pushes her sports buggy over, breathless, apple-cheeked from the morning walk.

Hi, Paul! Alex! Nice to see you both! We're great thanks. Let's get inside and get warm, eh, Alex? Alex smiles hi, yeah, let's go, trying to wrestle the changing bag unstuck. She finally drags it out and takes Izzy's hand; brings her round to kiss Daddy. He touches the bump under Alex's baggy jumper and it starts contracting, hard and tight. She tries not to cringe. Izzy turns and waves, *bye bye, Daddy,* as Alex leads her across the car park behind Ruth. Paul gets back in the car and looks at his phone. He'll start the engine once they're inside.

The church hall is boiling, plastic pears and aubergines rolling, wooden train track scattered, underwater din. The baby could be born now and survive. Ruth takes Alex's coat, and drapes it over a chair with her own. Her son rushes off, vanishing into a stripy tent. So perfect. Izzy is still clinging to Alex's leg. *Do you want coffee, Al?* Alex says I'm trying not to drink caffeine. The baby, you know? Ruth raises her eyebrows.

Alex smiles. Oh, go on then, I'd love one. Maybe it will help her wake up; kick to the surface. This noise. Ruth smiles – *a little bit never hurts* – and goes off to the hatch. Alex leads Izzy to the play-tent and kneels down: look, it's little Edward! Do you remember him? From when you paddled in the river? Izzy peeps in, shy, one hand on Alex's knee. Peekaboo with the flaps for a few minutes and they are laughing: Izzy crawls in to join the boy.

Ruth calls over from the chairs, a metallic red beaker in each hand, spill-proof. *I've got your coffee, come sit down for a sec. She'll be okay in there.* Alex joins her, takes the mug. Thank you. She never usually rests at these places. Ruth says *how're you feeling – you know, with the pregnancy and all?* Alex takes a sip of milky hot coffee and Paul is suddenly walking towards them, through the hall, making a beeline for her, looming bigger and bigger, stepping over bricks and tambourines. He is huge. Alex starts shuddering with cold, daughter not in sight, coffee in hand, too late now. Metallic mug shaking. Ruth smiles brightly, *hi, Paul – we didn't expect you so soon! Shall I get you a drink?*

Paul hands Alex a pack of baby wipes. Smiles at Ruth. *I'm not staying thanks – I just brought these – you left them in the car.* Alex says thanks, sorry, and he says *well, enjoy your coffee, ladies,* staring hard at Alex. Ruth tinkles a laugh, pushing a strand of hair back, *oh, we will, Paul! Sadly all decaf of course!* Flirting. Beautiful. Lying. *See you later on then!* As Paul walks away across the hall, Ruth reaches across and presses Alex's hand.

Lauren

Oliver and Daniel are hyped. I've got the football, filthy and frayed, leather hexagon flapping where Mum's terrier got at it. We're early for once – both boys scrubbed and in their new shoes and joggers. I had a bit of spare out of the loan, so paid back the minimum this month out of that, no sweat. I should have done it years ago. I usher the boys into the front yard. There's a few bangers going off already, and it's only October. That's what they're like round here though – rockets in broad daylight – money going up in smoke, same with the dogs and cars.

Oli does dragon breath at Dan in the pushchair, then races off down the street, roaring steam. My teeth chatter – I'm chilled to the bone. I've been wearing two pairs of tights under my jeans in the house but it makes no difference. The sun's lost its gold already – that picnic seems another lifetime ago. My hoodie and jeans aren't up to this – we shouldn't be having frost yet. I couldn't wear my anorak – the lining's full of holes and the metallic's all peeling – I don't want people looking down on me. I've been layering the boys up so we don't need the heating.

He's standing on the playing field when we get to the park, bright neon football under each arm – one orange, one lime – casual, beaming. *Hey, you*, as we approach, but no kiss. Sensitive about the boys. He crouches to greet them – *hi, boys! I remember you from the picnic!* I pull Dan out of the pushchair and prop him on the grass.

He offers the balls and the boys hesitate. I tell them yeah – go on. Then look at him. Thank you. They're perfect. Really thoughtful. You shouldn't of though. He squeezes my hand and Oli boots his ball hard, globe of light against the autumn sky. He races off, after it, while Dan stands smelling his ball – rubbing the gloss on his lips and saying nice. He's always smelling stuff.

There's another bag, one of those posh cardboard ones with cord handles. *We couldn't leave you out, Lauren, could we?*

I don't need anything I tell him, not taking the bag, but he presses it on me. *It's just a little something.* My hands are bluish and old-looking as they reach into the fancy tissue paper. An Armani puffer jacket all wrapped up in gold. I can't take it. I push it down and pass the bag back. He smiles, hands behind his back. *Come on, you deserve it! Put it on – let me see!* I shake my head. It's too much – it must've cost a bomb. He laughs. *Hey, I can't take it back now, I've chucked the receipt and cut out the tags – put it on!* He reaches forward and pulls out the coat and hands it to me, letting the bag drop. I push my arms into the silky lining. It's proper beautiful – not my usual style but gorgeous – deep blue with fur and thick duck down, like warm water. I zip it up and it's soft around my cheeks, perfect fit.

He beams – *I knew it'd suit you. You'll need it when we stay in Manchester – it's always bloody freezing that side of the hills!* I laugh. Only a couple of weeks til our first proper night away together. As long as my mum doesn't bail – you'd think I'd asked her to sit them for a fortnight, the way she's been going on.

He races off across the field after Oli, so I keep the jacket on and hang out with Dan, playing careful catch, not wanting to get it all muddy. My cheeks are hot. People are going to think I've nicked it. Dan cups his tiny hands together to catch the football but falls over nearly every time. He's getting better at throwing though. I'll tell my mum I got it from the charity. Pam says we always get first dibs – staff prices, dirt cheap. Perk of the job. The stuff some people chuck out.

Oli runs back for a drink, glowing and gives me a massive hug. It makes my throat hurt – how much I love him, how much he needs a man in his life.

He follows Oli over. *Did you get the form in?* he asks, getting his breath back. When I nod and smile, he rubs my arm – *nice one! That job's got your name all over it!*

It's a part-time, paid assistant with flexible hours. He helped me with the statement – I'd never have done it without him. He said they've advertised internally but it hasn't gone out publicly. Then he's running off back to the pitch with Oli for the second half. I ruffle Dan's hair and smile at a woman walking past with a pram. Nothing to be ashamed of for once.

Nancy

Luna has been laying eggs and eggs. It's since the escape. There was another clutch this morning. Bone white, thin-shelled. The staff think it's funny: the more they take, the more she lays. I told Gladys about when one of my auntie's budgies had chronic laying – calcium deficiency – thought the management might listen to her. Their model resident. I can't speak to them after Norman and the soup. I told Gladys that it's him they should be watching, but Bev made herself very clear at the meeting. *I've got my eye on you, Nancy. We all have.*

It turns out they won't listen to Gladys either, but she asks her son to bring in some golf balls for the cage, in case that helps. Apparently it works wonders for chickens. It's good of her, but I hope he's quick: there's already a shiver under Luna's feathers; a tremble of skin. Tail wagging. The other women surprised me, rallying round. Scrawny Joyce donated a string of beads as a distraction, and even mad Patricia's trying her best, belting out musical hits next to the cage. The clamping down has been bad for everyone: they're watching us like hawks.

Bev comes flapping in, *come on, ladies, give that poor bird some peace.* We scatter, back to our chairs, as she throws the blanket over the cage. *Don't get too comfy – it's autumn crafts this aft! Nancy, can you put that book of yours down for a second? I hope you haven't forgotten the harvest festival tomorrow?* How could we forget – the place has been pumpkin mad for weeks. Candles, soup, lotion, you name it. A never-ending stream of spooky crafts: paper-cup ghosts, yarn spiderwebs, haunted word-searches.

I stay in my chair, fiddling with my locket, while everyone traipses off to activities. It's a blessing my mother never had to put up with anything like this. Bev follows without even look-ing at me. I know exactly what tomorrow will be like. A parade of kids with dusty tins and giant cauliflowers; vicar beaming, harvest hymns from the front. Bev on her best behaviour, Luna's appalling eggs concealed under the blanket.

I sip my orange squash and write in my book. Patricia will be back soon: she never sits at anything long. I'm passing on what I know about bird-care to the others: they'll need it when I'm gone. I've worked it all out: Pip will give the tenants notice, and I'll stay with him while I'm recovering. That wife of his will just have to put up with me.

There'll be harvest flags tomorrow: they never miss a chance to plonk a flag in our hands. I did used to love dressing Pip up though, when he was little. There's a picture of him as a lady-bird in the box upstairs in my wardrobe: little boy with sparkly antennae boppers in a laughing ring of cowboys, cats and fairies, dark eyes fixed on the floor. So furious every year when he missed out to a clown or a witch in a bin bag. Angry little bug, face paint streaked with tears.

Just as I'm finishing my notebook, Patricia bursts in, covered in orange paint, activities girl hot on her heels, breathless. *Come on, Patricia, let's get you cleaned up before you get paint everywhere.* Patricia cackles and points at me – *it's her fault! She's the one you want!* I usually cringe from her when she's shouting, but today I look up and could swear she winks before she's ushered out.

Alex

Alex is walking along the river to the park, Izzy in the pushchair, weight of the baby pressing down. There is a harassed-looking girl with a buggy up ahead, blocking the path: cheap jacket, too much make-up. Pretty in an emaciated sort of way. Alex remembers girls like that from school. As she gets closer, the girl pulls out a half-empty bag of white bread from under her buggy. A snotty boy clings to her legs.

Alex takes a deep breath: the girl is not moving out of her way. She can't deal with anything at the moment. There is a smaller boy asleep in the buggy, scuffed toy car loosely cupped in his hand. Tatty handbag looped over the handle. The girl suddenly turns to Alex, startles her: holds out the bag of crusts. *Do you want some and all? For the ducks?*

Izzy tries to wriggle out of the pushchair to reach the bread, but Alex leaves her strapped in. No thanks, we're in a rush. Paul says ducks should not eat bread. The snotty boy grins at Izzy and lets go of his mum's legs. There is still not enough space for Alex to get round. The woman pulls a scrappy tissue out of her pocket and wipes at her son's nose, then rummages under the buggy. *I've got a bit more somewhere*, then steps closer, pushing another bag of bread towards Alex, ducks quacking madly from the water.

Alex backs away, knuckles white on the pushchair, excuse me, can I just get past? The girl stares at Alex, taking in the greasy hair, porridge-stained top and saggy jeans, then speaks more softly. *It's for your kid – for the ducks – I didn't mean for you to eat or nothing.*

Alex nods yes, I know, thank you, but we need to get going. Flustered. Izzy shouting to get out, *feed the ducks*, and Alex shouldn't have said it out loud, no, Izzy, bread is bad for ducks, we have to go, and that gets the girl riled, holding the bread bag high, the bigger boy snatching up for it. *Oh, right, it's like that – it's not good enough for you.*

Alex is on the verge of tears now, no, that's not what I meant – I don't want any trouble, can you just let me past? – Izzy arching her back, wailing to get out, and the woman says *keep your hair on, I was only trying to be nice*, squaring up to Alex, and Alex doesn't mean to shout, let me past, and the baby in the pushchair is awake and crying now too, and the girl says *look what you've done now, you mentalist*, and heaves her buggy to the side, then spins back to her kids and the ducks, swearing under her breath.

Nancy

I can't sleep, so I go down to see Luna in my dressing gown. I'm supposed to press my buzzer, but I'm only going to the lounge. When I pass Norman's chair I catch the high scent of soaked urine, cold reek of tea. Breakfast's not for three hours yet. There's a string of garish pumpkin lights around the window, flashing the room orange.

Luna chirps and fans her feathers when I sit down. I post a treat through the bars. More eggs in the bottom of the cage. She is worse. Lopsided. Not many droppings. Tail wagging again. Gladys's golf balls haven't helped.

There are nylon webs everywhere – all set for Halloween fun. I hear faint singing, from the river, and join in, murmuring the song to Luna. Sing me a song of a lass that is gone. Krystyna, on the night shift again, pops her head round. *Hello, Nancy – is everything okay?* I tell her yes thank you and she leaves me to it, silly Nancy, singing to her bird. Say, could that lass be I?

The bird watches me loosen my plait; untangle it with my fingers. Plait it again. Bird on the wing. I walk to the window, look out. Touch my mother's locket. Back to my chair. To the window. Loud the winds howl. Unplait and plait. Maybe I did it already. The singing in my head. From the river. To Luna. All that was good, all that was fair. Krystyna again. *Nancy – is everything okay?* Loop the loop, I thought she was nice. *Would you like a cup of tea?* Cog cog cog in the machine. All that was me is gone. *Shall we get you back to bed?* Unplait and plait. *Are you chilly?* My dog, where is my Ruby?

Do you know what year it is, Nancy? I rifle through my diary, my records, blotted with tears. A lass that is gone. Everyone out to get me. Nylon wrapping my face, mummified, giant spiders. *What year it is?* Loop. Chirp. Window. Knickers. Locket. Plait. *What year were you born, Nancy?* All that was me now is gone.

Lauren

He's coming round after work with Friday fish and chips. Oliver's mad to see him again. I tell him don't expect any more presents, then get the table set – vinegar, salt, mugs of tea, Coke for the kids. Check myself in the hall mirror when the doorbell goes: hair-sprayed bun, kohl eyes, red lips. I glance at the doormat where the pink envelope was when I walked in. Red writing. *FINAL REMINDER. TV Licensing.* I chucked it straight in the bin – the loan's gone so there's no use opening it now.

He sits on the sofa between the boys and reads them a glossy picture book he's brought while I unwrap the hot parcels. I tip them all onto plates – jumbo fish and golden chips, floury butter rolls, bright mushy peas, pickled onions and batter scraps – he's really gone to town.

We sit up at the table together, our spare chair full of his body. He changes the light in the room. I try not to gobble. I've just taken a big bite of butty, lips all floury, when he passes me a creamy envelope. *I've got you something, Lauren. You and the boys.* I giggle, dust my lips with a tissue.

I'm expecting a note or card or something, but inside there's three Virgin Active swipe cards. What the fuck. I look at him, cards in hand, don't know what it means. He is smiling at me. *I'll not take no for an answer – one adult, two juniors – so you can take the boys.*

He rubs at a smudge on his watch. I realise he's waiting for me to say something. I slide the cards back in the envelope. What, are they like guest passes or something? *No, Lauren* – laughing – *this* – sitting forwards – *being here all together – it feels like a massive step and I wanted to mark it – you know?* Hands behind his head, leaning back. *Look at us, we get on so well. You're champion, aren't you, boys?!* Oli and Dan beam at him. *They're a credit to you, Lauren.* I stare at him – still don't understand. What is this?

It'll give us somewhere to go – something to do – now it's getting colder. I've made you all members so you can go when you like, no limits. Nothing to pay. There's a crèche so you'll have a bit of independence as well – it's all free, so you can do your classes, or use the pool or whatever. I close the envelope, face burning, and sit on it: uncomfortable under my bum. It's so nice of you – but it's too much. Can we talk about it later?

The windows steaming up from the food. He's not getting the message. *There's soft play too – you'll love that, won't you, boys?* I help Oli scrape the batter off his fish. There's way too much food – they only need half a fish each. Loads will end up in the bin. Look, I tell him, we need to talk about this – let's not do it now. It's a lovely thought, thank you, but it's too much. *But you've been working so hard, Lauren, and for nothing – it's criminal. We get a discount anyway through work so it's only what you're owed.*

Oliver is nagging at me: *Mummy, what is it, Mummy?* I tell him eat your fish and not just your chips – it's good for your brain. Come on, no more chips until. Interruption. *Your mummy's going to take you swimming, Oli – we've got special tickets so you can go whenever you want!* Oli's face lights up like a pumpkin. He never goes to the baths like other kids.

I shake my head and put my knife and fork together on my plate. *Swimming, Mummy, swimming!* I pull out the envelope and pass it back across the table. We can't take these – it's too much. He laughs, takes it and puts it down on the table next to his plate. *Okay. I'll keep them. But I've signed the direct debit now, so they'll only go to waste.* He looks hurt then, and puts his knife and fork together too. *Look, I'm sorry, Lauren – I've obviously got this wrong – it's too much. I thought we were serious – that it was something we could do as a family – but I've obviously got the wrong idea. I'll sort it, don't worry. It was meant to be a good surprise – I thought it would be our place – fun, you know?*

Oli is staring at me, round owl eyes. Danny climbing down from the table, putting his greasy hands everywhere. I think of warm turquoise spangled with silver – of shiny tiles and hot showers. The smell of chlorine. The commitment he wants to make as a family. I tell him I'm sorry – it was just a bit of a shock. Of course, we'd love to go with you, Paul – we'd love to go swimming, wouldn't we, boys?! Come back to the table, Danny, come on. Only until I start the paid job though – then we'll pay our way – but it's really generous of you, you're right – it'll be ace – it's really sweet, thank you.

Alex

Izzy pushes her nose against the steamed dining-room window, peering out at the surprise dark. She picks up pebbles from Alex's collection on the sill. Alabaster, siltstone, spotted slate. Geode cracked open, hollow crowded with crystals. Alex's star find from her childhood beach, when she used to spend days searching, checking her beginner's pebble-spotting guide. Alex bends down to her daughter, shows her how the large oval of quartz glows when you hold it to the light.

Alex is still underwater, but a little closer to the surface today. She moves away to set the table. The clocks will go back at the weekend, the nights even longer. She texts Reema: would be lovely to catch up – it's been ages. She wonders if Reema has decided to try for a second baby yet.

Isabella calls *Mummy – someone eat the moon*. Alex smiles. It's called a new moon. Come on now, up to the table, tea's ready. Daddy's working late – he sent a message to say he'll get chips for himself on the way back, so it's just me and you for now. Alex wonders who he is with but never asks. She kisses Izzy's head; pulls her chair close, warm cheeks, giggles. Gently takes the large greyish pebble from Izzy and puts it back on the windowsill: that is a special one.

Camping at the foot of Scafell Pike, next to a thigh-deep beck: icy and clear, lined with shining cobbles of turquoise, salmon and lemon. Paul had hidden the grey pebble in his backpack as they hiked to the summit with a picnic. At the top he went down on one knee, rinsed the grey stone to duck-egg blue like magic, and balanced the ring on top: a simple band with an ethical Canadian diamond. A stone wetted for luck. He knew her better than anyone: would do anything for her. Worshipped her.

Alex and Izzy pick up the chicken bones now with their hands, suck the juices, grease dribbling their chins. Happy. Kitchen roll on the table, just in case. Alex listening for the door. Izzy chatters on about baby Hari from nursery. *I drived him in the dolly pushchair!* Lovely. And what did you have for lunch? For snack? Izzy says she had no lunch or snack. Or drink. She is utterly unreliable. Alex wants to smile more. Listening for the door.

She warms Izzy's towel and pyjamas on the radiator while she's in the bath. He is later than usual. She reads three books, *Pip and Posy*, popped balloons, stolen ice creams, all happy in the end, then lights off. *Stay, Mummy, stay*. Listening, listening. Alex climbs into the toddler bed and curls around Izzy in the dark, little thumb in her fingers, nose to cheek. Twinkle twinkle little star. Listening. She is too rigid: needs to relax to ease the girl into sleep. She takes a big inhale, tries to let it go. Like a diamond in the sky.

At last, Izzy's fingers loosen, slowly slowly, on Alex's thumb, and Alex tips herself quietly out of bed. She tiptoes out of the room. Hears the back door. Goes into the bathroom. Paul is coming up the stairs when she comes out. Alex braces, smooths her top, looking at him, waiting. He grins, triumphant, and raises his hands: two bottles in one hand – Cava and non-alcoholic spritzer – and a bunch of autumn freesias in the other. Fire, peach, heat. He holds his trophies towards her. *For you, my darling! I'm sorry I'm so late.* A kiss. He smells of fried fish and aftershave. They head downstairs. *You get comfy on the sofa, while I sort the drinks.* Paul brings her a frosted glass, clinking with ice, and they sit together and watch a nature documentary, his phone flashing messages next to him. He has the remote. *Come here, love.* She shuffles closer and he puts his arm around her. Alex leans into him, resting her head on his chest. Everything back to how it should be.

November

Lauren

Oli's been on about fireworks for weeks. I don't want him to miss out, so I said I'd take him to that big bonfire in the park. I asked Mum to come but she said no, as usual. There's always an excuse. *You know fireworks aren't really my thing, Lauren.* I get the boys wrapped up – two uncomfy bundles with sticky-out arms. Their toes and fingers'll end up numb, whatever. Paul's not coming now neither. He's staying home with his ex-wife, who he says he doesn't love. And a cat from the estate's run in and hid behind the fridge, shit-scared of the bangers. It better not piss behind there.

Oli leaps around like he's got ants in his pants, all the way to the park. *The moon's red, the moon's red!* The pavement's crammed when we get near so I can hardly get through with the buggy, fireworks flashing, making my heart jump. I used to hate watching Mum's boyfriend through the kitchen window – lighting rockets in the backyard, swaggering back to the house, swigging lager, taking too long. He was a dick – never used a taper like I said. Burnt the firework code I showed him from school.

Why's the moon red, Mummy? The buggy wheels slide around in the mud near the river. *When will it start?* Everything always has to happen now with Oli. I catch him looking at the ToffeeApplesHotDogsCandyfloss but he never asks for nothing. Sometimes I could cry he's such a good boy. I dig around in my bag – pull out two bags of budget cheesy puffs. Here you go – same as the picnic, remember?! I don't know how I'm going to the make the payment this month. I just haven't got it. I daren't ring Tania to ask what to do – she's always told me make sure you don't miss a payment and you'll be right.

I'll look online later. I help Dan with his cheesy puffs then get him out of the buggy and hold him up, above all the people, to see the bonfire on the other side of the field, cordoned off with tape. He's getting heavy. Then Oli wants a go so I lift him up there too, then bring him down and give him a big kiss. *My feet are cold, Mummy.* I know, Oli, it'll start soon. Do some stamping. I hold their hands in a little circle and we stamp around, ring o' roses, a bit wild, laughing, not caring what all the staring people think. Then I get Dan back in the buggy and give his cheesy puffs back, his lips powdery orange. He's hypnotised by a kid swishing a flashing wand. The fireworks'll be on soon – not long now, boys.

Dan starts crying as soon as the first banger goes up – *want to go home!* I lift him back up and hold him close – fat with jumpers under his coat, face into my neck, little gloves clamped over ears. Gold lace crackles, flares, exploding leaves. Oli stands next to me, face to the sky, cheeks lit by green fish, pink snaps, silver snakes. He's jumping up and down – *they're higher than the stars!* Hyped.

My puny arms burn with holding Dan, but I hold on in this field of bulky sacks on legs, idiotic. All whooping. My cheeks roasting, the whole world going up, flames reflected in the river. Then something moves in the bushes near my feet and I kick out, can't breathe, and I swear there's a shadow, but it's stupid, no one else even looks, it's all in my head as usual.

Oli drags his feet on the way home, whining. The smoky raspberry dark, fucking freezing. I'm sure I can smell piss, but can't get behind the fridge. When I finally get the boys in bed, I stumble down to the bottle of white on the side in the kitchen. There's only a bit left – warm and lemony but I tip it all in and plonk myself on the sofa in front of the dark TV. I search on my phone what to do if you can't make payment on a payday loan. Everyone else's fucking fun flashing through the curtains, rattling the glass. I'm supposed to check if there's an early repayment fee. Oli shouts down, crying. *We don't like it! The bangs are too loud! Danny's sad!*

Both of them whingeing. I go up with a drink of water, time to sleep now, and Oli says what if the cat gets hit by fireworks and what about the birds and I tell him go to sleep now, the cat's not even outside, and anyway cats can look after themselves – you're just tired, Oli, you'll feel better in the morning – I need some mummy time now, the bedroom flashing like a nightmare disco.

He whimpers so I stand on his bed and drape a couple of towels over the curtains to block out the flashes and then go back down to the sofa. Search instant loan low-interest payday. Paul in his cottage, mansion, apartment. Whatever. With her. Probably roasting chestnuts on their private bonfire. Triple-glazing, spotlights. I scroll down the results.

Instant online decision. Very high approval rate. I'll never get low interest until I've got a job. I don't even know why he's bothering with me. I fill in the application for £500 – to cover the lot – loan and interest, all in. The payment jumps to £89, but I can keep some to cover next month and I'll have the job after that if everything goes to plan. And it'll hopefully stretch to Christmas too. I'll get some sparklers to have at Mum's when I pick the boys up after my interview on Monday.

Gytrash

The birdlike nurse is marching home from work on the towpath, keys spiking through clenched fist, fingerkeyfingerkey. Armed crab, metalflesh. Phone ready, on speeddial. Hair tied up, stone-washed jeans, ready to be home. She tries to walk strongunafraid. The nights are drawing in: she'll have to start paying for the bus. But it takes longer that way. And there's still the walk at the other end.

The trees are gnawed to the bone now: spider shadows skittering the track. Yellow mushrooms on rotten stumps, but notimetostop notimetolook. She wants music but leaves the earbuds in her rucksack. Staysafe. At thistimeofyear. Sensible. Alert to any crackletwig shufflefoot.

Her ankles are swollen from standing all day. She always stays longer than her shift. Stones through the thin soles of her pumps. Jaw tight. The pain of women, in their eyes. She glances at the water: subdued today, glassy. The odd ripple, ribs. Dead air. Bats not out yet. Over half way now: only ten minutes left. She might be okay. No handgrabbedmouth, leapfromthebushes, flashofdick. She keeps her feet marching, outofbreath.

Alex

Paul bursts through the front door with a Magician's Family Box: soft fountains, cones, candles. Gentle but Elegant! No bangers. Then back to the car for the fire pit: *it's our lucky day – I got the last one in Argos!* Alex has the pies in the oven, as instructed. Paul wants it traditional, proper: the works. Izzy has been looking out of the window since 4 p.m. She is hungry, waiting for her tea.

Alex helps Izzy stamp woolly socked feet into yellow wellies. She fastens the small duffel coat, pops on a rainbow bobble hat and releases the girl to the patio to watch Daddy cracking firelighters into the steel bowl, petrol on his fingers. There's a neat pyramid of kindling and meticulously positioned logs. Alex shuts the bifold doors and leans forward over her huge stomach to stir the mushy peas in the pan. Two cans. His mother would have made all the food from scratch, of course.

It is all ready: hot pies, sparklers, metal pail of sand, sticky parkin in a tin. A spiteful pain in Alex's pelvis makes her wince. Reema never replied to her text: she'd understand this pelvic stuff. Alex is desperate to sit down but can't, with the baby head grinding down between her legs. Izzy waves at her through the glass.

Alex waves back; makes her face smile. The plates are warming in the oven. She pops her head out to tell them tea will be ready in five. Izzy wants to come in, but Paul makes her stay out. Alex's face tenses. Things have been so good lately; she doesn't want to ruin it. Chardonnay wood smoke blusters in with icy air: the neighbours burning oak chips in their chiminea. The pie and peas go down well. Not even a complaint about the sliced bread. The parkin is left in its tin: Paul has something more exciting from the baker's. *Gingerbread pigs – like Mummy!* Izzy looks at her mummy for a reaction. Alex chokes a laugh out of her mouth for them. *Pot-bellied.*

The fireworks are after the food: Paul parading the lawn with his headtorch, lining them up, then back to the kitchen for the taper. Tension rising. Rosy-tipped little rope. Tender. Safe. He wants everything perfect. Alex stands out with Izzy on the patio while he lights the first fountain. She can't pick her up with the big baby belly. Paul takes too long, laughing and lingering on the walk back, white spray firing behind him, as he steps onto the patio. Izzy shrieks; hides her face in Alex's legs. *I don't like it!* Paul looks at her. *Don't be a baby, Isabella.* He's back on the lawn already, glowing taper in hand. Izzy looks up. Whimpers, tears rolling now. *Daddy, come back!* He doesn't turn. *You'll like this one. Watch!* Alex squats down to the girl, baby pushing down. Be careful, Paul. He lights a Roman candle and saunters back. Wrong. *Do you think I can't light a few fireworks, Alex?*

Each bright puff sends a shiver up Alex's spine, crouching, wobbly, Izzy sobbing into her chest. She's scared, Paul, I'm taking her in. He's not interested. *It's pathetic. You've made her like this, Alex – it's your fault. Stay there, both of you.* Alex squats against the step, pelvis burning, sobbing toddler weight into her chest, fixed on the relentless glow of the taper, bobbing over the lawn, back and forth, flare after flare, clouds reflecting perfect peach. The neighbours call over from their open conservatory. *Happy plot night! Ours always loved the Catherine wheels when they were little! Isn't your daddy clever?!* Paul ducks in for the tin of parkin and hands it over the fence. *Alex made this specially for you – didn't you, love?!*

Then time, at last, for the Catherine wheel. Paul hammers it into the fence, Izzy screaming with each blow. *Make it stop, Mummy, ScreamStopScreamStop Stop, Daddy! I want to go in!* Alex shelters her: nearly over now. The wheel hisses sparks, too close to the shed, too loud, too bright. Paul stands back arms folded, smirking.

It fizzes into dark. It is done: they are allowed back inside. *After you.* Alex can't look at him: she takes Izzy's mitten and leads her in. Paul follows, red taper still in hand. He brushes past Alex on his way to the sink to douse it. It is an accident: doesn't touch her long enough to blister, only a trace of red on the back of her hand. It is too late: Paul saw her jerk her hand back. *I'm so sorry, darling, let me see, come here, hold it under the tap. You take up so much room these days – it's hard to judge – I'm sorry.* It doesn't hurt, Paul, it's fine. But he keeps it held under the tap.

Right, sit down, you two, I've got something to make you better. Paul pulls a Thorntons box out of his bag and puts it on the table next to his phone. Treacle toffee cracked into shards. Izzy climbs onto a chair and puts a piece in her mouth, bulging her cheek. Tears shiver on her chin. *You have some too, Alex. Open wide.* He drops a big triangle onto Alex's tongue, takes one for himself, and then fills a bowl with water and ice. *You need to keep your hand under for fifteen minutes, Alex.* His phone lights up: more messages from someone.

They sit at the table chewing, Alex's hand so cold it hurts, ice cubes tapping against the sides of the bowl. *I'm going to take Isabella up to her bath – you stay here and relax.* Izzy clings to Alex: *I want Mummy.* Paul picks her up and looks at Alex. *Mummy's hurt her hand. Have some more toffee, Alex. Your hand needs another seven,* then he carries Izzy out crying, leaving Alex at the table, jaw aching, hand fiery red in the water.

Nancy

I've done my research. Slips and trips. Hospital admissions. The risk of broken bones is high in women. All in my notebook.

Fragile bones, light with bubbles, mere tunnels of air. They herd us into the conservatory for the fireworks like children: trays on laps with pie and peas. The blow-heaters are up full, drying out my eyes. I flood my mushy peas with mint sauce. Can't eat for fretting about Ruby: she'll be quaking some-where, tail between her legs, every bang and pop plucking at her skin.

The staff have got us a box of fountains. *Nothing too wild.* I accept second helpings of pie, despite myself. Remember, remember. Bev snapping photos for the website. Roman candles. Sputtering blue showers. Old people smiling, tucked up in tartan with traditional fayre. Plotting. A guy on the fire at the end of the garden, blistering in the flames. Guy, guy, poke him in the eye. The smell of leaves and paper skin hissing; bandaged eyes, singed yellow hair. It's not the same without the kiddies. Put him on the bonfire, and there let him die. The body packed solid, refusing to burn.

They usher us into the lounge after, for sherry. It's impossi-ble to fall or trip in here. Carpets glued down, non-slip mats; everything mopped, lit, clear. I take a tiny sip of the sweet brown liquid: don't want to blur my resolve. But maybe it will be help with the pain. Treason and plot. The only way. I stop one of the girls on her way past, I'm off up to bed, love. *But it's bonfire night, pet – you want to stay up a bit, don't you?* The room flashes, jangling my nerves. I'm not feeling right, I tell her, an early night'll do me good. I nod slowly at Luna in her cage, then heave my body up, past the staring faces. Old Joyce, Patricia, Gladys. Goodbye, ladies.

I make my convoluted way to my room. Kerry waits for me to get decent, then pops her head round the unlocked door to check I'm tucked in. *Just buzz if you need us.* Will do. But I'm fine, really, goodnight. *Nighty-night.*

Clean nightdress, sparkling teeth. Face cleansed with Imperial Leather, creamy lather, tight skin. I'm all set. Brittle bones, hips like seashells. Handbag packed: notebook, clean hankie. I've left the bag in position, under the emergency cord. I lie on my back in bed and pull the string to turn off the light. Fireworks flare on the ceiling; snarled shadows of branches. And the sickly green glow of emergency lights; black smoke gathering at the window. Seven months I've been here. All of us left to rot, waiting for our bodies to give us up. Treason itself.

A stick and a stake, for King George's sake. But what if I end up somewhere just as bad? There's no point thinking it: I squeeze my eyes shut. Up a ladder, down a wall, a cob o'coal would save us all. The terror of the river, my cheeks burning with the creature's eyes. I turn to the window, very dark now, oily smoke seeping under the curtains. It is close. Blotting the emergency lights, green to black. I gag as burnt wool clouds my mouth and eyes and with an almighty heave flip my body away from the window, slamming my weight with the fall as hard I can to the floor.

The shriek: twisted and high. Cheek to carpet, searing pain in the marrow of my collarbone – the beauty bones – yes, bright white – the bones which have never been seen, always submerged in spilt grey flesh. Yes. I reach out for my handbag with all its provisions, then stretch up for the emergency cord. Just where I wanted it. I sink into the pain after that, close my eyes and let them find me.

Lauren

Mum's having the boys til teatime, so I walk to the gym after my interview. Paul said it'd do me good. They'll let me know tomorrow whether I got it. The adrenaline's still pressing at my lungs. The entrance to the gym's like a fucking hotel. I've only been there once, for the tour. I try to swipe in and end up dropping my purse and blocking the turnstile while I scrabble around on the floor, cheeks hot. People crowd up behind me. I try the card all different ways and eventually a man from behind says *black strip that way, love*, pointing.

The changing room smells likes a hotel as well – hand lotion, movie lights, hairdryers. I pull out the neon leggings and sports bra I got with the voucher Paul got me for my birthday. He thinks of everything. They were on sale, so I had enough to get

waterproofs for the boys, one each – red, yellow – a size too big.
I didn't know I needed a padlock so I hide my phone in my shoe
in the locker and pile my bra and rucksack on top. I bet Dee
comes here with her perfect body – bet she has a padlock. It was
just her and him across the table from me this morning – apparently she had to be at the interview as shop manager. Both of
them sitting at the table, judging me. He says it's a dead cert but
he doesn't know Dee. She's had it in for me from the off. She said
all the right things – *come on in, Lauren* – *make yourself at home* –
but it's all show with her. Anyone can see she's got a thing for him.

I follow the signs upstairs to Gym Floor. Even the handrails
shine like lemon lollipops. Upstairs it's a whir of crop-tops,
tanned bellies, heartbeat-pounding treadmills, Lycra. Those
skinny kandi-bracelet girls with giant eyes that Jamie always used
to go with, before he fucked off to Scotland. I shouldn't have
bothered – should've gone straight to get the boys. I'm everywhere – sagging back at myself from mirrored walls, flushed and
sloppy. Faces staring at me, looking down their noses at me like
that snobby woman on the river, standing there in my cheap
fluorescent kit.

I climb on a bike. The seat's too high so my feet don't reach
the pedals. And the machines are so complicated. I move to the
next bike and start peddling, ignoring the electric screen. The
TVs on silent at the front – everyone staring, headphones in.
The news flashes – poppies, obesity, a crash. There's a repeat of
that soap on another screen – pregnant lass sobbing – I saw it
last night already.

Paul talked me through the interview questions yesterday but
I still messed up. It was Dee's fault, out to trip me up. I go over
my answers in my head as I pedal. *Can you give us a little example, Lauren?* Teamwork, multitasking, organisation skills. SMART
targets. I was a disaster. I'll never get a job – I'll always be skint.
He'd be better off with her.

I manage six minutes on the bike, then sneak back downstairs, sweating, and gulp straight from the fountain when no
one's looking. The shower's worth it though – hot river rain,
rinsing me free. If I got that job I could buy the kids goggles and

these fluffy animal hood towels the other kids have got. He's in charge – not Dee – he'll make sure I get the job and we'll do sparklers together later – and now I'm here, where I'm meant to be – in the rush, the downpour – chest and bum stinging pink, free shower gel foaming the run-off, dizzy with heat, doused, nearly singing, clean. The boys'll love it here when I bring them.

Nancy

Monitor the resident for seventy-two hours after the fall. Symptoms must be clearly documented. Blood pressure, temperature, pulse. They keep coming in my room, bothering me. Bruising around the pelvis and collarbone. No head injury. No broken bones. Not even a wrist. Not even the beauty bones. *You were lucky, Nancy. We'll make sure it doesn't happen again.*

They didn't even bother to take me in. The nurse came out to check me over, *they'll be dead busy at A&E tonight, Nancy – it's best to monitor you here, in your home.* I said I need a proper doctor. This is not my home. Women patted and tucked, *what a shock,* saccharine juice and fuss. *We'll keep a close eye on you, don't worry.* Silly old woman fallen out of bed. The bed's like a cage now – side rails, header, footer – I'm all boxed in.

The nurse gave me painkillers for the bruising. *These should help, love. You might be a bit sore tomorrow. We'll up your normal meds if we need to.* I said nothing. We're not allowed to talk to the medication nurse when she's dishing out pills in paper cups. They watch us like hawks, but I'll find a way to stash the pills in my wardrobe.

The doctor will come and see you in the morning, love. I feel around the bed for my bag but can't find it. Someone must have taken it while they were getting me back in bed. The room's full of standing people, treating me like I'm senile. I ask for my bag. The nurse passes it to me, still talking. I look inside. My notebook's gone. I stare around at the people, where's my diary? It's not here. The nurse checks under the bed then pats my arm, *you've had quite the ordeal, let's look in the morning. It'll turn up.* She offers the beaker of juice again. *Just a little sip?* I ignore her, lifting the sheets, trying to get out of bed: I need my records. The room still flashing with fireworks. *Come on, Nancy, lay back down, you need your rest.* I let her take my weight in her arms.

You must let us know straight away if you feel sick or dizzy – do you hear? It's important. I close my eyes, stay quiet, try to think. My notebook. *Someone will sit with you for a while.* Notebook. *Nancy,* warm hand on my arm, gentle voice, *you mustn't be embarrassed, this happens all the time. Only last week Joyce fell out of bed.* My eyes snap open. What does she mean. Joyce never said: there's nothing like that in my records.

Alex

Alex bloats around the bedroom like a turquoise-veined ghoul. The huge baby visible through her skin. Izzy at nursery; Paul at work. Her skin has been thinning for weeks. The neighbours don't notice her any more.

On the towpath, people see only the curled baby, bobbing along, suspended under the jumper. They stare. Bulging jumper, floating. No woman head. Blink. Looking for scaffolding. Eyes playing tricks. Roar of river.

She hardly goes out now. Can't bear the static of the water. Can only stomach pale food. White cheese, milk loaf, plain pasta. Baby size of a cantaloupe. Antelope. Elope. Big white face, stuck. Bump distorting, warp to warp. Clench.

She is trapped, blistering images, necklace on her bedside table, splintered stone, fishing waters poisoned, acid-yellow river, people crammed in a lorry. Daughter lost, violent protests, thousands of women marching. Blood-black dog always waiting.

Your baby can see its first colour. Red. The inside of your uterus. Blood of womb, flesh. Blood pools in your feet and legs, dizzy when you stand. Red. White. Baby skull bones soft and separated, sliding over each other in birth. You are bleeding gums, filmy skin, subterranean labyrinth of bright blue veins.

Lauren

He invites me for coffee and a swim – a belated celebration about the job. Like our night in Manchester wasn't celebration enough. I'm still buzzing from it. He said he's never felt like this about anyone. I text back – will have to bring the boys. I can't go asking my mum to have them again yet. *Perfect, see you all in the cafe at 11 xx.* He gets there first – stands up for a kiss. Squeezes my arse. *Hello, gorgeous! Fancy seeing you here!* Big boxes for the boys. *Advent calendars for you two – special ones, with Lego in!* I tell him you didn't have to – Mum got them Disney ones already. But hers are knock-offs from next door – back of a lorry – cheap chocolate. The boys shriek, arms wide around the boxes, thank you!

Well, we have to treat our boys, don't we?! I tell them don't open them yet – we don't want to lose all the bits in the locker. If they'll even fit in a locker. He stays at the table. *Hang on – I thought we could try out the crèche before swimming – you'd like that, wouldn't you, boys?* Dan stares at his box, but Oli looks up, frowning. *You won't have to listen to our boring grown-up chat then – and your mum can have a bit of peace for a change!* I say I'm not sure – they're looking forward to seeing you – and swimming but he's already filled in the forms – ready to sign. *They'll be right here, Lauren – you can see the crèche from where we'll be sitting! It will be a good test run for the nursery anyway!*

I haven't slept since he rang me about the job – thinking about the boys, so little, with strangers, the vouchers, the money – how we'll keep up. I should be over the moon. I remind myself over and over – it'll mean I can pay the loan, buy what we need. It's a paid job. I look over at the crèche. *It's not like you're leaving them for a week, Lauren!* There's another woman dropping a tiny baby off in a car seat. I'm being silly. I pick Dan up and we all go over together, Dan clinging on. *No!* Oli looks serious. *Mummy – Dan doesn't like it – we want you – and swimming!*

I bob down to Oliver. I know. It's only for a little bit, then we'll go straight in the baths. Just give it a go – if you don't like it you don't have to do it again. Paul stands by the counter, arms folded, smiling at the girl. A conspiracy. The girl picks Dan up and carries him through the baby gate, sobbing over her shoulder, arms stretched out for me. Oliver follows behind, punctured. *Come on, Lauren, they'll be fine once they can't see you.* I follow Paul to the drinks counter, breathing fast. He orders my latte, asks for it skinny. *Well, this is nice – getting you all to myself!* I smile, not quite at him.

He taps his credit card on the machine. *Have you seen that special offer they've got on personal training?* I look at the poster – a pumped-up man with tanned biceps next to a grinning woman on a treadmill. *You should give it a go – my treat.* I shake my head. I'll stick to the pool for now. He nods at the fit girl in the black vest, now making my latte. *It looks like it's working for her, doesn't it?!* She sashays across with my latte and pushes it over the counter, ponytail swishing like Dee's. The drink is pale and watery.

His jacket is on a table by the glass wall at the back, looking onto the pool. There are stickers of waves and fish all over the giant window. I burn my tongue on the thin milk – trying not to look at aqua aerobics. Old biddies with dove-grey hair bobbing around. They should frost the glass – give everyone a bit of privacy. It's supposed to be soundproof, but I can hear Ace of Base – I've heard it before when we've gone past to the family pool. I think I can hear Oli crying. Paul tells me just relax for once. *You deserve it.* I ask about his daughter. *She's at nursery.* How's work? *I'm in between meetings. I'll need to get going after this – then the boys can have you back.*

What are we going to tell people? *Lauren, why so serious? Come on, let's enjoy ourselves – we don't often get the chance.* I tip another sugar in my coffee. Maybe I should just pack it all in. It's too much. New job, nursery, gym. This weird new family thing. It's a lot of pressure – especially since Dee's made it clear she doesn't even want me in the shop – *this is a huge step, Lauren my lovely – it's not only your future at stake – it's for everyone on the scheme.* Once a thief, always a thief. And those vile fucking women in the clothes that I'm always expecting, any second. My lungs squeeze. I gaze at the old women in the water – weightless and unapologetic, having a right laugh with each other. Mum always says *you're never happy, Lauren — nothing's ever good enough*. Maybe she's right. I look at him, scrolling on his phone. I try again — this is lovely. *Look, Lauren, I can tell you're not enjoying yourself — to be honest, I have a lot on if you don't want to be here.* I take his hand. No, honest, it's really nice. I'm just a bit distracted with everything — I'm sorry. He relaxes, puts his phone in his pocket, then takes my hands and looks serious. *Lauren — I've been thinking about houses for after the baby's born. Maybe it feels too much, but I thought it might make sense if we looked together?*

December

Alex

Your baby's head burrows deeper and deeper into your pelvis. Alex clings to her daughter. Trapped. Needs to walk, to swim. The hills are too far away. Her limbs will barely move. Your baby's gut now contains meconium. Alex is bloated. Sticky green-black substance. She cannot rid herself of it by washing her hands.

Look out for the signs. Back pain, trickle of water, urge. Her daughter cries Mummy in the night, but Paul will not let her go. *Leave her. She has to learn. You need your rest.* Hurting Alex's heart.

The stone strung up by the bed now, old wives' remedy for restful sleep, leaking splintered images, calls, wails from the river, flooding the room with murky river static, the reek of singed hair.

Two extra days at nursery. Alex not coping; Paul needs to work. Her eyes ache with missing her daughter. Red-raw hands. Green-black germs already in the womb, swollen ghoul. Dog getting closer. *Stop talking like this, Alex – you're scaring Isabella.*

Turquoise-veined bump, warping. Clenching. Your baby is trying out facial expressions now: frowning, smiling. Not connected to happiness or sadness. *I don't even recognise you any more.*

Translucent skin, baby grinning through. Alex examines its facial expressions in the mirror. Aquamarine map, veins to the nipples. Heavy down. The weight of it all. Hated grin. Glistening ghoul. River rushing, ghoul. Baby gushing, ghoul. The room speeding up slowing down. Diesel simmering in from the river. Your baby is ready to be born.

Nancy

Krystyna hands me my diary, like it hasn't been missing for nearly a month. *I found Patricia wandering around with it – it has your name in the front.* I snatch it, then want to say sorry. It's not her fault. I rifle the pages, stomach hurting, as she walks off. Looking for clues. The other women watch as I flick back to the start, working methodically through each numbered page. Nothing obvious but then my insides flip: twenty-six days of November ripped out. Nothing between plot night and advent.

I look up in shock. Everyone's gone back to their business: Gladys on her crossword, Patricia staring at the advent wreath, singing, Norman rasping in his new chair. His old one too sodden to salvage. I lick my finger and leaf through each page again, one at a time. I only catch it third time round. A single word in trembling letters. Green biro. I can hardly read it. Maybe *KITCHEN*. On 31 December. I look around. Joyce peering out of the window, more like an ostrich than ever. Gladys doing her puzzle with the blue biro from Bev's office. I've never seen Patricia pick up a pen, so it can't have been her. Old Norman wouldn't have the nouse.

I draw a new column in the back of the diary. Suspects. Ancient skin loose round my knuckles as I write, like little elephant knees. *Green Biro.* My own letters shaky. My words float around, looming up, making me nauseous: someone has been through my personal records, taken November and left a great dirty hole in my mind. I run my finger down the ruffle of torn paper: soft white wound. The hand is so frail and spidery: it must be an old person's. Maybe it's *KITTEN.* But there's no question it's 31 December.

Lauren

I walk up Mum's path, holding hands with Paul, slimy leaves plastered all over the concrete. *I can scrape them off for her, Lauren, if she has a shovel?* I squeeze his hand, let's see. The boys are in front, already banging on the door. *Nananana!* I suddenly want to grab them and leg it – this is a disaster. But she's already opening the door, click-clacking like always, best lipstick and zebra print. Cleavage on show, tanned and crinkled. *Come on in – how lovely to meet you!*

It couldn't be more different to how she'd been with Jamie. *I won't have anything to do with that boy or his family – not after what he's done.* Like I had no say in it: park, cider, bandstand, knickers round my ankles. Mum ushers us into the front room and asks Paul if he fancies a little lager. He looks at his watch. Smiles. *If it's not too early, that'd be lovely, thanks, Mrs Turner.* She laughs. *Oh no, love, call me Angie – I'm not that old – not yet anyway!*

I perch on the arm of the chair by the window, the kids shoving each other to pull out the tray of dusty dinosaurs from under the telly. *This is nice,* he says, looking round.

I cringe. I shouldn't have brought him. But he said he wants me, family and all. *I'll prove it, Lauren, I'll show you.* During that massive row after the gym. I'd texted him after a couple of wines, like an idiot – what's going on with you and Dee? He called me back – *what's all this, Lauren?* I told him anyone can see there's chemistry between you – and what about your wife? Let's be honest – I'm not really in your league – not like either of them – not from some posh family and posh place. I shouldn't even of got that job. He didn't say anything so I carried on. Maybe we should call it a day – fun while it lasted. I kicked at the pink envelope on the doormat while we spoke.

He sounded totally shocked – *Lauren, it's been over with my wife for months, you know that. And Dee's a work colleague.* Grim pause. *Men and women can talk without having sex, you know.* I started crying – I know, but it's all too much – I just want everything out in the open – but he said *you have to trust me, Lauren. I know* you've been hurt in the past, but I'm not like those men – I want us to do things properly.

I picked up the envelope and ripped it in half – another FINAL REMINDER – and sniffled through the rest of the call in front of the hall mirror, shiny red nose, smudged mascara. *I know it's been tough, Lauren, but we're getting there – we just need to wait that bit longer and we'll be together properly.*

I told him okay, sorry – I've had a shit day. It's hormones. He told me *you need a bit of retail therapy – why don't I take you out?* But I said it's okay, I'll take myself out. You're right, it'll do me good. Why not. I've the job now – I deserve some nice things for a change. My reflection pathetic. He carried on. *Lauren – it's you I want.* Okay, I told him, okay, rubbing my fingers on my legs to warm them up. I've got to go.

Fine. But let me prove it to you. Why don't I come and meet your mum, make it official like?

I'd agreed, then sorted out the loan. The second one hadn't gone as far because I owed more on the first than I'd borrowed, so I decided to stop fannying about and get enough to cover everything – that way I don't need to worry about the payments and can manage some proper presents for the boys, and get myself a couple of nice things as well. Surely I'll be able to pay it back after Christmas, with the job and everything.

And to give him credit, he's kept his word and now we're here at Mum's – Sunday roast and lager, wine, gas fire up full, Mum's boyfriend Neal slopping gravy like always. Pork chops, spuds and peas – she's made a right effort.

Mum tops up my glass. *It's good news about your cousin, isn't it, Lauren?*

I don't know what she's on about. She pauses. *Oh, didn't Hannah text?* I tell her come on, spit it out then. Mum looks shifty. *She probably wanted to ring you herself – I hope I haven't spoken out of turn. She's got a job on cruise ships – last minute – over Christmas – doing her beauty and hair and all that.*

I press my fork down, over and over, into my mash to get rid of the lumps. It's too watery. I start on Dan's when mine's done. Why didn't Hannah say.

So, love, Mum says to Paul, *tell us what you managers get up to all day long.* It's supposed to be banter – but I can tell something's up. It's the stress on *managers.* She doesn't like him. He doesn't let on – he's too polite – but I can't look at her. What the bloody hell is she playing at. I have a go at Oli's potatoes next, take a forkful and blow it hard, face wet with steam. Come on now, eat up.

Once we're done and Paul's headed off, I go into the kitchen and ask her straight. What's your problem, Mum? *Nothing, love – I don't know what you're on about.* She starts filling the sink for the dishes.

You don't like him, do you? She squeezes liquid in and swishes it around, not answering. No one's ever good enough for you, Mum. Look at me. She turns, hands dripping suds on the lino. *Lauren, it's not that. It's just I've seen men like him before. Just be careful – right?* I feel it like a slap. You'd think she could be happy for me, just once.

So I say it all, right in her thick-plastered orange face, too much wine between us, you always have to ruin everything – you've never had a man who treats you proper – who's actually bothered – who'll love your kids – look at Neal. My boys deserve better than what I got.

She turns back to the washing-up. You know what, Mum – you're jealous – jealous of your own bloody daughter.

I shouldn't have said that, but she always has to stick her oar in and she says *get out if that's how you feel,* so I get the boys wrapped up and storm out – then march them all the way back to our freezing house.

Gytrash

A woman in dark red slippers stands on the wet lawn, behind a high wooden fence. You cannot see the river from the care home, but its sound fills her ears like the rushing of wings.

The woman stands tall, unbent by her years, lead-white hair frizzing in the rain. Visitors flinch at the spittle on her lips; look away from the wild black eyes, embarrassed. Afraid for their futures.

When this woman shrieks in the night, haunting the corridors, tireless staff guide her back to bed. They are gentle and efficient but whisper that she is mad.

The woman's slippers are sopping: she will catch her death. She stares at the gap under the fence where the foxes pass through. Waiting. Her thin cotton nightdress shining silver with the moon.

When the shadow finally appears, pouring under the fence like black liquid, she takes a single step back. It gathers before her: an enormous animal with burning orange eyes.

This woman is brave but starts to shake a little. The creature's eyes bore into her: saucers of fire. She covers her mouth and nose for the stench, but stands proud in its gaze, resolute.

As she stares, the ragged fur becomes her little sister, packed off in disgrace, returned vacant and hollow. The niece she should have had. Pulse between her thighs as the girl she loves is whisked away, corrected by the priest.

It all flashes through her: shamed, disgraced, lost. Finally, when she can bear no more, the shedding begins. She sheds quickly, skins shrivelling like hair in flame, spinning quickly to grass.

Childless falls from her shoulders first, followed by mad: twirling, like seed pods, to the ground. Spinster is heavier: shrugging off like sodden wool, a stinking cardigan, heavy to the pile. She holds the creature's eyes: pathetic and useless join the heap at her feet, followed by weak.

She remains upright in her terror – charred tree, lightning-struck – raw but stripped clean. Standing in her power at last. When the pile is complete the creature dissolves at her feet in a pool of water: a dark stain spreading under slippers.

Alex

Alex's belly clinching to flint again. Endless. It's been happening all month. It was the same when she was pregnant with Izzy. *Just normal practice contractions* the midwife had smiled then. But this time it is grotesque. Protruding like a shelf.

She vomits when she wakes, lick of flame in her throat, sirens in her coccyx. She goes downstairs, blinking against the visions, smile mask for Izzy. Last day at nursery before Christmas: Santa coming to the woods, special. Paul tells Alex to go back up and rest. She gets in the shower when she hears them leave. No turning back now: the body unstoppable. The baby has to come out.

Plug of red-veined jelly. Alex makes circles with her hips for the crack of pain. The shudders sweep too fast: she is not ready. Boiling her up like pepper broth. Out of the shower, she can hardly dry herself. She makes it to the bedroom, pulls on a T-shirt. Retches. Can't reach the joggers. The birth plan. Move to hospital when it gets too much.

The kitchen door slams. *I'm back! I've got pastries from Grande Vita. Not that you need any more butter!* Loud thunder laugh. *I thought the baby might appreciate it.* Heavy tread on the stairs – *Alex?* Goliath into the bedroom. *What are you doing down there? – get up, Alex – look at the state of you with all your arse showing – my God – what's happened to your face? You're like a pufferfish.* Alex says help me. On all fours. *Alex? I can't believe this – why didn't you call me?*

She looks up at him, cotton-stuffed-wool mouth. I'm sorry. It's different to Isabella – I need the hospital now. It's too much already. Small laugh. Please.

You don't need the hospital, darling – I've only been gone twenty minutes. You're a dab hand at this – we don't want anyone interfering too soon.

But something's wrong, it's too fast, not like last time and another spasm through the body, clench. Kneeling, face into bed, Alex clamps teeth to keep her jaw on, swinging in the blood dark, muffle the cry, *you're always so dramatic, darling – just breathe softly like the hypnobirthing lady said – it's all natural,* but another wave cresting, I need a midwife, Paul, don't leave me and *I'm just here, darling – we'll be fine* but the purple in her eyeballs now, gagging her face, splintering, breath and vomit again and

I can't clean that, Alex, you're like a baby yourself. How am I supposed to look after you if you're throwing up everywhere? He is livid, Alex far from him now, almost unreachable. Her head swarming with red ants, stinging, face into the mattress, and someone might see the carpet so Paul goes for gloves and spray but she says don't leave me, I can't do this, I need help, ring for help now, hands and knees crawling for the phone, but he is there, kicking the mobile away from her, across the carpet, spraying, scrubbing, scathing, *I said we don't need anyone yet*

and Alex will die splitting the baby is coming fire and a silence of light – it has gone. Sudden peace. She opens her eyes.

Paul looks at her. *What now?* I don't know – it's just stopped. *Right. I told you we didn't need anyone. But you should have got me sooner – if anything happens it's on you, right? I'm off to put the kettle on – I'm knackered. Remember – you were like this with Isabella and then it took forever for you to get her out in the end.* But the purple is back coiled on the floor shitting and blood and I need to push, ring now, Paul, ring. It's back. Please. Ring! It's coming. I'm dying.

Paul looks at her and dials 999 – *right, they say I need warm towels, put the heating on – we need towels, Alex – why isn't anything ready? They say don't push, breathe through the push, they're on their way – can I see the baby? – on all fours, Alex – don't push! Why am I the one who always*

and fluid bleeding petrol and *yes I can see the head* to the operator – *she says you're doing really well, Alex – they're on their way – there's gunk – the head – she says big push for the next one – we're doing well – fuck it's coming, I have to catch it, why am I the one?* and Alex chokes on diesel sting, the push splinter she will never survive and the head is out, *oh shit, just its head – they say just wait like that with the head out, it's normal* and will the neck hold it, that thin snappable neck, head between legs, and it is rising again *massive push on the next, push now, push* and it is out in a slither of flames – *you've done it, Alex, we've done it* – wrap the baby in a towel or jumper – whatever you can reach, rub him now, clear his mouth of any mucus and no cry and rub him, he's mauve, what are we going to do and a cry slices the air like a silver arrow

and don't pull on him, the placenta is still inside, but there is blood, too much blood, they are just round the corner, *we'll be with you any second now, just hang in there* and Alex on hands and knees can't see Paul or the baby the tug of grey-purple pipe, dark blood swirling in her skull like a tea bag in hot water

and she wakes on a stretcher, plastic face, hammered and nailed, looking around, Izzy, where is my daughter?

A deep voice, *don't worry, love, we've got you – your baby's right here – he'll go in the ambulance with you. He's doing really well. Mummy and Daddy did a fine job! What an entrance, eh – he'll turn out to be a right one, you bet.* Alex closes her eyes, whining bees, strapped. Needs her girl. *You're in good hands now – let's get you to hospital so they can have a look at you.* Eyes shut to the flash of river and bumps of asphalt to nowhere. And Paul, bolt upright in his fold-down seat, chest puffed, proud as punch.

Nancy

Bev tried to have another private word last night. *A trim would do you the world of good, Nancy.* She moved in front of the TV, blocking the pregnant girl on screen, big as a Christmas pudding. *We want to work out a plan to meet your needs – just want you looking your best.* I tried to look around her. No one's touching my hair: I've managed nine months, I don't know why she thinks I'll change my mind now. Joyce tutted over at us, trying to concentrate.

Nancy, you do want to be ready for Christmas, don't you? I crossed my legs and looked sideways at the birdcage. *Let's sort this out, then you can get back to the telly.* I got a hankie out of my sleeve and dabbed my nose. We're all sick of turkey and tinsel. If it's not Halloween it's Christmas. Party magicians, choirs, nativities: she can't let anything rest. I put the hankie away and grip my diary. Luna's getting worse: the eggs are killing her. Swollen abdomen, constant straining, open-beaked breathing, blood in her droppings.

Nancy, if you don't speak, it's difficult to take your views on board. Talking down at me, in front of everyone. I stared at the cage, mouth sealed, until she went away. She'd ruined our programme by then: none of us could make head nor tail of the row in the pub. Joyce nudged me, leaning forward in her chair, *look at him!* head shaking side to side slightly with her tremor. She watches properly: me and her, we're not like the rest of them here. Watching everything as if it's *Cash in the Attic.* We're real people, part of the real world.

The pregnant girl with haunted eyes. She should keep quiet about what happened with her dad on the bridge. It was an accident. Some things are better kept to yourself.

It's still dark when I wake, Pip's Christmas roses on the side. Winter solstice. Plan B. I draw a blue circle around Christmas Crafts on my list. Two birds with one stone. A chance to inspect for green pens, and to pick up equipment.

After coffee, I sit near Gladys in the Activity Room, snowy hair freshly set again. She knows something's up. She slides her cardboard tree cut-outs together angelically, getting them ready for dangly gold thread. Jessie comes over, surprised. *Hello, Nancy, good to see you here!* She points at the main table. *Shall I show you the ready-mades?* Snowmen, candles, plum puddings. She's such a friendly girl. I tell her I want to make a tree like Gladys, and she sets me up. I fiddle with the cardboard for a decent enough time, then wander over to the craft drawers. There's a pot of mixed biros: anyone could have taken a green.

Everything alright, Nancy? Jessie calls over. I smile, yes thanks, getting a pair of safety scissors out. Round-ended like nursery school. I pick up two pairs and slide one up my sleeve. *Can I get you anything, love?* Jessie asks, coming over. I tell her I want to make a doggie card, for my granddaughter. They don't have a ready-made, so Jessie sits me down with brown card, glue and felt tips.

I make a total hash of it, but clear up after, and put my gluey scissors and cardboard mess by the sink to dry. Jessie's pleased

I've given it a go: a tick for my notes. Progress. Acceptance. *You'll have to come again!* I yawn, yes thanks, and head off upstairs to my unlocked room.

Things move all the time: they think we don't notice. I shake the scissors out of my sleeve by the drawers, stomach hurting. Open my top drawer, then slam it shut. I check the safe: pick up the pocket watch, heavy and cold. It was my husband's, worth a small fortune, promised to Pip when I'm gone. The only decent thing he left, except for Pip. I shove it back: it's too obvious to put the scissors in here. I push them in with the thimbles in the plastic bag instead: an innocent bag of junk at the bottom of the wardrobe. Pills, thimbles, scissors. It's only for a couple of days.

Lauren

It's the charity's Christmas do and they're paying for a meal for us all at Global Buffet to say thanks for our hard work. Like the picnic. But I'm there on my own merit this time – first wage due Monday. They pay us early, apparently, for Christmas. I hold the long black dress up on its hanger. Paul got me it specially. I smile at myself in the mirror – who would have thought, Lauren Turner going out with the top boss, wearing fancy dresses, going to the gym. Buying the kids proper presents on my own.

It's that long since I've actually been out, I don't even know how to act. Luckily Pam arrives in the packed lobby just behind me, shuffling her ankle boots self-consciously through the automatic doors, smart and square in shoulder pads. *Oh, Lauren, I'm glad you're here. Don't you look glam!* Fussing with her handbag and jacket, juggling something bulky in a carrier bag. *I wonder where the rest of our lot have got to?* Talking too fast, coral-lipstick blur. A peck on the cheek: powder, leather, tissues. Her face soft dough. The floor skitters under my heels like the ice rink. We're both out of our depths.

Pam spots old Leonard from the shop and bustles me over to say hello. He's with a group – they all turn and grin, ice clinkle on glass. Women in kitten heels and silky jumpsuits with matching handbags, cool and sophisticated. I'm dressed wrong. I don't recognise anyone – it's the area meal, not only our shop – but they act like I'm an old mate. *Hiya, Pam! Lauren! Nice to see you!* I look around for Paul. He said he might be late – his wife's not even up to doing bedtime now. Dee appears from behind Leonard, ever the chirpy manager. A dazzling giant glass in her hand, pink bubbles with thin straws.

Mum shoved a tumbler of warm vodka Coke in my hand when I dropped off the boys – *get that down you, love, quick – for your nerves.* Peace offering. I look over at the gleaming bar – there's at least ten sorts of vodka. Suddenly everyone's moving. I press close to Pam, who's magically got herself a Britvic orange. A waiter ushers us over to two long tables with crimson tablecloths, sparkly crackers and wine on ice down the middle. A right banquet. I want to take a picture for my cousin, but don't want to look like a kid.

I drag a heavy chair out and squeeze in next to Pam, legs together, trying to sit properly. I shiver – it's freezing. I've too much skin on show, out of place. Dee's at the other end of the table, halter neck rippling silk. The man across from me looks like my old science teacher but with flashier glasses. Bald scalp, trimmed grey beard, blue-winged specs. He puts his hand out, *how do you do.* Hand like a lettuce. *Red or white?* I say white please, and he leans across to serve me, like I belong. The waitress talks loudly over my head, trying to collect drinks orders. *You can help yourselves from the buffet now.*

I check my phone – nothing. My breath switches in my chest – something must have happened to Paul. I should have known the last few weeks were too good, that it couldn't last. I've given Mum and her negativity a wide berth, but maybe she meant well. I've been crying every day, leaving my babies at nursery, but everyone says it'll get easier. It's good for them to socialise. They get a hot dinner there and all. Paul even took us round Ikea last week to see what we might get for our new place, once his baby arrives and things settle down. We're on the countdown now. The kids raced round it like a theme park and he got us all hot dogs at the end. I thought he was serious, committed, but where the fuck is he now. I should have known she'll always come first.

I feel Pam stand up – *let's see what they've got, love* – *I'm famished.* I follow like a puppy, taking a warm plate from the pile. I trail behind her, watching her pile prawn toast, samosas and sausage rolls on her plate, my cheeks burning. All this food. *Come on, Lauren,* she calls – *you've such a lovely figure – you can eat whatever you want!* I lift a steaming lid on a tray of egg fried rice. I spoon a bit on my plate, wondering if you're allowed to come back for seconds. I don't want to look like I'm taking too much. Pam's still going on. *It'll go straight to my hips – but what the heck – it's Christmas!* Her eyes are bright, her neck blotching pink. *You only live once!* I wonder if someone sneaked a vodka in her Britvic.

Back at the table I wish I'd picked foods that matched. Hot saliva rising under my tongue at the cottage pie, bolognese, pizza and dal bleeding on my plate. The science teacher is *which shop are you based at, love?* as he tucks into his plate of sushi, like he's never heard any gossip about me and my probation. Pam answers for us both. I'm struggling to swallow, about to head to the loo, when Pam thrusts a Christmas cracker at me. I put my fork down, take the cracker and in that moment everything might be normal – food with friends, boyfriend running late, nobody suspects I'll nick their handbag.

And then I catch Dee smirking at me from the other end of the table, spite all over her face. She'll never let me forget my probation. My breathing goes fast again. Pam plonks a paper hat on my head, laughing. I straighten it up, try a nibble of pizza. Thick and cold – yellow, congealed cheese. The crust stained from bolognese. The science teacher's already back up at the buffet. A waitress swoops in to take his plate, only half empty. Surely they won't throw all that away.

I'm still on my pizza when Pam gets up. *Are you coming, Lauren?* I shake my head. She laughs. *I'll grab you a sausage roll while I'm up – they're good ones!* I'm like a turtle without its shell with her gone. Nothing to stop Dee laughing at my bony arms and posh frock – this dress she knows I'd never afford. Everyone knows.

I can't wait to see you in it, Lauren. We'll show them. Half the people up at the buffet, spats and spills, ripped hats and crackers all over the table. Dee charming everyone, long hair loose and shining, centre of attention.

I down my white wine and gnaw the pizza to the crust. A man goes round to talk to Dee – cosy. I realise it's that other manager – Paul's squash buddy. I haven't seen him since I first started at the shop. They whisper to each other, then Dee suddenly springs up, manically tapping her glass with a fork. Ting ting ting. *Can I have everyone's attention please?* Everyone shushes each other. *I have a little announcement!* She beams down the table. *Of course it would usually be Paul's job to thank you all for coming, but we've just had a text to say how sorry he is that he can't be here.* Everyone waits for more. Dee flicks her hair with her acrylic nails.

As you know, Paul's never missed a do – in all his long years of dedication to our charity! But he's got a good excuse this year – his wife has just had a little boy! The table erupts, everyone clapping and cheering. *Mum and baby are staying in for a few checks but they're both doing well!* Dee raises her glass. *So it's just down to me to thank you for all your hard work this year and to raise a glass to the newest member of our team!*

Pam and the science teacher stand up, so I copy, like a machine. *Here's wishing you all a beautiful Christmas and happy new year!* My glass is empty but I shove it in the air anyway, tears coming on. The science teacher spots my glass and tops me up, chuckling – *we can't be having that!* I down the wine, pepper in my throat, then march off to the toilets, ears ringing.

In the cubicle I check my signal. Fire off a text – what's going on? No kisses. Delivery notification. I wait a few minutes, sitting on the closed lid, listening to people going in and out, plastic walls swimming around me. I go to the sinks when I hear some-one leave – wet a tissue and dab under my eyes, like I do with the boys' chins. I'm about to send another text when a reply comes in.

Baby arrived – it's been a nightmare. We need to talk but can't ring now. So sorry x That's it. Pam pats my leg when I get back. The science teacher slurring, sweat patches under his arms. *Our team's going for drinks after – you girls should join us!* Baggy eyes behind his turquoise glasses. I look at Pam's plate of miniature puddings. She shakes her head, spoon in hand. *I'm done after this, love – I've a taxi on order. I'm no spring chicken, you know!* I pick up two paper hats from the table and fold them carefully along their original lines.

I tell science teacher I'm leaving with Pam, knife and fork together on the table. My plate gone. I say no to pudding – polite to Pam, but mainly I just sit there in silence. When we get up to leave, science teacher suddenly appears on our side of the table waving a biro, eyes goggling through his blue frames, telling my non-existent tits how much he adored my company – *I'd absolutely love to see you again, Laura.*

I write the wrong number on the back of his hand, pressing down hard with the pen. He shoves a napkin with his number in my hand. Holds on too long. Pam's velvety face wobbly with worry. I pull away, sweep the paper hats and a couple of cracker toys from the table into my handbag, and follow Pam outside.

Pam pushes the carrier bag at me. *It's only a little something from me to you – it came in last week, tags still on, and I just knew it'd be perfect on you.* I peep in the bag, shaking my head, and it looks like one of those posh jumpers – like a soft black baby lamb and there's a box of Black Magic too. Pam doesn't let me say that it's lovely of her but I really can't take them – *oh go on – it's nothing – I don't get to treat anyone these days. I'll not take no for an answer.*

I close the bag and say thank you, nothing else for it. We're still ten minutes early for her cab. I say I'll wait til it shows, grinding science teacher's napkin into the wet pavement under my pointed shoe. Pam says I should share, but I tell her I'm walking.

But she insists – *I'm paying – it'll make me feel safer if you come –* and seems relieved when I finally agree – links her arm through mine. I try to stand tall for her, sky pressing us into the ground, weight on my arm.

Pam pays the full fare when she gets out – tells the driver – *make sure you take her right to her door mind* – then pushes a handful of cracker toys into my lap. She must have seen. *They'd have only gone in the bin, love! And here's a quart of midget gems as well – my favourites – for the little ones.* She pushes a rumpled soft paper bag at me but then sees my face and looks horrified. *Oh, Lauren, I'm sorry, I didn't mean any offence by it.* I hush her, clutching her hand – no, it's fine, honestly – it's not that. Go on in now – I'll text you when I'm back. I'm fine.

As the taxi pulls off, tears stream down my face for her kindness, for being such a fucking mess, for being a shit mother, for being so gullible. When I get to Mum's I'm a right state, mascara panda eyes, blotched face, swollen lips. Mum takes one look at me and sighs *oh, Lauren* and sends me upstairs where she's squeezed a mattress on the floor in the back room between the boys' narrow beds. She brings up a pint of water and a spare nightie and tells me *get that down you and I'll see you tomorrow.*

Nancy

Christmas morning. There were no presents on my bed, thank the lord. I cut into my bacon, relieved. Gladys told me they sneaked into her room with a stocking last year. We're grown adults for Pete's sake. I handed out postcards for the staff yesterday morning. No presents on my bed, thank you. Nancy. Bev popped up right in the middle of our Christmas Eve special with a tinsel boa and sparkly boppers. The girl with the giant stomach on screen, sobbing in the dark on her settee, empty Moses basket beside her.

Nancy – my door's always open, you don't have to write me a letter! Shrill giggle. *Anyway, it's no problemo – Santa can leave your presents down here by the tree instead.* She was blocking the view for Joyce as well. The glitter balls on her headband bobbing up and down. Everything so special. So magical. *It's just a bit of fun, Nancy.* Joyce craned her long neck this way and that, trying to see. Alright, thank you, Bev.

Back in my room, I took pills out of three thimbles. I wrapped the thimbles for my favourite staff, then wrapped a souvenir spoon each for three residents: Gladys, Patricia and Joyce. Then set to work on Bev's present.

I put everything out this morning by Santa's empty sherry glass and carrot top. Bev's present not wrapped, but with an anonymous note. *To make your life easier.* I popped poor Luna a treat through the bars – Merry Christmas, little bird – and went for breakfast.

Krystyna was surprised to see my Santa hat. *Happy Christmas, Nancy! Do you fancy a little tipple in your coffee?* Poor girl, working Christmas morning. I said no thank you, same as Gladys: they only want us drunk so we'll doze off. Norman's already halfway through his. Gladys holds a cracker over the table towards me, already in her paper hat. I take the end and nearly pull her off her seat: light as a feather, that one. I go back to my Full English.

My head itches so I take the hat off and start chopping up my sausages. When Krystyna walks in she screams so loudly, I nearly jump out of my skin. *Nancy! What have you done?* I look at her innocently. Gladys is staring at me, hand over smile. Norman doesn't look up from the newspaper nearly touching his nose, snouting his head from side to side like a typewriter. He must be able to smell the ink, he holds it that close. I put my hand to my scalp. Tufts of stubble, like a cropped field. A bit like how my mum used to cut it, before I got wed. But more bare patches now: bald earth, packed hard. No need for mithering about washing and trimming.

There's another scream from the lounge. Bev must have found my present. Krystyna runs out, to see if anyone needs help. I chew my sausages, looking around, grinning. When I look at Gladys, I'm sure she winks. But then Bev walks in, calm and cold like a machine. Chilling the room. She stands at the door, mechanically waving people in, *Merry Christmas, ladies*, my long white plait gripped in her fist, down by her side. No one talking. All I want for Christmas is you. She doesn't look at me. My sausages start to stick in my chest, but I keep chewing. A battle of wills. I just want you for my own, more than you could ever know. She stays at the door until I swallow my last mouthful. I wipe my chin, fold the napkin and stand to leave. *All I want for Christmas is you, baby.* On my way out of the room Bev murmurs, *a word please, Nancy. Now.* My head knows I'm free to walk away, but my legs follow her to the office, lumpy-stomached, voices singing loud in my head.

Bev closes the door. *Take a seat.* Voice trickling sweet. She sits at the desk and lays the plait out in front of her, horizontally. I stay standing, the barred window to the river on my left. *What's the meaning of this?* Honey voice silking. I look away, at the windowsill. *You think you're too good for this place, Nancy – that you're oh so clever.* There is a ball of spider in the gritty corner of the glass, coiled and still. I try to settle my hands together in the same knotted clump. *I know you.* I dig the nail of my thumb into my palm. *Know your type. Trying to upset the apple cart – thinking you'll get one up on us.* I press harder with my nail to draw blood. *You've actually done us a favour, Nancy!*

I start shivering violently. The office is freezing. I glance back at Bev, but her eyes are fixed on the clock above my head. *You're not going anywhere.* I look around for a panic button. She is not allowed to do this. *I've put my life into this place, Nancy.* Syrup dribbling from her mouth now, dripping on the floor. Pooling. My slippers sliding. *Listen carefully.* Leaning forwards, her hands pressed on the desk, syrup pouring out of her mouth, off the desk. *This is how it is going to be.* She suddenly stares into my face. *We will have a merry magical morning and you will behave. In two days' time you will sit in the salon while we make you look decent.* I grip my convulsing arms, trying to hold myself still.

You will not ruin this special day for anyone else. She stands up, looking down on me now. *You will not make this place a disgrace.* Coming closer. *Do I make myself clear?* I look at her, looming bigger and bigger, like I looked at my husband all those times, face hot, knickers soaked with pee, and she repeats *do you I make myself clear, Nancy?* and I nod, like I've always done, reek of sweet perfume suffocating my face, and she opens the door and sends me out into the corridor.

Alex

Paul flicks the light on: tells Alex get up. It is dark out. Izzy still asleep, the baby in the basket. Alex shuffles to the toilet, puffy, sad and sore. Big shirt, leaking milk, breasts hard. He watches in disgust. The bathroom door shuts. *It's our first Christmas with our new family, Alex.* He raises his voice, through the door. *Don't go ruining it.*

Two days home, and all Alex can do is sag. Or squeeze Izzy when she is close enough. She hasn't spoken to anyone, except her parents who called from her auntie's computer in Brisbane to see their new grandson. Off on the retirement adventure they have worked all their lives for.

Alex oozes herself back into bed, tender. Grateful for feathers. For carpet, wood, cloth. The shine of hospital had been brutal; the lino too hard and infected for Izzy to play, the single time Paul brought her to visit. Too many spats of blood. The doctors kept Alex in three nights: everyone obsessing about home in time for Christmas.

Paul comes up with tea in a Christmas mug for her bedside table. Takes a photo and uploads it to the NCT group. The other mums will reply, *lucky you!* Paul sits on the duvet next to her; kisses her cheek. Strokes the hair from her forehead. *We missed you, darling, when you were away.* Alex is crying again. *Isabella called for you in the night. If you'd have managed at home like we said, she wouldn't have had to, would she?* Alex squeezes her eyes.

What's wrong, Alex? Tang of turkey seeping up through the carpet. *They'll cart you off if you carry on.* A laugh. He looks at her. *Come on, I'm kidding – it's bound to be tricky at first.* Alex opens her eyes. Please, Paul. I'm so tired. You're not being fair.

Wrong. He pulls his hand away; stands up. *Oh. But who got up at 5 a.m. to sort the dinner? Who drove for an hour yesterday to get a decent turkey?* Alex stares up at him with wet eyes. *Who's been up and down like a yo-yo all night with our children? Don't talk to me about fair.*

He marches off, downstairs, to double-check everything. She's blown it. Knows by now how he likes it. She'd wrapped all the presents back in November: Izzy will love them. Scooter. Play kitchen. Doll's house. Big cedar sandpit outside with eco buckets and spades. Alex creeps to Izzy's room and into her little bread-scented bed. Weeps into the sleeping girl's hair. Kisses her cheek, soft as sea. Happy here.

The baby starts making noises in the other room. Alex puts her hands over her ears, but it gets louder. She hauls herself away from Izzy's warm body, milky breath of morning, and stands next to the Moses basket, staring down. The baby's face is angry raw, mouth cavernous. You could get lost in there; blood-black abyss.

And suddenly Paul is next to her, scooping the baby, *why the hell are you just standing there watching him cry?!* She sees it then: brittle ribs. Careful! She didn't mean to shout. Paul's face makes a confused shape. Then angry. But she can see he is holding the baby too hard: an arm or leg could splinter in a blink. Alex backs away, towards the bed, and Paul brings him over for milk. Yellow blots of light in her eyes. She shakes her head: I don't want to hurt him. He murmurs. *Come on, darling, get yourself ready – he needs milk.* Chuckles, smiling into the bawling face. *I'm afraid I can't help you with that, little man.*

Alex sits on the bed, nursing pillow on her lap. Unclips her bra, pops out a breast. Paul puts the baby onto the pillow, tiny head next to the massive breast. Props her arms with cushions. *I'll leave you to it – I'll get you a fresh tea.* Alex sits and stares. *What's wrong, darling? Come on, you're a pro! Just relax – I'll take care of Isabella, and we'll be back in five to check how you're doing.*

The baby tries to gape its mouth wide enough for the ugly nipple. Swollen and cracked. It shakes its head frantically, side to side, can't get at the milk. Screams at her: this is your fault. Thin grey milk starts spraying its face: it responds manically, like a mole, snouting its head for the source. Surge pain in both breasts, and finally the baby clamps on with a sting. She holds the head still, electric flashing even when she closes her eyes. Yellow blotching. The skull still softly solid in her hand: not calcified brittle yet, like the other bones.

Izzy and Paul burst in with a fancy bag of presents – *for the best Mummy! Oh, sweetheart, you're doing brilliantly now! Just look at him. Come on, Isabella, up on the bed – you can help Mummy open hers.* There's an expedition compass and a superbright torch. They would be perfect. He's always bought her the best presents; still knows her better than anyone. Izzy snuggles in; chubby fingers on the baby's hair. *I love my mummy.* Oh, Isabella. I love you. Gripping the girl too tight. *Very much.* Blinking up at Paul. *I'm scared, Paul. I'm really scared.* Paul leans in to kiss her hair. *I know, darling. It's okay though, we're going to be okay.*

Lauren

Oli's been on at me since 4 a.m. *Has he been yet?* Santa this, Santa that, cuddled up in my bed. When he finally settles down I can't get back to sleep. Texts from after the work meal going round in my head. *Lauren, I'm worried about you. Please call me.* I didn't reply, hungover at Mum's, but they kept coming. *Nightmare here, I need you. Please, darling – can't get through this without you.* Kisses. I had Mum's jeans and a baggy T-shirt on – I couldn't exactly walk home in that long dress. When I finally replied – why didn't you text me about the baby? Why would you tell Dee? – he called me straight away. *Lauren – sweetheart – thank God you picked up. I've been worried sick about you.*

I told him hang on and went upstairs to the toilet so Mum couldn't earwig. What's going on, Paul? Are you with Dee? There was a silence. *What? What's Dee got to do with it, Lauren – why on earth would I be with her?* I looked at myself in the mirror, eyes still caked with last night's make-up.

A jumble of words in my ear. *Look, we need to talk, it all happened so fast – we got blue-lighted to the hospital.* A pause. *I texted the duty manager – you know Chris, who I play squash with – but there wasn't time for anything else.* But why didn't you tell *me*, Paul? I licked my finger and rubbed at the black flakes under my eyes.

Lauren – come on. It was an emergency. I couldn't exactly tell them to hang on while I call my girlfriend, could I? Girlfriend. Duty manager. Squash buddy. Talking to Dee at the meal.

I need you, Lauren. He was sniffing a bit. *I can't even leave her alone with the baby – she's scary – she won't even look at him.* I said hang on, slow down. It sounds like you actually need some proper help. He said *you're the one I want, Lauren – whatever it takes.*

Oli wakes up and starts kissing my cheek again. *Mummy, can we get up?* It's still dark out but I know how much the boys will love the sandpit. Paul brought it round last week, with buckets and spades and everything – before the baby – before all this mess. We filled stockings together – with cars and plastic animals and crazy slime I bought from the pound shop and I actually believed in it all. I got a new loan to cover the lot – presents, chocolates, the other loan and interest – best to start over before it all goes up again. I ended up owing more than I thought, but now I've got the job I'm just trying not to think about it. I just want to have a nice Christmas. Hopefully the new year can be a fresh start.

Last year, all we had was a couple of cheap games from Mum, a selection box from Auntie Eileen and my pathetic books from Kid Action. Tania told me she was sorting her kids on credit as usual, but I had to insist on doing everything the hard way. Mum gave me tuppences and satsumas in a stocking like she always does, and the sad thing was, the boys leapt about like it was all treasure. But it's different now – I'm doing right by them for a change.

Oli gets out of bed and runs in to wake Daniel. Dan's too little to properly understand, but I say let's get your shoes on, not bothering with socks – coats over pyjamas – then we go out the kitchen into the pitch-black yard. I lead the way with the torch on my phone, steadying little Dan. I set it all up last night. Oli suddenly pulls back towards the kitchen. *Mummy, I'm cold! I want go in.* I tell him come on – let's see what Santa's left outside!

I pull Dan towards the big blue plastic clam under the wall, at the end of the yard. It's freezing rain and he twists back – then Oli trips on a brick just behind me and that sets him off screaming loud enough to wake the dead. I haul him off the floor and shine the torch on him – his pyjama bottoms bleeding at the knee. I flash the light down at smashed glass – someone must have chucked a bottle over in the night again. The fuckers – they're always doing it. Then Dan's wailing – I'll have the social round if he doesn't pipe down. Fuck's sake, always a drama. I pull them back in and shut the back door, trying not to go off on one.

Okay, sit down – we'll go back out once it's light. I help Oli get his pyjamas down, and try and rinse his knee with a sopping tea towel as he sobs, wetting the pyjama legs on the floor. I glance at the flowers on the table: they came yesterday with chocolates and a note – *Merry Christmas, darling. Next year we'll be together. I love you. P.*

Loves me. Hadn't said that before. I root around under the sink for plasters but can't find any big enough, so sprint upstairs, two at a time, for a towel and some spare pyjamas. I run back, sort out Oli best I can, then tell them, come on, let's see what Santa's put in the front room!

Both of them go mad when they see – hopping around, not knowing what to do first. I grab their hands and jump up and down too, look at all this! Come on then.

I grab a wrapped selection box each and throw them at the boys. Oli rips his open. *Can I eat it now?!* I nod – course you can – it's special, innit! He rips open a Milky Way and stuffs it in, then looks at me worried, cheeks bulging. I nod at him. All for you. Then he gives me a massive bear hug that proper sets me off – tears leaking down my cheeks.

I got Oli a remote-control Ferrari on the loan, and a pack of batteries. He's beside himself when he gets it open – just standing there staring, box at arm's length. Then he starts hugging it. I laugh at him. Come on, monkey – get it out the box then! He shrieks when we get the batteries in. I love it. This is what it's like to be proper. I hug them both close and we laughscream. I'll be on the payments as soon as I get my first wage. We take it in turns with the car, crashing into the skirting boards. *Mummy, can I show, Paul?!* I laugh, he's coming over tomorrow, love – he's got a busy day – but we can take it to show Nana in a bit. And you can give her the nice perfume we got her.

The cards from their dad are on the sofa. They open them last – a tenner each. Typical. That's that for the year then. The boys wave the notes like flags, then Dan starts screaming *money my money my money* when I whip it off him to put it safe.

Mum's got a big turkey crown in – it's just her and Margery from next door again, so she won't bother with a whole bird. Neal's over at his sister's, like always. When we get there, I give Dan the posh cardboard bag to carry in. Shoes off, Oli, come on now, Nana doesn't want you treading muck in her carpets. The meat smells so good. I check my phone – missed call. And a text – heart and snowflake emojis. *Happy Christmas, sweetheart. Wish I was there.*

His wife's completely lost it by the sound of things. He says we need to wait a bit before we make any moves. It's awful with a new baby – I feel for her really. But she's treating him like shit. Dan totters up to Mum with the bag. She looks in, then closes it up, tight-lipped, and puts it down by my trainers. What's up, Mum? It's that perfume they always advertise. *You know I don't need fancy things, Lauren.* She's never been one for a great show but I thought she'd at least manage a thank you.

Mum! What are you on about? You never treat yourself. I look at her. It's not a rip-off, back-of-a-lorry job – if that's what you're thinking. Look, it's in the proper bag and everything – the real deal!

Lauren – I've told you before – having you and the boys here is enough. Oli watches us quietly. *I'm alright for perfume anyway – you have it.*

I take it back. I know she's proud but it'd be nice if she could show a bit of gratitude. Then I get it. She thinks I've nicked it. I march off into the lounge – don't say that I wanted her to have something proper for once – that I never get to treat anyone – that I don't want to be the only one gallivanting round in designer stuff bought by someone else.

The doorbell goes and it's Margery, looking down her nose as usual. Pale green blouse and trouser suit, like she's still skivvying at the hospital, hairy mole still sprouting on her neck. She's got me and Mum a bottle of cheap wine each. The boys scramble for the jigsaws she's wrapped and I push them forward after to say thank you properly. Go on, give your auntie Marge a kiss.

We eat our prawn cocktails, then I help Mum serve up the roast. I drown mine in gravy. The paper hats from the cheap crackers rip when the grown-ups put them on, but the kids love them. I chop Oli's meat up into tiny pieces. He's always so slow. The rest of us finish and Mum takes me in the kitchen once we've finished the wine. She pours two big vodkas, and tops them up with cheap lemonade. She holds one of the tumblers out to me – no fizz. Flat plastic lemon air between us. *Lauren, listen, please don't bite my head off. I need to talk to you.* I take the glass and sniff it. What's up now?

She takes a swig. *Where's all this money's coming from, Lauren?* I bang my drink down on the side, untouched. You just can't leave it, Mum, can you? What's wrong with saving up and buying a few nice things? She necks half her vodka. *Well, it's not exactly like you've been rolling in it, is it?* I look at her. *I'm only worried about you, love.* I pick my glass back up. Maybe she means well. I tell her I'm getting paid soon and I just borrowed a few quid to tide me over, nothing much, not prepared for her going totally fucking berserk, talk about overreaction, screaming at me, *how many times, Lauren, how many times have I told you not to get yourself in debt?* She downs her drink, shoves it on the side, and grabs the bottle.

I knew it. I told Neal it wasn't your own money! And don't give me that about a few quid – I know it's more than that. How many times have I told you – you know I lost my dad to it – the debt – it was the end of him. She unscrews the lid. *I never wanted you to go through what I went through.* I try and interrupt. I know she gets upset about her dad.

This is different, Mum – this is only a few quid. *Lauren – you should hear yourself – you sound exactly like him. You never*

152

come to me, thinking you're so above us all, but look at you now – thieving and going round with married men and lending, you're a disgrace.

Silver flecks swarm in the air between us. She's breathless red. She pulls the ice-cube tray out of the freezer, slams the freezer door, and whacks it on the side, shattering a bit of plastic off. My face is burning. You can't fucking help yourself, Mum, can you? This is the happiest I've ever been, and all you can do is slag me off. The room tips: too much wine. You just can't accept that someone loves me – that I've got what you always wanted. She pours neat vodka on the ice and knocks it straight back, ice cubes hitting her teeth. I put my half-finished drink down – she disgusts me. I tell her. You're pathetic. She looks like I've thumped her in the stomach. Just cause I want something better – you can't handle the fact I don't want to end up a miserable old slag like you.

She freezes, empty vodka glass in hand, staring at me, her voice cold and clear when she finally speaks. *Right. If that's how it is.* The ice clinks as she moves towards me, yelling in my face. *But don't come crying to me when it all goes tits up.* Margery bursts in and slings a flabby arm round our necks. She's pissed as well. *Now, now – what's going on in here, girls?* I throw the arm off and storm up to the toilet with my phone. They're welcome to each other.

There's another text with hearts. *You're going to love the baby. He's gorgeous – needs a mummy like you.* No photo. I flush my paper hat. She's trying to poison me against him, but I'm better than that. I sit on the toilet lid and refresh my search on Rightmove.

Oli bangs on the bathroom door as I'm scrolling. *Mummy! I want my car! Nana took it.* I blow my nose and wipe my eyes, then march down with him on my hip and sit him at the table in front of his Christmas pudding. It's soaked in brandy so he spits it all out. Mum comes in and pours him more pop, then puts the telly on and plonks herself on the sofa, ignoring me, pinched mouth, fresh glass of vodka and ice.

I grab Oli's Ferrari from the kitchen worktop and shove it in a carrier bag. Texts flooding in. *All I want for xmas is you. I'll pop round tonight – I'll tell her we need bread. Nightmare here.*

Come on, we're off, I tell the kids. I stuff the jigsaws in with the Ferrari, drag the kids' shoes and coats on, then storm out, leaving Mum on the sofa and Margery alone at the table with the whole sweaty pudding.

Nancy

Bev raps on my door to escort my stubbly head down to the salon. The nails girl is there in her spa tunic, bored again. She looks like Sindy. The girl you love to dress. *Morning, Carla!* Bev sings. *I think you've met Nancy before?*

Sindy girl shows me to the chair, not looking at my scalp. *What do you fancy, Nancy?* Fairy lights and gloss. Bev leaps in before I can open my mouth. *She deserves a full pamper does our Nancy, the works! No rush.* The chair spins as I try to get onto it. *We want you seeing in the new year as a new person, don't we Nancy?*

I don't answer. Knees pressed, hands clasped between them, staring straight ahead at my reflection. A lardy vulture. Sindy laughs politely, *perfect!* swirling and tucking the cloak around me. Bev heads off, while the girl dabs blue liquid onto cotton pads. *We'll just give your face a quick cleanse, and then get you washed up,* she says, swishing the pads across my cheeks in a butterfly. Stinging. I grip onto my legs under the cloak.

Right, let's get you into the sink. Sindy girl twirls the seat, and tips my head back onto a rigid rubber rest. *Are you comfy?* I flinch when the shower runs ice. She laughs, *God, I'm so sorry – it'll come warm in a sec.* I squeeze my eyes as she rubs pear shampoo hard into my head. It smells like the sweet shop. My neck is locked in, hairline itching wet.

When she spins me back, pink towel round my head, I think I might run for it – my last chance – but her hand is already firm on my shoulder, holding me down. I look up and her face is set: for all the Sindy look, she's Bev's machine – skin over high metal cheekbones, the lips glued on. I shrink down into the chair, deflating balloon, the barest puff. Only scraps of dead rubber, wrinkled grey pink.

My body won't move after that: I watch in the mirror, wilted, numb, the head moved from side to side, tufty white hair frothed and primped. The smell of pear drops on Sindy's hands. I watch her snip and snap, bolt bits of hair into rollers. Then she wheels over a giant space heater, burning red.

I watch my hands pulled out, claws clipped and lacquered fuchsia. The body gaping, surrendered. I can hear Sindy but still can't move. She tips the chin up and draws on eyebrows, then stands behind the chair to pluck the rollers out, one by one. The slightest jerk of the body, then the final submission as Sindy spins the chair to reach the pathetic face: violet powder eyelids, strawberry cheeks, and last of all the mouth. That dreadful mouth: a yawn of blood-red O.

Alex

Eat some turkey broth. Saffron salty with soft round carrots, oil floating on the surface. Alex sits up in bed. She stares into the bowl and sees tiny bones moving in the depths: she cannot eat. Spongy cartilage, tiny white eggs from the body. Unborn, soft-shelled. She slumps back to the pillow, staring. Paul stands above her. Baby in the basket again.

The midwife rings the doorbell, as expected, to do the newborn blood-spot test. Paul brings her up, sucking Alex's air. The midwife explains she will prick the heel, squeeze four drops of blood onto a special card. The baby jerks awake when she punctures his skin, shocked. A split second then screaming from his belly. Alex doesn't flinch.

It was different with Izzy: Alex felt it in her own body. This baby tries to yank his foot up, instinctive, bawling, as the midwife squeezes his pink heel harder in her squeaky blue gloves: two drops, three. *You're an awkward little man, aren't you?! Nearly there – we need four big blots on the card, otherwise they'll send it back to do again.* Fourth drop, fresh red. Alex stares at the card, saturated with blood, red soaking white, dripping onto the carpet now, seeping puddle. She squeezes her eyes, feeling sick.

The midwife brings the screaming baby over. *The boob will help him out.* Alex opens her eyes but shakes her head, hands by her sides under the duvet, no. The midwife turns to Paul instead. *Let's let Daddy have a go at soothing him then, and get these curtains shut so we've got a bit of privacy.* Paul stands, screaming baby in his hands, face twisted, blackened wick, angry.

She whips the curtains shut, and turns to Paul, hands out for the baby. *That's it – give him here, love – then you go down and see to the little girl, while we sort ourselves up here.* But Paul wants to stay. To help. *Isabella's fine – she won't want me interrupting* Postman Pat. *I'll see her when we're done.* The midwife turns her back on him: props Alex up with pillows and tries to latch the baby onto her right nipple. He's frantic. Paul folds muslins on the other side of the room, discreet. No latch.

Hyperventilating baby. The midwife takes him back. *Okay, let's have a little breather – we'll try again when we're a bit calmer – can you fetch us a nappy, Dad? That sometimes settles them a bit.* The midwife puts the baby on her shoulder; rubs his back firmly, bobbing up and down. Paul goes for the changing bag at the bottom of the steps. In earshot.

The midwife speaks gently to Alex. *These early days can be really tough, love. Can you tell me how you're doing?* Alex doesn't answer. Baby cry filling the room, splashing the walls, spraying her face, flooding up towards the ceiling. Threads of blood dissolving in the murk, spreading closer.

Midwife speeding up, slowing down, losing power, a terrible dread. Alex flushes hot, trapped, heartbeat thumping, something terrible, a drowning, bones like coral, big dog, women calling her down. She squeezes her eyes, terrified. It is hard to say anything underwater.

Lauren

Paul's in his car next to the For Sale sign when we get there, engine running. It's a semi in a quiet cul-de-sac, near good bus routes. Nice schools and all. Surely he must be serious to look at a house like this with us. I hardly slept last night, thinking it's all too much of a mess, for me, for him, the boys, but maybe this is just what real life is like – we just need to get through the next few weeks and things will get more sorted. Paul said the house has only just gone on the market – the estate agents said we can look outside for now, then get a proper viewing when they reopen after Christmas if we're still interested. The boys drag their feet, cold.

No one in my family's ever owned a house. When Paul started talking about it a few weeks ago, I said renting might be quicker but he told me *renting's a mug's game, Lauren.* Sometimes, I swear it's like we're from different planets. It's not that he ever looks down on me, but I'm shit-scared that one of these days he's going to wake up and realise that me and my family – we're just not his kind of people.

He gets out of the car, shadows bruising under his eyes, stubble. It's nearly dark, and it's only teatime. I shiver – should have worn that jumper from Pam. I nearly put it on this morning – thought it would feel nice under Paul's hands – soft and rich and luxury, not my usual cheap – but at the last minute I put it back in the wardrobe. I've moved my stuff around to find it a nice hanger – one that won't stretch the shoulders, but I've a funny feeling about it.

My phone pings – Mum's added me to the WhatsApp for her New Year's do. 7 p.m. til late, fancy dress, BYOB like always. She texted last night saying *you're still welcome, Lauren, let's put it behind us,* but I never replied. Too much has been said to go back: I'm on my own now.

Hello, boys! Paul crouches down to give them a cuddle, then straightens up for a kiss. *Hi, darling. I can't stay long. What a day.* We have a hard hug. I understand. His voice is hoarse. *This is all I want, Lauren.* I know, I tell him, I know. It'll be alright. He nods, stands back and looks at me, eyes glittering. *Lauren, it's hell. She totally freaked this morning. I shouldn't let her out of my sight – even this long.*

Oli looks up at me, quiet. Paul sees him and suddenly his voice is cheerful, total change of tune. *Come on.* He locks the car and bounces towards the house. *Let's have a squiz at this then. They're away seeing family – but we can have a nosy outside.* Paul stands back, checking out the roof and gutters, while Oli and Dan go to play on the weedy gravel strip on the drive. I walk up to the front window and peer in. The room looks cold and dark – there's a Christmas tree with lights off, and a three-piece suite with matching cushions. Ornaments and fake flowers lurking in the gloom.

The high wooden gate to the back garden is locked, so we head to the car. I hold both boys tightly by the hand. He turns to me. *You don't like it, do you?* I can't explain. It kind of feels a bit sad – the wallpaper and tiebacks and all that. I'm surprised when he nods. *I get what you mean. Listen, we won't jump at the first house we see – this is just the start.* He comes close, hands out for mine. *I need to get back.*

I know, I tell him, letting go of the boys and putting my hands in his. Good luck. I squeeze his hands. You can do this. He smiles, mouths *thank you*, then leaves me and the boys on the pavement, while he gets in his car. He chucks two packets of Monster Munch through the passenger window for Oli and Dan, then starts the engine. The boys blow kisses at the back of the car as he drives off, then I trail them both back to the bus stop.

Alex

Paul answers the door with the hungry baby, cough-crying for milk. It is the midwife again. *Can I come in?* Paul picks up the post from the doormat. *Sorry, Alex is still in bed.* He stands, awkward, hands full. *Can you call back later?* But the midwife is already coming in. *I just want to see how you're all getting on?* Cartoons blaring from the living room.

Paul yawns, pink-eyed. Stubble. *Excuse the mess.* Shuts the living-room door, leads her to the kitchen. *We're exhausted, to be honest.* Baby klaxon rising. *We just need some sleep.* He looks down at the baby. *He's not feeding.* Stacks of dirty cups and plates.

An open jar of marmalade on the side. *I need to see Mum,* she says, looking him in the face.

He puts the baby on his shoulder, rubs his back. *I'm sorry – you'll have to talk to me instead. She can't even get up.* His voice crackling. *You won't get any sense out of her anyway.* Pacing the room, angry tears in his eyes. *She's not washing or eating or anything. Won't even hold him.* He shifts the baby back into cradle position, bouncing, swaying. The baby's face deep red, higher pitched than ever. Paul is sweating, having to raise his voice. The midwife watches him. *Go on.*

It's like she's delirious – saying she's drowning, and his bones are fragile like coral – I'll damage him. Paul stops and swallows. *I don't want to make a fuss. I'm sure you're very busy.* He looks at the wall clock, then down at the baby. *I think he's hungry.* Paul slumps into a kitchen chair. *None of it makes sense. She keeps saying he's not hers.*

The midwife pulls a carton of formula from her bag. *I need to see her. Get a pan boiling while I'm up there. This needs to be sterilised for ten minutes, everything under the water, okay?* She hands Paul a new bottle and teat, still in plastic, leaves him with the baby. Upstairs, Alex is in bed in the dark, facing the wall, impassive. The midwife sweeps the curtains open, filling the room with grey river light. *Alex? Are you awake, pet?* Jolts the room into electric yellow. *Can you hear me?* Ten minutes later, she's back downstairs, helping Paul with the bottle.

He can't stop talking now, a torrent of words. *She burnt her hand on purpose not long ago – I just don't know what she'll do any more. I've had to hide everything – have even turned the boiler down so she can't scald herself – or the children.* The midwife snaps things in and out of her bag, clean and efficient, murmuring acknowledgement. *It's good you've told me – we can get you some help now.* He doesn't stop. *She's been raving about this dog, stalking her, everyone against her, even me.* He sinks to his knees on the kitchen tiles, sobbing now. The midwife dives down to scoop up the baby. *It's okay, Mr Sutherland, it's okay. Come and sit on this chair, your baby needs his bottle.*

She gets him sitting down; shows him how to touch the baby's lips with the teat; how to tip the bottle, then goes into the hall with her phone. *I just need to make a couple of calls.* They are lucky. There is a bed: only an hour away. Another midwife on the way already. And an ambulance.

She goes back upstairs. Speaks slowly. *Alex. It's only me again. Can you hear me?* No response. *Alex love. You're not well – we're going to take you to a special hospital where you can get better.*

No. Alex tries to swim up. What is this woman saying. Where's Izzy? She is light-headed, breathing too fast.

It's a fantastic place, Alex – the best. Your baby can stay with you, and your husband can visit. Alex is staring at the midwife, cloudy-eyed. It is like this woman is somewhere else.

No. Shaking her head. What about Izzy?

Your daughter's just fine – she'll be able to visit too. It's only until you feel better. My colleague Lynn – a nurse – is on the way – you'll like her. We'll help you get ready – and then you can go in an ambu-lance – nice and easy. The midwife's voice is soft. Kind. But it is wrong. The doorbell goes downstairs. *We'll follow in the car – and your husband too – we won't leave you til you're all settled in.*

Alex drags herself up onto the pillows, head spinning. Where's Izzy? What have you done with her? *Nothing, love, she's just grand. She's downstairs watching cartoons with her daddy. She needs you to get better for her and her bonny little brother.* Alex grips the duvet.

I know it's a lot to take in – we'll take it nice and slowly, there's no rush. There is a gentle knock on the door – the other nurse. She beckons the midwife. Whispers. *Dad's not happy. He doesn't want the baby going.* They agree to swap: the nurse will help Alex with the bathroom.

Paul is pacing the kitchen, baby asleep in his arms, in a milk stupor. Needs burping. Paul stops when the midwife walks in. *You didn't say anything about the baby! He's staying with me, where he belongs.*

She hovers in the doorway. *I know it's difficult, Mr Sutherland. But your wife needs to go to hospital for a proper assessment. This place is specially designed for mums and babies – it's best for them to be together and they'll be in the safest possible hands.* He walks towards her, moving the baby to his shoulder. Shouting. *You're not taking my baby to a nuthouse!* The baby belches milk down his back and starts crying. The doorbell goes again: the paramedics. The midwife lets them in and has a quiet word at the door. Paul is back on the wooden chair by the time they all come in the kitchen, paramedics with their jolly greetings, baby glugging more milk.

The male paramedic pulls up a chair at the table next to Paul as if they're in the pub. Sits down, legs wide. *I know this is rough, mate, but we're going to need your help here. Trust me – it's better to do it this way if we can. Otherwise we'll need a whole team of doctors and that'll be more stressful all round. Let's just get your wife to hospital smoothly so she can get the treatment she needs, eh?*

The female paramedic nods her agreement – *they're all experts there, Mr Sutherland – it's the best place for them both.* He seems calmer now so the midwife goes back upstairs. The nurse has got Alex to the bathroom. The midwife goes in too and locks the door. They help Alex pull on new pants and pad; joggers and a clean T-shirt. Alex slumps down in the clean clothes by the toilet, will do anything for peace. Vomits water in the bowl.

Izzy's voice comes from the other side of the door. *Mummy?* The handle moving up and down. *Mummy, where are you?* Paul's voice, *come back down, darling, Mummy's poorly. Let's get your shoes on – we're going to the park.* Two women under Alex's armpits, helping her to the sink, to wash her hands. Her body won't even struggle, her fingers swollen like tyres, her legs so heavy. *Mummy!*

Paul comes up to talk to Izzy on the landing. *Mummy needs to go to hospital to get better.* Alex looks in the mirror, water rushing her fingers cold: face wavy at the edges, like a blue jellyfish. Flaky lips, Izzy's eyes, but eclipsed. Like dread. Afterwards, she'll hate herself for this: surrendering, staring, weak, while Paul slips shoes and coat on her daughter, ready for the park. Ready for the new year without her.

They help Alex downstairs to say goodbye. *Mummy'll be better and back in no time.* She manages to crouch and squeeze the girl tight: longs to take her inside, eat her up, carry her safe like a cherry bun. I love you, baby, do you hear? She grips Izzy's arms and looks into her eyes. You're hot. Paul – she's hot – we need to find the thermometer. Alex looks into her daughter's eyes. Whatever anyone says, I love you – don't forget that, okay? And then she's wheeled away in a chair to the ambulance, like an oversized rag doll, weeping; the paramedic swinging the baby in a car-seat carrier; the neighbours watching the drama unfold from the safety of their nets.

Lauren

I spent all morning getting the house ready for Paul and Isabella to stop the night for the new year. I even went round on a chair with white vinegar to get at the black mould above the windows – changed all the bedding and vacced the stairs. I gave the boys a damp rag each, so they could help me wipe down the skirtings and windowsills. They love doing grown-up jobs.

Just as I was plating up their beans on toast, my phone rang. The whole place stank like a fish shop from the vinegar. *I'm really sorry, Lauren, but we can't stay tonight – it's too much for Isabella. She's so confused with everything going on. Can we just pop round for a new year's drink before bed instead?*

I went up to my bedroom and pulled the new lacy bra and pants out of the bag and chucked them in a drawer, labels still on. The boys needed fresh air, but I thought a cup of tea might help me pull myself together, so I stuck them in front of the telly after their beans.

I'm on the bed with my tea when I hear the rap on the door. I'm not expecting anyone so I peer down out the window. Fuck. He looks official. But surely no one would come round on New Year's Eve. He knocks again, louder. I run down, grab the remote and turn off CBeebies. Go on, upstairs, Oli, take Dan with you. We'll build a den after this boring man's gone and then go down the swings – go on! Oli wails – *it's not finished!* refusing to budge – but then sees my face and takes Dan's hand, *come on, Danny,* and leads him out of the room.

There's more rapping on the door and I shout coming! then wait til the boys are at the top before opening up. Go on, boys, quick now! When I open the door my heart flips. *Good afternoon, madam, I'm from TV Licensing.* Flashing his ID. He's only young, not much older than me. *Are you Lauren Turner?* I tell him yeah – what's up?

Miss Turner, it's on our records that you don't have a TV licence, and that you haven't responded to our letters. He holds out a piece of paper towards me. *Can I please ask whether you have a TV?*

I glance down at the paper – OUR RECORDS SHOW YOUR PROPERTY HAS NO TV LICENCE – then look him straight in his boyish face. He actually doesn't look like a dick. I'm probably older than him. I can sort this. I tell him yeah, we do, but don't watch it, sucking my tummy in and giving him my best smile, head tilted, one hip jutting.

He blushes a bit, but carries on anyway. *Madam, I have to remind you that if you have any recording equipment that can receive TV, even if it's not used, you need a licence.* Chatting his official spiel, like he's actually a man. *If I can just take a quick look inside to confirm, I'll be off.* I tell him no – we don't have anything like that – anyway you can't come in without a warrant. I turn round and Oli's at the top of the steps. Go in your room, Oliver – go and play with your brother. The boys vanish again.

The lad lowers his voice. *With respect, Miss Turner, I saw the light of a TV as I came up the path.* I fold my arms, shivering. He's letting all the cold air in. *Between us, it's best you just let me in for a quick look – to save the drama of coming back with a search warrant and all that.* He leans in, nearly whispering. *Prosecution's a lot less likely this way too. I'll be right quick – then you can get on.*

He's got me. Fine, I tell him, fucking fine. You don't need to come in – I have got a TV. Now what? He goes bright red and starts jabbering about a payment plan, and not risking prosecution and a fine of up to a grand. Prosecution. Mum once told me about a lass from school who ended up inside cause her boyfriend never paid the fine. I feel sick. My record. The boys.

I tell him yeah it's fine, I can pay it – I don't know how I missed – it's been mad busy yeah – just tell me how I pay. He looks surprised – says I can pay in instalments, a bit each month, fumbling in his bag for a letter with the details. I tell him no, I want to pay it all now, it's all good yeah, speaking so loud he steps back a bit.

He gives me a number where I can pay over the phone. I ask if they'll take me to court. Someone's letting bangers off a couple of streets away. He flinches with every bang – looks behind him, nervous like – then back to me. *Look – you've cooperated fully and you don't have any previous licensing convictions. You need to write a statement to say you overlooked it – just say you're very sorry.* He's whispering again. *Lay it on thick, say how much you've had on and all that.* He nods at the boys at the top of the steps. *To be fair, you do look like you've got your hands full. If you pay and set up a plan, it's not likely to go any further. They only do that as a last resort.*

Fine. I tell him again in my too loud voice. Fine. I'll do that. Thanks very much then. The boys come down as I'm closing the door. Oli saying *who was it, Mummy?* no one I tell him, it was no one – just a boring man selling stuff no one wants.

Nancy

Old Year's Night. I scratch at the nail polish, scattering fuchsia confetti on my bedroom carpet, then set to work on my hair, brushing the patchy curls madly to a fluff. Nearly time. I grind one of the pills from the wardrobe into powder with the back of Pip's special spoon. Three droplets of tea, mixed well on the saucer.

Once it's dissolved, I tip the solution into a teacup and drop the spoon in my bag. I scroll the combination on the safe until it clicks, then collect everything I need. Brooch, last will and testament, George's watch. Ready to cover everything with a scarf if anyone barges in.

I take off my tights, then pull two pairs of peachy knickers out of my top drawer. I write *Patricia* on the labels. This will confirm neglect once I get to hospital: mixing up residents' clothes. They won't be able to send me back this time. I put a pair in my bag and swap the knickers I'm wearing for the other pair. They fit perfectly. A gift all along. I drop the pack of green biros and my notebook in my bag, so thirsty, and put on the string of pearls that Patricia threw on the floor of the lounge last night.

After Sindy and the salon, my body gave me up for three days: I sat in the living room, like a disgrace, trussed up like a turkey. Not eating or drinking, even with all the mithering. Bev smiling down with satisfaction. Her victory. The green writing in the diary meant nothing, my wardrobe full of crazy rubbish, mystery knickers, all alone here with a bunch of senseless old people, a batty old woman myself: I would die here. The bird on her last legs in the cage.

It was mad Patricia who snapped me out of it: last night, in the lounge. Who'd have thought. I was staring at my slippers, cardigan wrapped tight, sherry untouched, thin brownish blood to the brim. The girl on telly blabbing about her dad and the bridge. Joyce's head tremoring side to side, pandemonium on screen as the girl's waters broke.

Patricia never remembers her seat: she just plonks herself wherever. I kept my eyes down as she took the chair next to me, madly ogling the side of my face. *You've even the face of a traitor,* she cackled. I ignored her. The noise on screen: sobbing girl, someone shouting down a phone, sirens. *Oi!* Patricia leaned in towards me, getting louder. *I'm talking to you.* I sighed and turned to look at her. Watery eyes and spittle lips. *Want a crisp?* she said, holding one out. I took it, even though I hadn't eaten for two days. Said thank you quietly.

She watched me crunch the crisp, then handed me another. *You have to keep your strength up,* she hissed. I sucked at the salt, eyes back on my slippers. Wondered what she was playing at.

That bird, Patricia suddenly screeched, pointing at the cage, *wants to be a traitor as well!* Everyone ignored her, but Krystyna popped her head round to check. Turned up the volume then left again. My crisp going soggy. Patricia still cackling. Then, a choking whisper – *but it never had the guts.* I whipped my head towards her. She was looking at me, sitting tall now, like a secretary; Gladys's neat pearls around her chicken neck. I've no idea how she got her hands on them, but suddenly snowy-haired

Gladys was right there too, nodding at me. And then Joyce, eyes fixed on my face, nodding along.

Green biro clutched in Patricia's bony fingers. Green! She started hissing then, stabbing the pen at me – *you! You've the guts*, Gladys and Joyce nodding, coven of three leaning in. I glanced up but no one else was taking a blind bit of notice. Patricia passed the biro to me and took off the pearls, a big grin on her face. Gladys whispered *you have them*.

I stared at the three of them: suddenly wondered if they've had me all along. *KITCHEN*, green ink. 31 December. Today. The code. Giving me knickers. Making me do things. Helping. But just as suddenly as I saw the conspiracy, it was gone: Joyce glued to the TV, Gladys intent on her crossword and Patricia up, toppling a side table, crashing and screeching, scattering crisps and pointing at Norman, lopsided in his chair, *he's a monster – get him away from me!*

Two girls hurried in to steer her out. I wondered if my starving brain was playing tricks on me, but as they escorted Patricia from the room, she jerked her head back at me, eyes wild. *Get out of here! You! Get away!* Pen and pearls on the floor as the sirens on TV blared.

I sat and stared. Then shook myself: sneaked my juice in a plant pot when no one was looking, then came up to my room: Old Year's Night, scratching at my nails, brushing my hair to fluff, so close to getting out of here.

Gytrash

A woman sits on a bench on the river path, telling her grand-daughter a story. Once upon a time, not too far from here, there was a sister and baby brother lost, deep in the woods. They wandered in circles all day, desperately searching for crusts of bread, but every last crumb they had dropped had been devoured by magpies and crows. The girl carried her brother on her back; they could not hear their mother calling their names.

The granddaughter looks up at her granny, eyes glittering. She does not like this story. The light is fading; she wants to go home. The granny draws her closer but carries on. When darkness fell the children were empty-bellied and cold. There was no way home now: all was lost. The sister made a nest of dry leaves under a black oak and huddled close with her brother in the crackle. The moon a bone white shining through the tangle of trees; the static of river in their ears.

The girl clutches her granny's arm now. Whimpers. I want Mummy. But the granny ploughs on, merciless. The baby brother in the story wept about monsters too, wanted his mama. But the big sister was brave. She put her lips in his shiny hair and shushed him, knowing there are worse things than monsters in this world.

But suddenly the big sister's scalp tingled ice. The moon was swallowed up by purple clouds and two flaming red dots appeared in the distance, moving closer through the dark trees. Twin balls of fire, looming though the dark.

The girl hides her face in her granny's coat. But the story must be told, there is no going back now. The burning eyes moved closer, a ragged body appearing around the glow. It was a black lion with raging red eyes. The brother screamed but the sister clamped her hand over his mouth.

When the creature was almost close enough to strike, it stopped and stared. They could feel its heat. Poised. Ready to pounce. The boy screamed through his sister's hand but she stayed still as a statue, eye to eye with the beast. And then suddenly she relaxed. It's okay, baby. We have to follow, she told her brother. He shook his head, but the sister was bigger, so she stood up, swung him on her back, and nodded at the creature. We're coming.

The girl on the bench looks up at her granny, eyes glittering. Sometimes her stories have happy endings.

And so the creature turned, and the sister followed it through the trees, stumbling, ankles clawed by brambles. It slowed for her, not using the paths: she tripped, skinned her shin, lost her right trainer to a bog, gripping her brother tight. The river always getting louder, closer.

The boy was heavy, his sister's arms on fire now. The earth ever softer under her feet. Suddenly they heard voices. But what if they were the wrong ones? The bad ones. It was too late now though. The creature picked up its pace. The sister's final choice.

She ran to catch it up. There was a sudden flash of search lights ahead, and the creature turned on her. For a split second it turned its hot eyes on sister and brother, and then it was gone, vanished into earth in a splash.

The granddaughter on the bench lets out her breath. But Granny doesn't pause yet.

The big sister raced forwards to where the creature disappeared: a soaked patch of river earth, red-black, nothing else. To the river it always returns. The torches were blinding, bright lights hurting her head. Blankets wrapped around them, people everywhere. The river crashing, the radio. We have them. A girl and boy. They are safe. Let the mother know.

And so, the granny says finally, straightening herself up, snip, snap, snout, the tale's out. They were lucky, that sister and brother: the girl was brave and the gytrash led them home to their mother. But others are not always so lucky, you know. The girl looks down, cheeks wet.

And that, the granny says, standing up and brushing herself off, is why we never wander in the woods at night.

PART TWO

December

Nancy

Everyone's downstairs, waiting for the new year bells. Five minutes to go. I sit on the bed, fluffy hair, nails stained red, making my final preparations. I check the time, get out the craft scissors and start snipping heads from the bouquet Christmas roses Pip bought me. No point letting them go to waste. He looked like he was going to throw up when he saw my butchered hair, but he'll get used to it. I pluck the petals and half fill the shoebox. It'll be a nice touch.

I double-check my handbag. Purse, gold watch, last will and testament. Fireworks flashing through the curtains again. I pick out the wedding brooch, roll up my sleeve, test my skin with the pin. Gilt butterfly laced silver. I've never been one to stand pain. I yank down my sleeve and open the wardrobe to put everything back: I can't do this.

Then I see the safe and remember Patricia's blessing – *get out of here – you – get out!* Gladys and Joyce nodding. I can't get my mind straight. Surely it can't be a coincidence. They must have done the writing, the knickers, the lot. I don't remember doing any of it. I touch the pearls in my pocket. Bev's voice. *We want you seeing in the new year as a new person, Nancy.* I need to get out: she's sent me mad.

I close the wardrobe, slide photos of Pip and Ruby into my bag, then turn off the light and lie on top of the duvet, roasting then shivering, fully dressed, listening to the countdown in the dark. My locket still at my throat, my mother always with me. There's cheering at midnight, fireworks blasting outside, then a commotion while they herd everyone to bed.

I look at the clock once the din has simmered to the usual hum of machines: as quiet and dark as it gets in here. 1 a.m. I pull the cord light. There are a few scrapings and thuds upstairs: I think it's my husband George, then remember about the night carers. I'm dying for a drink – it must be twelve hours since I've had anything. My arms are flu-like. No sound of Patricia screaming, but there is singing, loud from the river. All that was good, all that was fair. All that was me is gone. I look around, blinking at the light, then clamber around the bedrails and pick up my handbag, box and cup of medicine tea.

I tiptoe into the corridor, downstairs to the lounge, through the dark to the bird. I pick out the butterfly pin and rake it quickly down my arm. It hurts less than I thought. Blood rolls, deep enough, but not much more than a surface wound. Good. I drop the pin back in my bag, pick the key from my purse, then open the cage. Come on, Luna – it's okay. She's already heavy from the tea I slipped her earlier. Sedated. A mess from the egg illness: bloody tail and legs. Cloacal prolapse, lame. Bev says she'll get the vet in the new year, but it'll be too late by then. Luna tremors in my hand, so I hold her close.

Nobody thought of her, under her blanket, with their cups of kindness, belting out Auld Lang Syne. I tip her head back, prise open the beak: pour in more tea solution. From morning sun till dine. Cradle her small weight to my chest.

I stand still, listening, before carrying Luna out of the lounge. The most dangerous part. Two one oh four. The code from Gladys's mirror. Not the code for the front door, but I have a second chance with the kitchen. I think of my diary. Kitten. So similar to my writing, but it must have been the three women helping me. A few distant noises, deep in the building, but nothing on this level. I creep into the corridor, equipment in one hand, Luna close to my chest. Kitchen. Authorised Staff Only.

There is a sudden movement at the end of the dim corridor. My stomach lurches. It's mad Patricia, floating towards me, barefoot, nightdress pale green under the emergency lights.

Her face is twisted, snarling, eyes pinkish, coming closer. I stumble back, panicking. What if the whole thing is a trick: a set-up? She's in on it with Bev.

But in an instant she's Patricia again, tall and serene in her long nightie, slippers squeaking as if they are wet. My throat hurts: I wasn't expecting her. She must have come to see me off. She nods at me and watches. The kitchen door isn't shut properly: there's no need for Gladys's code after all. It is all meant to be. I whisper the code anyway, for luck. Twooneohfour. Push the door. I glance back at Patricia as the door gives. She looks like she's blowing a kiss and then she's walking away.

The fluorescent glare of kitchen hurts my forehead: I need to act fast. There are footsteps in the corridor and Patricia's making a commotion, screeching her distraction, buying me time. I spot the knives, deep in a wooden block, safely stored for the night. I remove Luna's limp body from my breast: barely conscious now. For Auld Lang Syne. Mercy, not slaughter: her soul will fly at last. The seas between us broad have roared: she has been caged in her body too long; couldn't grasp the freedom I offered. It is time.

I heave a white chopping board onto the steel unit. For innocence. Select a knife. Pick up a rolling pin. I've seen the block enough times: my husband always had the butcher and barber in him, twisting white and red. I have jointed enough lumps of meat in my time. I look at her, peaceful, trusting body. Knife in my hand, pain in my throat. I am so very sorry.

I can't move. Another scream in the corridor, more footsteps. I breathe into my belly and lift my arm high, then bring it down fast, and split her, head from heart. I raise the bloody body to my lips, taste iron: make my promise to join her. In time.

And then, the betrayal. I use her – wipe blood on my chin – smear it over the scratch on my arm, soak my blouse. It has to look bad enough. When I'm done I lay her down gently, ever so carefully, to rest in the box of petals, close the lid, and tuck her in next to the bread bin on the steel worktop. Rest in peace, Luna. Chef will find her tomorrow, but by then I will be gone.

Everything ready now. I hit my skull as hard as I can with the heavy rolling pin, the pain making me reel: it puts me off balance and somehow twists me to the floor. The pain attacks like an animal, sinking its teeth into my hip – this wasn't the plan. I am not prepared for splintered bone. I let the rolling pin go, waving the bloody knife above my head, screaming for dear life. There's running in the corridor, then the door swooshes open and Krystyna bursts in. *Nancy. My God, what has happened?!* I'm sorry I tell her, wielding the knife at her. For a split second she stops, stares at me – off-kilter – like she doesn't know me. Frozen. I'm sorry she had to find me. I gave her my second-best spoon at Christmas.

She's moving again. *Help! Nancy – you are hurt!* I keep waving the knife. *Nancy. Come now.* Her voice slows. *I need you to put the knife down now. Please.* I shake my head, tears streaming. *Nancy. You can do this.* I slide the knife across the floor to her and bang my cheek down onto the floor. Cold and hard. There's more screaming, people crowding in now. *Phone 999! There's blood.* So many voices. *Stand back, everyone, we need to keep calm!* Krystyna stands at the sink, guarding the knife behind her.

I force myself to breathe faster, concocting each gulp, fleshy and loud in my throat. The deputy tells people not to crowd then two paramedics march in, brisk spearmint with black boots. The man crouches down, feels my pulse, stretches an oxygen mask over my face. I pray it is bad enough. *Nancy, can you hear me?* The man checks my arm, looks puzzled. The woman passes wipes. *The wound isn't deep, but we need to check for other injuries.* He calls out behind. *We need a list of her current medication. As soon as you can please.*

I start gasping, as fast and screeching as I can inside the mask, tasting metal. *Nancy, try not to panic. Breathe slowly now, in and out. In and out.* They are suspicious. What if I need to do more. I shout they are coming, they are coming, watch out! jabbing my finger at the crowd. Throw my head back and laugh my bloodied mouth inside the plastic.

Krystyna turns away, ashen and vomits in the sink. The paramedics talk in hums *she is clearly distressed — we need to stabilise her — possibly delirious — fever — maybe a fracture — needs an assessment.* They are agreed. *Right then, Nancy, we'll just get you on here — gently does it,* lifting my body onto a stretcher, the pain cutting deep, making me shudder and sweat cold in their grip, my face ugly under the mask, *that's it, nearly there. Nancy, we're going to take you to hospital so we can check you properly.* Bev glaring down at me, fury on her face, as they strap me down. I swallow and grin back up in triumph.

They carry me into the corridor and I turn my head towards three women in dressing gowns, looking on. So many people, but among them: neat Gladys, mad Patricia, scrawny Joyce. Here to wave me off. I try to smile as they carry me past. This is what I wanted. Tears roll into my hair as I lift my hand slightly under the strap to wave goodbye, farewell, to the only friends I've ever had.

Alex

There is a sink with pink liquid soap; wads of blue paper towels. The water runs brown when Alex washes her hands: she scrubs at her nails, webs, thumbs, but the flow remains rust. The midwife pats the bed, *come and sit down, it's okay.* Another nurse cradling the baby in a blanket, good with him. They have filled him with bottle: bad for his bones.

Alex slumps onto the bed, maternity joggers sagging, shattered. The nurse offers the bundle: *do you want him for bit?* But Alex shakes her head no, I do not. Wants Izzy; has failed her daughter. Tells the nurse, I need to get a message to my husband. My daughter's not well — he needs to monitor her fever. She has a terrible fever. The nurse puts the baby in the cot, *there, there, little one* and comes over to sit next to Alex. *We'll let him know, love.* Alex shifts away: knows even her breath is lochia and rot. She will never have energy to get clean.

She'll be just fine, Alex. You focus on getting better. Nursery Nurse Niki will be here in a sec to give you the tour — then you can settle in.

Alex's eyes seep, always leaking. Paul has taken her Izzy, like he always said he would. Without her mummy, sick, while Alex is here in this airy laminate place, miles away, a blister on the clean, weeping. She has abandoned her girl, broken her promise. Stuck with a baby she has vowed never to love, in this place pretending to be a hospital, with pastel murals and security doors.

Alex closes her eyes and collapses into the bed, head on stiff pillow, feet dangling, not to muddy the duvet. She hears the women go out, and then the Niki girl is knocking and skipping in: chirpy little wren, shiny dark hair, tiny and strong. Alex opens her eyes and sees Niki peeping into the cot – *hello, poppet, aren't you gorgeous?* – then she comes over and perches on the bed; asks Alex how she's doing.

Alex lifts her head but doesn't sit up, so Niki hops to the chair. *It's really lovely to meet you, Alex.* Looking into Alex's eyes like she really cares. *I know you're exhausted – we'll make it a very quick look around, just so you know where you are, and then you can get some rest.* Alex's body is too heavy to lift. Oil in her mouth. *Alex, you'll get better, you know.* Niki leans forward. *I've met lots of mums like you and they all do. We'll make a plan together once you're up to it. And I'll be here with you all the way.*

Niki stands. She is never still. Her hair gleams under the strip lights. *Amy here will watch Benjamin.* Alex looks around, shocked. Another one. Women popping up everywhere. She is sweating, freezing. Niki offers a hand; helps her up. Alex follows her down the shiny corridors, rainbows and giraffes laughing down. Kitchen, playroom, women-only lounge. Light and modern. Like Ikea. Empty chairs around a TV. A girl spoon-feeding mush in the kitchen. Another slouched on a beanbag in the playroom, breast-feeding. Niki's lanyard operates doors. Women in blue dresses smile up at her. *Welcome, Alex! It's lovely to have you here with us.*

Lauren

I rang the TV Licensing and paid in full. The woman on the phone might as well have been a robot talking about my 150 quid. There was some kind of fucking woodpecker in my head at the same time banging short now short now you're short now. Short on the next payment. I'd planned it all out and all – I'd enough left for nearly two months at £166, but now I'm short thirty quid for Friday's payment on the loan.

I take the kids to the park for a bit but my head's messed up and I end up giving them a bollocking over nothing, then feel bad. Some New Year's Eve this is turning out. They'd be better off at nursery. I get them pink Mini Milks from the Spar on the way home to make up for it because I'm short now anyway so what difference will a couple of lollies make. Might as well do it while I can.

We're just walking in when Paul rings again. *I'm so sorry, Lauren, Isabella's having a total meltdown – she can't understand where her mummy's gone.*

I'm trying to get the kids' muddy trainers off before they run in, so I drop the phone and miss the rest. Hang on, Paul. I sort out the boys and send them in the front room, trying to calm my breathing. Go on – I'm here now.

I was just saying that staying up late for new year won't do Isabella any good – she needs her routine right now. I'm really sorry, we're going to have to cry off completely.

My throat hurts when I speak. The boys are really looking forward to it, Paul. We're doing one of those early countdowns – same time as India – it's only for a bit. We've got everything ready.

He says *I know – I'm gutted as well. But I need to put her first, you know how it is.* I do know. But I don't know what to say. So I say what I've been saying all day. Fine.

He asks *can we meet up in the day tomorrow instead?* I tell him I've got plans with the kids – I'll let you know. He knows that's crap, but he says *have a nice cosy evening then, I'll be thinking about you – I'll wait to hear later on.*

I twist crack the metal seal on the quart of dirty vodka that Mum got me for Christmas. It's paint stripper with a red label – rip-off Smirnoff. I don't have any mixer so make up some squash for the kids and top my glass up with that. Fuck it. I get them on the sofa and sit between them, under the quilt, so we can watch Casper the Friendly Ghost with our bright orange drinks. I love them so much it makes me cry.

When Casper's done, I grill fish fingers and stick them in butties for the boys, then make myself another orange squash vodka. I get a countdown on my phone and we do that together in a tiny circle with sparkly blowers before I get them in bed.

Back downstairs in my frayed dressing gown, I open the sweet yellow wine Marge got me, and sit on the sofa with my phone. There's loads of texts. One from Mum – *Come over with boys? Xx.* She'll be wasted with her mates by now. Oli loved being a pirate for her party last year.

I reply – Sorry, still busy. Spk soon. There's a message from my cousin on her posh cruise – *Hey, sweets, how you doing? Hope all your dreams come true this year. Kisses to my fave boys. Love you. Han.* Hug and heart emojis. I delete it – can do without her pity. A reply from Mum. *Suit yourself.*

Another text from Paul. *Missing you, darling xx.* Drunk round robin from the boys' dad with a comedy photo of his new baby in a Santa hat, wishing everyone on his phone a happy new year full of champagne emojis. You think he'd make a bit more fucking effort with the mother of his own kids.

I turn on the telly – it's that girl finally giving birth. Longest pregnancy in the history of TV. I gulp the wine – her waters have broken, total madness, sirens blaring, sobbing. I nearly jump out of my skin when something massive hits at the window. I ignore it – it'll be those twatting kids from down the street chucking firecrackers again. Looking out only makes them worse.

I press mute so it doesn't wake the boys, racking my brains for something to sell. Short for Friday. I've nothing worth pawning. I neck the wine and pour another glass then go and get my Armani puffer from the hall. I take a couple of pictures, then text them to Tania. Can you sell this for £30? Like new.

She replies straight back. *Yeah no probs got the bag?* I reply – Yeah bag & tags but cut off. I need it quick though. She replies yellow okay emoji. Finger and thumb O. Perfect. I look at the telly. The girl's in hospital now. Another text from Tania. *Wanna come out?* I text back – no babysitter soz. She replies. *Shame. Next time girl.*

I have to blink to focus on the words. I haven't seen anyone much since Paul. I put my phone down. To be fair, I've hardly even seen him since the baby arrived. No more texts now. I stare at my bare, bitten nails: I never opened that sparkly nail polish upstairs. Maybe I can flog it.

The screen shines silently in the corner. The monthly payments are nearly as big as my first loan now and I've no clue how. Tania said the only rule is never ever miss a payment – or they'll fleece you for everything. The jacket money should just about put me right for Friday.

The man on telly who's having an affair with his daughter's friend downs his pint, so I follow suit with my wine. His mouth gapes open and closed like a wet fish. Blah blah. I need a second job but then I'd need more nursery and I can't afford that. And there's my record – they're bound to check up.

The work's all shit anyway. I don't want to end up like that girl from school, sitting in the pub all day with the old man who growls. She says he's alright – at least she doesn't need the gas on while she's out – but I can't stomach that.

I scroll my phone, all the girls from my old class posting selfies from a bar in town. Like teenagers. I've said no that many times that they've stopped asking me out.

Another text from Paul. *Happy new year, my beautiful Lauren – the year we found each other.* Red love hearts. I finish the wine, head spinning, and turn off the TV.

That's it then. I stumble into the kitchen with the empty bottles to check the back door. Lights off, front door, upstairs to bed. Mascara wet and itchy under my eyes. I bang my head hard on the bathroom shelf when I lift up for a towel to dry my face, hot pain in my skull. Dizzy. I want to text him, but I can't.

This was supposed to be proper – a sleepover with us all. Not just shagging – waking up together and everything. His wife's not even there. And I've got all the stuff in for a fry-up in the morning as well. I sit on the toilet, forehead on my knees, phone on the floor at my feet. Then I reach down, head spinning, and hold the button until the black screen.

When I get to bed, the room's churning. It's worse when I shut my eyes, but then if I open them it's all coloured lights spinning. I try to breathe slower. Jamie with his new Scottish baby, short on the payment now, that massive dog, Paul's big gingerbread house but I'm short now. Pond weed slithering under the bed. Women in bags. Something moving in the wardrobe.

I make it to the toilet to be sick – sour orange. I'm there ages, in a heap. When I finally pull myself up, I scrub my teeth hard with minty froth, burning my tongue, wipe my lips on a rough towel from the floor, then drag my duvet into the boys' room. I'll be better on the floor between them.

January

Lauren

I wake up on the floor – stiff neck, cardboard mouth, icy feet, but warm in the middle – Daniel's climbed out of bed in the night to curl on the floor with me. I blink wet onto his hair, a right state. I cover him with the duvet and heave myself up, head banging. Need water.

My phone's on the bathroom floor, battery gone. I go down and plug it in and put the kettle on. The kitchen floor's freezing. Happy new year. I'll ask Dee for some extra hours in the shop. The empty booze bottles on the side make me queasy, so I go collapse on the sofa with my eyes shut. My phone beeps in the kitchen when it comes on.

There's a big bruise on my foot but I don't know how I got it, and my skin hurts all over. I suddenly panic that I sent something stupid on my phone. When I fetch it from the kitchen, there's three voicemails – two from Paul, one from Mum. A shitload of happy new year texts. I look through. I didn't send many replies, so that's something at least. I'm getting an ulcer on my tongue. I touch the back of my head where it's sore while the kettle boils.

I pour hot water on a tea bag and breathe in steam. There's loads of texts from Paul – *I'm serious about us, Lauren. I love you.* Another. *We should have come round – I'm sorry. Call me.* Another. *I'm worried about you. Your phone must be off. Let me know you're okay.* Another. *We'd love to meet tomorrow. Ring when you're up.* I squish the tea bag hard against the mug, then flip it in the bin. Serves him right. I don't know what he's panicking for. Milk, two sugars. But I'd better reply. Happy new year, will call later, love Lauren and the boys x.

I go up for a two-minute shower, then head to the long mirror in my room. I drop my towel, shivering; squeeze at the wrinkled skin of my belly – it doesn't match the boniness of my ribs and arms and legs. He didn't choose me yesterday. I lean closer to my reflection, my face a cragged hangover.

I put two tops under my hoodie to try and get warm – then smear foundation on my nose, and across my cheeks and chin. It makes the dry skin orange, even worse. I have to think of Oli and Dan. They love him already and fuck knows they need a proper dad. But I can't have them let down again.

I sit on the bed and check my bank. Even with the money from work, it'll never stretch to Friday's payment. I hope Tania sells that puffer in time. I scroll – my benefits came in but less cause I'm working. It doesn't look right – you're supposed to earn so much before they dock you, but they change the rules every two seconds. I can't do anything about it now anyway – they shut on bank holidays. Last time, that narky woman wouldn't say anything except go on the portal if you've an issue.

Dee wouldn't give me extra hours in a month of Sundays – she hates my guts. Maybe Paul can have a word. I can't always go crying to him though. I look round the bedroom. We've nothing else to sell except the telly. Paul's messages going round in my head. I'm serious about us. Worried about you. Love to meet. He really wants to see me – maybe he's just trying his best for his daughter and it's all gone twisted in my head. I respect him – a lot of men wouldn't do that for their kids – just look at Oli and Dan's dad. Twenty quid, job done. There's someone who doesn't give a shit, always making excuses that he's got his hands full already, with his other kids. I'm going to put my foot down with him, like Mum says – it's only what he owes us.

I text Tania – Shall I drop the jacket round later? She won't be up for ages yet. I look in the mirror – just imagine if I turned up at hers with Paul, in his sharp clothes and car! She'd think he's a dealer. I want to show him off – prove to everyone I'm not a total loser – but we can't hardly go anywhere as a couple. I just need to talk to someone – anyone but my mentalist mother. Maybe Pam at the shop – she was so sweet at that work do. She must know anyway, so it can't do any harm.

The boys wake up and come find me on the sofa. They're still warm with sleep. I pull them up and give them both a big squeeze – my team. Oli says he loves me. Asks if we're seeing Paul and Isabella. I try not to breathe alcohol in his face. I say we'll see.

Mum's always saying *you're your own worst enemy – pushing folk away when they mean well.* Paul says he loves me – people like him, he's a good man. I just need to see myself through his eyes and stop going all fucking paranoid. All I want is someone to walk me through the park with a bag of salty chips soaked in vinegar and be told everything will be alright.

I go to the fridge. We've the eggs from the fry-up and nearly a full loaf on the side. I get the boys dressed and text him. Would love to see you both. I'll bring sarnies. We'll be at the swings from 11.30.

Nancy

Morning, Nancy, another young nurse sings to me. *I just need to do your obs.* She has tired eyes, clogged up with turquoise kohl. She reminds me of the girls from the home. I smile up at her, stiff white sheets tight across my middle, legs lumpy blue and useless underneath.

There's a bloke making a commotion behind my curtain, shouting and bawling like a drunkard. The nurse sees me looking. *Don't mind him – we get a lot of that in A&E, especially this time of year.* She clips a grey plastic peg on my finger. Her fingers red raw from washing. *How are you feeling now?* I tell her fine thank you. She nods. *Your urine sample showed an infection this morning, so the doctor wants to start you on some antibiotics – she'll be round soon to have a chat. We should have your X-rays back then too.* I say thank you.

The nurse looks at a screen, takes the peg from my finger and puts something plastic in my ear. Those chapped fingers never stop dancing. She waits a few seconds then nods. *Your temperature's still high.* Thank you, love, I tell her. I make a kind old woman's smile. I've been good as gold since we got here. Butter wouldn't melt. I should be ecstatic to be out of Bev's place.

She asks my date of birth; what year it is; who's on the throne. Pointless questions, wasting time. I answer confidently, then look down at the tape wrinkling the grey skin on the back of my hand, fixing the needle. Fluids for dehydration. There's no way they can send me back now, the state I came in. Wrong underwear, raving, covered in blood. Dehydrated, dizzy, confused. Found in a hazardous area, seriously injured. Maybe they'll even shut Bev down.

I press the needle through tape and skin while the nurse busies with the clipboard. Her soles squeak on the lino like puppy toys. It stinks of bleach, everything scrubbed clean: floors, bedrails, curtains. No cappuccino cushions or artificial flowers. No dust, ribbons, flags. At least it's honest.

She vanishes through the curtain. I rest my head back on the starched pillow and stare at the tiles on the ceiling, milky and soft, blurring in and out. I raise my fingers slightly from the sheet: three women in the corridor, waving me off. The bird's desecrated body in her cardboard casket in the kitchen. All abandoned. And now I'm here, stuck: can't even get out of bed.

There is a faint sound of women singing in the distance, but I shake my head hard: this won't do. I try to focus on the ceiling; clear my vision. I'm lucky to be here, at last: there's no point dwelling. I've never wanted to make a fuss but I need to talk to Pip: tell him straight now. Then he can give the tenants notice, and I can get home. He'll go back to doing my odd jobs, and if they really don't want me near the cooker, Gladys said there's some meals-on-wheels people who aren't so bad.

I've a sour taste in my mouth when the doctor appears. I must have fallen back asleep. She stands next to me and says hello as I try to lift my head, then asks how the pain is.

I don't need to move: I know it's very bad. She frowns. *Your X-ray isn't showing any fractures. I just need to check your movement. I'm still hoping you've got away with some bad bruising.*

That can't be right. I tell her – I'm broken – I can't move – you can't send me back there, I won't go.

The doctor soothes me like a child. *Nancy, you're not going anywhere just yet – we need to make sure you're well first. The X-rays will be double-checked by the team, but for now let's just have a little look.* She presses my hips, gently, then moves to my feet, cradling the weight of each heel in her hands, lifting them, slowly, ever so carefully, bending, nudging, asking how it all feels. It turns out I can move after all: the doctor is quite happy, but says I might be sore for a few days.

She shows me how to use the electric button to adjust the bed. *We're going to move you upstairs, but right now my priority is to get your temperature down and treat this infection. Your urine sample was very concentrated, but the fluids will help. We'll send your sample off to the lab. For now, let's get you on some antibiotics.*

Okay, Doctor, I say, the drunk man behind the curtain quiet now: probably having a good earwig at the old woman's disgrace. *Also, Nancy – there was a trace of blood in your urine. It might be the infection, but we need to keep an eye on it.* She's looking right at me, her voice ringing out clear and loud. *Have you ever noticed that before?*

My stomach contracts. Twenty years without bleeding, and then it came back suddenly when I moved to Bev's. It's the stress – it'll go away when I get back to my proper home.

I whisper, it's nothing. It must be a mistake. Nothing to fuss about. Where's my son? I need to see him so we can get me home. She says visiting's later on: Sister will have phoned your next of kin. *I'll ask her to pop in and let you know.* She asks more questions about pain passing water and blood and I don't know what I say.

She says not to worry then. *Once you're upstairs, we'll get you sorted.* She smiles down sympathetically. *You're a tough cookie, Nancy – nothing broken after a fall like that. I'm sure you'll be back on your feet in no time.*

Right, I say, thank you. I have to be good: don't want them sending me back to Bev. I'll show them: I'm fit to live in my flat – better out of that awful place. I'm so tired my eyes keep blurring the doctor's face, the words jumbling together. I say yes, no, I don't have any questions, yes, that's fine, thank you very much, Doctor.

Alex

Niki props Alex in the pink chair with inhospitable arms; adds cushions, brings the baby over. *Come on, gorgeous Benjamin, let's see Mummy!* They have been topping him up with bottles, but say breastfeeding is still possible. Alex refuses to pump like cattle, but will not give him formula: cannot tell Niki that she has seen that it will make his bones worse.

Niki tries to put Alex's left breast into the baby's crying mouth but it is no good: he clamps and slips off again, wailing. Alex can't hold him properly: he will fall off and shatter. She can hardly touch him. The baby is furious – scarlet – but Niki perseveres. She has a strangely soothing voice for such a little wren. Alex's breasts are painful and hard: too big for his mouth. Hot. Her eyes ache with exhaustion. Women bring her steaming cloths against mastitis.

Niki bobs out and comes back with a frothy bottle of warmed milk. She does not walk on eggshells like some staff, or speak to Alex like she is a child. Everyone thinks she is the one at risk, not the baby, even with his body packed with strands of spun sugar, so easily cracked. Even though she does not love him, she sometimes says a silent prayer to help his bones. She shakes her head at the bottle, so Niki sits down instead and takes the baby: shows Alex how to cradle him upright; brush the teat against his lips: *see how he opens his mouth and draws it in.* He likes Niki.

Alex looks out of the window, keeps catching strange shadows in the rhododendrons. Niki says Alex has been in the hospital two days. Keeps making promises about feeling better – *you're doing brilliantly, Alex — we just need to take this one hour — one minute even — at a time.*

She spoke to her parents on Skype again this morning. They perched on two chairs in front of her auntie's computer in Brisbane, leaning in so they could both get in the picture. More worried-looking than she expected. Tired. Evening there already. Her dad talked too loudly, as always on the computer. *Shall we fly back, sweetheart? You're more important than any of this.* Alex shook her head. They have worked too hard for this trip.

I'm alright, she somehow said. There's no point anyway. There's nothing you can do here. Doesn't want to wreck everything for them too. *Well, let's see how you get on in the next couple of days, eh? We've got insurance.* Her mum nodding along. *How's the baby getting on?* Niki held him up to the camera and her mum moved in closer and waved. *Hello, little one. Oh, sweetheart — look at all that gorgeous hair. He's the spit of you when you were little.*

Alex shifts back to the bed now. Her breasts make it too painful to lie on her side, even her back. Still pulpy between the legs from the birth. Heavy bees, roaring inside the breasts, burning to get out. Rocks on the bedside table. Paul put them in the suitcase with her extra clothes. A few nice things, to make her feel at home. Large grey rock with fawn-coloured circle, a giant eye from her childhood beach. Skimming stone, proposal pebble, limestone oval from the afternoon with Ruth. Her rare rhomb porphyry: frothy diamonds popping in its cola-coloured lava. Drilled pebble on the necklace. River wanting. Images flashing. He is always so thoughtful. She just needs to get right so they can go back to the way they used to be.

Something flicks in Alex's peripheral vision. She spins but when she looks it has gone again. She flushes hot, dizzy. The visions have followed her here, but they have turned in on themselves now: inverted flashes, matt, sucking light. The dark blooming underbelly of migraine lights. River stone forced, splintered, the magnetic pull of the water, more urgent here. No longer heart of a saint returned, world cup, moors on fire: it is closing in. River rising, fever, daughter. Her head splits at the fracturing futures: she does not know what is real.

Alex tries to focus on Niki rubbing the baby's back, his body flopping with milk now. Niki listens so carefully to Alex when-ever she speaks, believes her. She tucks the baby into the cot, fleecy sheet to his armpits, asleep, then starts folding and tidying, moving bits of Alex's life around. The baby would be so much better off with this lovely woman.

Nancy

They've wheeled me up to the top floor with the old people. I should count my blessings: I've got a window and haven't been sent back to Bev. It might as well be night-time for all the light the window lets in, especially with this weather. Sleet constantly blathering at the glass; clouds pushing up like old bruises.

It's stifling as well. Women keep popping through my curtain with monitors, milky tea, handfuls of bourbons in crackly wrappers. I think about the people outside. The hospital looks like Blackpool illuminations from down there: I've seen it enough times, on miserable days like this, walking Ruby by the river.

The humming's even worse than the care home. I look around for air conditioning. Maybe it's the river, or taxis idling outside for visitors, headlamps lighting up the spray. I turn to the window again: a square of fog. And then I realise: it is the women from the river, they have followed me here, wanting. Voices curling up from the river, through the vents, urgent, louder, getting angrier. Tracking me down. Sailing souls, come to the water. Loud the winds howl, loud the waves roar. All that was good, all that was fair. In my head, around my head. Even if I could get out of bed to the window, people wouldn't see me, not from right up here.

There's clattering and TVs and croaky voices behind the curtain and I'm trying to shuffle my legs across, heart pounding, to swing myself out of bed to get away, the pain practically gone, when a nurse bustles in to fuss my feet back into place, empty wrappers still crinkling in my hand. *I'll take them, love – don't be bothering yourself with the rubbish. You just rest back.*

The woman across from me is shouting *excuse me* again, always wanting something. She just sits there, lady muck, curtain wide open, shameless. I've told Pip to bring me some cotton wool for my ears so I can block her out.

I ask the nurse for my handbag, and she passes it up from my cupboard, then goes off. Everything's there except my pills. Notebook, will, gold pocket watch. The soft worn paper bag of pear drops, which Pip brought me yesterday. He came as soon as he heard: he's a good boy. I pop one in my mouth to calm my nerves.

I lean back, and the next thing I know, I open my eyes and Pip's there again, chatting with another doctor like old friends. Darling. My voice croaks. I reach my hand out, Pip, come here, sticky drool on my chin.

Mum. He comes over and kisses my cheek. Thinks I don't notice him flinch at my hair. *You were out for the count. How're you doing?* I'm fine now, love, I tell him, still holding my bag. He looks at the doctor, eyebrows slightly raised. *You've had a shock, Mum – they're still trying to work out what happened.* The doctor starts saying something to me but I ignore him and pat the bed: come sit down, love.

Pip comes over to the plastic chair next to the bed, and the doctor says he'll see me later. I'm much better now, I tell Pip, ready to go. I wipe my mouth with a tissue. But. I take a deep breath. Darling, I know you've always wanted the best for me, but I'd much rather go home – to my old place I mean – I've given the care home a good go, like we said, but I want to go back to my real home now. Pip looks shocked, little-boy shocked.

Mum, you're not serious? Did you hear the doctor? He holds my hand, eyes glittering. *You're not well – you need proper care – I've been beside myself with worry.* I tell him there's no need, it was just a funny turn.

It's not the first time you've said that, Mum. It's just not practical – you need support. Look what just happened. First your hair, and now all this. *Imagine if you'd been at the flat and no one had found you.* He puts my hand down, exasperated. *You know I can't be there twenty-four/seven to look after you.*

But I don't need watching like a baby, I tell him – I just need to get on. We can get people in to do my meals if you're still fretting about the kitchen?

It's a weight off my big body, saying all this: I'm like a soft fluffy loaf, full of air. But then he's looking at me like I've gone mad, and my stomach sinks, full of stones.

Mum, you're in hospital on a drip. The tenants have got a lease – we can't just evict them. And how would we pay for your care without the rent? Live-in carers don't come cheap, you know.

I smile, prepared for this. Then I'll come and stay with you, I tell him. He stares at me. *What?* You've space, haven't you? Your spare room's not doing anything. Like you said before, it's time we moved on: me and your wife need to make our peace. Then I can help out with the kiddies as well.

He suddenly wilts into himself. He wipes his palms on his jeans, then leans forward. *Mother. You're not thinking straight. It's all a muddle but the doctors know what they're doing – they want to help you.*

I'm not muddled, I say, I'm not. I'm not going back there – look what they've done to me, raising my voice to him like I haven't since he was little. Pip takes my hand and squeezes gently, his fingers like ice. *I'm sorry, Mum,* he says, *I know I've let you down. What were they playing at? They were supposed to be look-ing after you. I'll find you somewhere better, please, don't cry – I'll sort it, please, okay?*

Lauren

I wake up at 4 a.m. again, soaked in sweat. Those fucking women from the bags keep waking me, like a shot of speed in the chest. Horrendous nightmares, open mouths, heads flinging back, screaming with laughter, lips gaping wide, jaws stretching below their necks, tits, waists, swallowing themselves whole, until only the thick black smoke of their guts is coming for me, fast, to suffocate my face.

I toss and turn, fretting about the money. Due tomorrow. I got us some milk and a bit of fruit from the supermarket yesterday with my vouchers, but they never go far enough. I gave the boys an apple each after swimming, all the posh mums taking their darlings to the cafe for organic snacks after their lessons.

I put the duvet over my head, all the bad things I've done whining round my head. Stealing, throwing myself at lads, sleeping with another woman's husband. What am I doing. I shouldn't have shouted at the kids. I think about my cousin Hannah, in one of those tiny cruise ship beds, lurching side to side. I hope she's not too sick, so far away, in the middle of the sea – I bet there's loads of bitching on those ships. Lads taking advantage. I should have replied at new year – I wish she was back at her mum's so we could have a brew.

I end up turning the light on at 5 a.m. and checking my bank. Same as yesterday. I need to get cash in today to stop the payment bouncing tomorrow, but Tania's being well slow with the jacket money. I can't let on I'm that desperate for thirty quid.

I send Hannah a message – happy new yr darlin cuz! Miss you here. Tell me everythin. When u back? x

I delete all the messages in my phone from my mum, then take ages doing a message for Pam. Happy new year! Bursting to tell you about me & Manager Paul getting together! Will tell you properly at the shop. Lauren x

I feel a bit better for telling Pam – it's not like we can keep it a secret forever. Not with kids and houses and exes involved. And now his mum's in hospital – he needs me even more. I wish he'd let me go with him to see her – I only want to help. With his wife away we could be spending more time together, but he's so worried about keeping everything normal for his daughter. I guess I'd be the same though, putting the kids before everything.

It'll be good to talk to Pam anyway – someone who's known him for longer – who understands how sensitive he really is underneath. I put the light off and fall so fast asleep that Oli has to shake me awake at 8 a.m.

Alex

Alex is out for fresh air, Niki pushing the baby in a pram. Alex's socks filled with cement, dead weights to lift, one after two, never-ending. They walk through the grounds, up to the golf course, the grass frosted white. The path crunches, gritted for the patients; pram wheels crusting brown salt.

Niki says Alex has been in hospital four days. Her body is like jelly, without scaffold. Shapeless fleck of blood in raw egg white: a spoil on this ice-bright day. The sun is low, cutting black silhouettes of the trees. Alex blinks and looks down at her trainers: one, two, one.

Her feet follow Niki, heavy as sandbags, plodding the daily loop. There is only weight. She glances up at Niki's hands on the pram handle, strange creatures moving. Sea stars. Then back to the feet.

There is a harsh sound above, and Alex stops and looks up. Wild geese. *High in the clean blue air.* Niki stops too; puts the brake on the pram.

They stand together, heads back, arms touching, gazing up at the skein of geese. The baby is asleep. Each bird has its place, wind in their wings, lifting; guttural barks rushing through air.

The women stand motionless as the birds pass over. Eventually they are gone: dissolved into sky. Niki moves first. One hand to the pram, she unhooks the brake with her toe, ready to walk. She turns to Alex, sees her wet cheeks and rubs her arm. *That's good, Alex*, she says. *That's good.*

Nancy

I'm trying not to hear the morning TV babbling from the bed opposite when a doctor sweeps in. They're always in, prodding and talking. What I'd give to be in my own bed with a bit of peace. The doctor says *morning* and plucks my file from the end of the bed. He gives the papers a brisk once-over, then starts speaking quickly, announcing my business to the world. *You're making good progress, Nancy. I'm pleased with your response to the antibiotics. Your temperature's down and your urine sample this morning was encouraging.* I nod at him, trying to follow. I can't remember if I've seen him before.

We'll remove the drip this afternoon, and in the meantime we'll do the usual, wheeling it along with you to the bathroom. It's good to stay mobile. You'd think the whole ward needed to hear. *We'll monitor you for another couple of days, but if things carry on like this, you'll be home soon.*

I look at him, my hands folded neatly on the sheets in front of me, thank you, Doctor. He pops my file back, *someone will be round to help you dress in a bit*, and he's gone in a swish of curtain.

I stare at the wall. At some point an older woman with purplish hair appears. *Hello, love, I've come to be helping you change.* I tell her I don't need help thank you, her scent of Parma violets filling my cubicle, but she says *the drip can be a bit of a faff and there's not enough room to swing a cat in here and a little hand always comes in, doesn't it? It always does – we'll have you organised in a jiffy.* She sounds like she's snipped up a magazine and jumbled and swallowed the scraps.

I hold my breath as she rummages around and pulls out a fresh pair of knickers from the bag Pip brought from the care home. She steadies me gently as I step out of one pair, and into another, then carries on chatting in her peculiar way until it's all done and I'm on the plastic chair and she's stripped back the bed, flapped and tucked new sheets, and folded me back in, ever so discreetly. But once I'm settled she says quietly, *Nancy, I noticed a smidgen of blood on your smalls.* I feel my face burning. *It's alright, I've seen everything, have you noticed it before?* I say no, too loudly, too quickly. It must have come from someone else.

How stupid. But she pats my hand, *okey-dokey, don't be fretting, pet, get your head down now and I'll have a word with Sister – she'll look to it, not to worry.*

I want to grab her hand: ask her to stay with her funny way of talking; to watch over me while I have a proper sleep; keep me safe from the river singing. But instead I look away and say nothing, ungrateful old woman, stomach hurting.

Pip arrives at visiting time and sits on the plastic chair. He tells me they've booked me an appointment downstairs with the gynaecological clinic for next week. *It's women's stuff, Mum, have they explained it?* I ask him to pass me a tissue: I can't find my hankie. He passes the box, then balances it on my cupboard where I can reach it. He fidgets. *Did you hear me? Do you want me to get one of the girls from the home to go in with you? I could leave work early and give them a lift across?*

I'm taken aback: don't know what he's talking about. I push the crumpled tissue under my pillow, avoiding his eyes. Love, you're always so thoughtful – but I said before – we can manage now – I'm feeling much better thank you.

He sighs, then changes the subject. *Did you get your programme last night?* I tell him yes, thank you, you're so good. He's loaded up the big white robot TV above my bed, but I don't want him using all his money up. I'd pressed my buzzer to get a nurse to pull it across so I could see the screen. That girl, sitting in the dark with the new baby. I had to switch it off halfway though: couldn't get Joyce's tutting out of my head, or Patricia's yelling, or Gladys pretending she's ignoring it all, concentrating on her crossword, but knowing all the storylines, just the same.

It's madness here: each of us paying to watch the same thing behind our little curtains. I tell Pip. What a waste of money. He fidgets; asks what I had for dinner. I tell him I've no idea: it all looks beige. I want to go home. He takes a deep breath. *Mum, you're right. We need to get you out of here before you catch something.* His voice is low, gentle. *You're right that we need to find a new place for you when you come out as well.*

My heart lifts. I nod, but don't want to interrupt. *Riverside say they can't meet your needs, not that I'd let you back there anyway, but it's a bit complicated. They're saying you need a proper assessment – they think you need more care.* I blink to refocus on his face, my hands twisting the sheet.

The social worker rang to talk about where might suit you. He pauses, to see how I'm taking it. I sit very still; speak calmly. Pip, the best place is my own home. I should have been clearer from the start, I'm sorry. He carries on. *Mum, you haven't been* back to the flat for months — *you're not remembering it right. What about the accident?* I reply quietly. We've been over that, Pip — you know it could have happened to anyone. He carries on. *Okay, let's not rake it all up — like you say — we need to get it right this time. Make sure you're happy. They've given me a list of places that have space, say you could go to one of them temporarily while we wait for a full assessment.* I shake my head, looking at his face. He's trying so hard. He carries on. *There's that beautiful place on the way out to the hills, but there's quite a wait apparently.*

I can see how close he is to tears. I know he only wants what's best. I look down at my hands. Take a deep breath. Well, why don't I come home to you, just while we get the tenants out? His voice shakes. *Mum, we've been over it, you're not safe by yourself. You know I can't look after you.* He puts his face in his hands.

His shoulders judder then, crumbling down. Cliffs into the sea. Like when his dad died. My stomach drops. Pip, what's wrong? You're not telling me something. *Mum, you don't understand. I don't know what to do. It's all a mess.* I swing my legs so I can sit round to him, my feet dangling a foot above the floor. What is it, darling? You're scaring me. Come here.

He looks up and leans in, eyes red, *I just want you to be happy — and safe — but I keep getting everything wrong.* I ask him, but what, what's wrong? What is it? He pulls his chair closer and leans on me.

Mum. You know I'd take you home if I could — make sure you're properly looked after. But I can't, not now, not with Alex and everything.

I'm suddenly livid. I knew it — it's that woman again, isn't it? What's she been saying now? It's your house as much as hers, Pip — you can't let her push you around.

He blows his nose. *It's not that, Mum. She's ill this time — it's not just attention-seeking — she's in hospital.* I look at him, bewildered. What do you mean? She's here? Where? She can't be. *No.* He lowers his voice. *It's like a mental hospital place.* He looks down. *And she's taken the baby as well.*

I can't believe it. I hold him at arm's length so I can see him properly. What are you saying? Where's Isabella? Look at me, why didn't you say so before? He's sobbing now. *I don't know, Mum, you've enough on your plate, I didn't want to worry you. Isabella's at nursery. I'm managing everything on my own.*

It's okay, Pip, we'll work it out, I tell him. He shakes his head, cheeks wet, nose running. *I don't think so this time.*

Okay, take a breath, I tell him, we're going to be fine. We always have been, haven't we? I'm here. I'll do anything to help you. He nods, eyes watery, looking at me. *Thanks, Mum. Thank you.*

We sit there for a minute, then he blows his nose. *I'll ring some places on the list then. And once you're settled you could come and stop the night at ours – you're allowed, you know, I don't know why we didn't think of it before.* He's excited now, his eyes glittering and feverish, like a child, *yes, that's it – we can do that. We just need to get you out of here – please, Mum – give it a try, for me. It'll be temporary, just while we get the assessment.*

I look at my hands. I'm sick of it in here too. But it has to be temporary, Pip. *Yes, he's nodding, yes, just to get you out of here, get you safe.* Okay then. Just a short-term place while I wait for these blessed tests that will show everyone I'm fine to go home.

Lauren

I wake up and check my phone. Nothing. I double-check my signal. Pam still hasn't replied to my text about Paul. No texts from him neither. Even Hannah never bothered replying – too busy with her fancy new cruise mates probably. Nothing even from the loan company. I'm totally on my own. I check my bank again. The payment bounced on Friday. I don't know what I was expecting – bailiffs or cops or whatever – but when they couldn't take the money nothing happened. I've had a couple of texts about it, but that's it.

So maybe missing the payment's not as bad as Tania made out it'd be. She couldn't get the cash for the puffer jacket to me til Saturday, but the payment'd bounced already by then so I put the money on the meter instead, and now I've nearly enough in my account for the rent. I feel sick when I think about it, but maybe the company won't do anything, and by the time they really want the money I'll have been paid again.

When I put the bin out the front, there's smashed glass all over the doorstep. I slam the door and fetch the pan and brush – the sooner we're out of this shithole, the better. My boys deserve better. I wonder about messaging Pam again – my heart racing whenever I think about seeing her at work – but I've done enough damage – I just need to shut my mouth now. Why did I even go gobbing off in the first place.

I flick the telly on in the front room. Paul's off to visit his wife today, and the baby. I shouldn't be jealous of someone that poorly – God knows I wouldn't wish it on anyone – but I can't help thinking about him and her making a baby and her on top and their proper home and life and I know my cousin would say stop torturing yourself but I can't help it. He keeps promising we'll all go to some bright white villa in Spain by the sea in summer – salty warm, sparkling sunlight, sandcastles, fancy cocktails – but I just don't know any more. But what else can I do – I've no one left and fuck all else to sell.

I hear the postwoman and start sweating. I can't breathe properly, and when I hear Oli and Dan racing for the doormat like they always do, I go all dizzy and have to lean back into the sofa. They share the letters out, like good boys, one each, and run in to deliver them to me. *There's two, Mummy – open them, open them!* Jumping up and down. I glance at the envelopes and put them on the arm – it's just boring bills – you two go back up and play now. They stop leaping around and look gutted – this is our special game and I'm pushing them away.

Oli's about to start wailing so I pick up the first envelope and try to play along. Oh yeah, whoops – there's nothing boring about this one, high-pitched and excited, it's a letter from the Queen! I rip open the envelope and the writing swims but I keep playing our game in my happy voice, you are invited to tea, please contact us immediately, at Buckingham Palace, late payment fee, garden party, charges and interest, please don't be late, wear your very best clothes, court action, default, may have to, marmalade sandwiches and sugar plum cakes, fancy that, debt collection, please reply please reply today.

The boys pick up on my excitement, *yeah, Mummy – let's go, let's go!* and I jump up as well, rip the letter in pieces and throw them in the air, and I'm laughing and crying at the same time, confetti, I'm fucking screaming my head off and my phone rings but I knock it to the floor, and we leap on the sofa and jump and jump holding hands, jumping, the Queen the Queen, out of breath laughing God Save the Queen at the top of our fucking voices.

Alex

Niki walks Alex and the baby to the playroom. There are no chairs: only beanbags and a jigsaw of giant foamy mats. Niki sets up a little tripod camera on the side, then comes over and sits next to Alex on the mat, cross-legged, chirpy as ever. She says they will do a short recording for Alex's care plan: as they discussed. Alex has been here nine days. They will watch the recording together later. Everything will be deleted when Alex leaves hospital.

The walls are fresh lemon. Jungle curtains and giant stickers on repeat. Fluffy bunny books, crinkly fish. It could be a baby group but for the grey medical bin lurking under the sink, and the health and safety posters: giving the game away. Hot Drinks Not Permitted in the Nursery Environment. This Playroom is Suitable for Babies 12 Months and Under.

Niki rolls the baby onto the gym for tummy time, under a dangling tiger. He hates it and protests by smashing his face into the mat. Alex can't stand it: she reaches in and flips him over to his back. He stops crying and starts waving his arms and legs like he wants to fly. Niki smiles at Alex: *look at that! Look how happy you've made him.* Alex slumps back into a bean-bag: knows it is not true. Time on his stomach is crucial for muscle strength and motor development. His bones need to increase in density. She closes her eyes. She has denied him what he needs. Could have shattered ribs, flipping him like that. Alex's head clamped in a vice, Niki singing a little song in the background.

Later, Niki takes Alex to a computer to watch the recording, baby in a bouncer at their feet. Niki points out how well Alex responded to one of his cues. *Look how you're leaning in there; that's lovely eye contact. Look at Benjamin focusing on you!* Alex stares at the screen.

There is something strange about the clip. Her face is too puffy; her ponytail too low. She is wearing the same faded red top, with scuffed gold buttons on the cuffs. But there is definitely something not right about her face.

Alex glances sideways at Niki, to check whether she looks different to the video. Maybe it is fake. That woman wearing her clothes: it might not be her. The Niki next to her looks the same though: bright body, rich brown skin, neat French plait, gleaming cheeks. Hard to tell. Niki pauses the clip and looks at Alex. *How do you feel watching yourself with Benjamin?*

Alex says she doesn't know. Doesn't feel much. She doesn't mention the suspect recording. The blots lurking at the edge of her vision. River weeds wrapping her ankles, daughter crouching under the table, the terror. She glances down: the baby has bounced himself asleep. Niki scoops him up and into the bassinet. *Okay, I think that's enough for today – you've done super.* She shuts the computer down and stands up, ready to wheel the bassinet. *We'll do the same again in four weeks – then you can see what's changed. Let's get you both back to your room.* Alex heaves her body up and follows Niki back to her bed, where she is finally allowed to lie down.

Lauren

I drop the kids off at nursery on the way to the charity shop, my heart a raw steak, flopped on a plate. I hope Dan starts settling soon – they had to prise him off me.

I got all these missed calls from Mum last Wednesday when I didn't turn up to drop the boys at hers – like we can't manage without her. It's not like I'm just going to pretend like nothing happened – it was her who said not to go crying back to her.

I don't know how I'll manage the extra nursery day though – maybe the free hours'll cover it. I need to fill the form in. I'm dreading seeing Pam in the shop – she still hasn't replied about Paul. When I go in, she says *morning*, polite like – tight lips – but carries on sorting the books. I go in the back, hang up my cracked old metallic jacket, and fill the kettle.

Pam says she's already got a tea, so I make myself coffee and get on with the steaming. Smell of old dishcloths. While I'm waving the hissing wand around, I try and work out if there's any way I could make enough for the loan by doing more hours in here. Even if I could stomach it, and by some miracle Dee gave me extra shifts – it'd all get swallowed up by the nursery anyway. I look in a plastic bag, wondering about the women. There's a shimmer, but nothing much. My tummy rumbles. I don't know what we're going to have for tea.

Pam gives me the cold shoulder all morning, not even making small talk about the weather. I swear everyone's being funny with me – Dee pops in and out without so much as a hello, and even old Leonard won't look me in the eye. Surely Pam hasn't blabbed to everyone.

I make another coffee and start hauling old clothes out of the pile of bags – can't face the shop floor. Why would Pam under-stand anyway – she's a judgemental old cow – I always knew. I'm pathetic – someone's kind to me a couple of times and I go spilling my guts and now I can't take it back – home wrecker – not that she says it – but that's what she's thinking.

On my break, there's a load of missed calls from an unknown number and texts from the loan company. I can hardly breathe. They must have properly clocked the missed payment. There's a text from Jamie as well. *It's tight after Xmas Lauren – I'll send the boys money at the month end. Let's sort it between us – we don't need to involve any authorities.* He'll probably send twenty quid again next month, job done. But

I haven't the energy – and the court aren't exactly likely to rule in my favour – it's not like I'm the perfect mother. What if they decide the kids are better off with him, up in Scotland. It's better left alone.

But I can't ignore the calls forever. The selfish bastard – like it's not tight for everyone in January. Get in contact immediately to discuss repayment. I corner Pam after my snack noodle. She's at the till, counting jigsaw pieces. I ask if she got my text. She nods, chin juddering back into her jowls, all the leathery pouches of her face wobbling. *Yes, Lauren, I did.*

I wait, but that's it. She doesn't say another word. I front up to her. Well? Don't you want to know then? She looks up at me. *It's really none of my business what you get up to. In fact perhaps it's better I don't know.* She carries on sorting the jigsaw pieces into stacks of ten. So that's it? She looks up again. *I thought you were different to that, Lauren.* To what? I ask, staring right at her.

I stand there, waiting. *You do know that you're not the first young girl he's been involved with from the shops, don't you?* I look at her, winded. The bitch. What's she on about.

Her mouth softens a bit. *Surely you didn't think?* She sweeps all the jigsaw pieces back into one big heap. *Anyway, it's that wife of his I feel sorry for.* I put my hands on the glass counter to steady myself, staring at her. *And the wee ones.*

A God-awful screech suddenly comes from the window display, jagged with spite. A woman in a crimson ribbed polo neck, clutching at her throat, laughing, eyes fixed on me. I yelp and trip closer to Pam but she's still messing with her jigsaw, oblivious. My cheeks are roasting – I can't think straight.

I don't know what you mean, I tell her. A bit of jigsaw falls on the floor. *They never do,* she says, stooping to pick it up. I suddenly remember Dee smirking with her shining hair at the Christmas do, the other women in silky jumpsuits and kitten heels, but he said they were work colleagues, that grown-ups can talk without shagging, and I'm racking my brains to think if he's ever mentioned anyone else, but surely this is different, he's met my kids, we're serious, aren't we.

Pam looks at my face and softens a bit. *Anyway, look — you've made me lose count now — I've said my piece — let's put it behind us and get on.*

Nancy

Pip wheels me down to the clinic in a chair, like the nurse told him, even though I'm perfectly capable of walking. He'll bring me back up once we're done, but I'm so much better now. They're getting a room in the new home ready as quick as they can.

He's moving my things across from Bev's place this week. Another burden on top of everything else he's got on. He's such a good boy. I've worked so hard to make up for his dad; to make sure he turned out decent.

He brought my post last week, and a bunch of daffodils from the care home. There was a package too, in crumpled Christmas paper with no label. I told him to bin the flowers. He left the package on my bed; didn't know who it was from. A few objects tumbled onto the sheets when I ripped it open: a small marble egg; one of those little lavender bags that Joyce used to make with scraps from the craft room; a new diary and a green biro. I no longer know if it was me or them that got me out.

I picked up the egg: smooth and cold on my palm. Later on, when the social worker came to see me, the egg warmed in my hand as I squeezed it tight. I'm not sure exactly when it was: all the times and days blur on the ward, even with the new diary. I've made a list of the objects, but already know who they're from. The three women.

The social worker was friendly but agreed with Pip and the doctors: I need to be looked after until they've done the forms properly. Mind you, with all the prodding and bleeping and the singing, it'll be a blessing to be out of here, wherever I end up.

Pip wheels me to the clinic reception where a woman asks my name and date of birth, looking mainly at him, then sends us down a corridor to wait with all sorts of people. I look around: it

202

sets you wondering. It looks like a normal waiting room. One of the girls is quite young: I wonder what she's doing here.

Pip tries to distract me. *Mum, I brought you Midget Gems, your favourite.* Thanks, love, I tell him. I take one and pop it in, but keep looking around. Pip picks out a couple of greens – he always liked those – then hisses. *Mum, stop it!* I look at him, questioning. What? He smiles. *Stop staring.*

I laugh. I'm not staring.

And take that cotton wool out of your ears, it's not helping one bit. I pull both pieces out, agreeable as you like, and drop them in my pocket with the marble egg.

I tell Pip I don't like being stuck in the middle of the room in the wheelchair, and clamber out to sit on one of the seats by the wall, like everyone else. He asks if I want to take my jacket off, but I shake my head, I'm fine as I am thanks, love. I'm finally getting settled, when I hear my name. *Nancy Sutherland.* I look over at the lady doctor calling me, and Pip says *come on, Mum, back in the chair* but I tell him I don't need to, and stand up.

The doctor comes over, *hello, Nancy.* She looks at me, then the wheelchair. *We're not going far. You can leave it by the wall if you can manage, it's fine by me.* She talks to me, looks at me. I tell her thank you, grinning, and loop my arm through Pip's so we can follow her down the corridor. She talks about the dreadful weather as we go, *what a day!* cheerful as you like.

The room is tiny and hot, but at least it's got proper walls so everyone can't hear my business, and even the singing is quieter in here. There's a smiling nurse, and Pip says should he come back later? His face is flushed: it's not the kind of thing a son wants to hear. But the doctor says *you're welcome to stay while we chat, and you can always wait outside if we need to do any checks.* Pip mumbles okay and sits down.

Then the doctor turns to me. *I'm Jackie, a consultant here – I look after patients with symptoms like yours.* She smiles at the nurse. *And this is Wendy, a clinical nurse specialist. We're basically both here to make sure you understand everything – to help you decide what's best for you.* I take my jacket off and Pip helps me get it on the back of my chair. The doctor waits until I'm sorted, then carries on. *Obviously, everyone's different, Nancy. The most important thing is that we do what you want. Do you have any questions before we carry on?*

My voice shakes – no, thank you. I don't know why I'm so nervous, it's ridiculous: I'm a grown woman for Pete's sake. I twist round to get the egg out of my pocket.

The doctor asks about the bleeding: says it's much more common than most ladies know. I cringe: know Pip doesn't want to hear it. It's a bit of a blur as she talks me through every-thing. *We usually start with some questions and basic checks – blood pressure, sugar, weight, that sort of thing – and then there are lots of options, depending on how you'd like to go forward.*

She talks calmly about speculums and scans and little cameras and tubes in this bleached room, like we're discussing the sand-wich offer at dinner, but she says it in such a kind way, like there's all the time in the world, and how some ladies find the tests a bit uncomfortable, how it's all my choice how we go ahead. Pip keeps looking at his knees.

I say what do you think, Pip? And he looks up, red-faced, and says *I'm obviously no expert, but I think it's best if we do the checks and get sorted as soon as we can – just in case they find anything – you know, to be on the safe side.*

The doctor says gently *there's no rush to decide everything now* but I can see Pip's right and say yes, I know what you mean. I'll have the tests please.

She smiles. Okay, well, we don't need to do everything right away. We can start with an internal today if you're sure – it's a bit like a smear test – and a quick scan too. Then we can book any follow-ups, if we need them.

Pip goes to the waiting room, then the specialist Wendy woman helps me onto the bed and pulls the curtain round, while the doctor types something in. She helps me get ready, with a sheet over my middle, nothing showing, but I'm so hot. She reminds me of the Parma violet woman – I wonder if it's the same one with new hair – but she was upstairs, it can't be her, I need to keep a grip, they're so nice in here but this place is getting me so mixed up.

Alex

Alex is in the family lounge, waiting. She can't sit still, the black plastic chair squeaking beneath her: Paul is visiting with Izzy. Her daughter is poorly: it is spinning in her head. She has never spent a night away from her before this.

The slight change in light makes her jump. Niki shows Paul into the room, both of them laughing. He comes towards her, arms wide: *darling, it's so good to see you!* Alex stands up; looks behind him. Where's Isabella? He laughs: mock offended. *Well, that's nice, isn't it?!* He puts his arms round her: *come here, you! We've missed you!* He stands back to look at her.

Alex is frantic. What's happened to Izzy? Is she in hospital? Paul replies, under his breath, *Alex – she's confused. I don't want her upsetting any more. She's not sick. I'll bring her next time – they say you'll be improving by then.* Paul stays standing when Alex sits down. White light burning in her eyes. She wants to strike him hard. She bites her nails. He looks at her disapprovingly then launches into *where's my boy then?* diving into the basket and murmuring over his baby. *My little George – oh my days – look how big you've got already!*

Niki glances at Alex, then goes out to give the couple some privacy. Paul picks the sleeping baby up and sways him, humming. Alex looks at him. Where's Isabella really, Paul? He stops swaying. *You don't need to worry – we're doing perfectly fine without you.* But you said you'd bring her – where is she? She was so hot – I think she's really poorly, Paul. She needs a doctor. Please.

Look, Alex, I've just booked her in for an extra day at nursery – it's no big deal. She's been unsettled and it's better that we keep her routine.

But surely she shouldn't be in nursery if she's got a fever.

Paul shakes his head at her.

I'm serious – I think she needs to see a professional – you need to act quickly with infections – she might need antibiotics.

Alex, you're like a demented rabbit. He stands above her in the chair, the baby still sleeping in his arms. *You need to focus on getting better like they say. Isabella's fine.* Alex looks at the carpet. He laughs. *I always said you'd end up in the nuthouse, didn't I?!*

The blue-grey carpet goes wavy in her vision. *Look at me, Alex.* She moves her eyes to his face. *Come on, I'm only kidding.* She doesn't respond.

Alex? She looks up at him. *I know everything about this place. Don't forget, will you? I'll always be with you – even when we're not together – I'm right here.* He taps his temple. *In your head.*

The baby stirs; starts to whimper. Paul paces slowly around the room, shushing. *We're missing you. We can't wait to have you home. Keep on trying hard, won't you?* He smiles at Alex. His phone beeps in his pocket.

Are they looking after you properly anyway? Alex nods. It's fine. A couple more circuits of the room, then he returns to her, sits down and gets his phone out.

He smiles again; shows her the screen. *Some good news at last – one of the girls I've been mentoring has got employee of the month.* Alex inhales sharply at the photo. It is the skinny woman from the river with the tatty pushchair and white bread for the ducks.

She's pretty, isn't she?

Alex nods, says nothing. A pause.

He taps back to his home screen. More agitated. *I'm waiting on a call from the hospital.* Alex looks at him, surprised. What? Why? Her heart turns over.

It's Mum. Paul suddenly looks different, as if his insides are collapsing in, eyes glittering.

My God, Al, I don't know what to do. What me and Mum have been through – you're the only one who knows. I can't do all this with-out you.

What's wrong with her, Paul? Is she okay?

He stares at her. *They're doing tests. It's too soon to know.* Alex leans forward, puts out a hand.

He pulls away. *Not that you're actually bothered. You've never liked her.*

The baby starts to cry. It was never meant to be like this. Alex stands up to reach for the buzzer. Paul shakes his head, nods her back to her chair with a grim smile. *No need for that, Alex. We can handle this ourselves.*

Gytrash

The woman on the bench is bundled up: anorak, scarf, gloves. Grey hair tucked in her hat. She does not come here often, but today a carer is sitting with her husband so she can go out for a couple of hours.

She stamps her feet to keep warm; stares at the icy river. Finally out, but with nowhere to go. She fumbles for a sweet in her pocket: pulls the twist of silver; drops the sweet. She grinds it under her ugly shoe; pulls the scarf closer around her dough-soft face, trying to seal out the chill.

The trees are stripped bare; the ground hard. Desolate. She is about to stand, continue her walk, when she senses movement on the opposite bank.

She freezes, heart beating thick. It was foolish coming here: the woods are too lonely. She has read, in the papers, what they do to old women.

A shadow pushes its way out of the undergrowth, huge and ragged. It is a kind of dog. But with the strangest red eyes. The woman stays still, knees pressing tight. There is no point running.

As the creature stares into the woman, she sees herself judging: the way women dress, their children, the tidiness of their houses

disapproving; their manners, their tears, and she goes to jelly, trembling jowls, whimpering; her own husband on the doorstep, ghost-faced, sick in the light; lost without her; women she'd like to see, to be, has been; young girl dancing, narrow-waisted flare skirts, huge pram, keeping house, getting tea on the table for when the husband gets home

and she stands up straight, resolute, and faces the creature, determined to open her heart.

Nancy

I'm on the bed, feet together, knees apart, draped with a sheet, nude from the waist, being looked at again at the clinic. There's two of them down there: the same doctor and nurse as last week. I'd forgotten their names but they seemed pleased to see me when I came in, like I was some sort of old friend. *Hello again, Nancy, it's lovely to see you – we're Jackie and Wendy from last week.* A nice change from the ward upstairs.

Wendy's chatting away down there by my legs as if we're having afternoon tea in this antiseptic place. The doctor's trying to be gentle, but the metal feels sharp inside. *Relax your hands now, Nancy,* Jackie says, *give me a nice breath in, and then out.* Wendy meets my eyes as she chats on, passing the doctor a metal instrument.

Pip's in the waiting room. He wants me to have everything – as soon as I can. They're getting a sample today – a bit of tissue or something – to send off. They say to see if the cells are typical. I clench, and Wendy soothes, *it's okay, Nancy, nearly there, keep those hands soft, relax your knees down towards the bed.*

I look away, at the wall, and take a deep breath of disinfectant. I miss a lot of what they're saying but I do know that they're looking for typical. Standard carrots and strawberries – and those that stand out – the funny ones, with legs, or noses, or bumps in funny places, the carrots no one wants, on special offer, even though they go just as nicely in a stew – the strawberries even sweeter, diced, tossed with sugar, piled in a cut-glass bowl with meringue and carnation cream. I flinch: I'm too old for this.

Wendy pats my hand. *You're doing ever so well, Nancy – we know it's not very comfy.*

When they're done, Wendy tells me I can sit up and asks if I want a hand to get dressed. I feel a bit faint and say yes please. *You might have a bit more bleeding than before – but we'll give you some pads – just keep an eye on it and let someone upstairs know if it's soaking through.*

The doctor takes her gloves off; tells me I've done ever so well, and goes out, while Wendy helps me up. When I'm dressed she gives me a tissue to wipe my eyes. She says *come and sit down here, love, and have some water while you come round a bit.* I sip from the blue plastic beaker, trying to pull myself together. Sorry, I tell her, it's not like me to make a fuss, I'm not sure what's up with me.

She says it's no fuss at all, it's very normal, and drags another chair over to sit beside me. My thighs spill over as usual, everything designed for thinner people.

You know, whatever the tests come back with, Nancy, you have a lot of choices – you don't have to do anything you don't want to. I nod at Wendy. Yes. Thank you.

She pauses and lets me sit in peace. It's nice of her to give me some time, then I realise I'm keeping her – say I'll let you get on – you must be very busy. She says *no rush* and leans in with an elbow nudge and cheeky smile, *between you and me, it's nice to get a sit-down for once,* so I keep looking into my plastic cup, the water turquoise as a swimming pool.

I'm not sure how long we sit, but she makes me jump when she speaks again. *Nancy, I'm here to help you say what's best for you.* Her voice ever so kind. I look up from the blue water.

You know, she says, *it's okay if what you want is different to what your family wants.* I can't speak, the tears coming on again. She hands me a tissue. *A lot of ladies feel like they're letting someone down – we're programmed like that, aren't we?! But in the end, all that matters is what you want.*

Alex

Niki knocks on Alex's door – *just to let you know that Paul's arrived!* Bang on time, but a day later than expected. He phoned yesterday to let them know he wouldn't be coming, but never said why.

I have this for you too. Niki puts the parcel on Alex's bed: her friend Reema's name and address on the back.

Niki walks Alex to the communal lounge with the baby. Alex is sick to see her daughter, but knows in her heart that Paul will not bring her. He is sitting there already, chatting with the receptionist who escorted him in. He jumps up when they walk in. *Hello, darling! You're looking better!*

Alex knows this is not true. Niki parks the bassinet and says merrily, *will you look at those windows?! We can't leave them like that.* She pops out to fetch spray and cloth. Alex has been here seventeen days. The baby wakes and starts crying when Paul picks him up. He glares at Alex. *Look – he doesn't know me. Doesn't know his own father.* The receptionist stays until Niki skips back in with her cleaning kit. Paul frowns at her: it is obvious she is not wanted.

Niki squirts the windows liberally as Paul marches around the room, baby on his shoulder, rubbing his back: wailing louder every lap. Alex is pale in the chair, tiny stars of sweat on her face. Eventually she murmurs, I think he's hungry. Paul snaps back – *rubbish, he just needs to get to know me.* Still pacing the room. Alex asks about Isabella, about his mum, but it is impossible to talk above the crying.

Niki puts her cloth down and looks over. *Do you want to try feeding, Alex?*

Alex shakes her head so Niki goes off and comes back with a bottle. Paul takes it from her, fuming, and sits down with the baby while Niki goes back to vigorously buffing her windows.

Lauren

Look, Lauren, we're going round in circles. Why would I have told my mum about you if I wasn't serious? Paul pulls over onto the double yellows in the bus lane, and stops the car to look at me. I didn't realise he'd told his mum about us. I know how much she means to him.

He leans over to take my hand. *That girl Pam's talking about was nothing – it was a one-night stand – years ago – a cry for help. I was desperate – you know how it's been.* I want him to kiss me, for everything to be normal, to get to nursery so I don't get charged for their tea.

We've been driving round since I finished work. He passes me his wallet. *Can you get a couple of tenners out please?* I get them out and pass them to him. Here.

No. He laughs. *I meant for you – to treat yourself.* I shake my head. As I push the notes back, I spot a driving licence with a woman's photo. I stare. It's a spit of that stuck-up woman from the river, that time we were feeding the ducks. Surely not.

I pull it out to have a closer look. Alex Sutherland. He looks over, to see why I've gone quiet. *Come on, Lauren – put that away, it won't do you any good.* I say who is it? He laughs. *Who do you think? I'm not in the habit of collecting driving licences from random people, you know.* I look at him, waiting.

He sighs. *It's my wife's – I said I'd get it renewed for her at the post office – come on, put it back now.*

I close his wallet, pass it back, then look at my phone. It's on silent to stop that fucking loan company interrupting me every five minutes, but I have to keep checking in case the nursery needs me. I can't think, my brain a mess. At the river, that woman. That's his wife.

I put my phone away, undo my seat belt and tell him I can't do this – I'm not going to be his bit on the side – I have to think of the boys. I reach for the door handle. A taxi blares its horn at us. Paul gives it two fingers and turns the engine back on.

Lauren, come on, what're you doing? This is different – this is real. My mum wants to meet you – says you sound lovely. We deserve a fresh start. Get your seat belt back on.

I look at him, not moving.

Please – we'll sort out a date to see Mum in her new place this week – it's been tricky finding time with work and the baby and Isabella.

I pull my seat belt over. Click it in. Are you sure your mum wants to see me? *Honestly, Lauren – she's dying to meet you – she wants me to move on as much as I do.*

He kisses me deeply when he drops me off at nursery, holding as I pull away. I still don't know, but he worships his mum – surely he wouldn't let me see her if he wasn't serious. I don't know what to think any more. I check my bank as I go down the slope to the door – Jamie's put money in, like he said. Not loads, but more than I thought. A boulder lifts from my chest.

I press the buzzer. Maybe everything'll work out after all. I mean, we're not asking the earth – I only want my kids to have something decent, and he wants that for me. He's been through the wringer these last few weeks – and he's so good with the boys. And I'm going to meet his mum. And that woman on the river – she was a bit of a state. This is no fling – it's different. Pam just doesn't understand how complicated it all is.

The boys race out of nursery at me, *Mummy Mummy!* I swing them up, one at a time, into a massive squeeze, and they hug me back hard, passing on all the small hurts of the day – *someone took the toy, someone pushed me* – and somehow I can take it – come here, you two, I love you I love you – your dad's sent us some money at last – let's get out of here – we'll stop at Asda on the way home to get hot dogs and chips and ice cream.

Alex

Alex is frantic in her room: Paul is supposed to be here; has not phoned to cancel. Niki leaves him a voicemail. What if there has been a crash, Izzy in the back. Or she is in Children's Hospital with an infection.

Paul returns the call late afternoon: so sorry, important test results tomorrow, excuses excuses. Alex knows it is revenge for the baby wailing on his shoulder.

Niki says she will pass on the message to Alex; discusses a Skype call. *Your daughter needs to stay in touch with her mummy. Alex is really missing her. Isabella can see her little brother too – it'll do everyone good.*

Paul agrees to meet online at 5 p.m., after nursery pickup. Niki promises Alex she will sort the tech. *I can see you're worried. Would it help to talk?* Alex wants to say something but is underwater again. They sit for a while in silence. *Don't worry. There's no rush.*

Niki logs them on ten minutes early. They shift around in front of the webcam, to get Alex and the baby fully in the frame. Niki has put him in a rainbow sleepsuit: nice for his big sister. Alex feeds him a bottle while they wait. They have been working on breastfeeding in her room.

Niki texts Paul at ten past. *We're online – are you having trouble connecting?* No reply. Alex should have gone to pee before they sat down: she is stuck now. They phone Paul at twenty past; leave a voicemail. It is dark out. Alex does not move, bladder bursting: maybe he thought Niki said six o'clock.

Alex wants to wait out the hour. She knows Niki is busy – has important things to get on with, but Niki stays all the same. The screen splinters, flashing oddly. Maybe it is a connection problem.

Niki tries calling Paul one last time just after 6 p.m., then rubs Alex's arm and stands up. *I'll get someone from the health visiting team to check in on them. Come and get some food.* Alex stays in the chair, rocking side to side with the baby. She cannot stand up: what if Izzy comes on and thinks her mummy didn't turn up; what if he has said she doesn't love her.

Nancy

Mum, they're only saying it's not urgent so they don't scare you to death. Pip's brought me to the hospital canteen for a cup of tea before he drives me back to the new home. I'm all over the place. I haven't talked to anyone in the new place really, not unless you count the polite good mornings, like you do in old-fashioned hotels. I'll be out of there in two weeks, once they've asked their questions; done their forms.

Pip pours milk from a tiny carton into his coffee and stirs it with a wooden stick. I can't think when he's this worked up. *We can't wait until next week – it might have spread everywhere by then. I'm going to ring them again as soon as I've dropped you off.*

I woke up this morning with dreadful nerves in my stomach, like a split melon inside. Doctor Jackie told me about all the results calmly, explained everything, normal as anything. Wendy was there too, smiling and nodding.

This is never easy. But it's different to what you might have heard about some other cancers, Nancy. This is what we call a low-grade cancer – it means it evolves very slowly. It means we have time to explore all the different options – it's important to get this right for you.

Pip must have been in some kind of shock. He went silent and gripped my hand while she talked about different ways of stabilising it – medication, some kind of tablets, check-ups. The option of surgery, but they'd have to balance the demands of it on my body with the risks of the cancer.

What's right for someone else doesn't have to be right for you.

That seemed to jar Pip into life and he started saying *you want the full operation – don't you, Mum?* I shifted in my seat, still a bit sore from the tests. Told them I think you might've got it wrong, it's probably nothing. Pip saying *we need to get it all out as soon as possible, don't we?*

We looked at the doctor. *When can you get her booked in?*

It's all a bit hazy after that. I just wanted some peace. The doctor said something like *I know it's a shock, but it's not a rapidly progressing condition. There are lots of ways we can stabilise it.*

She gave us some leaflets and talked about websites. Wendy patted my arm and said she'd give me a ring in a couple of days for a chat. *My number is on the leaflet if you need to talk, I'll be your main point of contact. We're not going to decide anything today – you both need time to let it all sink in.*

February

Alex

Niki pops her head into the kitchen and makes Alex jump. *Hiya. Your husband just called – he's visiting at lunchtime today if that's okay?* Alex stops, milk bottle suspended over her cornflakes: he was only here two days ago. And even Alex, with her cloudy head, thought it was a weird visit: he brought carnations to say sorry for missing the week before, but was strangely vacant and flat.

Alex is back in her room with the baby, doughnut pillow on her lap, shirt flapped open, veins showing, when there is a knock at her door. Alex can tell by the bright sound that it is Niki. Come in! Niki bobs in – *you look like you're doing a stellar job!* – but Alex can tell from her face that something is wrong. What is it?

Niki sits on the bed. *Alex, Paul's here already.* Alex's lungs fill with black smoke. It is not even 11 a.m. *We've asked him to wait in reception, with him being so early, but I said I'd let you know.*

Alex starts shaking. The flowers, the strange mood, turning up so early. All the warnings. She covers herself, doesn't speak; unlatches the baby, asleep at the nipple.

Niki waits; gives her time. Alex stays in the chair, stroking the baby's forehead. It is a milk stupor, not real sleep. Drunken. He will wake in a minute, raging for more. She has made a new pact with this baby: she will loan him her body, but only until he finds somewhere else.

215

Niki speaks quietly. *There's no rush.* Alex looks at her, tries to inhale clean air. Tears in her eyes. Niki folds a blanket as she speaks. *Alex. You're safe here. You can talk about anything you want – we'll support you.*

Alex puts the baby on her shoulder and rubs his back to rouse him for the other side. I need to get ready, she says, he's waiting. Niki smooths the blanket, kitten-soft. *Alex – you seem quite worried.* She puts the blanket on the bed. *Even afraid?*

You can talk to me. Alex latches the baby on to her left nipple; picks up a muslin to cover herself. There's no time. I don't know what to do. Benji has to finish his feed and needs changing and look at the state of me – can you help us – help me get ready – I can't manage.

Niki tells her *of course I'll help, it's okay, there's plenty of time. Your husband changed the plan, so he won't be surprised if there's a little wait.* Alex looks at her strangely. *We can talk later instead if you like?* Okay, says Alex, yes, her voice juddering. Yes. That would be good.

Lauren

I sneak in for a shower at the gym before I pick the boys up, to use the free soap to sud up my hair. As much hot water as I want. It's quiet in the changing room, so I wind the roll of blue paper round and round my hand and shove it in my bag. It's not stealing. We'll tear it into little squares later so it doesn't block the loo.

My feet are killing me after the shop. Pam pretending like nothing happened. She gave me a bag of books for the boys like she's sorry, but I know what she's really thinking.

I sit on a cushioned bench, floor tiles warm under my bare feet. Four missed calls, not from the nursery. Another text. Final warning. *If we do not hear from you in the next 48 hours your details will be passed to a debt collection agency.*

Twenty-four-hour news on silent on the wall. I can't pay – there's nothing left. My January wage went before I even got it – electric, food, shoes for Dan. Bus fares, a bit of the nursery

bill. I've told them there's a hold-up with my childcare vouchers – I don't know what I'm going to do. My universal credit's
gone AWOL.

I delete all the texts, get my socks out of my boots and pull
them on. I could stop all day in here – so warm – I could fall
asleep and never come out.

I look in my purse – enough to get a bag of chips for the boys
after nursery. A treat – hot in our bellies, no nagging about veg.
I zip up my old shiny jacket and walk out of the lobby, into the
icy wind.

Alex

Alex drops two slices of white bread in the toaster. Another
mum does the same at the second toaster: most of them eat it
dripping yellow with butter; as much as they like, unlimited.

The other mother is Jade: often in the kitchen with her baby,
Sam. He is in the high-chair sucking on a rice cake. Cute. Jade
has a thick dark fringe, hollow cheeks and black-lined eyes:
beautiful chic, like rock and roll.

Jade has been here longer than anyone. Alex has never talked
to her properly, but she has picked up the scraps of Jade's story:
postpartum psychosis, spitting snails, coughing up grit.

Niki comes in and smiles at them both, *evening, ladies!* It is
5 p.m., still light: snowdrop hope. Surely time for Niki to be
heading home.

*Alex, Freya's offered to bath Benji for you, so we can have a look at
your notes if that's okay?*

Alex says that's fine, glancing up from her buttering. Jade stands
by her toaster, pretending not to listen. Niki beams *fab – see you
in ten then*, and bounces out. Jade looks over and shakes her head.
I don't know where she gets her energy from, that one. Pushes her toast
back down; likes it well done.

Alex smiles, polite, and awkwardly carries her plate and baby
away to her room. In exactly ten minutes, Freya appears to take
Benji for his bath, followed by Niki with two mugs of camomile

tea, and Alex's file tucked under her arm. She has come to talk. *How are you doing, Alex?* Alex says okay. A bit of a weird day. But okay.

Niki asks more questions; Alex's file closed on the drawers. She asks if Alex would like any other visitors – reminds her that she is welcome to phone friends, call her parents as much as she likes. Alex starts talking about Paul: he visited today to tell her about his mother; her diagnosis. Cancer. No wonder he's been acting strangely, under so much pressure.

He was devastated, crying. I've never seen him like that. Even when she had her accident and went in the home. This is another level for him.

It all pours out. It's why he couldn't come last week – I get it now. Him and his mother, they've always been close. It wasn't good with his dad – they've only ever really had each other. He wouldn't want you to know. Alex lowers her voice. But it's come as an awful shock. He thinks he's going to lose us both. It's so hard for him, managing everything alone. He didn't want to burden me, but he's always needed me, right there by his side.

Niki listens carefully, sipping the hot yellow tea. *It sounds tough. And how do you feel about it all, Alex?*

Alex looks at her, guilty. She has never got on with his mother, but she can't bear to think of her like this. She should have gone to see her in the home, even though it was Nancy who'd given strict instructions for her to stay away. Told her straight. *If you wanted to see me, you wouldn't have put me here in the first place.* But Alex feels terrible now, wishes she could make amends.

Niki suggests Alex writes a letter but it feels impossible: she is so exhausted she can barely even read a page of a magazine.

Take your time, Alex – you're not well either, remember. We can come back to this together if you like?

Alex says yes, and drains her camomile tea. It tastes like spring hay. She is ready for bed. Niki nods. *Just before I leave you to it, I want to ask how you're doing.*

Alex is confused – they have just talked about this. Like I said, it's all a bit of a shock. Niki nods, but presses gently. *I mean you personally, Alex – in yourself? You seemed really anxious this morning? I mean, before you heard about Paul's mother?*

Alex stumbles. Yes. I think I was getting mixed up. It's the stress making everything tricky, but it's fine now – I just need to get better so I can be more useful. Paul's having to deal with all this, and I'm just sitting here like a lump of lard.

Alex stands up; she has said enough. Niki stands too, touches Alex's arm gently. *Before you go, Alex, I need to ask. Have you ever felt Izzy's in any danger at home? From your husband I mean?* Alex steps back, says no, angrily. Paul's a good dad – he always has been. He'd never let anyone hurt our daughter. Niki nods, *okay, thank you. I'm sorry to have asked – but we have to, you know, as part of our jobs,* then she lets Alex go to her room and finally heads home herself.

Alex lies on the bed with her eyes closed until Freya comes in with a freshly washed baby. *Some of the others are in the TV room, love – why don't you go join them? I'll walk you down if you want?*

Alex usually says no, but for some reason lets herself be led down the corridor. It's women-only: no visitors. They go in together: Jade is there again, on the sofa with baby Sam, watching the soap that never stops. Jade looks up, *alright?* nothing more. Alex picks a chair, positions Benji on a cushion on her lap, and starts feeding.

The girl on screen tips a bottle for her baby in the cafe. Her boyfriend's mother leans in to adjust it: the helpful grandma. The boyfriend breezes in from the garage, overalls oily: kisses the girl on her hair. Alex smells grease and jasmine. Jade in her peripheral vision, always moving, twinkling like a spider.

The boyfriend's mother takes the baby for burping, cloth over her shoulder: she's an expert.

He's fit. Jade's words surprise Alex: she wasn't expecting any chat. Alex smiles back, agreeing quietly. She's not used to thinking like that any more.

She'd do my head in though. Jade nods at the boyfriend's mum: the soap mother-in-law. Alex laughs, knowing. Not daring to speak it out loud.

They go back to watching the doting boyfriend and granny. Lonely girl in the middle. The grandma pushes the pram out of the cafe; tells the girl she always left her babies outside in the snow. *Babies need plenty of fresh air, you know.*

Alex catches Jade's eye and sniggers. Jade's face cracks into a snort, and suddenly both women are laughing, tears in their eyes, laughing so much they are crying so much, babies asleep on laps of hysterical women, so far from the world, in the world, these crazy heartbroken women, laughing wild at what they know to be true.

Nancy

Look at them, I tell Gladys without lowering my voice: the lot of them have dementia. Gladys looks around, upright and impeccable, as always. Her son drove her over when they heard I was out of hospital. He's so good to her: like a chauffeur. All except her anyway, I say, nodding at the woman in the corner. I whisper. Old Annie. Forty a day and a blue rinse to keep the yellow out of her hair. Gladys grins. Annie's like a chimney, but she's alright: I give her my biscuits now I've lost my appetite.

Anyway, I say, voice back to normal. I'll not be here long. I glance at Gladys's son. He's next to her, relaxed as anything. He doesn't look like a solicitor.

I mean, the social workers are doing my assessment next week, and then I'm off home. I laugh. I'm looking on this as a little bonus holiday.

The son smiles grimly, says if I ever need any help with my affairs, he's always happy to help friends of his mother, without charge of course, not looking at the worn carpets or thickly glossed woodchip, but Gladys laughs along with me. She's completely out of place here: so neat and proper with her tartan skirt, like the Queen on her throne in a backstreet B&B.

The son asks if supported living is a possibility. *We were looking at that for you for a while, weren't we, Mum? If your mobility was better.*

Gladys nods, smiles and touches his hand. They are so warm with each other. I thought solicitors wore suits. I say I'm not sure.

Gladys asks him to leave us to it for a bit. He says, *yeah fine – I'll go for a stroll and be back in half an hour or so, if that's alright?* As he heads out, a girl arrives with a tray of mugs, tea bags stewing, milk already in. No teapots or little jugs in this place.

Gladys leans in to ask quietly how I'm really doing. Overheard the staff in the old home talking about a diagnosis. I say I don't know. I'm sick of moving around. I'm tired. They say I can have an operation to sort things out. But I'd rather hear what's been going off in Bev's place since I left.

Gladys opens her bag. *We've missed you.* More lavender pouches. *Joyce sent these.* A decorated cardboard lamb. *And this is from Patricia.* Gladys smiles. *They've got us on the spring crafts early this year! We were only doing snowmen last week!*

I press her tea bag against the side of the mug apologetically, embarrassed to be offering her this excuse for tea.

· *Bev's off on sick – the deputy's standing in.*

Kerry. I liked her. *Bev's off with stress apparently.*

I drop the tea bag on the tray and look at Gladys. The tea bag is hard and distorted, like compacted mud. *To be honest, I don't think she'll be back. They've new security on some of the doors, but apart from that, everything's much of a muchness.*

I tut and shake my head. Gladys takes the mug from the tray politely. *Oh, you won't have heard about old Norman though, will you? I look at her blankly. You know Norman – the spilt-soup fellow?*

I remember. The grumpy old bugger who was vile to the chair-aerobics girl.

He passed last week, God rest his soul. Gladys has always been a churchgoer, but there's a glint in her eye.

I offer the plate of Rich Teas. Good riddance.

Gladys takes a biscuit and balances it on her knee.

Did they get another bird?

Gladys shakes her head. *They put the empty cage out on the car-park skip after you left. It sat there a week or so – such an eyesore – big heap of broken chairs, stained carpet, frayed Christmas trees, you name it – I couldn't see a thing from my chair. Thankfully a lorry came in the end and took the lot.*

I let out a sigh of relief. Gladys asks did I say something about an operation? *What does it involve? When can you have it?* I blow on my tea. There's so much to remember: I'm not completely sure. I'm too old for all this. Gladys nods. She's never surprised.

We sit in silence for a bit. The whole thing has pulled the rug out from under my feet. My main priority is to get back to my flat. But I'll be as much use as a chocolate kettle if I go for this surgery malarkey. I'm sure they said there won't be anything like the chemotherapy, but I couldn't take it all in. I don't know now. They don't seem in any mad rush.

I take a sip of the treacle tea. I've a hard enough job convincing everyone I'm fit to go back to the flat as it is, without all this.

I can't win. Gladys nibbles her dry biscuit, lets me be. Everyone assumes I'll say yes to it all. They're giving me tablets. But the nurse keeps saying I can choose. Pip's in pieces – can't bear it, and I'm still wondering if they've made a mistake. But what if I get too poorly to manage on my own.

Gladys's son comes back in. Gladys kisses her fingertips then presses them on the back of my hand. Her hands always so cold and white, like snowy doves. Time to go. He helps her up. Before they leave, she murmurs *you know best, Nancy, don't you forget. We'll be back soon, don't worry, whatever happens, we'll be back.*

Alex

Alex is at the computer with Niki watching another two-minute clip. Her hands are soft from the baby massage oil; Benji sound asleep on her chest now, hot cheek to skin.

On the computer screen: two women and a baby in the play-room. The same lemon paint, pastel zoo animals, butterflies. Niki goes off-camera, leaving Alex on foamy mats with the baby. They always watch the recordings through once without stopping. Second time round, Niki pauses at 39 seconds.

Tell me what you see, Alex.

Alex leans in.

Take your time.

It looks like her. Alex speaks slowly. I think I see me. And a baby. *Okay. And can you describe what you're doing there, Alex?*

I am stroking the baby's forehead.

And do you remember doing that this morning? Alex looks at Niki and hesitates. Yes. Yes I do. Niki smiles.

Anything else? Alex looks down at Benji's hair. Yes. I can see that the woman is his mother. Alex's stomach cramps. I'm sorry. I need the toilet.

She passes the baby to Niki. When she returns, the woman and baby are still frozen on the computer. *Alex, you're doing really well.* Pointing at the screen. *Look at how you're touching him, so tenderly – can you see what an amazing mummy you are there?* Alex shakes her head. It is his baby, not hers.

Alex says no. She can't. Niki gentle, hand on her shoulder. *What is it, Alex?* Alex shakes her head again, folds her arms across herself, a hand on each shoulder. And then the pathetic tears flow, hot, making Alex's nose run as always, a disgrace. It would only be more to lose.

Lauren

It is hot in the church hall, my cheeks burning up. I don't look at the others. A woman in a sparkly jumper shows me what I can pick from the different sections. She's given me matching carrier bags – so no one outside will know.

Except they're Co-op bags, and everyone knows I'd never show my face in there – not since the arrest. What if he sees, what if he sees.

I pick up pasta, beans and tinned peaches. My throat blocked. The boys will love them. A packet of Bourbons. I always said I'd never stoop this low. Going begging. Bread, soup, sauce.

The radiators down the edge boxed in, in cages. It smells of dust and old wood. Shreddies, tinned sweetcorn, juice. The woman asks about allergies. Dietary requirements. I say nothing, heart hard in my chest.

I don't stay for a hot cup of tea. Thank you. No thank you. So fucking rude. I pull my hood up before I rush out, head down, plastic carriers cutting into my hands.

Alex

The baby wakes Alex again at 5.30 a.m. She props herself up in bed; provides milk, thin light seeping under the door. She can't stop thinking about Paul's mother.

She glances at the Neal's Yard creams on her bedside table: gleaming blue glass. She only opened them yesterday. Reema's parcel came a month ago, with a sunshine Get Well Soon card, in the dread, when she couldn't move properly. Alex has not seen her since summer.

Niki keeps asking if there is anyone other than her parents that she'd like to ring. They are happy to see her looking brighter on their regular calls, but Niki says that reaching out to more people is an important step for planning her return home. Alex is relieved her parents did not cut their big trip short: hopes to be out for April when they fly back.

Niki is on the early shift today. Alex takes her time with the feeding, ties her dressing gown tight, and carries the baby to the office. Niki is there already, through the window, writing notes, sparking energy.

She looks up and waves when she sees Alex; comes to the door. *You're an early bird, Alex!* Alex smiles back. Can I talk to you, Niki?

Of course, come on, let's find a room. Niki thinks she knows what this is about. There are two square-cushioned chairs, and a box of tissues on a low table. She fills translucent blue cups from the cooler, clicky, glad to see Alex: talking always helps. She slides cushions under Alex's elbows to take the strain, then sits down at an angle, legs and arms uncrossed, deliberately open, encouraging.

Alex asks if Niki can get in touch with Reema and sort out a phone call? Things are going round in her head. Paul's mother, her daughter, what happens next. Niki nods *of course — that's brilliant you'd like to connect up with your friend.*

Alex keeps talking, releasing her worries. She is getting better at this. Niki listens carefully; asks questions. Suggests again she writes a letter to Paul's mother, even if she doesn't send it. *I'll pop some paper and pens in your room in case you ever feel like it. Sometimes it helps to write things down.*

It begins to get light outside. *Alex, it seems to stir up some very strong feelings when we talk about going home?* Alex agrees: she is desperate to see her daughter. But Niki's questions about her husband roll off her like water on oiled feathers.

Alex changes the subject. I remembered something weird in the night, she says, from when I was little. Niki nods, go on.

Have you ever seen a creature around here? In the grounds. She hesitates. Maybe connected to the river?

Niki looks at Alex holding her baby close. She is more natural with him now: a stranger would assume he was hers. But Niki knows they still have some way to go. *What sort of creature?*

Alex's thoughts are jumbled: it's hard to say — a bit of a blur — like a dog, but not — like black smog and fur. Like something bad. She speaks quickly. I'm worried it's come back — that it's connected to my daughter — she's not safe. I've been thinking it for a while to be honest. What if it's a bad omen? I've got to get home. Alex is talking quickly now, sweating.

The look on Niki's face is peculiar. Alex sees she is taking her seriously, but regrets saying out loud about the dog: it sounds madness. Just when everyone thought she was getting better.

Alex, take some deep breaths now. You're okay. Hand on her knee, gentle; giving time. *Alex, this is a safe place — your room is secure. And you've met Debs, our security, haven't you?* Niki smiles. *No one's getting past her.*

Alex can see that Niki wants to believe her.

225

I can hear that you're very afraid, Alex.

Alex is shaking; passes Niki the baby. *Are you scared of someone, Alex?* Niki cradles the baby, still sleep. *Of someone hurting you? Or your daughter? We can help you.*

Alex stands up. No. No – it's nothing like that. It's the river. It's nothing anyway. I'm just overtired.

Niki says *sit back down. Come on – I'm glad you've come to me. I don't live near the river, so probably wouldn't see the same things as you. We can talk to Dr Menston about it together – she'll want to help. You're bound to feel anxious about the future – there's so much going on right now.*

Alex reaches down for the baby. Niki gently hands him up. *You don't have to go yet.* I do, Alex says, I need to get back to my room before his next feed.

Nancy

One of the home staff comes to find me in the lounge with the phone. Old Annie watches from her corner. I don't get many calls.

It's Wendy, the specialist nurse from the clinic. Ringing for a chat. Says last time we spoke I'd agreed with my son that I'd do anything possible to get the hysterectomy. That he's been in touch since, pressing for a date.

There are lots of things to weigh up though, Nancy. I want you to know it's not the only option. Do you have time for a quick chat now? The voices from outside are suddenly louder, out-of-tune cacophony, like punk shouting. My stomach twists: I can hardly hear her.

The girl who brought the phone asks if I'd like to take it to my room to have a bit of privacy? I say yes please: it will hope-fully be quieter there.

Wendy waits until I'm settled. Asks how the bleeding is.

I say fine.

And how are you feeling in yourself, Nancy?

I don't know really. Fine, I think.

She tries to explain some things. *The surgery is definitely an option but there are lots of things to think about first. The recovery. The risks. The treatment options are different for everyone.*

A hormone treatment I could try. To stabilise the cancer. It is a low-grade, slow-growing cancer – this could work very well. Tablets. A special coil. Regular check-ups.

I've never been very good on the phone.

I know it's a lot to take in, Nancy. We have time to explore all the options. Why don't we get you back to the clinic for a proper chat? Maybe someone from the home could drive you in?

I go out to the garden after, stand with Annie in the smoking area. I say no when she offers me a cigarette, but stay with her until she's done, all the same.

Alex

Alex carries the crying baby into the family lounge. He permanently needs milk: Niki says it's a growth spurt. She watches Alex: notices the change. Paul walks over and kisses them both. Alex sits down; unclips her bra and feeding top.

Paul looks away. He has seen this with Isabella hundreds of times, but it bothers him more with this baby. Benji, with his flailing limbs, skilfully latches on and pounds his jaws, extracting milk with mechanical precision. It is a big step.

Paul notices something different in Alex too. Her body has somehow relaxed to make a space for the baby: they slot together now, like a foamy puzzle. Paul leans back and looks at the ceiling. *Let me know when I'm needed.*

Alex tells Niki you can leave us, we're fine. Honestly, we'll buzz you if we need to – then turns to Paul. I'm so glad you're here. I miss you so much. She means it. A day without so much dread.

But when he looks sideways at her he is excluded. Her body giving the baby what he cannot; what she will not give him.

Alex talks into his silence. I made something for Isabella. She leans over but can't reach her bag with the baby. It's an embroidered square with the four of us.

Alex laughs. You probably can't tell it's us, but I wanted her to know how much I miss her – that I'll be home soon. They do all sorts of art therapy things in here. Paul looks back at the ceiling, his lip curling. *God help us.*

Alex is confused. Paul, I've been trying really hard. I thought you'd be pleased. I know it's been so tough for you, but I really am getting better now. Honestly. I'll be home to help soon. Ask Niki. Tell me about Isabella. Please. How is she? And what about your mother?

Paul turns to her and sighs. *I'm sorry, darling – it's been one of those days. It's really stressful with Mum. But Isabella's fine.* He smiles. *She'll love whatever you've made. I brought a painting she did for you actually. I'll get it from the car after. We can't wait to have you home.*

Lauren

It's taking forever to sort a date for me to meet Paul's mum. He's so busy – with work, and his daughter, and the drive to the hospital. I know he's trying his best, but we need this to work so much. I'll have to go see her myself if he can't sort it soon. I can't just sit around on my arse waiting for him – I'm not that sort of person, and anyway, he keeps saying she wants to meet me so it'll save him a job if I just pop round and say hello.

I've been finding it harder to look him straight in the eye – even when we do get to meet up. Everything's a lie – if he knew how much I owe – that I'm more of a fucking charity case than the place we work in, he'd want nothing more to do with me – I just can't let him know, I've no one else.

The debt people are on at me, day and night. Shouty messages and twenty-five missed calls a go. They've said they'll send door-step collectors round. It's too cold to stay out all day so I've got the downstairs curtains pulled when we're in. I tell the boys it's an adventure.

Mum'd go ballistic if she knew, not that she wants anything to do with me either. The kids keep asking about Nana. Even about her dickhead Neal. I say they're busy, we'll see them next week. Hopefully they'll stop asking in a bit.

If we can sort this move with Paul, we won't need them anyway. I just want to put it all behind us – dirty nappies and glass in the front yard, bailiffs, freezing fucking beds. I can't stop thinking about those women in the bags at the shop and what Pam said about other girls but I just want to go off to work in the mornings like normal people, and Paul to drop the boys and Isabella at a nice school with kids from good families, and I just want to pick them up at home time with apples and cookies so we can be warm and full and happy ever after.

March

Alex

Alex sits at the computer sobbing. Niki puts an arm around her, but it is no use: the damage is done.

Paul cancelled both visits this week after seeing her and the baby getting cosy: sent a message through Niki to say that he was needed more at home.

When they showed up on the Skype meeting this afternoon, Izzy started crying as soon as she saw her mummy. Paul got irate with her for hiding under the chair – *come out, Isabella – tell Mummy about your new nursery.* Izzy stayed crouching on the floor.

Alex said what do you mean, what new nursery? She was happy where she was, Paul, and he said *you're not even here, Alex – what would you know? She needed more hours than that old place could give – so we've moved her up to the new one by the Castle Pub. It's much better – modern and organised, and the staff have got a bit more about them, if you get me.* He laughed then, his mouth blurring pixels, opening red, ha ha, ha ha. *She loves it.*

But Paul. She was settled where she was – surely it's not a good time to move her? She loves playing outside – in the mud. Niki sat very still at the edge of the screen, watching. That wooden train, Paul – she loves that, what will she do? And what about her friends? Jack and Hari?

Alex, if you're just going to give me grief, I'm off – can't you see I've enough on my plate as it is? He looked down, under the chair. Alex tried to apologise but Izzy still wouldn't come out, and after a few minutes she said she'd let Paul go. *Isabella? I love you,* Alex said, voice cracking like a stone at a windscreen. *Can you hear me, darling? I promise I'll see you very soon.*

Nancy

Pip took me back to the clinic. I agreed with him. Told them I wanted it over and done with – I'll have the operation, put it all behind me.

It's started to sink in a bit. Cancer in the lining of my womb. Quite common but not well known. In the place where I grew Pip; lost the girl. Betrayed again by my body.

Dogs are so much stiller than people when they listen. Feathery ears and sad-eye listening. I need Ruby to help me work everything out. Where are you, little dog.

We want it all out. Womb, tubes, eggs. The tiny fingertip imprints in the walls of my flesh. All sent to sluice. They've booked me in for the end of the month.

My mind keeps wandering; thinking of Pip as a child. Call and response: goodnight, my apple pip; goodnight, my mummy. Once upon a time in your bed, lights off, sweet gingerbread breath hot on my face, small fistfuls of hair.

Billy goats butting the troll hard into the river to be washed away, never seen again. I would gobble you up, I loved you loved you.

Your dad saying you were old enough to go to sleep by yourself. You'll make him soft. Like a girl. Made me stand downstairs with the wireless on, ironing shirt after shirt, crying you to sleep, tears splashing hot cotton.

It might take more than a year to recover. It might be too much. I can climb a flight of stairs: I am healthy enough. There's four weeks until the operation – I said to Annie, I'm not sure about any of it.

231

I told her about the woman on the ward with her purplish hair and funny way of talking, wish I could remember her name.

Annie used to have a dog: a collie. But she's never going back to her council house or sheepdog. She accepts things – not like me – says it's just part of getting old.

She says I need to get on with my life. I'm starting to think she might be right. That there hasn't been a mix-up with the tests. I still have my son: and we've always been there for each other. The only thing to do is get on with it.

Alex

Niki convinces Alex not to cancel her phone call with Reema after the Skype disaster with her daughter. *It'll do you good to get another perspective, Alex – it's an important step.*

Alex uses the landline in one of the small meeting rooms. Reema's voice flatter than usual. Alex thanks her for the parcel, strangely formal: it was very thoughtful of you. I'm sorry I didn't have chance to thank you sooner. Reema says *don't be silly – you haven't been well. It's me who should be apologising – for not being there at Christmas when you were ill.*

Alex says no one could have known. She didn't even recognise the signs herself. But I'm working hard now on understanding my symptoms. On things I can do to help myself stay well when I get home. Awkward. Reema is so subdued: it sounds like she has lost her bouncy tracksuit and eyeliner. Are you there, Reema?

Reema says *yes, sorry.* Says she has bumped into Paul a couple of times with Isabella. *Everyone will be so glad to get you home, Alex.*

Alex asks about her daughter. Tries to complain about the new nursery but it sounds too feeble now: Reema nattering about him *juggling everything like a star – you mustn't worry.* Alex says it'll be good to meet in the cafe when I get back and then Reema's voice breaks.

I'm so sorry, Alex – I should have replied to your text months ago but I couldn't – I know it makes me an awful person, but I just couldn't see you so pregnant and happy. Alex tries to say it's okay but Reema carries on. *We had a miscarriage at the end of October. All I can think about is Rudi never having a little brother or sister. We're trying again but it's not quick like last time.*

Reema stops with a noise like a sob. And now Alex knows she can't say she has a baby that she doesn't love; that Paul is not always what he seems; that she doesn't want her daughter to swap nurseries. It is all pathetic. So she says she is deeply sorry for Reema's loss: I had no idea. I will pray for good news. Keep in touch, Reema, then the call dwindles away.

Jade is in the kitchen stirring a pan when Alex walks past to her room. She calls out her usual *alright?* Expects an answer. Alex says fine but Jade tells her *come in then* and nods at a chair – *pull up a pew.*

Jade gestures at the liquid in the pan with her wooden spoon – *there's too much for us, do you want some?* Alex lets the tears roll, yes please. She stands up to put Benji in one of the wooden cribs. He'll wake soon, but at least her hands will be free for a bit.

Jade's baby, Sam, is in a high-chair sucking a hunk of baguette. Jade wrestles him into a red bib with long sleeves: he looks ready to go splashing in the rain. She blows her fringe up out of her eyes. *He always gets in a right state with soup.*

Alex tries to laugh, but this makes her cry more. Jade puts a bowl of warm soup and bread in front of her. *Get that down you. Root veg. It's from a carton but it's proper healthy.* Alex dips her spoon and sips. She's never been able to make a good soup.

I'm sorry.

Jade laughs. *No need to be sorry in here – we've all seen worse. Been worse. What's up?*

Alex says she spoke to a friend on the phone – a good one – but she didn't understand. It was awful, we just couldn't connect or something – it's like I've lost her – well, lost everyone really.

Jade dips Sam's soggy bread in her soup and blows on it gently, nodding. *Yeah. I totally get it. It's not like they aren't trying – but it's hard for people out there to understand.*

Baby Sam grabs the soupy bread from his mum and smears his mouth and chin. *You've got to keep at it though.* Alex glances at the baby, waiting. Paul hates people dunking bread in soup.

Keep talking I mean. Some people do get it — you've just got to find the right ones. Alex wipes her nose and eyes, and butters her bread. She thinks of Ruth at the church baby group: she understood, without Alex saying a word. She'd told Paul the coffee was decaf, covered for Alex with the car seat. But maybe she is remembering it wrong.

Jade smiles at her. *Don't get me wrong — there's people I thought were mates out there who've totally blanked me. They're scared as much as anything — don't know what to say. But there's a couple of good ones who've got my back.*

But Ruth is the wife of Paul's best friend. Colleague. His squash buddy. Paul will find out if they talk. It is too risky.

Jade nods at the rainbow of footprints on the wall: other babies who have been in the hospital; other mums who have got well and gone home. *You'll get better, you know. Look at me — out in a couple of days, even though I've been here longer than anyone.* This sets Alex off again, salty tears on her lips.

Listen, why don't we swap numbers? We've got to stick together — I'll let you know how we get on out there! Alex nods, and smiles. Yes. Takes a breath and plunges her bread deep into the warm liquid. I'd like that. And she means it: the soup and sleeping baby and bright tiny feet all give off the faintest shimmer of hope.

Lauren

I'm in the loo when the banging starts at the front door. The boys are in their room doing Lego. I hiss at them leave it, come in here, quick. They wander in and I lock the door. Tell them shush.

We crouch on the lino and I sing ten green bottles to keep them quiet, and when we get to no more bottles I go back up to twenty and start again, and keep singing, on and on, until I'm sure the banging's stopped.

I'm shaking. The boys won't go back to their Lego, clinging to me like limpets, hanging on my legs while I sort their tea. In

234

the end, I send them in the front room to watch telly. We need to get out of here. I check Rightmove. Text a newly listed three-bed to Paul.

I peep out the gap in the curtains then put their tea on the table. Text him again. Can we come over? Can't invite him here – what if they come back. It would be the end of every-thing – if he saw me for what I really am.

He's busy tonight. Why don't we have a nice family day out tomorrow? You bring the boys, I'll bring Isabella.

I reply straight away. Yes. What time?

But I need somewhere now. I'm all alone – there's no one else. Not my mum; not my cousin, away on her cruise. I text her just in case. When are you back Han? Miss you. L x

Alex

Alex pushes the pram towards the river. These daily walks are in her care plan now: building confidence, independence. Fresh air. Preparation for home. Jade left two days ago: promised to keep in touch.

She walks the usual loop, Benji in the pram. He squawks; ramps up the volume when they pass the memorial bench. Like his sister: she always hated the pram. Alex is irritated that this thought pops into her head about this baby, as if he belongs.

She'd always wanted to carry Izzy in a sling, but Paul's mum said it would make her too clingy. He agreed. Niki suggested it for Benji, said they could try a few from the sling library. At the church toddler group, Ruth said she should borrow her rainbow wrap. Alex will ask her about it tomorrow when they speak again on the phone.

She spoke to Ruth this morning, while her squash buddy husband was at work. Niki set the call up; took care of the baby so they could chat in peace.

It was a surprise when Ruth said hello in the same voice as before: as if Alex was the same Alex. She babbled the words, warm: *it's so lovely to hear you, Alex! How are you doing?* She asked how she was healing after the birth. Said they missed her at the group. A laugh. *Actually, let you into a secret – I bunked off again last week and had to go to the river all by myself!* Alex laughed with Ruth.

She could see her, in her home, beautiful and cross-legged on the sunlit polished floorboards, barefoot, surrounded by books, silk scarf in her hair, breastfeeding her toddler.

She spoke to Alex like she was at home too. Phoning about a play date or something normal. Called her daughter Izzy. Said *why don't we chat again tomorrow afternoon? There's too much to catch up on for one little call. When my husband's out again – that way we won't get disturbed.*

Alex sits on the bench and gathers Benji up, out of the pram to feed. He is bulky in his snowsuit; awkward to manoeuvre. The crocuses sprouting around her are weedy and pale: as if forced to grow under stone.

Alex calls hi to Niki when she gets back to the unit, face flushed cold, then heads off to change the baby. Niki knocks on her door after a while: *how are things?*

Alex has propped herself on the bed, Benji on a pillow on her lap. She smiles fine, telling the truth. She has colour in her cheeks. The baby has a clean nappy and a tummy full of milk. The dread is lifting, a bit each day. Niki says it's brilliant to see her doing so well. Says Paul rang to say he's visiting at 2 p.m. Alex's mouth distorts.

That's in half an hour. Niki pulls a chair across and sits down. *Alex. You're safe here. We'll support you.* Alex shakes her head, looking down at Benji, hand on his warm stomach.

Niki changes the subject. Speaks lightly. *Alex, why does your husband call the baby George?* Alex rubs gentle, clockwise circles on the Babygro.

That's his name. Niki waits, but nothing comes. *But you call him Benji?*

Alex nods. But he's really George Benjamin – after Paul's dad. Paul wanted to do it right. First son. Tradition and all that. It's his baby anyway. Benji's just my name – silly really.

You don't have to see him, Alex.

Alex looks up at Niki. Her hand stops rubbing, the tiniest quiver, almost invisible. Butterfly fingers.

I have to.

Well – why don't I just pop Benji down to the visiting lounge to see Dad – and let him know you're not feeling up to it today? No drama.

Alex's hand goes back to the circles. No reply.

Alex, just look at him – you're doing such a brilliant job.

Niki pauses again. *There's no access to this corridor for visitors.*

He will kill her. Alex looks up, then passes Benji awkwardly to Niki, two-handed, struggling with his head, saying you're right, I'm actually not feeling that well – I could do with a lie-down. Send Paul my love – tell him I'll see him next time.

Niki nods, lowers Benji into the pram, still sleeping, and props the door open. Alex follows her to the doorway. Niki?

Niki turns, waiting, but Alex says nothing.

Niki comes back and rubs her arm. *Listen, I'll be back with Benji before you know it. He's not going anywhere.* Alex nods okay and goes over to the desk in the window. A pile of nappies, a muslin cloth, pen and paper, pushed to the side.

You take advantage and get some rest. I'll get someone to check in on you. Alex thanks her, and sits down at the desk. She listens to the tack of rubber wheels down the corridor, then picks up pen and paper and begins to write.

Lauren

I'm washing up after tea when I hear stamping upstairs, then silence. The boys are in the lounge in front of the TV, there's no one up there. I'm being paranoid now. I trudge up the stairs, breathlessness pounding blood shushing over the noise of cartoons. I call down – stay there, boys, I'll just be in the loo, the banister creaking as I lean into it.

Then the stomping goes again, like crazy stamping dancing. It's coming from the bedroom. Someone's fucking hammering the floor with clogs. I look up – the landing is dark but there's nothing there. I'm proper losing it this time.

At the top I dive for the light switch. There. I knew it was nothing. It must have been the pipes clanging or some shit – the whole place needs modernising. I can't wait to get out, but everything's gone quiet now, it's fine.

I'm about to go back down when I see something moving in the dark bedroom, blackness moving, stench of wet dog. A kind of flapping. Then the stamping feet start again, nearly going through the goddamn floorboards.

Hello? My voice echoes. The noise stops, and everything goes still, and then I know it's all in my head, but then there's a swoosh at my face, open mouth coming at me across the landing, scream spewing, stink of burnt hair, cave-black eyes passing through my face, and then back again, back into the bedroom with a shriek.

I rush across to the bedroom light and then I see her, lit up on the bed, the woman in the black cashmere jumper from the shop slumped there, head hanging down, all the dance and flap gone out of her.

I'm suddenly livid. I could tear her to shreds, invading our home like this, and now I know it's not about the shop or Pam or Dee – it's all me. I ignore the tears glistening on her craggy face, the manipulative bitch, and pick her up and smash her in the bottom of the wardrobe like she's rags, then slam the doors, and shove my hairbrush through the handles to wedge it shut until I can find a proper way to get rid of her.

Gytrash

The woman with lilac hair has nipped out of the hospital, down to the river for fresh air. She rarely gets a break: when she does, it is usually a quick tea in the canteen, or a smoke under the shelter.

She glances at the bench; wants to take the weight off her swollen ankles. Wet and splattered with bird mess. Upturned can of lager on one end.

She stares hard at the flowing water; thinks of the stories her grandmother used to tell. The gytrash comes from the river; to the river it always returns. She always wonders what she'll see out here.

But there is only the sound of the river. The woman finishes her cigarette, grinds it carefully under her toe into wet soil. She picks it up, drops it in the bin, then trudges back up the path to the ward.

Nancy

I'm sitting at the back of the dingy lounge, to get a bit of light from the garden. I fold the letter as many times as I can, and shove it in the pocket at the back of my diary. It's too thick: won't close properly now. I strap the covers tight with the special elastic. That woman's a cheek. Writing to me like that. Feeding me a pack of lies about my own son.

I can hear Annie crooning to herself in the garden, the words sailing in with the draught. For all her smoker's voice, she sings as if she's pegging out washing in the icy sun; lullabies for a babe in a pram. I pull my wool scarf closer around my neck.

I get the letter back out and smooth it on my lap, writing creased, nursery songs still shivering on the breeze.

Red stockings, blue stockings, shoes tied up with silver.

Nancy, we are not so very different, you and I. Like I don't know she forced a wedge between me and my son, turned my grand-child against me, pushed me out of my home. Abandoned her husband, took his baby. The audacity of it. We're like chalk and cheese.

A red rosette upon my breast, a gold ring on my finger.

She's never been right for him. She's only come crying now because she thinks I'm about to pop my clogs. Probably after my money. I press my knees together, freezing.

Paul hardly talks about his dad, but I know you had it tough. The barber shaved the mason. *There are so many things I wish I'd asked you. About the fifties, your mum and dad's bakery, the ivory scar on your chin. Your husband and his barber shop.*

Cut off his nose. And popped it in a basin. Speaking of my life like she knows anything.

I know we haven't always seen eye to eye. Paul told me you've been ill, in hospital, but won't tell me anything else.

The writing looks like it came out of the pen in a rush. Pat-a-cake, pat-a-cake, baker's man. Bake me a cake as fast as you can.

Nancy, I'm in hospital too. I'm getting better though. I've started to think I'm not mad after all. The women here – they believe me. They see me when I speak.

Oh my darling, oh my darling.

I don't know what you know. You have a new grandchild. He has your eyes. Paul's eyes. But this child – you will meet him – this child was not made with love.

Oh my darling Clementine.

It is not the baby's fault. Paul hates me but will not let me go. Lost and gone forever. *I'm sure there's been other women, younger girls than me.* Dreadful sorrow.

I think he might be seeing one now. I used to be jealous all the time, but now I'm just glad when he leaves me alone.

Made you look. Made you stare. Made the barber cut your hair. He cut it long. He cut it short. He cut you with a knife and fork.

I know you don't want to hear this about your son. I know he means the world to you.

See how they run. See how they run.

But I can't get away, Nancy. I have nothing. The children. The house. The money. He has me trapped.

Cut off their tails with a carving knife.

I know we haven't been close. I haven't been the daughter you've always wanted. I know you blame me for taking your son, for your move to the care home. That you miss your lovely spaniel.

Oh where, oh where has my little dog gone.

You're the only woman he respects.

Oh where, oh where can she be.

The only one he truly loves. Please ask him to let me go, Nancy. You are my only chance. With her tail cut short and her ears cut long, oh where, oh where is she.

I hope that you will find it in your heart to believe me.

I've put up with this too long. I fold the letter back up and ask one of the girls for paper and pen. It's time I gave that woman a piece of my mind.

Lauren

I sign in. Visitor for Nancy – Paul's partner. *How lovely,* the woman with the high cheekbones and glam hijab gushes at me. *She'll be made up to see you.* She takes my umbrella. I feel scruffy next to her, especially after a day sorting other people's crap. I did my best in the work toilet, but I'm soaked and know my red lipstick looks cheap.

She walks me and my shit bunch of dyed flowers up the corridor to the lounge. They were on yellow sticker – will probably be dead by tomorrow – but I didn't want to turn up empty-handed.

It's all worn-out carpets and ugly ornaments of kittens and bunnies. Grim. I hope I never end up somewhere like this. I clocked off early to come see her – me and Paul still haven't been able to sort a date that works for us all, but he keeps saying she's dying to meet me so I just thought I'd take my chance and pop in. All that women's stuff she's been dealing with at the hospital – it might help to talk to another woman.

I pause in the doorway – don't know which of the four women is Paul's mum. Luckily the glamorous woman comes to my rescue, singing *Nancy – look – you've a visitor!* The large woman in the corner looks up blankly. She's nothing like Paul said – she looks sour and floppy and vacant – nothing cosy about her. I'd been expecting the perfect granny – floury apron and rosy cheeks – with everything Paul's said.

The glamorous woman points to the chair next to Nancy and asks if we'd like a drink. The telly's blaring on the wall – one of them home-improvement programmes. I'd love a tea, thanks, I tell her, nearly having to shout. Nancy keeps staring at me as the woman goes out. *Are you from the social?*

I tell her no, I'm Paul's new partner. She stares at me, frowning. He said he told you about me? She clearly she has no idea who I am. Oh my God. I can hardly breathe – maybe it's a massive mistake coming here. She's been through a lot though, she's bound to be confused.

Paul said you'd like to meet me. She looks above my head, nose in the air. *I don't know who you are, but I don't recall saying any such thing.* I offer the flowers. She looks at them. Then her face changes and she reaches for them.

Do you mean partner as in work? I tell her yeah, we've worked together – relieved that she seems to be getting it – but we're trying to keep that separate to our relationship, you know – it's all a bit sensitive still. I'm like his girlfriend, see, but it's a lot more serious than that.

She sits forward, putting the flowers on the side table, doughy face looming closer.

He thinks the world of you, I tell her. She stares at me. *I'm not sure who you think you are?* she says.

I stutter about maybe there's been a mix-up – Paul said you'd like to meet me as we're serious together now, the flowers between us on the table.

She spits her words – *coming here, telling me all this –* the last thing my son needs is another trimmed-up girl throwing accusations around. You're not the first, you know. I know your type.

I stand up and say I know you're not well but you can't talk to me like that – anyway it's not what you think – it's not like that, having to raise my voice even more, all the other women gazing, not bothered, like they have slanging matches in the middle of the room all the time. She mutters up at me. *You know he's married – don't you? And with kiddies?*

The woman closest starts cackling as I try to say no, it's over with his wife – it's been over a long time, we're serious about this, you know – I've kids as well, we're going to be a family – it's not some kind of dirty affair – but she spits *rubbish – that's rubbish and you know it.* I stare down at her, spilling out of her chair, my cheeks slap red.

She stares right back at me, hard as nails. *I think it's time you went, don't you? Go on — and take those as well.* She thrusts the flowers at me. *Go on. Take them and get out.*

Alex

The letter from Paul's mother is bitter as rust. Alex will tell Ruth about it on the phone this afternoon. Ruth will find something sardonic to say, make Alex laugh. They have been chatting every afternoon, while Ruth's husband is at work. She is easy to talk to, although Alex is careful not to let anything slip about the suffocating visions. She is trying so hard to be normal.

Alex takes the letter to her morning meeting with Niki. They sit on the low chairs, Benji asleep on Alex.

Niki asks *how do you feel about it?* Alex is not sure. The reply does not hurt as much as she thought. She is more at peace for trying, at least. Has said all she can say.

When Paul arrives, Alex asks Niki to take the baby to the visiting lounge without her again. Eyes shining. Niki nods; understands.

Alex knows she will pay for this. That without his mother on side, there is no hope. But there is Ruth.

Niki brings the baby back too soon. Her husband is still in reception. They have had to call security. No one messes with Debs.

Alex paces the room, throat burning. This is not like him. He is never angry in front of other people. She is shaking, doesn't know what this means. It is a different game. Niki sways, rubbing the baby's back, humming a quiet song. Another woman knocks. Takes Niki for a word outside.

Niki comes back and asks Alex to sit down. *He's gone.* The sobs bubble out of Alex's face, ugly noises: buried too long.

Niki soothes, sways the baby while she waits for calm. Murmurs that they need to make a plan. *We can work this out together.*

Alex nods. What did he say? Niki hesitates. *He was different to usual. Said he'd known this was coming – one of his colleagues told him you've been talking to his wife. Paul said he knew you were up to something.*

Alex looks up at her, chalk white.

Niki tries to sit next to Alex, but whenever she stops swaying, the baby starts squawking. Surely not Ruth. Alex trusted her.

Niki stands back up and keeps swaying. *I know it sounds alarming, Alex. But we'll find you somewhere safe when you leave here – it's going to be alright. We need to start thinking about what you need – making some lists.*

Alex shakes her head. I don't need anything like that. There's been a misunderstanding. I wasn't well today: just needed a rest. My husband's been under a lot of stress with his mum. And my daughter on top of it all.

We've always been committed to each other. My home is his home. He knows me better than anyone. I need to talk to him – let him know I'm better now. He needs me. We have made our vows.

Lauren

I dump the flowers on a bench and somehow stagger on the bus to nursery, head spinning. I left my umbrella in the care home, so get soaked to the skin in seconds. What if this whole thing is a lie. It's not just that she's forgotten that he told her about me – she was vicious.

What if she's right. What she said – the same as Pam, and Mum. All of them sounding so sure. *You're not the first, you know. Another trimmed-up girl. I've seen men like him before.* None of them want anything more to do with me. I rack my brains for someone to call. Tania would just laugh – *were you born yesterday, Lauren? What did you expect, getting yourself involved with a married man?*

But he's not really married – not in the proper sense. No one gets it. They haven't seen how he is with me. He said it's over with his wife. But what if it's not. And these other girls. I shake myself, don't have a choice – I've got to believe him, everything's riding on this – me and the boys have nothing without him and the job and the house, no one left. We've got to make it work – it's not like anyone's perfect – and surely what we've got is different to any one-night stand.

I rub my eyes hard, lean into the steamed window of the bus. I can't let a deranged old woman get in the way of our happiness – proper job, dad for the boys, getting them off the estate, into a decent school. I can't let anyone fuck this up now.

Nancy

I turn on the TV in the bedroom. It works. I'm surprised, to be honest. I haven't watched my programme since the hospital. Not much has changed by the looks of it. The girl with the baby still crying, the boy loving her all the same. A lonely noise in this room.

The girl confessing to the boy. Her father didn't fall from that bridge. But he knows that already. Has always known. He loves her anyway.

Pip came to see me just before tea with a bunch of fat orange tulips. Isabella at nursery. I asked after Alex. He shook his head. Angry. *No idea. She won't see me. She's not right in the head.* Got his phone out. *I've got these though.* He swiped through bright photos of the new baby.

My eyes blurred the sweeping colours.

She sent me a letter last week.

His head jerked up, phone still shining. *Who did?* His face jagged.

Your wife.

What do you mean, she sent you a letter? She doesn't even know where you are.

The old place forwards all my post.

He leaned towards me. *Well, where is it then? Let's see what she's got to say for herself.*

245

He stood up, flushed, hand out for the letter. When I told him no need, he moved forward too quickly, forgetting himself.

I told him sit down. Everything suddenly clear. Not made with love. Glad when he leaves me alone. Damp bricks, my cheek to dank carpet, boiling spoon to big thigh. Breathing river, retching mould. He is more like his father than you know. I've been a fool.

I told him that's enough. I've binned the letter and that's the end of it. Tulips flashing at the edge of my vision.

He talked about the weather after that. Squash. Work. Waiting for incompetent people to ring him back. Social worker. Consultant at the clinic.

Kissed me on the forehead to leave. *I need to get Isabella. I'll pick you up Friday for the hospital.* My operation. *It'll be okay, Mum, you'll see.* Worry contorting his face.

Goodbye, darling, I told him. As he walked across the room to leave, I spoke quietly from my chair. By the way. A woman came to see me before. More a girl really. Cheap-looking. Red lips, black eyes, skinny as a rake. Half your age. Said you were involved.

He turned, stunned a second time. Stuttered. *What?* I waited, in silence.

It must be that mentalist at work who's stalking me – she's obsessed. I'll get onto it, make sure it doesn't happen again.

See it doesn't, Pip, I told him. Beckoned him back to press his knuckles to my lips. My cheeks wet. Goodbye, my darling. Promise me you'll not let something like this happen again.

Alex

Niki leaves Alex with the phone; takes the baby into the corridor to wait. Alex stands by the window, lead in her belly, watching raindrops puncture puddles. The cloud thick as soot; earth sodden from days of rain. Alex dials her house number.

There is a slight snag when he answers, his voice caught on a nail: she has surprised him.

She takes her advantage. Hi, Paul, it's me. I've been so poorly – I'm really sorry I missed you again last time – I know it was such a waste of your time coming all this way. Flustered words rushing out. I'm so sorry. I think I had some sort of sick bug.

She looks at the water trickling down the glass; merging. Selects raindrops to win the race.

We miss you. I'm so much better now – do you think you could squeeze us in again this week, now I'm better?

He finds his voice. *I can't make any promises – it depends how Mum's operation goes in the morning.* His voice deadly sweet, clawing back control. *I'll do my best, but it'll be a stressful day.* He thinks someone might be listening in to the call. *I'm glad you're feeling better.* A pause. *I seriously hope you don't have another relapse.*

Alex has not convinced him. Don't forget. I am inside your head. She looks at the towering clouds: storm brewing. Cumulonimbus. King of clouds.

They say you'll be out soon – maybe even next week.

Alex looks for the usual birds: always flitting between the bushes and feeders. The seeds and nuts deserted; not a bird in sight.

We won't need anyone once you're home.

Alex used to love thunderstorms. As a child, on the lawn, barefoot: mouth wide open to the sky, rain on tongue, face, arms; twirling. Too dangerous for the beach. As a student, up north, away from her family, studying formation and features.

It's my fault – I should have known better than to leave you at the mercy of that hippy bitch Ruth when you were so defenceless.

Nothing living in sight, not even a pigeon or squirrel.

All you needed was some time with normal mothers at a proper baby group, but she had to go dragging you off to the river, putting ideas in your head.

Feet to soil, face to sky.

It's down to her that you're there now, you know that, don't you, Alex? She's done this to us.

Alex knows better than to reply.

It's lucky Chris went home early yesterday to get his squash kit and caught her on the phone. Like I said – I know everything that goes on.

Wet, wet, soaked to the skin. Ruth. Paddling feet, children in the play tent, silk scarf. Covering for Alex, every time: decaf, loose baby seat, death trap. Talking to her while her husband was out. Alex was wrong to doubt her.

She won't be hassling you once you're back anyway. I'll see to her, don't worry. It'll just be the four of us – and Mum – that's all we need.

Alex says yes, it will be so lovely. I have to go now. Fear like rocks rising in her windpipe: what if Ruth's husband is like Paul. Baby George needs feeding now – I hope your mum's operation goes well. Speak soon, Paul.

Niki peeps through the door to check Alex. Frozen at the window, looking out.

Is everything okay?

Alex spins round. I need to get a message to Ruth.

Lauren

We get back to a pile of letters after nursery. I tell the kids to go watch TV but they want to set up the pizza cafe for Paul and Isabella. We haven't spoken since yesterday when I saw his mum, but tonight's been planned for ages, so I unwrap the red-and-white-checked cloth to stop their pestering, and lay it all out with cutlery and candles and send Paul a message to make sure they're still coming over. We get it looking really special, like a proper Italian, then I send the boys off while the oven warms up.

I get changed into a dress Paul got me, then go back down and open a couple of letters. From the debt collectors. I chuck the rest without opening them and glance at my phone, chest tight. Still on silent. Ten missed calls since I left the nursery. Four texts. Warning. *Contact us immediately to avoid immediate court action.*

My head's buzzing with wasps. They want the full amount. They're going to take my kids this time. I just can't think. I stare around for something to sell, then run up and get the black cashmere jumper and push it in a carrier under the pushchair, trying not to look. I leave it by the front door – I've been waiting for bin day, but I might as well take it round to Tania's to see if I can get anything for it. I shove the pizzas in the oven. The bailiffs could be back any second.

I peep through the crack in the curtains and ring Paul. *Ah, Lauren – I've been meaning to call you all day* but I don't let him speak and ask can we come over and do this Italian cafe thing at yours instead – we can bring all the stuff, I mean we've set up here but there's a problem with our oven and it'll be easy enough to bring it all over – it'd be better all round, but he just stays silent. Paul? Are you there?

Yeah – I'm here, Lauren. Where are you though? I say what? What's he talking about. His voice is scary – so deadly calm. *I went to see my mother yesterday. It seems you've developed a habit of turning up in surprising places.* Oh that, I say, relieved – I need to talk to you about that, it was a nightmare to be honest – I was just trying to take the pressure off a bit, you know?

No, I don't know, Lauren – it sounds to me like you're trying to stir trouble. The doorbell goes. I scream. Leave it, boys, don't answer it. Just get back in the front room. Paul's still talking, but I hiss I've got to go and hang up.

I mute the TV and sit between the boys, clinging on, telling them to stay quiet. Little Dan whimpers, asks if it's bad men coming. I tell him no, but we sit, frozen for ten minutes, then I creep to the window. I can't see anyone. I put the sound back on the TV, but down low, then run to turn the oven off and ring Paul back. Can we come over with the Italian cafe stuff now? We've got a bit of an emergency here. We can talk about everything at yours.

There's nothing to talk about, Lauren – there's not going to be any Italian cafe. The same weird voice. What's up with him. Paul – please – we need to come over – it's not safe here. There's a pause. We're not safe.

You've got to be kidding, Lauren – you can't just turn up here – at my family home. In this weather. What will the neighbours think? I start to say surely that doesn't matter now, it's a bit late in the day for thinking about neighbours, but he cuts me off. *Look – I've got to go – it's really stressful here. Isabella's having another meltdown – and now Mum's upset – on top of Alex – and right before her operation. My family need me, Lauren.*

My throat constricts. But we're your family. My voice so quiet. He doesn't skip a beat. *Not right now you're not.* The boys have come into the kitchen, after the sweet melting smell of cheese. Oli crouches down to peer through the tarred oven window, then looks up at me – why am I just standing there, not talking. I want to tell Paul the pizza's ready, the boys are waiting, the bailiffs are ready to pounce, any second, they're about to get me – that I just need to get out, away from the door and calls and letters, that I just need some fucking help.

I sink to the lino, phone still at my ear. The floor's mucky and peeling at the edges. There's clattering at his end in the background. I should tell the kids stand back from the oven, it's hot. Dee'll sack me without him, this house isn't safe, we've nowhere to go. Oli sits next to me and kisses my arm. *It's okay, Mummy.*

I owe everyone – nursery, housing, loan. In too deep. I've been such a fucking idiot. Even my own mother hates me. He speaks first. *I've got to go – I need to give Isabella her tea. You're not the priority right now.*

Oli is staring at me. *Mummy?* It's all wrong. I say fine, bye then, Paul, hang up and drag myself standing. I grab the boys' coats and push their arms in, come on, we're going to Nana's. *But she's on holiday, what about pizza cafe? – Mummy, we're hungry!*

It's all a lie.

I drop the lukewarm pizzas in a carrier bag, push their shoes on and shove them through the front door. I need to get them out – get them safe. I'll never pay it off – too deep. They'll be better off with Mum. It's the only way.

I ram my feet into trainers, gritty under my tights, then put Dan in the pushchair and lock the front door, both boys wailing.

Hoods up in the pouring rain, we march round to my mum's, heavy plastic bag swinging, and I bang on the door, sobbing. She opens up, glass in hand, and I push them in with the bag of soggy pizza, saturated with rain.

Lauren! My God – what's happened? I tell her I can't do this any more. You win. And she's saying *come in – Lauren, come back, what're you playing at, we can sort this* as I run down the path, away, the boys' cries in my ears, but I keep on running, rain blurring my eyes, whipping at my face.

Nancy

Rain-mate tight under my chin, I dash through the car park with my handbag, stomach coiling. I hope the downpour will hide me long enough. They'll be after me in no time.

It's absolutely belting it down: I can't even see where I'm going properly. The voices so loud, singing so loud. My left foot plunges in a puddle, freezing water pouring into my leather mules. Bits of grit under my feet.

Gladys and her son called in this morning to wish me well with the operation tomorrow. Everyone's been fussing. I needed a bit of help with my will and a few papers, and he was so patient, what a lovely man. Gladys is lucky to have him. When they left, I told them there was no need to worry about the operation. I'll be fine now.

Once I'm on the cul-de-sac to the park, I try to shove my brolly up, fingers frozen, but it blows inside out. I wrestle it back and stuff it in my bag. Sirens behind, not far away. They're out looking for me already.

Or maybe it's the fire brigade arriving at the care home. I was first out when the alarm went, because I'm mobile. Ready in my coat at the front door, old Annie on my heels, unlit cigarette in hand. The ones who can't move took longer – they have special plans – staff occupied with safe-zone plans, buying me time.

I said goodbye to Annie in the car park, raising my voice above the storm. She squeezed my arm and nodded me on with a chesty laugh. *Go on then, get your skates on. Look after yourself.*

I reach the side gate to the park and turn left towards the woods by the river. The playing field is swamped so I stick to the tarmac path, all the way round. There's not a soul in sight: everything deserted in the mist: boating pond, cafe, swings.

There was never much of a playground where we lived when Pip was a boy. But I used to walk Ruby past this one, before they made me go to Bev's: I'd let her off on the field, then we'd watch the kiddies and share a cone from the van.

I struggle forwards on the path like a bloated cod against the current, gale blowing me back, tossing me about, drenched. My bones aching cold in the marrow.

I hear the river before I see it. I've not known it this swollen in all my years, smashing, debris sweeping past: trees, garden chairs, snakes of plastic. The towpath is still high enough to be clear. I stumble on, even slower now: I have made my choice. One sopping foot at a time, heading for my old wooden bridge, the path sodden, tide coming in fast. More sirens.

I'd moved the metal fire bucket to the conservatory and got Annie to drop her lit cigarette in, then told her to turn her back while I added lint from the dryer out of my purse. Balls of cotton wool. Damp leaves and sticks. I waited just long enough for the orange flames to dampen to smoke, then we dashed into the main house to raise the alarm.

The fire bell causes panic every time, even with so many false alarms. There was the usual pandemonium, but me and Annie were on our best behaviour: even helped a couple of old ones round to the car park down the side.

I hope they're not too hard on Annie. They'll be looking for a smoker, but I've left a note on my bed claiming full responsibility. Saying I'll be back. I hope it's enough. It won't take them long to notice I've gone.

There's a strange oily smell on the wind, disconcerting in the rain. I glimpse a movement in the trees on the opposite bank, but when I look, there's nothing there. My stomach lurches: it's my eyes playing tricks. Impossible to see anything in this rain.

When I get to the bridge, a thin layer of water is already flowing over the wood, clear as glass. I grip the old railing as I cross, freezing water flooding my mules, water to my ankles. Ear-splitting singing, voices ringing out. I pause in the middle of the bridge – take my husband's gold pocket watch from my bag. I hold it above the water, pause, then let go, quick as a flash. The singing rises to a scream. It was supposed to go to Pip, but he's had quite enough from his dad. I should have realised sooner.

I cross the bridge and take the path into the trees. Not far to the clearing. I approach, out of breath: circle of tree stumps, fire pit, mud-kitchen. Ruby always running loved it here, early morning, before the toddlers arrived for their learning in the forest. It has changed over the years: it is a safe place now, pastel bunting flapping wild between trees. Pip would have loved it when he was little: he hated being inside. Always playing rough with sticks and ropes: this place could have changed him. Given us a chance.

The fire pit in the centre is iron, orange with rust. I set everything up, look around: I feel watched. A rustle in the bushes. Probably rats, fleeing the storm.

It takes me both hands to haul the heavy lid off. Dry cinders underneath. I let out a sigh of relief, but the rain is against me – I have to be quick. I force the brolly up again, but it is dislocated spokes; wild nylon. I hurl it to the mud, useless, then grab the bag of fuel and make a careful pile on the rain-pocked ash: two handfuls of cotton balls thickly coated in Vaseline. Hand-sanitiser drizzle. Dry-lint garnish. Annie promised me it would burn.

I spark the lighter and the lint catches first time. A surprise: I thought it would take longer. More sanitiser. I lean over to protect the small flames with my big body, rain battering down. I am ready. It is time.

I pull the thick creamy paper from my pocket, bile rising. It has to be here, by the river, where no one can stop me. I unfold the paper, greased corner to flame. It goes straight up. The last will and testament of Nancy Sutherland.

I keep hold of the paper until the flames flick my fingers, then drop the last scrap into the small blaze, fingerprints blistering. Tiny black fragments curl, attempt to rise, forced back by rain.

I look into the feeble flames, shivering. Not letting me stay after the fire in the flat, forcing me into Bev's care home. Hardly seeing my granddaughter. Losing Ruby. Why would he do this to me. *Please ask him to let me go, Nancy. You are my only chance.* I've been blind. He'd been on at me for months about going into a home. But I realise now it was never even about me: it was about control, about her. I remember her letter. *He has me trapped.*

I poke the blackened paper with a stick – soggy, only the tiniest white corner still intact. I grind the pulp into ash, destroying the evidence, rain dousing the flames. Not glorious, but done. I've ignored what is right in front of my face for all these years. Longing for him to be different to his father.

They'll all be back inside at the home now – when they realise it was only smoke in a bucket. The search party will be out for sure though; they'll be here any second.

I rip the rain-mate off, hood back, face up, water streaming down my cheeks, and scream into the sky.

The new will is at the solicitor's, signed and witnessed this morning by Gladys and her son. I got Pip's girlfriend's name from the visitor book. Pip written out; two women written in. Everything split between the wife and the girlfriend – for the children's sake.

I can go back now and face the operation in peace, whatever happens – I have broken the cycle.

Once I'm sure the fire is out, I heave the iron lid up and turn back to my path, but stop short at the bridge – water gushing over now, foaming, knee-deep.

Lauren

I run down Mum's street – away from it all. The storm blasts at me, soaking my hair, roughing me up, blowing me about.

I blink mascara, trying to see, stinging blind. There's no one about – everyone tucked up inside. Hiding. I owe too much – nursery, loan, rent – I've fucked it all up for the boys – lost them another dad – chance of a better life, school, home. A proper family. The wind roaring in my brain. My job'll be gone, everyone hates me.

I trip over a fallen branch at the junction, and scrape my knee, one hand on the pavement, rain spilling down my face, like the gym showers when you pick ice-drench, electric blue, all those stupid fucking posh people paying to suffer, when you could choose tropical, choose red. I stand up, tights ripped at the knee, bleeding, and look around. Realise I'm holding the jumper bag. Rain fizzing orange in the street lights, trees creaking danger. The wind's wrestled everything into it, breakers in my ears like white foam.

There's a black shape far down the street – too big for a cat, too black for a fox. I can't work it out but don't know what else to do so follow – down the street, over the main road, down the snicket to the river, sobbing. At the river I lose it, but the water brings me up short – I've never seen it that high. Churning brown, smashing up the banks – wrapping tree roots – carrier bags and cones and all sorts flying past.

The words thump in my head like a crazy nursery rhyme – *but we're your family, not right now you're not, but we're your family, not right now.* On and on. All a lie. My tongue burnt like scalding pizza. I can't go back now. I run on through the puddles on the towpath, tights itching and soaked, my trainers flooding cold river, sirens on the wind.

I race towards the shadow by the bridge, screaming into the rain – the wind nearly knocking me off my feet. At the bridge, the shadow's gone, but I clamber down the bank – there's a tree down there, with branches overhanging the water and I skid down and grab the trunk, to see the water – washing everything away, taking away the shit.

I yank my phone out of my pocket and chuck it into the water, shouting, have it, fucking have it all. Just leave me alone! It's sucked down without a splash – it's nothing – does nothing. It's not enough – they'll find me anyway. I could walk away – be someone else. Find the boys when they're older, explain

but I'd still never be free. The boys'll always have people knocking at their door as long as I'm around – they deserve so much fucking better. I step forward, the mud soft and sucking, water spraying my toes. I pull the cashmere jumper out of the bag, shudder of face staring back at me, and hurl her down too. She's gone without a trace, swept off in black water. My face streams with tears. Goodbye. Pam. Mum. Hannah. Even Dee, who gave me a chance, who was looking out for me, even though I was too stupid to see it. Who've I been kidding – I can't even look after myself.

I shift my weight – this will finish it, the mess, everything I touch – and step forward, let go of the trunk and stumble into the raging water, but a sudden movement near the bridge makes me panic and I grab up for a branch, get a fistful and hang on, thigh-deep in freezing river.

Alex

Alex is in her wellies in the lobby, hood up, drilled pebble necklace in her pocket, Benji wrapped sleeping at her chest, Niki got her one of those long stretchy slings from the library. Alex lumbers a little; an awkward bear: zips her giant pregnancy cagoule over the sling.

The sky is a wet purple, dark and low; torrential rain. Niki says *you don't want to be going out in this – it's nearly dark out, even at this hour.*

Alex says the air will do us good, animated, full of energy. Niki sees how well she looks.

No one expects it, Alex – not when it's tipping it down – it won't go against you or anything like that.

Alex says walking helps me think. Her body wants to be outside: she has not been out in rain like this for years.

Well, why don't you leave Benji here?

Alex picks up a huge golfing umbrella from the bucket by the door. Honestly, it'll do us both good – we'll take this and we won't be long. He sleeps better when I'm walking. We're well wrapped up – they're always out at Izzy's forest nursery, you know – no such thing as bad weather, just bad clothing. She pauses. Izzy's old nursery, I mean.

Niki hesitates, about to say something. Alex is so much better now.

But the river has been swelling all week, intent on rising. Stealing things from the banks: traffic cones, wild garlic, old shoes. Alex has to see it. The geographer in her. The explorer.

We'll stick to the paths around the unit. I've got my phone if you need me.

Niki nods. *Alright.* They will be fine on the paths. *But don't go far – just do the usual loop.*

Alex smiles in agreement. Don't worry, we'll be back in no time. She strides away, up to the golf course, the loop, one hand on Benji's compact body, curled to her, heart to heart, the other wrestling the heavy umbrella. The slugs are out: the ones with orange flashes. A siren in the distance. Her wellies slosh the baby's favourite rhythm, water splashing from her boots. She slips the pebble with its visions from the chain, spits on it, drops it over her left shoulder, turns and presses it into saturated soil with the toe of her boot. It will settle, sink, find its way.

The wind is even wilder up here; the umbrella impossible. Alex laughs, dumps it by the path, then, with a glance back, changes direction, across the green, heading for the shelter of the woods, rain battering down.

The trees roar as she approaches: limbs writhing; battered and wrenched by invisible waves in the air. It is not safe. The sky an ocean, raging. Alex should turn back: knows the danger of falling branches, flying debris, but she pushes on into the copse, ice rain numbing her lips.

She is reckless, laughs into the wind: cares nothing, only wants to be free. Turns right at the fork, the path waterlogged to the left, staggering a little in the mud, stepping high over splintered bones, wrecked and fallen from the sky, almost dancing.

She has walked these paths before but sees nothing she knows: the storm has changed it all. There is only the narrow track in front of her; thunder trembling in the distance.

She can hear the river coming up, crashing. The baby jerks his head. Alex pauses to peep in her raincoat. Trying to keep out the rain. Only a dream: he is quiet now, warm against her body. Still breathing.

To be water, wind: it is the only way. To be free, wild: a relief for everyone she has snarled in her mess. Niki, Reema, Ruth.

He will always find her. Her breath catches and she halts again and fumbles for her phone with frozen fingers: holds the off button until the light goes black; drops it in the bushes. The tracker off now, but too late.

He will be here soon.

Alex stumbles towards the ragged noise of river. Emerges onto the towpath, but steps back, shocked: the banks brimful, white water smashing past, wrapping trees, dragging black shapes in the churn.

There is no return now. She faces the rapids and opens her mouth wide to the spray, lets it batter her face and rip her hood back, cries a long guttural noise into the roar. A noise of abandon, of orgasm; a noise of sex with someone you want.

Alex swipes at her face; then pushes on again on the towpath, knocked about by the gale, past the stepping stones, submerged now, slick stone, swallowed rock, then see sees the old bridge ahead: recognises where she is.

Alex's heart squeezes: there is a flash of movement by the bridge. It can't be him. Surely not yet. She strains her eyes through the rain for clear edges, then sees. There is a woman in the water.

Gytrash

A triangle of women by a raging river. Smack of thunder in the dark: sky in shreds, whipping, rain thrashing down. Three women lit in a flare of lightning.

Nancy, stuck on the far side of the bridge, roiling trees behind her; cropped white hair plastered to her head.

Alex, on the near side, baby wrapped to chest, poised on the towpath, ready to lunge.

Lauren, thigh-deep in water, clinging to a branch, willing herself to let go.

The sky shakes off the light: three women pitched into darkness. Taste of burnt diesel: they retch at the same time; blood oil, singed hair. The river foaming yellow, seething.

Another flash of lightning and the creature is there between them, huge shadow peeled, in the centre of their triangle: matted mane, frothing jaws, ragged head. Turning slowly, eyeing each woman in turn.

In the dark, only the eyes remain. Blazing coals, big as saucers. Three women trapped. Searing pain in the stomach, the chest, the head. Time buckling.

The gytrash stares into Alex. Migraine fire, skull splitting: women who hurt her; women hurt; women who believe her. Fractured futures clashing. Health visitor, hospital, soup. Decaffeinated lies. She wrenches her eyes away; strains to see the figure in the river. Might be too late. Spots her. Employee of the month, white bread for the ducks, bedraggled, two kids and a tatty pram, malnourished.

Alex struggles for breath; looks back at the creature, clutches her head. Blinding. If she helps that woman, she will be dragged down too, with the baby. The creature wants them all. But there is no choice: Benji was never hers to protect. Pathetic wife, weak mother. It will be a mercy. A tragic accident to end it all.

The gytrash stares into Lauren. Her chest constricts. Aching to breathe river. The shame of stealing, debt, begging. Lungs burning pepper oil, hacking for the women let down. Cousin, mother, old friends. Pam in the shop. The whole fucking lot. Her boys, crying, bag of soggy pizza swinging. Shit mum. They will never forgive her.

She clutches the branch, feels it slipping. Glances up: sees the woman on the path, mouth gaping, silent noise. Photo in the driving licence; woman from the bench by the river. Lauren sobs. Wife. This woman should stamp on her fingers, send her under. Lauren decides: she will let go; save the woman this shame, at least.

The gytrash stares into Nancy. She doubles in pain, stomach screwing. Hands to womb. Sees women laughing without her, baby lost, only child. Double buggies. Women looking away from purple cheekbones, black eyes. Women used; women helping. Care homes, hospital, clinic. Metal-boned make-up women, forced red lips. The treachery of the body, over again.

Then she starts: two women on the other side of the river. Women she has failed. Betrayed. Women she owes. The river is rising on the bridge. She needs to get across; make it up to them. Wind batters her old body: nearly takes her off her feet. She puts one foot on the bridge.

The wind drops, the trees become still. Clear air, bright stars. Only the sound of the river. The moon stripped of cloud; the creature between them bleached out by moonlight, a pale shadow now, pencil grey. Three women in the eye of the storm.

They look around, stunned. Time suspended. Gaze at each other, over the creature. The scene has changed.

Nancy, standing tall on the bridge, one hand on the rotten railing; shining film over her entire body, wet in the moonlight: radiant. She glows against the sky.

Alex, feet planted strong on the earth, hands on the curve of her baby, power of birth in her muscles; animal quickening.

Lauren, soaked in bridal-white foam. Hanging on in the face of these women who hate her, lulled by the static of the river.

Three screams split the peace: the sky plunges back, wind snatches their hair. The froth turns sour again, yellow brown; rain battering down. The creature is angry now, ferocious. It turns, as if backed into a corner, lunging at each of them, in turn. Snarling. Who will go first.

But the women see now. Horrified. Each faced with herself in that matted mass of fur. A self coiled with selves, poison dribbled in the ears of sleeping women, should be, could be, entering the bloodstream, faces of women, had it coming, singing, disgrace, asking for it.

Each woman snared in the mesh of dark threads, electric, women hurt, powerful, raped. The creature is them only and them all. Hannah, Pam, Gladys. Ruth, Reema, Annie, Dee. Hauled up and carried. Hauling themselves. Hauling the women who came before them.

Alex faces the gytrash head-on, legs planted wide. It is hungry, wants more than her. She shakes her head slowly. No. He is my baby. Curled, compact in me. Seashell. Mine.

Nancy stands strong, holds on. No. Not like this. Thinks she hears a shrill yap from behind, cutting the wind, scuffle of small paws racing towards her.

Lauren. Time to let go. She screams back in its face. No. Reaches higher up the branch and grabs, palms bleeding. My boys need me.

Three times denied. Three times these women find themselves. It is enough. A dreadful splash: the gytrash dark liquid, soaking red black: returning to river. From the river it comes; to the river it always returns. The water will rise fast now, ripe to blossom; ready to burst its banks.

Alex rips off her coat, starts unwrapping the baby. Nancy pauses in the centre of the bridge, water to her knees, looks back at the woods, longing for the sound of her dog. Lauren holds on for dear life, waist-deep in water, bawling for help.

Alex

Alex unwinds the length of material, pulls Benji out from the hot cave of her body and up into the wind and rain, dangly legs clenching up, head jerking, startled. Bald cry rising.

Alex runs with him to the bushes, kisses his face and wraps him in the coat, I love you. Wedges him with the rucksack, safe, in a dripping rhododendron grotto, I'm coming back. She cannot see Lauren: hopes she is still there.

The baby flails on his back, a star screaming: heat, milk. I'm so sorry, Benji. Alex tucks him in. I promise I'll come back.

She runs: sees Lauren's pale face and hands, clinging on. River rising fast. Sobbing, please help me. Alex untangles the sling, lashes one end to a tree and loops the other tightly around her middle.

She tests the knots then rushes forward, arm stretched out, sling rope pulling taut at her waist. The other woman reaches, grasps. Fingertips nearly touching. But not quite. Their rope is too short.

Alex trips: Lauren slips and goes under. Alex frantic. Where is she. Can't see the other woman. She races back to the tree, unknots the loop from the trunk and runs back, cord trailing from her waist.

Lauren has surfaced gasping, head and shoulders showing, fingers clinging to a root, the rest of her body streaming like fronds of weed with the water. She won't hold long.

Alex runs upriver, flings herself belly to mud, anchors her toes; makes a loop in the end of the sling. The material is sodden; heavy. Only one chance at this. She yanks the loop to check it will hold and hurls it at the woman in the water.

Lauren reaches and grabs: Alex feels the weight jerk into her rope. Yes! Hold on, screams Alex, wrap it round your wrists; then starts to haul Lauren in, shaking with the strain, arm over arm. That's it, keep coming.

The weight eases off as Lauren gets a foothold, but then she slips back again, jerking Alex forward. No. Not now.

Alex thrashes on her stomach, rams her toes under a root. Benji's cry cutting the wind, Izzy waiting for her at home. Both her children.

No question. Searing migraine lights, hot and dizzy. He will not rob her again. His face will curl at the edges but she will keep breathing, look him in the eye: he will not win.

She grips, knuckles white, hauling the sling, hand over hand, ancient fisherwoman, heaving her catch, drawing it in.

And finally, there is slack in the rope, Lauren on solid ground, staggering hands and knees, both women slipping towards each other, crying, clashing to drag each other up, a tangle, soaking skin and bone embrace, shuddering, teeth clattering.

And then Alex pushes Lauren away, fierce. The crying in the rhododendrons has stopped. My baby. I need to get my baby.

Nancy

The bridge creaks under me, black rotting wood battered by the river. The water rising too fast, dark shapes hurtling past on either side. The bridge won't last, but I can't leave this place, not now. I wait, clinging to the railing with both hands, numb.

I used to wait here for Ruby to catch me up: bounding from the trees, spaniel blur, ears flying, tail wild corkscrew of joy. Scrap of copper. I would crouch, clasp her to my chest, licking my face, soaked fur to skin. It is where I belong.

I see the two women on the bank. Tangled. Risking their lives for each other. These women who should hate each other, rivals, running together to the bushes, pulling something out.

A baby. My grandson. I am ashamed. I think of the women at Bev's care home, seeing me off. Helping me all those months, ungrateful old crone, expecting nothing in return. Gladys and her son, sticking by me, even in that godforsaken care home. Old Annie with her cigarettes, clasping my arm. *Go on. Get your skates on.* Wives of men in the barber's, mothers at Pip's school: all pushed away. I never gave anything back.

I've been a fool. It was never enough to burn the old will in the woods. This has gone too far, too much damage has been done. My son must not become his father. His wife's words echo in my head. *You're the only woman he respects. The only one he truly loves. My only chance.*

And now three letters in the drawer: Alex, Lauren, Pip. My mother's locket, with a new miniature parchment: *My darling Pip. From my body, my love. You must make a better path. Your own path. I will always love you. Your Mama.*

I can only stand aside now, make way: it is my time. Here, where I've longed to be all these months. No operating table,

263

no fear: this is everything. To make my own way; to finally give back to the women who have shored me up, expecting nothing in return.

A massive tree appears round the bend in the river, crashing towards my bridge. The two women on the bank scream up at me, horrified; eyes and mouths black holes. Run!

I could. But I stand proud instead, facing the torrent, victorious at last, without pain, I give myself to the water.

Lauren

I'm right behind Alex as she pulls the silent bundle of coat and baby out from the bush. Fuck. She turns to me, clutching the lot to her chest, eyes massive.

We stare at each other, frozen. There's no cry. River crashing, sirens in the distance.

She goes to pieces – shaking, white as a sheet – shoves the baby at me, whimpering, *what have I done?*

I move in, but then it happens – clean as a needle through the roar of wind and water, the piercing cry of baby birthed, baby breathing.

She keeps shoving him at me. *Oh my God – take him. What have I done?* Over and over. I spin her to face me, grip her arms hard. Look at me. Come on – listen, but she's beside herself

so I shake her hard to bring her out of it. Look at me. Get a grip. Look! He's okay. He needs you. She nods, sobbing. I help her pull out a boob, press the baby's face in, cover them with the coat, hold his weight up to her, everything soaked, sucking, swallowing. Milk heat. But then she's sinking down, crumbling under me, and I shout no. Not yet. We have to get away from the water.

I walk them both, ever so slowly, shuffling away from the river, holding the baby up to her body. Sirens so close now. She's doing it, saving her baby, and I have to stop to throw up. I'm sorry, I tell my sopping legs, I'm so fucking sorry. What I nearly did to my boys.

I scan the banks for Paul's mum. There's a shape on the bridge in the dark. She can't be – what the fuck's she still doing on there?

I tell Alex, stand there – don't move, I'm coming back – but she grips my arm. *No. Please. Don't leave me.* Deadly calm now. *He'll be here soon. He's on his way.*

The lightning flashes mad shit crazy and we see Paul's mum lighting up on the bridge, clear as day, like the fucking Blackpool illuminations, and there's a massive crash up the river – some great fuck-off tree ripping down – and we scream at the top of our lungs. Run! But she strobes silver in the foam, smiling and shakes her head, then turns back to the tree smashing towards her bridge and it hits, splintering wood, and it's under and she's gone. Gone.

We stagger back, clinging to each other, screaming ring 999 but we've no phone and there's no point now anyway. Cause they're already here. Flashlights on the path, loud voices coming from the park. We hold each other tight, baby between us in the tent of our bodies

and then he's there, Paul, at the front, pushing through the hi-vis jackets towards us. When the care home phoned to say his mum was missing, he knew she'd come here. Always the old bridge on the river. I scream at the cops, there's a woman in the water. Paul stops like he's been shot

and a couple of them crowd in with blankets, asking questions, saying *that's it, deep breaths now, we've got you*, radios blasting while others wade to the water. I jerk my head after them, rain pouring down my face – she went under.

Paul plunges forwards, *you lying bitch, what've you done, what are you even doing here?* and he's pushing, trying to get through, words whipping away in the wind, *get away from her, Alex, she's poison*, and Alex presses into me, shivering hard, calls *Izzy?* and he shouts back *she's with Reema*, and we're still holding the baby tight between us and the woman cop with the blanket says *can you please step back, sir, and give us a bit of space? – I know this is distressing but we just need to check everyone over* but Paul's still shoving towards us, grabbing, *where's my baby, give me him*, and Alex speaks so quietly, *no, get off*, I don't even know if it's her or me or the river, *we need help*, and then one cop's nodding at another, bulky jacket flashing in the rain, *sir, if you don't calm down, sir, we'll have no choice but to detain you*

big cop moving in, but Paul's still pushing, arms swinging like fucking windmills, *get off me, they're psychos – she's got my baby*, and the woman gives the nod *can you please move this gentleman out of the way?*

and the bulky cop escorts Paul away, punching, writhing, baying for blood, and leads him through the driving rain into the darkness of the park.

Alex leans into me and I squeeze her hard, baby crying, tell her hold on. It'll be alright. She looks at me and nods. We're in this together now.

Acknowledgements

TK

A Note on the Author

RACHEL BOWER is an award-winning poet and short story writer from Bradford. She is the author of two poetry collections and a non-fiction book on literary letters. Her poems and stories have been widely published in literary magazines, including *The London Magazine*, *The White Review*, *Magma* and *Stand*. Rachel won *The London Magazine* Short Story Prize 2019/20 and the W&A Short Story Competition 2020. She has also been listed for the *White Review* Short Story Prize 2019, the RSL V. S. Pritchett Short Story Prize and the BBC Short Story Prize.

A Note on the Type

The text of this book is set in Bembo, which was first used in 1495 by the Venetian printer Aldus Manutius for Cardinal Bembo's *De Aetna*. The original types were cut for Manutius by Francesco Griffo. Bembo was one of the types used by Claude Garamond (1480–1561) as a model for his Romain de l'Université, and so it was a forerunner of what became the standard European type for the following two centuries. Its modern form follows the original types and was designed for Monotype in 1929.